THIS BOOK
BELONGS TO

_____

_____

SWALLOWS·AND·AMAZONS·FOR·EVER!

VINTAGE CLASSICS

OTHER BOOKS BY ARTHUR RANSOME

Arthur Ransome

SWALLOWDALE

Illustrated by the Author

SWALLOWS·AND·AMAZONS·FOR·EVER!

VINTAGE BOOKS
London

Published by Vintage 2012

4 6 8 10 9 7 5

Swallowdale was first published by Jonathan Cape in 1930

Vintage
Random House, 20 Vauxhall Bridge Road,
London SW1V 2SA

www.vintage-classics.info

Addresses for companies within The Random House Group Limited can be found at:
www.randomhouse.co.uk/offices.htm

The Random House Group Limited Reg. No. 954009

A CIP catalogue record for this book
is available from the British Library

ISBN 9780099572824

Typeset in Minion Pro by Palimpsest Book Production Limited,
Falkirk, Stirlingshire

Penguin Random House is committed to a sustainable future for
our business, our readers and our planet. This book is made from
Forest Stewardship Council®

Printed a   s plc

Contents

List of Illustrations

TO
ELIZABETH ABERCROMBIE

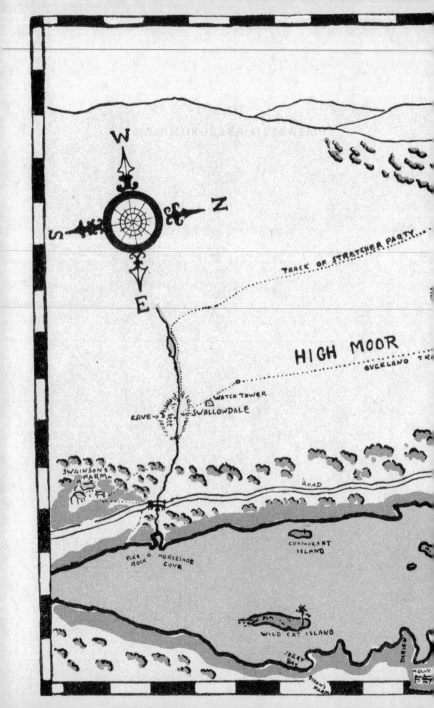

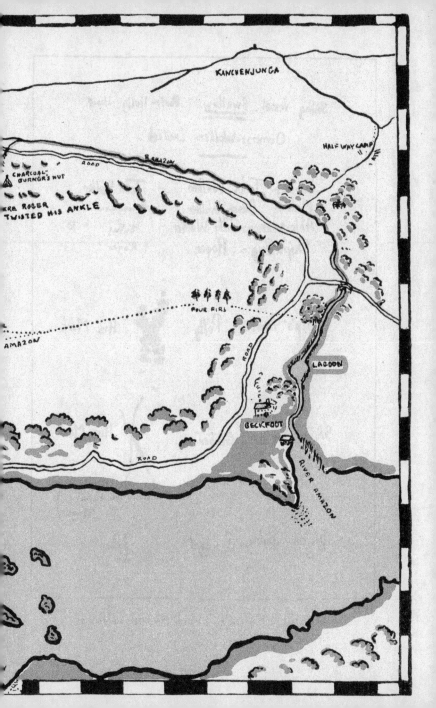

Sailing Vessel. __Swallow__. Port:- Holly Howe.

Owners:- __Walkers Limited__

Master:- John Walker   John Walker
Mate :- Susan Walker   Susan
Able-seaman:- Titty Walker   Titty   A.B.
Ship's Boy:- Roger   Roger

Ship's Parrot:- Polly   His Mark

Ship's Monkey:- Gibber      His Mark

(I held his hand.
Roger)

Ship's Baby:- Bridget   B

THE ORIGINAL SHIP'S PAPERS (INKED AT HOME)

1

The Swallow and her Crew

'A handy ship, and a handy crew,
Handy, my boys, so handy:
A handy ship and a handy crew,
Handy, my boys, AWAY HO!'
Sea Chanty

'WILD Cat Island in sight!' cried Roger, the ship's boy, who was keeping a look-out, wedged in before the mast, and finding that a year had made a lot of difference and that there was much less room for him in there with the anchor and ropes than there used to be the year before when he was only seven.

'You oughtn't to say its name yet,' said Titty, the able-seaman, who was sitting on the baggage amidships, taking care of her parrot who, for the moment, was travelling in his cage. 'You ought to say "Land, Land," and lick your parched lips, and then afterwards we'd find out what land it was when we got a bit nearer. We might have been sailing about looking for it for weeks.'

'But we know already,' said the look-out. 'And anyway there's land all round us. I'll be able to see the houseboat in a minute. There it is, just where it used to be. But (his voice changed) Captain Flint's forgotten to hoist a flag.'

*

The little brown-sailed *Swallow* with her crew of five, including the parrot, had left Holly Howe Bay, and was now beating across the open lake that stretched away to the south between wooded hills, with moorland showing above the trees and, in the distance, mountains showing above the moorland. A whole year had gone by. August had come again. The Walkers had come up from the south yesterday. John, Susan, Titty and Roger had been at the window with the parrot as the train came into the little station, thinking that their old allies, Nancy and Peggy Blackett, would be on the platform to meet them, perhaps with their mother, or with Captain Flint, that retired pirate, who lived in the houseboat in Houseboat Bay and was really Mr Turner, Nancy's and Peggy's Uncle Jim. But no one had been there. All the morning, while Mother, little Bridget and

Nurse had been unpacking boxes and settling into the old farmhouse at Holly Howe and they had been down at the boathouse loading *Swallow* for her voyage to Wild Cat Island, they had been sending scouts up to the high ground, to look up to the northern part of the lake to see if a little boat about the size of *Swallow* had come out of the Amazon River, where the Blacketts had a house, away up there towards the Arctic, under the great hills. Every other minute they had been looking for the little white sail of the *Amazon* at the mouth of the Holly Howe bay, expecting to hear Captain Nancy's jolly shout of 'Swallows and Amazons for ever!' and to see Mate Peggy hoisting the Jolly Roger to the masthead. Then the *Swallow* and the *Amazon* would sail down to Wild Cat Island together, calling on their way on the houseboat to say, 'How do you do' to Captain Flint. Everything would be just as it had been last year. But they had seen no sign at all of their allies and when afternoon came they could wait no longer. Mother and Bridget had gone off to the little town to buy stores for them and were going to bring the stores down to the island in the native rowing boat from Holly Howe. Whatever happened, they had to get the camp ready before Mother arrived, so that she could see that all was well for the first night. It was no good waiting for those Amazons. Nancy and Peggy were probably in the houseboat with Captain Flint. Or, more likely still, they were already on Wild Cat Island, plotting either a welcome or an ambush. With Nancy you never really knew. So the four explorers had set sail. The thing they had been planning for a year was at last beginning. It had indeed begun, for once more they were afloat in *Swallow*, and sleeping at home in beds had already come to an end.

*

'I do think he ought to be flying his flag,' said Roger, the look-out.

'Perhaps he didn't think we'd be sailing so soon,' said Titty, the able-seaman, who was resting a telescope on the cage of her parrot, and looking through it at the distant houseboat.

'He'll hoist his flag all right when he sees us coming,' said Susan the mate.

John, the eldest of the four of them, said nothing. He was too busy with the sailing, now that *Swallow* had left the shelter of the bay and had begun to beat down the lake against the southerly wind. He was looking straight forward, feeling the wind on his cheek, enjoying the pull of sheet and tiller and the

4

'lap, lap' of the water under *Swallow*'s forefoot. Sometimes he glanced up at the little pennant at the masthead, a blue swallow on a white ground (cut out and stitched by Able-seaman Titty), to be sure that he was making the most of the wind. It takes practice to know from the feel of the wind on your cheekbone exactly what your sail is doing, and this was the first sail of these holidays. Sometimes he glanced astern at the bubbling ribbon of *Swallow*'s wake. At the moment, it did not seem to matter whether Captain Flint was flying a flag from the masthead of his houseboat or not. To be on the lake again and sailing was enough for John.

Mate Susan, too, did not mind that there was no flag on the old houseboat. She had had a tiring time the day before, looking after her mother and Bridget and Nurse and the others and all the small luggage during the long railway journey from the south. She always took charge on railway journeys and was always very tired next day. But nothing had been forgotten, and the number of things that would have been forgotten if Susan had not remembered them was very great. And then, this morning, there had been lists of stores to make out and check, besides the stowage of cargo in *Swallow*. So Susan was resting and happy, glad that for the moment everything was done that she could do, glad no longer to hear the din of railway stations, and glad, too, not to have to listen to strange voices in that din to make sure that they ought not to be changing trains.

Even Able-seaman Titty was less disturbed than Roger at seeing no flag on the houseboat's stumpy little mast. She had so much else to think about. At one moment she felt that this was still last year and that they had never left the lake and gone away. All that long time of lessons and towns was as if it had never been. And then, the next moment, it was just that time that seemed real, and she could not believe that it was the same Titty who had had such awful troubles with her French verbs who was now once more the able-seaman, sitting in *Swallow* with the parrot-cage and the knapsacks and the stores, looking back at the Peak of Darien from which she had first seen Wild Cat Island, and looking down the lake at the island itself, sketches of which with its tall lighthouse tree had filled, almost without her knowing how they came there, the two blank pages at the end of her French Grammar. This feeling of being two people at once in a jumble of two different times made her a little breathless.

But Roger, wedged in his old place in the bows,

had been sure that their old friend, Captain Flint, would have had his flag at the masthead, even if he had not dressed ship to welcome them back, and he had been looking forward to seeing the houseboat's great flag dip and *Swallow*'s little pennant dip in answer. After that, of course, there would be a puff of smoke and a saluting bang from the little yacht cannon on the houseboat's foredeck. And now, there was the houseboat without any flag at all.

'He may be asleep,' said Titty.

'He can't be asleep if Nancy and Peggy are with him,' said Susan.

'They've probably gone on to the island. We'll know in a minute or two,' said John. 'This next tack'll take us into Houseboat Bay. Ready about.'

The little *Swallow* came up into the wind, Titty and the mate ducked as the boom swung over, the brown sail filled again, and the *Swallow*, now on the starboard tack, headed across the lake towards Houseboat Bay.

'Steamer on the starboard bow,' called the look-out. 'Miles away though.'

'There's one much nearer coming up astern,' said Captain John, 'out of Rio.'

Looking back they could see the wooded islands off the busy little port they called Rio, and through the islands glimpses of the broad waters of the northern part of the lake. The steamer was coming out of the Rio channel between Long Island and the mainland.

'Fisherman broad on the beam,' said the look-out, as they passed a rowing boat with two natives in it, one at the oars and the other holding a fishing rod.

'Towing a spinner for pike,' said the captain.

'Shark,' corrected the look-out.

The *Swallow* crossed the bows of the steamer that was going south from Rio. She crossed them with plenty of room to spare. The steamer swept past, the captain upon the bridge of the steamer waved a cheerful hand, and the crew of the *Swallow* waved back. They got a tossing in the steamer's wash that made them feel they really were at sea.

They were now nearing the sheltered bay where the old blue houseboat was lying to a mooring buoy.

'There's nobody on deck,' said the look-out.

Last year, when they had seen the houseboat for the first time and Titty had guessed that Captain Flint was a retired pirate, they had seen him sitting, writing on the after-deck with his green parrot perched on the rail beside him. This year there was no pirate to be seen. As for the parrot, he could not be on the houseboat for he had joined another ship. Titty was talking to him.

'Look, Polly,' she was saying, 'that's your old ship. That's where you used to live before you came to live with us.'

'Two, Two, Twice, Twice, Two, Two, Two,' said the green parrot.

'Pieces of eight,' said Titty. 'Say "pieces of eight". Don't bother about "Twice Two". It isn't term-time any more.'

'Let's have the telescope, Titty,' said the mate.

'I can't see his rowing boat,' said John. 'It isn't there unless he's got it hauled up along the port side.'

'The houseboat's shut up altogether,' said Mate Susan, looking through the telescope. 'The curtains are drawn in all the windows.'

Captain John and Mate Susan looked at each other. Even if they had not, like Roger, been dreaming of dipping flags and salutes of guns, they had been as sure that Captain Flint would be in his houseboat as that the big hills would be in their places round the head of the lake.

The *Swallow* sailed right into the bay, under the houseboat's stern and then, coming about, easily cleared the mooring buoy on her way out again into the open lake. Everybody had a good look at the houseboat, but they could see no sign of life aboard.

'He's covered up the cannon,' cried the ship's boy with indignation. Indeed the whole of the foredeck of the houseboat was protected from the weather with black tarpaulin sheets.

'It does look rather as if he wasn't there at all,' said Captain John, as the *Swallow* slipped out of the smooth water of Houseboat Bay to buffet once more with the little waves of the lake.

'I know what he's done,' said Titty. 'He's shut up the houseboat and he's on the island with the others.'

The others were really more important than Captain Flint, and, after all, it was just like Captain Nancy Blackett to plan that they should meet once more not in any mere railway station, or even in her uncle's houseboat, but on the desert island where they had met last year.

'Wild Cat Island abeam,' shouted the look-out as *Swallow* left Houseboat Bay. . . . 'Cormorant Island right ahead. . . .'

On this tack *Swallow* headed across to the western shore of the lake towards a low island of loose stones and rocks, with two dead trees on it, one a roosting place for cormorants, and the other long ago fallen down, its naked roots waving in the air, over the place where, once upon a time, Titty and Roger had found Captain Flint's treasure.

'There go the birds,' shouted the look-out when, as *Swallow* slipped across the lake towards them, four big black, long-necked birds got up off the dead tree and flew away over the water.

The able-seaman was looking not so much at Cormorant Island itself as at the water not far from it. Was it possible that she had ever been anchored out there, in someone else's boat, alone, in the middle of a pitch-dark night?

Mate Susan hardly looked at Cormorant Island. The voyage would soon be over and there would be tents to pitch and cooking to think about. She was looking through the telescope at the larger wooded island on the other side of the lake.

'It's a very funny thing there's no smoke,' she said.

'They must be there,' said Titty. 'May I have the telescope now?'

Captain John glanced over his shoulder.

'Ready about,' he called. Round swung the little *Swallow*, and this time headed for Wild Cat Island, of which the whole ship's company had been dreaming ever since they sailed away from it last year. It certainly was a funny thing that if Nancy and Peggy

Blackett were waiting there to meet them, no smoke should be blowing from the trees. Nancy Blackett was always one for making most tremendous fires.

'Nancy would have hoisted a flag, anyway,' said Captain John.

'Perhaps she couldn't get up Lighthouse Tree,' said Titty.

'Nancy'd get up anything,' said Captain John.

'Hullo,' shouted Roger, looking above the island at an old white farmhouse high on the farther shore of the lake. 'There's Dixon's Farm. There's Mrs Dixon. Feeding geese. Look at those white spots.'

'They may be hens,' said Susan.

'Her hens are all brown,' said Roger. 'Of course they might be only ducks.'

'Where are you going to land?' Susan asked the captain.

'I can make either end of the island on this tack.'

'The old landing-place is nearer the camp.'

'Oh, let's look into the harbour first,' said Titty.

The harbour was at the southern end of the island. It was sheltered by high rocks, and there were marks on shore to show the way in through the dangerous shoals outside. The landing-place was on the eastern side of the island, the side nearest to the mainland. It was a little bay with a shingle beach, close to the place that they had used for a camp. It was always best to bring boats to the landing-place instead of to the harbour when there was much cargo to be put ashore.

John steered for the southern end of the island, and, keeping well clear of the outer rocks, passed outside the entrance to the harbour.

'*Amazon*'s not in the harbour,' said the look-out.

Secretly everybody had thought she would be. There might be no smoke and no flag, but that would be natural if Captain Nancy, making sure that they would come straight to the landing-place, had hidden *Amazon* in the harbour and was waiting in ambush somewhere on the island. It was just the sort of thing she might do.

'There's the stump with the white cross on it,' said Titty. 'There's the high mark, the forked tree. There's the rock where I saw my dipper. Oh, isn't it jolly to be back!'

'They've painted the cross again on the low mark,' said John. 'It jolly well needed it, too.'

'They must be here,' said Titty. 'No one else would have bothered to do it. No one else knows about it.'

The moment they had sailed past the entrance there was nothing to be seen but grey rocks. No one who did not know would have guessed that a snug harbour was hidden among them. For its size the harbour on Wild Cat Island was certainly one of the finest harbours in the world.

John put up the helm, hauled in his mainsheet, jibed the boom carefully over, met his vessel with the helm again, and let the mainsheet out steadily and not all in a rush. *Swallow*, with a following wind, was running up the channel between the island and the mainland.

'There's the landing-place,' shouted Roger, as soon as he could see it. 'But *Amazon* isn't there either.'

John sailed on and then hauled in the sheet for a moment while he headed *Swallow* for the little strip of smooth beach.

'She'll do it now,' he said to himself, and let the sheet out again until the sail flapped idly in the wind while the *Swallow* slid more and more slowly into smoother and smoother water. She was moving at last so slowly that the crew hardly felt her as she stopped with her nose on the beach. The ship's boy, painter in hand, jumped ashore.

'Lower away now, Mister Mate,' said the captain.

Susan had already scrambled forward over the cargo. She loosed the halyard and paid it out hand over hand. Down came the yard and was unhooked by the able-seaman, while the captain gathered boom and sail into the boat.

The parrot was the next man ashore, handed out in his cage to the ship's boy. The able-seaman followed the parrot. Then came the mate and the captain. They waited just long enough to pull *Swallow* well up before hurrying to the old camping place in the open ground among the trees. Roger, Titty and the parrot got there first.

There was no one waiting for them. But, not far from the fireplace, left from last year, there was a large stack of driftwood all ready for burning, and on the top of it was a big white envelope, pegged in its place by an arrow with a green feather.

'The Amazons,' shouted Roger. 'It's one of their arrows.'

'One of your old feathers, Polly,' said Titty, putting down the cage, and the parrot, seeing his green feather in the arrow twanged his beak on the bars and let out a long angry scream.

Susan pulled out the arrow.

On the envelope was written in blue pencil: 'TO THE SWALLOWS.'

'Open it,' said Captain John.

Inside it was a sheet of paper on which was written in red pencil:

'TO THE SWALLOWS FROM THE AMAZON PIRATES. WELCOME TO WILD CAT ISLAND. WE'LL COME AS SOON AS EVER WE CAN. NATIVE TROUBLE. CAPTAIN FLINT IS STUCK TOO. HAS TITTY REMEMBERED THE GREEN FEATHERS? THESE ARE OUR LAST. SWALLOWS AND AMAZONS FOR EVER!

NANCY BLACKETT, THE TERROR OF THE SEAS, CAPTAIN OF THE *AMAZON*.

PEGGY BLACKETT, MATE.

P.S. – WE'LL BE WATCHING FOR YOUR SMOKE.'

Opposite the two signatures, a skull and crossbones had been drawn in pencil and then blacked in heavily with ink.

'Have you got the feathers for them, Titty?' said John.

'Of course I have,' said the able-seaman. 'They're in an envelope rolled up in my sleeping-bag. I haven't lost a single one.'

WILD CAT ISLAND FROM THE SOUTH

2

Wild Cat Island

'I WONDER what they mean by "native trouble",' said Able-seaman Titty, when she had read the letter carefully through to herself.

'That's just Nancy,' said Mate Susan. 'She always thinks there's no fun without trouble, so she'd put it in anyhow.'

'But it's very queer about Captain Flint,' said John.

'They'll probably be here before we get the camp ready,' said Susan. 'And Mother and Bridget are coming to tea. Let's get to work.'

'We'd better start the fire first, if they're watching for it,' said John.

'We'll rouse them with the red glare like the burghers of Carlisle,' said Titty. 'But, of course, it's the smoke that matters. They could see that if they've gone up the hill behind their house.'

No one was so good at starting a fire as Mate Susan. In a moment she had a flame licking up her handful of dry leaves, and setting light to the little wigwam of dead reeds and twigs she had built over it. A moment later the fire was taking hold of the larger sticks she had built round it, with every stick pointing in towards the middle. There was a pleasant crackling of burning wood, and a stream of clean blue smoke from the dry fuel poured away through the green trees. Wild Cat Island was once more inhabited.

'Now for the cargo,' said Mate Susan, standing up again and blinking the smart out of her eyes. 'Where's that boy?' She took out her whistle and blew it. This brought Roger running back from the look-out post under the tall tree at the northern end of the island, always his favourite place.

'No exploring till the camp's pitched.'

'Turn to, my hearties,' said the able-seaman. 'That's what Captain Nancy would be saying.'

'Turn to, then,' said the mate.

'All hands to discharge cargo,' said Captain John and the whole crew set to work getting the things out of the boat, and carrying them up through the trees to the clear space where they meant to camp.

As soon as the *Swallow* was clear of cargo, Captain John rowed her down to the foot of the island, and then, sculling with one oar over the stern, brought her into harbour, steering her in through the rocks awash and under water by keeping the two marks on shore (the stump with a white cross on it and the forked tree) exactly one behind the other. Then he rolled up the sail, coiled the ropes, and moored *Swallow* with the painter over her bows to the stump with the white cross on it and a warp over her stern to a stout bush on one of the rocks, so that his little ship lay afloat and as snug as any ship's captain could wish. He looked her all over. Everything was as it should be, and he hurried back to the camp by the old path from the harbour. It had grown over again a good deal since Titty had trimmed it last year.

In the camp the fire was already roaring in the stone fireplace under the big black kettle brought from Holly Howe. Each of the four new sleeping-tents lay where it was to be put up and the mate was only waiting for the captain to help her to sling the stores tent on a rope between two trees. This did not take long, and as soon as the tent was hanging from its rope, the able-seaman and the boy were kept hard at it filling the pockets along the bottom of the tent walls with little stones to keep them in place. Then one of the old groundsheets was spread inside, and in about two minutes the mate had bundled in everything that was not going to be wanted at once. The sleeping-tents needed no trees, but it was a hard job to find places where the stony ground would take the tent pegs. There were stones almost everywhere close under the mossy turf, but by shifting a stone here and a stone there, and making holes ready for the pegs before trying to drive them in, the explorers managed very well, and soon all four tents were standing, arranged so that anybody lying in any one of them could see the fireplace through the doorway. Then the guy-ropes were tightened up, the groundsheets were spread, the sleeping-bags unrolled and a little candle-lantern fixed in a safe place at the head of each tent, well clear of the walls.

Almost everything was to be kept in the stores tent, but Roger had got a new fishing rod and would not let it be stacked with the others, but wanted it with him in his own tent. 'It doesn't take any room longwise,' he said, 'and I might want to fish with it any time.' Titty would not be parted from her box of writing things. And, of course, John kept in his own tent the tin box with the ship's papers, and had his

THE ISLAND CAMP

21

watch and the little barometer he had won as a prize at school hanging from hooks on the bamboo tent pole at the head of his tent, so that he could unhook them and look at them in the night without having to get up.

'It's a far better camp than last year,' said Titty, looking at the four sleeping-tents and the stores tent that once had been hers and Susan's. 'And it'll be better still when the Amazons have put their tent up in the old place. Let's put some damp stuff on the fire to make a smoke they can't help seeing.'

'It doesn't matter how soon anybody comes now,' said the mate.

Titty and John pulled handfuls of damp green grass and threw them on the fire until a thick column of bitter grey smoke poured up and nearly choked them.

'Is the boy up at the look-out point?' said the mate.

Roger crawled hurriedly out of his tent where just for a minute he had been practising being asleep, ready for the night.

'Can we explore now?' he said. 'And can I take the telescope?'

'It's in the captain's tent,' said the mate.

'No. I've got it,' said the captain, and handed it over to the ship's boy, who dashed off with it at once to Look-Out Point, to lie there hidden behind a clump of heather with the telescope poking through it so that without being seen he could look far up the lake, as far as the islands off Rio.

The parrot, who had been quiet for some time, suddenly called out, 'Pieces of eight! Pieces of eight!'

Titty opened the door of his cage.

'Come on, Polly. You can come out and enjoy yourself like everybody else.'

The parrot scrambled out at once, but took no notice of Titty who offered him her hand to perch on. The parrot had its cold eye on the arrow with the green feather that Roger had stuck in the ground by the woodpile, and the moment his cage was opened, he made straight for it. Titty saw what he was after and quickly pulled up the arrow and put it out of the parrot's sight, on the top of the woodpile.

'No, no!' she said. 'You know you'll only chew them and rumple them till they're no good for anything. It isn't as if you moulted such a lot of them. There aren't any to spare. Susan, may I give him a lump of sugar?'

But the parrot was not to be comforted with sugar. What he wanted was his own green feathers from the Amazons' arrow, and as he could not have them, he went back into his cage to sulk.

They left the parrot to forget his bad temper, and

hid the arrow behind some of the boxes in the stores tent because, as John said, the Amazons were sure to want it, and as Titty said, Polly didn't seem to like seeing his feathers being useful after he'd thrown them away himself. The captain, the mate and the able-seaman went together along the path by the western shore of the island down to the harbour to see *Swallow* lying there in her old snug berth. It was no use waiting for Roger. After all there would be the boat from Holly Howe, bringing the best of all natives and the ship's baby. And then there might be Captain Flint in his big rowing boat, and at any minute the little white sail of the *Amazon* might come into sight from among the Rio Islands. There was really some sense in being a look-out, and nothing would stir Roger from his post.

On the beach in the harbour there were the marks of several boats. One, of course, showed where John had landed in the *Swallow*. The others, they thought, must have been left by the *Amazon*.

'They probably beached her here while they were putting the new paint on the leading mark,' said John.

'And piling up all that wood,' said Susan.

'They've painted it very well,' said Titty, looking at the white cross painted on the tree stump that served, with the forked tree behind it, to show the way to mariners who wished to bring their ships in safely through the rocks outside. 'And the nails are still there where we had the lanterns last year.'

'Mother says, "No more night sailing,"' said John, 'and I've promised, so we shan't want the leading lights.'

'We can easily plan things that don't need night sailing,' said Titty. 'There's lots of the Antarctic unexplored and all the Arctic at the other end of the lake.'

'It's no good talking about that till the Amazons come,' said John.

'And Captain Flint,' said Titty.

There was a great deal to look at. There was the rock where Titty had lain flat on her stomach and seen the dipper bob at her and fly under water. There was the rock she had hidden behind when Nancy and Peggy had come ashore with a lantern in the dark and she had been alone on the island. John, looking at the little waves lapping on the rocks outside, was remembering how Nancy had first shown him how to use the marks. Susan, looking down the lake, was trying to find the place where she had made a fire on the shore after their visit to the charcoal-burners up in the high woods. This year there was no trickle of smoke up there among the trees, and, indeed, Mrs Jackson, the farmer's wife at Holly Howe, had told them already that the charcoal-burners were not working on this side of the lake but up beyond the moor on the other side, in the next valley.

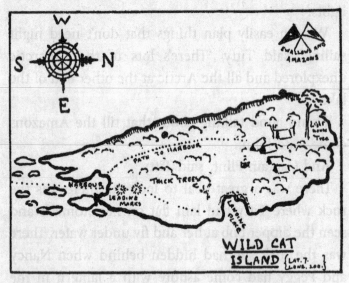

All three, even Susan, who, as mate, felt herself in charge of the others, for John, though captain, was a boy and not to be counted on in some things, walked on their toes, springily, and talked very quietly. To be back on Wild Cat Island was almost too good to be true. Titty dipped her hands in the cool water of the harbour, just to show herself that she was really there. They went slowly back, pushing their way through the bushes above the western shore, looking out through the leaves at the bright glint of evening sunshine on the lake below them. They had been all over the island and were just thinking of bathing, when they heard a shrill yell from the look-out point.

'There they are!'

All three of them ran up through the camp and under the tall tree. Roger was lying on his stomach at the edge of the cliff that dropped down there into the lake.

'Where? Where?' asked John, looking everywhere for the little white sail of the *Amazon*. There were rowing boats, motor boats, a few big yachts and a steamship, but no little white sail was to be seen.

'Mother and Bridget,' said Roger.

'Let me have the telescope,' said the mate.

She took one look, then gave the telescope to Titty, and ran down again into the camp.

Titty looked. Already this side of Houseboat Bay she could see the native rowing boat from Holly Howe. Mother was rowing and Bridget was sitting in the stern in the middle of a lot of parcels.

Titty ran down into the camp to help Susan. Susan was right. There was no time to lose if a kettle was to be brought to the boil, and everything else made just as it should be. John and Roger waited together up on Look-Out Point, watching the rowing boat grow larger until even without the telescope it was easy to see who was in it. At last the rowing boat was within hailing distance. Bridget waved and Mother looked over her shoulder as the captain and the ship's boy called to her over the water. Presently they were looking down into the rowing boat as Mother rowed past, and then they ran down through the camp to join the mate and the able-seaman at the landing-place.

Mother brought her boat in just as they got there.

'Last year we rubbed noses,' said Titty, as Mother stepped ashore. 'Do you remember being a native?'

'I don't see why we shouldn't do it again,' said Mother, and she did, and after that, of course, the ship's baby went native and had to rub noses with everybody all round.

'Tea's all ready,' said Susan, 'but we came away without any bread.'

'That's all right,' said Mother. 'It was on my list, not yours. Bread *and* bunloaf.'

'And you were going to bring us some milk.'

'I've brought you enough for tonight. But you'll get the morning's milk from Mrs Dixon's. She'll be expecting you. We sent word along from Holly Howe.'

Everybody helped to carry up the stores from the

boat. Susan hurried on ahead with the loaves and the milk-can. Bridget ran after her with a big packet of candles for the lanterns. Mother stayed till the last of the stores had been taken out of the rowing boat. Then she helped John, Titty and Roger to carry them up into the camp.

'It's a very good camp,' she said as she came into it and saw the four little tents and the stores tent among the trees. 'And I must say you haven't been long in getting a grand store of wood together.'

'The Amazons did that for us,' said Susan.

'What?' said Mother. 'Were Nancy and Peggy here to meet you? I half thought you might find them here. How jolly! And have you seen your friend, Captain Flint?'

'We haven't seen them yet,' said Susan. 'But they'd been here and left the wood for us.'

'And a letter fixed with one of their arrows. Green feathers, you know, Polly's, from last year,' said Titty.

'Peace or war?' said Mother.

'Oh, peace, of course,' said Titty.

'To start with, anyhow,' said John.

'But Captain Flint isn't in his houseboat,' said Roger. 'And he's gone and covered up the cannon with a black sheet.'

'Really,' said Mother. 'He must be stopping with his

sister at Beckfoot. I had a note from Mrs Blackett after you started. She's coming over tomorrow afternoon to Holly Howe with her brother and Miss Turner. Mrs Jackson at Holly Howe wanted to start cleaning the whole farm up as soon as she heard Miss Turner was coming.'

'I didn't know there was a Miss Turner,' said John.

'She's Nancy's and Peggy's great-aunt,' said Mother.

'Why a great-aunt?' asked Roger.

'Because she's aunt to Mrs Blackett and to your Captain Flint. And so she's great-aunt to your allies. What's become of Bridget? Bridget! Bridget!'

There was no answer. But Titty pulled Mother's sleeve and pointed to one of the tents. Anybody could see that there was something crawling about in it.

'I'd forgotten that she was ship's baby,' said Mother. 'Susan, Mister Mate, would you mind blowing your whistle to let the ship's baby know it's time for tea?'

Mate Susan blew her whistle and a moment later the tousled head of the ship's baby showed at the door of the captain's tent as she came crawling out.

'I shall soon have to be making a tent for Bridget,' said Mother. 'Next year she'll be wanting to go to sea like the rest of you.'

'Couldn't you make a tent for Gibber, too?' said Roger.

'I don't believe he'd really like it,' said Mother.

Gibber and Bridget were both on the ship's papers, but for different reasons were not really members of the crew. Bridget was too young. She was only three, and though she was growing up fast and everybody had stopped calling her Vicky because she no longer looked like Queen Victoria in old age, she was hardly old enough and strong enough for the hardships of life on shipboard or on a desert island. She was to stay at Holly Howe with Mother. Gibber was the monkey. He had been given to Roger by Captain Flint, after last year's adventures. He was very active and tireless, and Mother had said that he would be altogether too much of a good thing in someone else's farmhouse. Roger himself, when asked if he would really like to share his tent with the monkey at night, had agreed that perhaps it would be as well if the monkey had his summer holidays at the same time as the rest of the Walkers had theirs. So the monkey had been packed off to spend a happy month, staying with relations, at the zoo.

That first night on Wild Cat Island the explorers ran tea on into supper. It did not seem worth while to have two boilings and two washings-up when tea was late already. So, after tea had really begun, there was a great scrambling of eggs in the frying-pan by Susan, a great buttering of bunloaf and bread by Mother, a lot of stoking of the fire by Titty, while the boy took a big mouthful of bunloaf to last out and went down with the captain to bring up the saucepan full of water so that it could be put on the fire the moment the kettle came off and the eggs were cooked. Then, when supper was over, Mother lent a hand with the washing up and it got done much faster than most people would think possible.

Then Bridget had to see the parrot put to sleep in the stores tent, with his blue cover over his cage so that he should not wake the camp by loud shouts at dawn. Then both the visitors were taken all over the island and shown even the harbour, which had been kept secret the year before. At Look-Out Point, Bridget was allowed to look through the telescope. But it was already after her bedtime and Mother was in a hurry to take her back.

'Time for Bridget's watch below,' she said. 'She didn't get half the sleep she should have had last night, after the railway journey, what with all the chattering there was between decks.'

The others laughed.

'It was the first night of the holidays,' said John. 'At least, the first that really counted.'

'Well,' said Mother, 'she's got to make up for it tonight.'

The four explorers took the best of all natives and the ship's baby down to the landing-place and saw them into their boat.

'I think you should be all right,' said Mother, saying goodbye.

'We jolly well are,' said John.

'Remember what Daddy said, and don't go and be duffers and get drowned. And, of course, if you want anything, give a note to Mrs Dixon in the morning when you go for the milk.'

'We'll send a mail, anyhow,' said Titty.

'Push her off now, John. Good night. Don't stay up late. Get a good sleep. Let me see. What was the word in native language? Glook, was it? or Drool? Drool. Drool.'

'Never mind about talking native,' said Titty. 'We've been teaching you English all this year.'

'So you have,' said Mother. 'Good night. Sleep like old trees and get up like young horses, as my old nanny in Australia used to say.'

'Good night. Good night. Good night, Bridgie.'

The four explorers ran up to the look-out point

once more, partly to wave to Mother on her way up the lake, partly in the hope that they might yet see the little white sail that would show that Nancy and Peggy were coming to the island.

'It's too late for them to come now,' said Susan.

'You never know with Nancy,' said John.

'They'd think nothing of coming in the dark,' said Titty.

'Well, we've left the place for their tent,' said John.

They watched the Holly Howe rowing boat grow smaller and smaller in the distance. At last it disappeared behind the Peak of Darien. Roger, who had been following it as long as he could, shut the telescope with a click, yawned and rubbed his eyes.

They went down into the camp. There was some tidying-up and some washing of hands and faces at the landing-place, a last expedition to the harbour to see that *Swallow* was comfortable for the night, and then Mate Susan began to hurry the crew to bed. She found it easy enough to persuade the explorers to get into their new sleeping-bags and to lie down in their new tents. But this first night on the island, after a whole year away from it, nobody could settle down to sleep at once. One thing after another came into somebody's head. Sometimes it would be John who thought of it, sometimes Titty, very often it was Roger, and sometimes even Susan had something to say that she was afraid she would forget if she left it till next day. Long after the captain had said 'Lights out' and the little lanterns had been blown out in each tent, talk went on. It stopped at last. Roger was asleep, and perhaps Susan. Titty whispered very quietly, 'John.'

'What is it?'

'What do you think yourself Nancy meant by native trouble?'

'Oh, I don't know. Go to sleep, or they'll come and find us not up in the morning.'

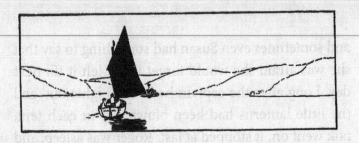

3

Horseshoe Cove and the Amazon Pirates

TIRED as they had been the night before, the explorers woke early. As the sun rose above the wooded hills on the eastern side of the lake it poured down through the trees on the island and splashed the little white tents with light so strong that nobody could sleep, and it was easier to look at the green outside than at the dancing, dazzling patches on the tent walls.

Roger woke and listened. There was a rustle of leaves in the trees and the noise of little waves splashing on the rocks. It was lonely, waking up for the first time in a tent with no one else in it, and Roger crawled out at once and made sure that the other tents were there, and then looked in through their open doorways to see that the rest of the crew were inside them. John and Susan might still have been asleep, but Titty was propped up on one elbow and looking out.

'Hullo, Roger!' she said, when the ship's boy blocked the doorway and looked in.

'Hullo, Titty!' said he.

'We're really here,' said Titty.

'I know we are,' said Roger.

'I never thought we would be again. Let's go and bathe.'

'John and Susan are asleep.'

'Hullo!' said John. 'Have the Amazons come in the night?'

'It's only Roger and me.'

'Go to sleep,' said Susan.

'We're going to bathe,' said Roger.

'What's the time, John?'

'Half-past six.'

'They can't go for the milk for an hour yet.'

'May I open up the fire and put some wood on to make a smoke?' said Titty.

'Bother you fo'c'sle hands,' said the mate.

'It's no good trying to sleep now,' said the captain. 'Let's all bathe.'

A few minutes later the cheerful screaming of a parrot brought out into the sunshine and four big splashes in the shallows by the landing-place showed that all five of the ship's company had agreed that the day had properly begun.

'Put your head right under, Roger,' said the mate. 'Put it under right away. You can do what you like afterwards.'

'Pouf!' said Roger, blowing and puffing and spluttering as he came up again. 'I went right down to the bottom. This is better than swimming-baths. Come on, Titty. Let's see who can pick up most pearls in one dive.'

After the bathing there was the fire to make up and the kettle to boil. There was not much hurry about the kettle, so as soon as the fire had burnt up well the boy and the able-seaman brought handfuls of damp leaves from the water's edge and threw them on the flames so that a great column of smoke poured up through the trees and drifted away to the north.

'They ought to see that if they're looking,' said Titty.

'They're probably asleep in bed,' said Susan.

'I'm jolly glad we're not,' said Roger. 'Isn't it time now to go for the milk?'

'We'll all go,' said Susan.

'What about the mail for Mother?' said John. Titty

dived into her tent for the box with the writing things. The box made a good desk to write on. Titty did the writing but everybody suggested things to say. This was the letter:

'My (crossed out) Our dearest Mother,

Good morning. Everybody slept very well. Everybody is very well. We hope you are very well. Love to the ship's Baby, and Nurse and Mrs Jackson. We've just bathed. No Amazons yet. Wind south. Light. Sky clear. Now we are going to get the milk.

Much love from   John, Susan, Titty, Roger.

P.S. – Love from Polly.'

She addressed the envelope to Mrs Walker, Holly Howe, and wrote 'Native Post' in very small letters in the top left-hand corner.

While the others were putting their names to the letter and Titty was doing the envelope, John went off to the harbour to fetch *Swallow*. He paddled her out through the rocks and round to the landing-place where the others came aboard. It was not really far to row, but with such a friendly wind blowing, making it an easy reach both ways, it seemed silly not to sail, even across Shark Bay to the landing-place for Dixon's Farm.

DIXON'S FARM

'They *were* geese,' said Roger, as soon as they had climbed up the steep field and come through the damson trees to the farm. 'I knew they were.'

'Aye,' said Mrs Dixon, coming to the door. 'Geese they are, but don't you be afraid of them.'

'We're not,' said Roger. 'At least (as the old gander stretched its neck towards him and hissed) not really.'

'Shoo,' said Mrs Dixon. 'Shoo,' and the geese went off to the other end of the yard. 'Just you say "Shoo" to them and make as if you'd give them what for if they didn't shift, and they'll not trouble you. Well, and I'm rare and pleased to be seeing you all again. Many's the laugh I've had, thinking how I had to come down to you with a bucket of porridge after the storm, and you taking your breakfast out of the bucket. You won't be seeing so much of Miss Ruth and Miss Peggy just now. Nor their Uncle Jim neither.'

(Ruth was Nancy's real name, but she liked being Nancy better.)

'They're coming,' said Titty.

'I was thinking that with old Miss Turner staying at Beckfoot they'll maybe be wanted at home. She's terrible stiff is Miss Turner, and always was. She never did hold with their rampaging around in a boat. Well, Miss Susan, and where's your can? Quite like old

41

times, it is, to be having you coming for milk in the mornings.'

In a few minutes she came hustling back with the milk-can full to the brim.

'Deary me,' she said, just as they were going, 'and where are the toffees I laid out for you?'

She went back into the kitchen and the explorers outside could hear her say, 'Go on now. There's nowt to be feared of. They're nobbut childer.' And then there was the noise of iron-shod boots scraping on the slate floor, and Mr Dixon came to the doorway wiping his mouth with the back of his hand.

'It bids fair to be a grand day,' he said.

'How do you do?' said the explorers.

'Champion,' said Mr Dixon, 'and – and I'm right glad to see you.' He went back into the kitchen.

'He means that,' said Mrs Dixon, coming to the door again with a bag of toffees. 'Dixon never was a one for talking.'

And then the explorers thanked her and went down the field to their ship and sailed back to the island.

*

For a long time after breakfast was over and washing up done they kept watch on Look-Out Point for the coming of the *Amazon*. Again and again they dumped armfuls of damp leaves on the fire. But they looked in vain for the little white sail. The early steamers passed the island on their way up and down the lake. Launches began to run to and fro. Here and there a rowing boat drifted along the edge of the lake while a fisherman, seated in it, searched the shallows with his flies. Two or three of the larger yachts came out to air their sails. All the life of the lake seemed to be astir in the sunshine and still there was no sign of the Amazon pirates whose arrow with its green feathers had been waiting for them in the camp.

'It's very funny about their not coming,' said John.

'I wonder what Mrs Dixon meant,' said Titty.

'Perhaps they're not coming till tomorrow,' said Susan.

'Let's begin exploring without waiting for them,' said Roger.

'Where?' said John.

'Where we left off last year,' said Titty eagerly. 'Let's go to Horseshoe Cove. It's a lovely place. We had no time really to look at it. We don't know what there is if you go up the beck. Let's go up the beck to its source and put it on our map.'

'Horseshoe Cove is a good harbour,' said John, 'and it's in sight of the island. We could see if they came here after we'd gone. What about rations, Mister Mate?'

'It's nearly dinner-time,' said Susan.

'Let's have dinner in the cove,' said Titty.

'Why not?' said John. 'Let's have pemmican, Mister Mate. We haven't had any since last year.'

'Come along then, you fo'c'sle hands,' said Susan.

Half an hour later the camp on Wild Cat Island was deserted except for the parrot, who was left on guard in his cage with a good store of sugar to keep him happy. The fire had been put out, for the mate did not like to leave it burning with nobody but the parrot to look after it. A knapsack full of bunloaf and apples and tea and sugar and chocolate, a jar of marmalade, the paper bag of Mrs Dixon's toffees (molasses), a tin of pressed beef (pemmican), a bottle of milk, one spoon and enough mugs to go round had been loaded into *Swallow* and she was pushed off from the landing-place.

The captain hoisted sail, the mate steered, the able-seaman took care that the cargo did not shift or spill or break, and the boy kept a look-out before the mast. They sailed first with the wind to have a look into Houseboat Bay, thinking that perhaps Captain Flint was back in the houseboat and his nieces with him. But the houseboat looked as dreary as ever, with its tarpaulin over the foredeck, and white curtains drawn across the cabin windows.

Then they beat down the lake, past Wild Cat Island to Horseshoe Cove.

Horseshoe Cove owed its name to its shape. It was a little bay, shaped like a horseshoe, shut in between two rocky headlands on the western side of the lake. It lay just about south-west from the southern end of Wild Cat Island. There were woods that came down to the water's edge there, though a little farther south there were green fields. Some way behind the cove the woods climbed steeply up the hillside towards the heather and bracken of the fells. Three or four tacks brought the *Swallow* to the entrance so that the mate could sail straight in between the headlands.

'Rock on the port bow,' sang out Roger, just as they turned in.

'A beast, too,' said John. 'I don't remember seeing it last year.'

'It's all right with this wind,' said the mate, 'but I wouldn't like to run on it in the dark.'

'The day we were here was the day after the storm when the lake was very high. It must be much lower today.'

They looked at the waves breaking on a sharp-pointed rock that showed, awash, opposite the southern headland of the little cove.

In another moment they had left the open lake. *Swallow*, her pennant drooping, her mainsheet slack, was slipping across the smooth water of the sheltered cove towards a beach of white shingle below thick green trees.

'Don't steer for the mouth of the stream,' said John. 'There's a bit of a bar there made by the stuff the stream brings down. Nancy showed it me last year. The best landing-place is this side. That's right. Couldn't be better. Ready with the painter, Roger?'

'Aye, aye, sir,' said the boy, jumping ashore as the boat touched.

As soon as the sail had been lowered and the kettle filled over the stern of the *Swallow* and carried ashore, Susan went to look for the old fireplace that she had built last year by the side of the stream, just where it joined the lake. Hardly a trace of it was left after the winter floods, but there were plenty of stones to build from, and while she was making a new fireplace, John, Titty and Roger were picking the best bits of driftwood they could find lying along the high-water mark in the cove. There were plenty of dry leaves for kindling, and dry reeds for the first little wigwam over the burning leaves. No one had been in the cove this year, so plenty of the larger driftwood for the real fire that was to boil the kettle was lying ready to be picked up. The kettle had already been filled, and the fire was burning up well, when the explorers were startled by a loud, cheerful shout from the lake.

'Ahoy! Ahoy! Swallows! Ahoy!'

A small varnished dinghy, about the size of *Swallow*, but with a white sail instead of her tanned one, was sailing in between the headlands. At the masthead was a black flag with the skull and crossbones on it in white. Two red-capped girls were the crew. One was steering. The other waved her hand as she started forward to be ready to haul up the centreboard.

'It's them,' shouted Titty. 'Hurrah! Now we can really start.'

'Hullo, pirates!' called Roger.

'Hullo, Nancy! Hullo, Peggy!'

'Hullo, my hearties!' called the girl who was steering. 'Up with the centreboard, Peggy. That's right. . . . Stand by with the halyard. Lower away.'

Down came the white sail and the little ship, on whose bows could now be plainly seen her name, *Amazon*, slipped on across the smooth water of the cove and grounded close beside the *Swallow*. The whole crew of the *Swallow* had left the fire and run down to be ready to lend a hand. They hauled her up a little and Nancy and Peggy Blackett jumped ashore and there was some tremendous shaking of hands.

'Did you see our smoke?' asked Titty.

'Uncle Jim saw it last night when he went up the fell for a smoke,' said Nancy. 'Aunt Maria doesn't like tobacco in the house.'

'We couldn't get away until late this morning,' said Peggy. 'And then we saw *Swallow*'s brown sail going into the cove soon after we had got past Rio Bay.'

'We waited a good long time,' said John, 'and we thought it would be all right coming here because we could see if you went to the island.'

'We could have given you the slip and got there without your knowing,' said Nancy. 'You never knew we were on the lake till we hailed when we were coming into the cove.'

'We were busy with the fire,' said Susan.

'But where's your tent?' asked John. 'We left your old place for it. We've got four tents this year, and one of the old ones for all the stores.'

'The new tents are beauties,' said Roger. 'I've got one of my own.'

'Shiver my timbers,' said Captain Nancy, 'don't you understand? We put it in the message we left with the wood. We told you there was native trouble. We're jolly lucky to be here at all. We've got to be back and into best frocks for supper. We can't camp. What about the feathers, Able-seaman? How's the parrot?'

'He's not been moulting very well,' said Titty, 'but I've got about eight really good ones. Polly's looking after the island.'

'You don't mean real native trouble?' said Susan.

'It's as bad as it can possibly be,' said Nancy. 'We've only got to make a plan and it's scuppered at once. No camping. No gold-hunting. No piracy except just now and then between meals. And best frocks every evening and sometimes half the day. Native trouble? It simply couldn't be worse.'

'Where's Captain Flint?' asked Titty.

'He can't come until tomorrow,' said Peggy.

'Didn't we tell you he's stuck too. He's on duty today. That's how we got away.'

'He's going to tea at Holly Howe,' said Susan. 'Mother told us last night.'

'We saw he wasn't in the houseboat,' said Roger. 'He's covered up the cannon.'

'He isn't allowed to live there,' said Peggy. 'He has to sleep at home.'

'But aren't you coming to Wild Cat Island?'

'Not until she goes.'

'Until who goes?'

'The great-aunt, of course,' said Captain Nancy. 'And she only came the day before you did.'

'But you needn't bring her,' said Titty.

'If we could maroon her we would,' said Nancy. 'We'd tie her to the anchor and send her to the bottom in forty fathoms. We'd feed her to the sharks. We'd leave her on a rock to be eaten by land-crabs. We'd hang her in a tree for crows – or vultures. Vultures would be better. We'd . . . There's nothing we wouldn't do. Can you think of anything really good?'

'Nancy thinks of something new each night for us to dream about while we're going to sleep. Last night it was land-crabs. The night before that it was white ants.'

'You know,' said Nancy, 'eating her up, like the fox ate up the Spartan boy. It's nothing to what she deserves. Why couldn't she come in term-time, when it wouldn't have mattered so much?'

'But it'll be all right if you're camping on the island with us,' said John.

'But we can't come,' said Nancy.

'We've got to be on view,' said Peggy, 'all the time.'

'Our aunts aren't like that,' said Roger.

'Nor are most of ours,' said Nancy. 'Some of ours aren't native a bit. One of them might almost be a pirate. But the great-aunt's altogether different. There's no help for it. We've got to be mostly native till she goes. If she ever does. It isn't as if it was only us. We'd bolt, but she'd have Mother and Uncle Jim as hostages. They're much more afraid of her than we are. You see, she brought them up.'

'Won't you be able to come at all?' said Roger.

'We'll always have to be back for some beastly meal,' said Nancy.

'The kettle'll be boiling in a minute,' said Susan, reminded of the dinner she was getting ready. It was a dreadful thing that all their plans were going wrong. But dinner had to be eaten just the same. 'Have you got mugs?' she called over her shoulder as she hurried back to the fire.

'Rather,' said Peggy. 'And we've got our rations in the boat. There's a cake and mugs in the knapsack. That other thing's a meat pie. It was meant for native dinner last night, but the great-aunt said it was too salt, so cook said this morning we'd better have it and if the great-aunt wanted to see it again she'd have to do without. So we swiped it. It isn't a bit too salt really. We dipped our fingers in the juice and tried what it was like while we were sailing down.'

She climbed back into *Amazon* and passed out the knapsack and then came carefully ashore with the meat pie.

'Sorry we've got no grog,' said Nancy. 'Cook's had no time to make any, being so busy with the great-aunt.'

'We've got plenty of milk for tea,' said Susan.

The four Swallows and the two Amazons were soon sitting round Susan's fire, drinking tea and disagreeing altogether with the great-aunt's poor opinion of the meat pie. When the meat pie was done, John used the tin-opener in his new knife to open the pemmican tin. Then he used the knife itself to cut the pemmican into six bits. They did not last long. But there was bunloaf and marmalade for pudding and then cake, and after that apples and chocolate to fill up with.

'Let's keep the chocolate for rations while we're exploring,' said Titty. After all, even though everything might be going wrong with their plans, they had set out today to explore the stream that ran into the lake at Horseshoe Cove, and there was nothing to stop them from doing that.

'Where are you going to explore?' asked Nancy.

'We're going up the beck,' said Titty.

'You'll only come to the road,' said Peggy.

It very soon became clear that there would be no exploring that day if it depended on Nancy and Peggy. What they wanted to do was to talk about the great-aunt and about schools and about all sorts of things that had been happening since Christmas. They were both tired of having only each other as listener. And you had only to look at John and Susan to see that they were quite content to sit by their fire in the cove and listen for just as long as Nancy and Peggy cared to talk.

The able-seaman and the boy listened for a long time and sometimes even asked questions. But at last Roger began trying to keep two little stones in the air at once, and one of his stones fell in his mug and might have broken it if there had not been a little tea left in the bottom. He had stopped listening. And the able-seaman, remembering all those blank spaces on the map got up and beckoned to him.

'Where are you going?' asked Susan.

'Exploring,' said Titty.

'Don't go far from the stream,' said Susan, 'and don't be away too long. . . . What was that you were saying, Peggy?'

The able-seaman and the boy pushed their way into the bushes and disappeared behind a green curtain of leaves.

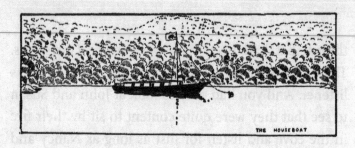

THE HOUSEBOAT

4

The Able-Seaman and the Boy Explore

'By mutual confidence and mutual aid
Great deeds are done, and great discoveries made.'

POPE'S *Homer*

FOR some time, as the able-seaman and the boy pushed their way through the bushes and small trees by the side of the stream, they could hear the talking of the others, Nancy and Peggy very loud and clear, John and Susan not so loud. Then they could hear only the voices of Nancy and Peggy. Then Nancy's voice alone was stronger than the rippling of the stream at the explorers' feet. Then they heard even Nancy's talk no more, though now and then, faint and far away as it was, there was no mistaking her cheerful laugh. After that, they could hear nothing but the noise of the water toppling over six-inch waterfalls and down pebbly rapids. The stream was too wide to jump across, but there were places where it was possible to hop from stone to stone and to get across with dry feet if you were lucky. The trees grew close to the stream, and in some places the water had hollowed out a way for itself almost under their roots. There were little pools, foaming at the top where the stream ran in, and smooth and shallow and fast at the hang before it galloped away again down a tiny cataract.

'There's a fish,' said Roger.

'Where?'

'There isn't one now. But there was. Look! Look! There's another!' But that fish too was gone before the able-seaman had seen just where the ship's boy was pointing.

'They needn't be frightened,' said the able-seaman. 'It isn't as if we were herons. Keep still when you see the next one. Don't point at it.'

The boy hurried on with his eyes on the water close ahead of him. Suddenly he stopped dead, like a dog that smells partridges in a field of stubble. Titty crept up, stooping low, till she was close beside him.

'There,' said Roger. 'By the stone with the moss on it. Look! He's sticking his nose out.'

A widening ripple was washed away with the

stream, but it had been enough to show Titty where to look. There, in the clear water, she could see a small speckled fish which stayed almost in one place as if it were hung in the stream. As she looked it suddenly slanted up and broke the water again.

'He isn't a bit like the perch we caught in the lake,' said Roger.

'It's probably a trout,' said Titty.

'I wish we had our fishing rods,' said Roger. 'We'd catch dozens and dozens and take them back to feed the camp.'

'We couldn't fish in all these trees,' said Titty.

'Well, there are lots of fish,' said Roger.

'Anyway, we can't fish now. We are explorers, sent out into the jungle by the rest of the expedition. We mustn't think of anything else. At the very moment when we were looking at a fish there might be a yell. . . .'

'A blood-curdling kind of yell?'

'Of course blood-curdling. Boomerangs and arrows might come whizzing through the air. And even if we weren't killed at once the savages would tie us up and take us away, and then when the others came to look for us they would walk into the very same trap.'

'What's that noise?' said the ship's boy suddenly.

It was the noise of a motor horn. They both knew what it was, but it was far too good a noise to waste.

'The trumpets of the savages,' said Titty. 'There's probably a causeway through the forest. We must be near the edge of the jungle.'

Another horn sounded, on a different note, and they could hear the fierce throbbing roar of a motor bicycle.

'Trumpets and tom-toms,' said Titty. 'The savages have their scouts on the road trumpeting to each other. We shan't be able to go much farther. Peggy said we couldn't.'

'Well, let's go as far as we can,' said Roger.

This part of the wood was all smallish trees, growing thickly together. There were hazels, oaks, birches, and here and there an ash, and here and there a stout prickly bush of holly, or a lonely feathery pine waving high above the rest. There was honeysuckle, too, tangling bough with bough. It was as good a jungle as anyone could want. And through this jungle ran the little stream hurrying on its way to the lake.

The able-seaman and the boy pressed on. Suddenly they saw what looked like an opening in the trees away to the left. They crossed the stream and pushed through the bushes towards the opening, and found a cart track, which led through the trees to a gap in the stone wall along the edge of the wood. Perhaps there had been a gate in the gap once upon a time, but there was no gate now, and the ends of the wall had fallen down. Beyond the wall lay the road, and on the other side of the road was another wall of loose stones covered with moss. Beyond that was another kind of wood, larches and pines and a few firs climbing steeply up into the sky.

The able-seaman saw the road first. She dropped flat at once on the ground by the side of the cart track. The boy waited for half a second and then dropped beside her.

'We don't know whether they're friendlies or not,' said the able-seaman.

'The only people we know on this side of the lake are the Amazons,' said the boy.

'Well, we know where they are, so anyone on the road must be someone else.'

A motor car flashed across the gap in the wall. For a moment they caught through the trees the glint of sunlight on something bright; then they saw it in the gap; then it was gone. Then three natives on bicycles passed the gap, going the other way. Then came a noise which promised something better. It was the noise of horses' hoofs clumping on the hard road.

'Trotting or walking?' said Roger.

THE EXPLORERS

'Probably walking,' said Titty. 'It usually is when it sounds like the other. A lot of them, anyhow.'

The horses were a long time coming into sight, but when they came they were worth waiting for. Through the gap in the wall the able-seaman and the boy saw them pass by, three huge ruddy-brown horses, harnessed one before the other, and after them the thing that they were pulling, the trunk of a great tree chained down to two pairs of big red wooden wheels, a tree four or five times as big as the tall lighthouse tree on Wild Cat Island. One man was leading the first of the horses, and another man was resting, smoking a pipe, sitting high in air on the thin end of the great tree which stuck out over the road behind the second pair of wheels. He had his back towards the explorers, or he might easily have seen them from so high above the wall.

'Where is it going?' said Roger.

'Probably to be made into boats,' said Titty.

The larch wood at the farther side of the road looked easier going than the tangled jungle through which they had come.

'Can't we wriggle a bit nearer to the road,' said Roger, 'and then rush across when none of the natives are looking?'

'It's no good,' said Titty. 'There's someone passing every other minute.'

As she spoke another motor car went trumpeting by.

'I say,' said Roger a minute or two later. 'The natives couldn't see us if we went under their road instead of across it.'

'Of course they couldn't,' said Titty.

'There must be a bridge,' said Roger, 'where the stream comes through.'

'That's a jolly good idea.'

'I thought perhaps it would be.'

'We'll get back to the beck at once,' said Titty. They could hear it, not very far away, when they listened for it, and indeed they had left it only when they had been tempted by seeing the clearing where the cart track ran through the wood. They jumped up and plunged back into the bushes, found the stream and hurried along its banks. Not more than fifty yards from the place where they had lain watching the road through the gap in the old wall, they came to the bridge, a low, wide, ivy-covered arch. The road ran over it, but the ivy was so thick and the trees below the bridge grew so close to it that the explorers found that they could follow the stream right into the arch without being seen by anybody, unless some native happened to be looking down from the bridge at the moment. Looking through under the archway they could see the bright greens and browns of the larch wood and the glitter of sunlight on the water at the other side.

The able-seaman sat down. 'Take off your shoes, Boy,' she said.

'Aye, aye, sir,' said the boy.

'Tie the laces together so that you can hang them round your neck.' Her own shoes were off as she spoke. It was easier to untie them when there were no feet in them to put them into awkward positions. She untied them and then took the end of a lace from each and tied the two ends in a bow. 'You needn't tie yours so tight,' she said, looking to see what the boy was doing. 'You'll want them when we get through. Now, then. Put your feet exactly where I put mine.'

She stepped into the water. It rose to her ankles at the first step she took, and nearly to her knees at the second, but after that it got no deeper, and at one side, under the bridge, it was quite shallow.

'Slip in here,' said the able-seaman. 'I wish your legs were a bit longer. Don't let your knickers get wet. Roll them up as high as you can. Keep to this side.'

'Aye, aye, sir.'

'And whatever you do, don't tumble down.'

Steadying themselves with their hands against the low arch of the bridge that curved over their heads, and paddling in shallow clear water over stones slippery with moss, they crept carefully through under the bridge.

A big motor lorry passed overhead, making the old bridge shiver. The boy looked with scared eyes at the able-seaman. But this was one of those dangers that was gone before you had really had time to know it was there, and the able-seaman was already feeling for steadier stones in the pool above the bridge to find the best way to the bank.

'It's all right,' she said. 'Keep close along the wall. Don't step on the big stone. It waggles, but there's a good one here.'

There were no accidents. Both the explorers climbed safely out on the bank. Sitting so close under the wall that nobody could have seen them from the road, they dried their feet on their handkerchiefs, put their shoes on again, waited for a moment when nothing seemed to be passing, and darted forward in among the larch trees.

They climbed now, up through the steep larch wood, where the beck came noisily leaping down stone stairs to meet them. Up they climbed, keeping close to the stream until the larches ended and they were once more among hazels and oaks like those in the wood they had left on the other side of the road.

And then, suddenly there were no more trees, and the able-seaman and the boy stood under the open sky at the edge of the forest, looking out over mile upon mile of green and purple moorland, green with waving bracken, purple with knee-deep heather. And beyond the moorland, the sunshine searching their gullies and crags, rose the blue hills that from up here looked bigger, far, than they had seemed when looked at from Wild Cat Island or from Holly Howe.

'We must have one of them for Kanchenjunga,' said Titty.

'Which one?'

'The biggest.'

The stream came tumbling and twisting across the moorland to drop at their feet into the woods. In its winter strength it had washed away the earth round great stones and carved a deep gully for itself, so that though they could see where it was they could not see the water except close to them.

'Are we going on?' asked the boy.

'We can't get lost if we keep close to the beck,' said the able-seaman.

She started forward again along a sheep track that led through the heather close above the stream. The boy ate a piece of the chocolate he had saved, and hurried after the able-seaman. Sometimes the bracken grew so high that they could hardly see each other. Sometimes the sheep track wound down along the edge of the stream, turning this way and that round pale grey stones, and then climbed up again to twist its way among the tough clumps of purple heather. There was the stream to guide them, and now there was a new noise to draw them on. This was the noise of falling water, the same noise that they had had close beside them while they were climbing through the larch wood, but much louder now, and different when heard on the open moorland instead of under the trees.

'Look,' said the able-seaman suddenly. 'There it is.'

They hurried on until they stood below the waterfall. Above them the water poured down noisily from ledge to ledge of rock, and they could go no farther without climbing up the rocks beside the falling water or getting out of the long winding gully that the stream had carved for itself in the moor.

The able-seaman hesitated. This time it was the boy who wanted to go on. Before she had made up her mind, he was already climbing. A moment later she was climbing too, and they came together to the top of the dry rocks at the side of the fall.

'That was easy climbing,' said the boy. 'Hullo! . . .'

Neither of them had expected anything like what

they found when they scrambled over the top. It was a little valley in the moorland, shut in by another waterfall at the head of it, not a hundred yards away, and by slopes of rock and heather that rose so steeply that when the explorers looked up they could see nothing but the sky above them. In there it was as if the blue mountains did not exist. The valley might have been hung in air, for all that they could see outside it, except when they turned round and looked back, from the top of the waterfall they had climbed, to the moorland, the woods and the hills on the other side of the lake.

'It's a lovely place for brigands,' said the boy.

'It's just the place for Peter Duck,' said the able-seaman. 'It's the most secret valley that ever there was in the world.'

Peter Duck had grown up gradually to be one of the able-seaman's most constant companions, shared now and then by the boy, but not taken very seriously by the others, though nobody laughed at him. He had been the most important character in the story they had made up during those winter evenings in the cabin of the wherry with Nancy and Peggy and Captain Flint. Peter Duck, who said he had been afloat ever since he was a duckling, was the old sailor who had voyaged with them to the Caribbees in the story and, still in the story, had come back to Lowestoft with his pockets full of pirate gold. Titty had had a big share in his invention, and now she made him useful in all sorts of ways, sometimes when she and Roger were together, but mostly when she was by herself. Anything might happen to Peter Duck and he would always come out all right. Dolls meant nothing to Titty. Peter Duck was a great deal more useful than any doll could have been. He could always tidy himself away. He never got lost. He had no sawdust to run out. And she had only to think of him, when there he was, ready for any adventure in which he might be wanted.

'He could hide here from anybody who wanted to bother him. I don't believe he's ever had a better place. Let's see what it looks like from the top.'

Roger was already on his feet and crossing the stream, jumping from one dry stone to another.

'You go up that side,' Titty called to him, 'and I'll go up this, and then we'll see if it's as secret as it looks.'

They climbed up opposite sides of the valley and looked back at each other. They found they had only to go a few yards from the edge of it not to see that it was there. Titty in the heather above one side of the valley and Roger in the heather above the other side would never, if they had not known, have guessed that a valley lay between them.

'It's absolutely perfect,' shouted Titty.

'I think so, too,' shouted Roger.

They scrambled down again to meet in the bottom, and followed the stream to the upper waterfall. In several of the little pools on the way they saw small trout, and in the big pool under the waterfall, just as they got there, a larger trout jumped clean into the air after a fly and dropped again into the pool in a splash of silver.

'Peter Duck'll be able to fish,' said Titty. 'He always liked it. Do you remember how he was always trailing a hook for sharks over the stern of the schooner?'

'We'll fish too,' said Roger. 'What about our tea?'

That was the worst of Roger. He might get hungry at any minute.

'Have my chocolate,' said the able-seaman. 'I don't want it.'

'Really?' said Roger.

'Of course,' said Titty.

'Let's wait and see if that fish jumps again,' said Roger, 'and I'll eat the chocolate while we're watching.'

Titty handed over her chocolate and looked back down the valley and out through the V-shaped gap at the foot of it to the hills on the other side of the lake, and to other hills beyond them, hills so far away that she might have thought them clouds if the sky overhead had not been so very clear. From this upper end of the valley she could not see the moor below the waterfall, or the woods through which they had climbed. She looked at the valley itself, and its steep sides, one of them, on the right, almost a precipice of rock, with heather growing in the cracks of it, and the other, on the left, not so steep, with grass on it, bracken and loose stones. She was wishing she had her map with her, to mark in it the stream and the newly discovered valley, when, on a warm stone close to her, she saw a tortoiseshell butterfly, resting in the sunshine, with his brown and blue and orange and black wings spread out and all but still.

'Isn't he a beauty?' she said, and as she said it the butterfly fluttered off the stone and away down the valley, never far from the ground.

'He'll perch again and open his wings in a minute,' she said, and indeed the butterfly presently dropped on a clump of heather growing low down in a cleft in the steep slope of grey rock at which she had been looking.

Titty, on tiptoe, followed to look at him, but when she was almost near enough to touch the heather on which he had settled, she forgot all about him. When the butterfly fluttered away once more, she did not even see him go.

'Roger! Roger!' she cried. 'It's a cave!'

Roger heard her, in spite of the noise of the waterfall. He did not hear the words, but there was something urgent in her voice that was enough to put the trout out of his head. What had she found? He came, running, and found her looking under the clump of heather into a dark hole in the wall of grey rock. It was a hole, narrower at the top than at the bottom, big enough to let a stooping man use it as a doorway, and yet so well sheltered by the rock which, just here, leaned outward over it, and so deep in the shadow of the thick bushy heather that was growing out of cracks in the stone above it and on either side of it, that it would have been easy to think it was no more than a cleft in the rock, and easier still not to notice it at all. The two explorers crouched together, and tried to see into the black darkness inside.

'Fox,' said Roger, 'or perhaps bear. It's big enough for bear.'

'I wish I had my torch,' said Titty. 'Today I haven't even got a box of matches.'

They picked up stones and threw them in. Nothing came out at them, though they almost thought that something might. Titty held the heather aside and reached in the full length of her arm, just for a moment.

'It gets bigger inside,' she said. 'Higher too. I believe we could stand up in it. Shall we go in? It's not much good in the dark. Or shall we?'

'Let's go and get torches,' said Roger.

'Come on,' said Titty. 'We'll go and fetch the captain and the mate. We'll leave Peter Duck to look after it till we come back. It's his cave. I expect he's known about it always. Come on.'

They ran down the valley, scrambled down the rocks by the lower waterfall, and raced along the sheep tracks through the heather and bracken. Just where the beck left the moorland to tumble headlong down through the steep woods, Titty pulled up.

'The Amazons are there too,' she said.

Roger looked at her, more than a little out of breath.

'They've discovered almost everything there is to discover,' she said, 'but perhaps they don't know about that. We'll tell them about the valley, but keep the cave a secret, for us and Peter Duck.'

'We'll tell John and Susan.'

'We'll get them to come to see the valley and then have the cave for a surprise. A cave's far too good a thing to waste, and it's wasted if too many people know about it. Of course,' she added, 'if they won't come to see the valley, we'll have to tell them about the cave.'

They dropped quickly down through the trees, tore off their shoes and splashed their way under the bridge. They put their shoes on again without waiting to do much drying, and came breathless altogether to the shores of Horseshoe Cove.

*

They found, like many explorers before them, that somehow, in their absence, they had got into trouble at home. Tea had been made and drunk, scouting parties had been out to look for them, the Amazons were in a terrible hurry to be starting back, and the mate wanted to know why they had been away so long. The tea that had been saved for the able-seaman and the boy was nearly cold, and they were quickly bundled aboard the *Swallow* and told to drink it on the voyage home, for unless they started at once the Amazons, who were late already, would have to go without seeing the new tents.

But while the *Swallow* and the *Amazon* were being launched, the able-seaman and the boy began pouring out their story. They both began talking at once, but the boy soon gave up. After all, Titty could do it better. And Titty told of the moor above the wood, of the waterfall, and of the little valley above the waterfall, a valley so secret that anybody could hide in it for ever.

'Honest pirate?' called Nancy, who was already paddling *Amazon* towards the mouth of the cove. 'Honest pirate, or is it a Peter Duck story?'

'Peter Duck's in it, of course,' said Titty, 'but it's all true.'

The two little ships got under way. Nancy and Peggy in the *Amazon* waited for the *Swallow* outside the cove, and they sailed for Wild Cat Island within comfortable talking distance.

'That's the Pike Rock,' said Nancy, pointing out the rock opposite the southern of the two little headlands. 'You wouldn't be able to see it if the lake wasn't so low.'

'We saw it when we were coming in,' said John.

'It's awfully jagged,' said Peggy. 'Uncle Jim saw a fisherman sink his boat by rowing into it.'

In *Swallow* Titty was still talking of the secret valley. 'Nobody would find it,' she said, 'if they didn't know it was there.'

'She may be quite right,' said Nancy, from the *Amazon*. 'We've never gone up to the moor from this side. Are you sure about it, Able-seaman? A real secret one?'

'You couldn't tell it was there at all if you hadn't gone right into it,' said Roger.

'It might be just the place to go to when the great-aunt says we mustn't sail,' said Peggy.

'Do you think I haven't thought of that?' said Captain Nancy.

'You'll make me upset the mug,' said Roger, as Titty prodded him gently with her finger.

'They don't know about it,' she whispered.

'What about going there tomorrow?' said Nancy across the water.

'Say yes, say yes,' said Roger and Titty together.

'I don't see why we shouldn't,' said Captain John.

John and Nancy sailed their ships past the harbour at the foot of the island, up the inner channel, and brought them in at the landing-place.

'Just for one second,' said Nancy. 'We're late already.'

'We always are,' said Peggy. 'But the great-aunt makes being late seem much worse.'

They raced up from the landing-place and looked round the camp. Susan thanked them for the wood-pile. Titty dived into her tent and brought out the envelope with the eight green feathers she had saved for them. John brought the arrow from behind the boxes in the store tent. Both the Amazons said, 'How do you do' and 'Pieces of eight' to the parrot, but the

74

parrot had seen the green feathers and so would do nothing but squawk at them, though Titty tried to make him show off. They looked, sadly, at the place where their own tent used to stand. They said how good were the new tents of the Swallows, and then they hurried down to the landing-place, tumbled into the *Amazon* and pushed off.

'What about tomorrow?' asked Susan at the last minute.

'We'll go to see Titty's valley,' called Nancy. 'It might be very useful. Mother's taking the great-aunt out to lunch, so we needn't be in till tea. We'll sail straight to Horseshoe Cove in the morning. Be there before you are. Bet you anything. So long, Swallows!'

The four Swallows went up to Look-Out Point to watch the little white sail grow smaller and smaller as the *Amazon* sailed away towards the Peak of Darien.

'I don't see why they shouldn't have come here in the morning,' said Susan.

'It's beastly for them not being able to camp on the island when we can,' said John. 'After all they knew the island first.'

When the *Amazon* had sailed away so that the pirates could not hear shouts, let alone whispers, it was hard for the able-seaman and the boy to keep their secret. But keep it they did, though they came near giving it away.

'There's something more we discovered,' said Titty.

'Something better than anything we've told you yet.'

'What is it?' said Susan. 'Probably a caterpillar.'

'Well,' said Roger, 'a butterfly did help.'

'If it hadn't been for the butterfly we wouldn't have found it,' said Titty.

'What is it?' said John.

'It's the very thing Peter Duck's always been wanting.'

WILD CAT ISLAND FROM THE SOUTH

5

Captain John hangs on

'The old man said, "I mean to hang on
Till her canvas busts or her sticks are gone" –
Which the blushing looney did, till at last
Overboard went her mizen mast.
    Hear the yarn of a sailor,
    An old yarn learned at sea.'

MASEFIELD, *The Yarn of the Loch Achray*

IN THE morning Captain John had everything ready for pushing off and hoisting sail. He was waiting only for his crew and his crew were busy tidying up the camp after breakfast, because the mate would never allow things to be left dirty between one meal and the next.

'She likes the camp to look as if no one had ever eaten even a biscuit in it,' said John to himself, rather grumpily, though he knew the mate was right. But he had a reason for being in a hurry.

Long ago the *Amazon* had been sighted, sailing fast down the lake, along the farther shore. The explorers on Wild Cat Island had slept so well that there was never any chance that they could beat Nancy and Peggy Blackett in getting first to Horseshoe Cove. Nancy had said *Amazon* would be there first, and she would be, first by any amount. But that was not all. Captain John had seen what a good wind she had out there. Through the telescope he had seen that there were pretty big waves on that side of the lake. From the rock above the harbour he had watched *Amazon* race past Cormorant Island and on and on until she reached the narrow entrance into Horseshoe Cove. Then, watching through the telescope, he had seen how Nancy and Peggy jibed her smartly, brought the sail over on the other side, and shot out of sight into the little bay. While he was watching, he was planning, of course, exactly what he would do in sailing *Swallow* across there. The wind was north-east, so that it was blowing directly from Wild Cat Island to Horseshoe Cove. Captain John made up his mind that he would run down wind to the cove with the sail out on the port side. By doing that, he thought, he would be able to turn into the cove without having to jibe in the rough water and harder wind that he could see that he would find there. He had this plan clear in his mind, and now he wanted to be sailing and getting across there before the wind changed or something happened to make the plan no good. It seemed to him that the wind was getting stronger and he did not want to have to reef when, as he had seen, the *Amazon* had carried full sail. He wanted to be off at once and today everybody else seemed to be busy about something that did not matter at all. It had begun at breakfast when Titty had started making a fuss about torches, as if anybody wanted torches on a summer day. He had been a donkey to give in to her and to let her have his torch to put in with the rest of the luggage.

At last he heard the others coming.

Roger came first with the kettle. Then came Titty with a basket of eggs and a frying-pan. Then mate Susan with two knapsacks, one full of towels and bathing things, and the other with rations for the expedition. 'We shan't want much,' she had said, 'because the Amazons have got to get back to tea.' As she came, she was going over the things she had put in. 'Biscuits, bread, seed-cake, spoons, knife, marmalade, butter . . .'

'You haven't put in egg-cups,' said Roger, 'because we don't have any.'

'Botheration!' said the mate, dumping the knapsacks on the ground and turning to run back to the camp. 'I've forgotten the salt.'

There was really nothing much in this to bother the captain, but it did bother him all the same. He was in a hurry to sail, and had been waiting a long time, and perhaps it was just that little bit of bad luck in the mate's forgetting the salt and keeping back the ship for two minutes more that made the captain not quite so careful as usual.

At last everything was stowed, the crew aboard, and *Swallow* was pushed off, stern-first. And then it was discovered that in her haste the mate had forgotten to bring her torch.

'We shan't want it anyway,' she said.

'No one's going back for it now,' said John. 'Do hold the tiller amidships while I paddle her out.'

'It's all right,' said Titty, 'we've got the other three.'

'There's quite a lot of wind,' said the mate, when they were clear of the rocks outside.

'That's why I was in a hurry,' said the captain. 'Now then, see that the mainsheet is free, so that the boom can swing right out. I'm going to hoist the sail up now. Are you ready?'

'Aye, aye, sir,' said the mate.

John shipped his oars, hooked on the yard, and swayed up the brown sail. The boom swung out free, so that the sail was no more than a big flag. John hurried aft to the tiller. He hauled in ever so little on the mainsheet, so that the sail held the wind and *Swallow* began to move. Then, putting the tiller up he let her bear away until she was heading straight for Horseshoe Cove. The little pennant flew out straight before her from the masthead. The water creamed out from under her forefoot as she gathered speed.

'Shall I go forward now to be look-out?' asked Roger.

'No,' said John, who was beginning to feel how strong the wind was. 'We want all the weight aft. Both you and Titty come as far aft as you can.'

The wind was dead aft and stronger with every yard that they moved out of the shelter of the island and the hills on the eastern shore of the lake. With Susan beside him in the stern-sheets, and the boy and the able-seaman crowded aft on the bottom boards at their feet, it was all that John could do to keep the *Swallow* steady on her course. The wind pressing on her sail seemed to be trying to lift her rudder out of the water and that did not help to make steering easy.

'She's going faster than a motor boat,' said Roger.

'Oughtn't we to have reefed?' said the mate.

'The Amazons hadn't,' said the captain, with his teeth tight clenched, hanging on to the mainsheet with one hand and holding the tiller as hard as he could with the other, doing his utmost to keep *Swallow* from yawing about.

'What's that you're saying, Titty?' asked the mate.

'I was telling Roger the bit about the old man who meant to hang on,' said Titty, 'the bit Daddy read to us at Falmouth.'

'Well, her canvas won't bust,' said John, 'and she's got a jolly strong mast.'

But he spoke too soon.

If the wind had been steady, it would not have been so bad, but it was never the same strength for long together. Every now and then came a harder puff, so sudden and so strong that it forced the nose of the boat round before John could meet her with the tiller and put her back on her course again. Every time that this happened it began to look less and less likely that John would be able to carry out his plan of sailing into the cove without having to jibe twice over, once to bring the sail across to the starboard side, and then again to bring it back to the port side for running into the cove. Each of these gusts that was a little too hard or too sudden for John left the *Swallow* further to the north of her proper course, and this meant that the wind was no longer directly from aft but was blowing over the quarter from the same side as that on which was the sail. The little pennant was no longer blowing directly forward over the stem, nor was it blowing out with the sail, when it would have shown that all was safe. There was the sail out to port, and there at the masthead was the little pennant fluttering to starboard, showing that there was a danger that the wind might catch the leach of the sail and swing it right over. A jibe of that kind, not done on purpose, was what John was trying to avoid. He had made up his mind that he could get across without having to jibe at all.

'We ought to be able to do it,' he said aloud, and really because he began to be not quite sure.

'Remember the rock we saw yesterday,' said Susan.

'The Pike Rock,' said Titty.

'We're much more likely to hit the rocks on this side if we get a gust like that one just as we are going in,' said John. 'We ought to have reefed, really. It's blowing much harder than it was a few minutes ago. But it'd be an awful job to bring her head to wind and reef here. Besides we're very nearly there. I'm sure she'll do it. . . .'

'There are the Amazons,' called Roger.

With his eye all the time on that warning pennant at the masthead and watching for a tremble in the leach of the sail, John saw Nancy and Peggy waving on the rocks at the entrance to the cove. That settled it. He could not give up his plan now. In another minute they would have done it and be safe between the headlands. Another twenty yards. The leach of the sail was ashake. Another ten. Could he do it, or could he not? He could. Surely he could.

'Look at the waves breaking on the Pike Rock,' said Roger.

And at that very moment, off the mouth of the cove, only a few yards from safety, the wind, leaping at them in a last furious gust, caught the wrong side of the sail and whirled it across.

'Keep your heads down,' shouted John, but for that there was no need. Titty and Roger were crouched in the bottom of the boat and the mate had ducked in time. So had John himself. The boom crashed over, but broke no heads. But John had been pulling hard on the tiller to keep the *Swallow* on her course. She was moving very fast. The moment the sail lifted there was nothing to balance the rudder. A moment later and the full force of the wind caught the sail on the other side, not working against the rudder but working with it. The *Swallow* spun round, out of all control, and ran with a loud crash on the Pike Rock. The rock stopped her dead. The mast broke off short above the thwart and fell forward over her bows, taking the sail with it.

There was a shriek, but it was from Peggy Blackett on the rocks at the entrance to the cove. There were no shrieks in *Swallow*.

It had all happened too quickly. Everybody had been jerked forward as the boat struck the rock. Everybody was holding fast to whatever had happened to come nearest, thwart, gunwale or tiller. Roger spoke first, as the *Swallow* slipped back off the rock.

'The water's coming in,' he said.

It was not so much an exclamation as a plain statement of fact. *Swallow* was badly holed below the waterline in the bows. The water was spouting in and she was filling fast. Already the water was nearly up to the thwarts. Hundreds of times they had had imaginary shipwrecks. This was a real one.

'Over you go, Roger, and swim ashore,' said Captain John. 'Go on. Don't get caught in the halyards. Go over this side. Hop out.'

Roger looked at the mate and then at John to see if he meant it. Then he looked at the shore. It was only a few yards away. Peggy was standing on the headland down at the water's edge. Nancy had disappeared.

'Go on,' said John. 'Don't wait. She'll be gone in a minute.'

Roger rolled himself over the side. For one second

he hung on to the gunwale. 'Isn't it a good thing I went on with the swimming lessons in the winter?' he said, and then splashed off on his way to land and safety.

'Now then, Titty. You, too, Susan. Be quick.'

Susan and Titty went overboard one after the other. Titty swam ashore as fast as she could, holding something above the water as she swam. Susan trod water for a moment, waiting for John.

'Come on, John,' she said.

But John was fumbling under water in the bows of the boat.

'Look out,' he shouted. 'Be quick, out of the way.'

He stood up with *Swallow*'s little anchor and threw it as hard as he could throw towards the headland. The effort of throwing it overbalanced him, and he slipped. At that moment the boat lurched sideways as the water came over the gunwale. John tumbled out, and kicked himself off with a foot against the sinking *Swallow*. He was not a second too soon.

Nancy, as soon as she had seen what had happened, had rushed round to the *Amazon*, which lay, beached, in the cove, had grabbed a coil of rope that she used as a stern warp when mooring in the harbour on the island, and had come racing back to the southern of the two headlands, opposite the rock on which the

SHIPWRECK

Swallow had run. She had hoped to throw the rope as far as *Swallow*, so that John could catch it and between them they could pull *Swallow* ashore before she sank. But the wind was against her, and the rope did not reach the *Swallow*. However, it fell close to Roger, who caught hold of it and was rescued in the most proper way, Nancy and Peggy together hauling him in hand over hand. Susan and Titty splashed their way ashore close behind him. After them came Captain John.

There was nothing of the *Swallow* to be seen, except a couple of floating oars and one of the knapsacks, drifting in between the Pike Rock and the headland.

'She's gone, she's gone!' said Titty, standing dripping on the rocks and looking at the place where *Swallow* had been.

'We had to swim for our lives,' said Roger.

'It was horrible,' said Peggy.

Captain Nancy looked at Captain John. For once she had nothing to say.

'I've got the telescope,' said Titty at last.

'Good old Titty,' said Captain John.

Captain John knew all the bitterness of a captain who has lost his ship. Now that it was too late he was telling himself that he ought to have guessed that the wind would be so much stronger. Yes, it was clear that he ought to have reefed. If he had reefed, the jibe would not have mattered so much. Besides, it was not as if they had been racing. He could quite well have sailed some distance down the lake with the sail out to starboard and then jibed carefully or even come up to the wind and gone about so as to reach the entrance to Horseshoe Cove with the sail out to port just as he wanted it for running in. It was all his fault. And now *Swallow* was gone and it was only the third day of the holiday. What was it his father had said about duffers? Better drowned. John thought so too. And then a new flock of black, wretched thoughts came crowding in like cormorants coming to roost. *Swallow* belonged to the Jacksons at Holly Howe. What would they say? It was all very well for Peggy and Roger to chatter about shipwrecks. He knew what Titty was thinking as she stood there dripping, looking at the waves breaking on that hateful rock. For Titty and himself, *Swallow* was something alive. And now, with *Swallow* gone, how could they live on Wild Cat Island? How could anything lovely ever happen any more? What would Mother say? After all, they might easily have been drowned. Mother was very good at understanding things, but wouldn't even she put an end to exploring for this summer at least? Things looked worse and worse whichever way he looked. It was as if the summer itself had been the cargo of the little ship and had gone with her to the bottom of the lake.

'Hullo, what's become of Susan?' said Peggy suddenly, looking round for the other mate.

And just then they heard her whistle, shrill, but not quite as clear as usual, from inside the cove.

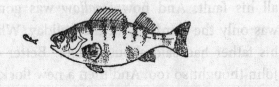

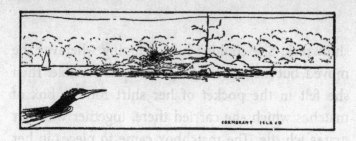
CORMORANT ISLAND

6

Salvage

MATE SUSAN always knew the right thing to do, and she knew now that even if it were the end of the world nobody who could help it ought to hang about in wet clothes. The right thing to do was to make a fire and to make it at once. While the others were still thinking about what had happened, Susan had gone at once to yesterday's fireplace on the beach, where the stream ran out into the cove. There were dry, charred sticks left there from yesterday's fire, and she gathered a few dead leaves and built her usual little wigwam over them of dry twigs and scraps of reed as if this had been a picnic instead of a shipwreck. She couldn't help dripping wherever she moved, but she kept the twigs as dry as possible. Then she felt in the pocket of her shirt for the box of matches which she carried there, together with her mate's whistle. The matchbox came to pieces in her fingers. The matches were soaked. The wetting did not hurt the whistle, though there was a good deal of water in it, but it was no good even trying to strike wet matches. Susan blew the whistle instead.

'Go and see what the mate wants,' said Captain John. Roger went off as hard as he could go.

The others were still out on the point, watching to see if anything else would float up from the wreck and drift ashore. Both the oars had been rescued in this way, and Peggy was using one of them to catch another piece of flotsam, the knapsack full of towels and bathing things. It was waterlogged and almost sinking. Peggy scooped it towards the shore with the oar and as soon as she could reach it picked it up and went off with it after Roger.

'Captain John,' said Nancy Blackett at last, 'why was it you threw the anchor out just before she went down?'

'Because I want to try to get her up,' said John. 'If we can get hold of it, it'll help us to get her into shallow water.'

'She wants matches,' they heard Roger shout.

Nancy felt in her pocket, but they heard Peggy call out, 'I've got some.'

As soon as she had lit the fire and seen the first flames licking up among the sticks, Susan took the rescued knapsack from Peggy and emptied the wet bathing things and towels out on the beach. 'That's lucky,' she said. 'Off with your things, Roger, and get into your bathers. Then you can go on getting as wet as you like while I'm getting your clothes dry. We'll all change. What are the others doing?'

'They're out on the point,' said Peggy.

Susan blew her whistle hard two or three times.

'She wants us too,' said Titty.

'Coming,' shouted John and Titty. Nancy and he hurried over the rocks from the point and joined the others by the fire.

Roger was already struggling out of his wet clothes.

'You'd both better change,' said Susan.

'I'm going to, anyway,' said John. 'I'm going down to have a look at her.'

'And you must, whatever you're going to do,' said Susan to the able-seaman. 'And then turn to and get more wood.'

'That's the way, Mister Mate,' said Nancy Blackett. 'Keep your crew on the jump and there'll be no time for mutiny.'

In the end the Amazons changed too, for company's sake, and then, running about like savages, they gathered wood and built up a fire big enough for a corroboree. Susan took the rope that had been used for rescuing Roger, and made it into a clothes-line. They squeezed as much water as they could out of their sodden clothes and then hung some of them on the line, and spread others on the stones near the fire.

Presently Susan said that the fire was big enough, and John and Nancy went off again to the point off which *Swallow* had gone down.

'Can we go too?' asked Roger.

'The moment you begin to feel cold,' said Susan, 'go into the water and swim as hard as you can.'

Titty and Roger went off after the others, leaving the two mates with the fire. They reached the point in time to see John dive in, bob up again, and swim towards the Pike Rock. Suddenly he turned half over and went under without a splash. The wind was veering to the south now, and not as hard as it had been. It was as if it felt that after sinking *Swallow* it might take a rest. But there was still a good ripple on the water and the morning sun was in the eyes of the watchers on the point, so that they could not see at all what John was doing.

He was under a long time, but came up at last close

to the Pike Rock. He rested there, holding to the rock with one hand. With the other he held up Susan's black kettle.

'Hurrah,' cried Nancy.

'Susan,' called Titty, 'he's got the kettle.'

John pushed off from the rock and swimming with one hand and carrying the kettle in the other, keeping it under water so that it was not heavy, he swam ashore.

'Did you see the eggs?' asked Susan. She and Peggy had come running from the fire when they heard Nancy's shout.

'Or a frying-pan?' asked Titty. 'I had a frying-pan as well as the basket of eggs.'

'The frying-pan's there all right,' said John, 'but I didn't see the eggs. They must have floated out in the basket and then been swamped. Half a minute and I'll go down again. It's not as deep as I thought it would be.'

He swam out again and went under, coming up with the frying-pan, which he threw ashore.

The next time he dived he brought up the knapsack with the day's food in it. He brought it to the top of the water and then kicked himself ashore, swimming with his legs only.

Susan opened the knapsack anxiously. 'The

pemmican's all right,' she said, as she pulled out the tin, 'and the spoons and the knife and the marmalade, and the butter. . . . But the bread and the seed-cake are all soppy . . . and the sugar's soaking through everything.'

'We've got some bread,' said Nancy, 'but we counted on you for the tea.'

'What about the milk?' said Susan.

'The bottle's all right,' said John, 'but the milk's just a cloud in the water.'

'We can get milk at Swainson's farm,' said Peggy. 'We often do. It's not far.'

'Is *Swallow* very much hurt?' said Titty. She had been wanting to ask each time John came up.

'I simply can't see,' said John. 'There's such a tangle round the bows with the broken mast and the sail settling down there. I know she's stove in, but we can't tell how badly she's hurt until we get her out.'

'*Can* we get her out?' Nancy, Peggy, Titty, Susan and Roger all asked that question at once. Indeed, looking at the rippled water, with nothing showing above it but the wicked point of the Pike Rock, it was difficult to believe that the *Swallow* had not disappeared for ever.

'I don't know,' said John.

'They often do get up sunk boats,' said Peggy.

'It'll be all right,' said Nancy. 'Captain Flint's coming today, and he'll howk her up in two jiffs.'

That settled it. It was bad enough to have lost the ship, but for Captain Flint to come for the first time this year to join the explorers and to find the *Swallow* at the bottom of the lake would be altogether unbearable. John climbed up out of the water and sat on a rock to rest and consider what he would do next.

'We mustn't let the fire go down,' said Susan. 'Come on, you two. I want all the wood you can get. And you must keep moving and not hang about while the clothes are drying. Let's see if we can do anything with the seed-cake.'

'It might get all right if we dried it by the fire and then fried it in slices,' said Peggy.

The two mates, the able-seaman and the boy went back to the fire.

When they had gone, Captain Nancy looked at Captain John. 'Have you got a plan?' she said.

'It may not work,' said John.

At the very moment of *Swallow*'s sinking, with the shore so near and yet out of reach, the plan had come into his head. Somewhere, in some book, someone had done something like it. It was this plan, so shadowy that it could hardly be called a plan, that had made him at the last moment use all the strength

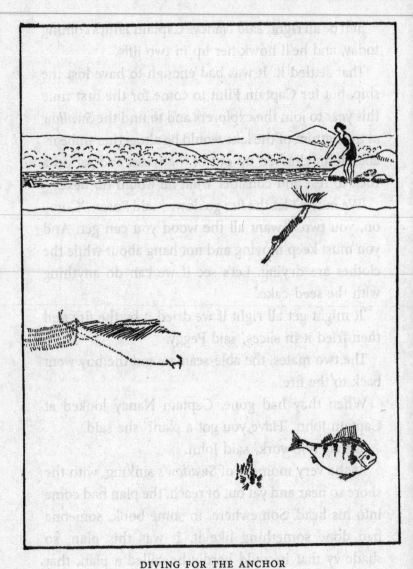

DIVING FOR THE ANCHOR

he had in throwing *Swallow*'s anchor towards the shore. He had often wished she had a heavier anchor. Today he had been glad that it was light. But, after all, what had he done? Not much. But he had been down to *Swallow* under water. The water was not as deep as he had feared. There was no doubt in his mind that Captain Flint and a few other strong natives could get her up. But he wanted more than that. He wanted to get her up without them, and, thanks to that anchor, lying somewhere between the wreck and the point, he thought he could. For the anchor rope was fastened to a ring-bolt in *Swallow*'s bows, and it was just there that he could not safely go without the risk of being mixed up in sail and ropes. If he had had that rope to fasten there, he might have had to give up his whole plan. But, it was fastened already, and if he could get hold of the anchor and bring the rope ashore. . . . He was almost glad the others had gone back to the fire. He almost wished Nancy had gone too. But someone would be wanted if the plan worked at all.

He swam off again and, carefully judging his distance from the Pike Rock and from the shore, dived down once more to the wreck. Dim and misty she lay down there. It was only when he had his eyes close to a bit of her that it looked solid and he could be certain what it was. It had been easy enough getting kettle and saucepan and knapsack. He knew where they were in her, stowed in the broadest part of her, by the middle thwart. He could hold on to that and find what he wanted as much by feel as by sight. It was different now. He dared not go too near that tangle of mast and ropes and sail about her bows, and yet he wanted the rope that led there, the rope with the anchor at its other end. Down he went, down to the stern of the wreck. Then swimming with his legs and using his hands to keep him close to the stones on the bottom he tried to swim in a half-circle round the wreck and between the wreck and the shore. Somewhere in that half-circle he must find the anchor rope. This was harder than picking saucers off the bottom of the swimming-bath at school. He counted to himself . . . Fifteen, sixteen, seventeen . . . at twenty he would have to come up . . . eighteen, nineteen, twenty . . . twenty-one. . . . There! There was the rope, but he was already shooting upwards, and a moment later was spluttering and blowing on the surface.

He got his breath again and dived once more. There was the wreck. No need now to begin his semicircle from the stern. The rope was more than half-way round it. It would be close to him now. Now . . . there it was . . . a long, grey, thin snake squirming away into the brown shadows. He grabbed it, lifted it off the bottom and swam along it, letting it run between his thumb and first finger. . . . He saw the anchor just before he came to it. He let go the rope, took the anchor by a fluke, and, using his feet on the bottom now, shifted the anchor a yard, two yards, three yards, until the rope drew taut and he could hold his breath no more.

'I've found it,' he spluttered as he came to the top. 'And I've moved it a good bit farther in.'

But there was no Nancy. For a moment John thought he had stayed under so long that she had run off to tell the others he had got stuck. But before he had let out a cheering shout to show that he was all right, he saw Nancy hurrying over the rocks to the end of the point. In her hand she had *Amazon*'s anchor rope.

'Have you found the anchor?' she called.

'Yes,' said John.

'Why not make this rope fast to it, so that we can haul it in from the shore? It'll be a dreadful job shifting it under water.'

He knew it was. Nancy really was a sailor. That was something he ought to have thought of himself. He came ashore, rested a moment, and then swam off with one end of Nancy's rope, which she paid out from the point.

'Let's have a lot loose,' he called, and then, taking the end in his mouth, for he did not think he could swim down with one hand, he dived again, found the

101

anchor, this time without difficulty, made fast Nancy's rope to it, shot up and swam ashore.

Nancy was already hauling in on her rope. In it came, and then straightened, tautened. There was a jerk.

'It's coming.'

The rope fell slack and tautened again. She hauled in, and John suddenly splashed under water from the point. *Swallow*'s anchor was in sight. He seized hold of it and clambered out.

'Well done, Nancy,' he said. 'It would have taken ages if you hadn't thought of that.'

'You've got a jolly good crew,' said Nancy. 'If they hadn't coiled your anchor rope as it should be coiled it would have jammed, as sure as eggs is eggs, and you might never have been able to throw it clear.'

Even to be ashore and to hold *Swallow*'s anchor and to pull the rope taut and feel *Swallow* at the other end of it was enough to make things seem more hopeful.

'We could shift her now,' said Nancy.

'It's an awfully rough bottom,' said John. 'All stones. I'm going to try to get the ballast out of her first.'

'How much is there?'

'Six pigs of lead, five little ones and a big one.'

'I wish I could take a turn at the diving,' said Nancy, 'but it's no good. I simply can't keep under.'

'It's all right,' said John. 'I'm not tired a bit. I'll take

102

your rope and make it fast to a pig of ballast. You start hauling when I give two jerks.'

He fixed *Swallow*'s anchor among the rocks on the point, unfastened Nancy's rope and swam out, towing the rope behind him. Down he went, grabbed the thwart of the *Swallow* with one hand, got a grip on it with his legs, and quickly, as quickly as ever he could, counting to himself as he did it, pushed the end of the rope through the loop on the top of a pig of ballast, tied two half-hitches, lifted the pig over the side, jerked twice on the rope and shot up in a hurry.

'How many did you say there were?' asked Nancy.

'Five more,' he panted. 'But the rest'll be easier. I know how to do it now.'

'Tie two of them together,' said Nancy. 'They don't weigh much under water.'

But it was just the tying that was the trouble. The little bit of extra work, in threading the rope through two of the stiff rope loops on the pigs of lead instead of through one, was just too much, and he had to come to the top to breathe without making the rope fast at all. So he gave that up and they were content with one pig of lead at a time. Five more times he went down. Five times Nancy felt two eager jerks on the rope and was hauling a pig of lead ashore as John's dripping head shot up out of the water.

'Now then,' he said, as he swam ashore after making fast the last pig. 'It's no good trying to free the mast and sail. If the sail gets torn we'll have to mend it. Let's try if she'll come now. Her bows aren't pointing this way though. Let's try, gently.'

They took hold of *Swallow*'s anchor rope and pulled, gently at first, and then harder. Something stirred far down and sent a quiver through the rope into their fingers. They pulled again and it was almost as if they could hear *Swallow* move on the bottom of the lake.

'Steady now,' said John. 'I'm going down to have a look.'

He was gone with a splash, but was up again in a moment or two.

'Her head's come round a lot,' he said. 'It's all right.'

Again they pulled. The rope came in and they could feel *Swallow* lifting over the stones. With her ballast out she weighed very little more than water.

'I can see her,' said John, almost under his breath, as if he were telling of a miracle.

'We can't do anything with her here,' said Nancy, 'with the rocks dropping down so steep. We must get her round into the cove to beach her. Hi, Peggy! Peggy! We must get some of them on the rope, and we'll go down into the water to fend her off.'

Peggy came running.

'You take the anchor,' said Nancy, 'and crawl round the point. Don't pull too hard.'

'They've got her up,' yelled Peggy, at the top of her voice.

'They've got her up,' echoed Roger shrilly, dropping the bit of driftwood he was carrying and setting off as hard as he could go for the point. Titty hurried after him, and Susan, after one more look, to see that none of the clothes were in danger of scorching, went after them.

'Half a minute,' said Captain John, who was in the water again up to his neck, feeling round the bows of the *Swallow*. 'I'll cut the halyard, so that we can get away the mast and sail. Anybody got a knife?'

As everybody was in bathing things, nobody had.

'Get the ship's knife, Peggy,' said Nancy. 'Stir those stumps. I'll hang on to the anchor while you're getting it. It's with our clothes in *Amazon*.'

'No need,' shouted John, who was feeling about in the water. 'I've got the yard unhooked from the traveller. It ought to come now. It's stuck. Oh, bother it, I forgot the boom's fastened down.' He struggled with the soaked ropes, but was glad at last that Peggy had brought the knife after all. A cut, a tug or two, and yard, sail and boom were free from the rest of the wreckage, while the broken mast, held only by the halyard (neither *Swallow* nor *Amazon* have shrouds) bobbed in the water like a tethered log. Nancy came down into the water to help. Susan and Titty slid down the rocks to meet them as they lugged ashore the brown sail, heavy with water and almost black, still fastened to its spars. They hauled it up.

'Is it much torn?' asked John, who was now busy freeing the broken mast.

'There's one awful tear,' said Mate Susan, 'and a little one that doesn't matter. Nothing we can't mend.'

'Spread it on the rocks to dry.'

The broken mast and the halyard came ashore next. The stump of the mast had somehow jammed and was still in *Swallow*, under water. But under water though she was, even those who were on the rocks could see that John and Nancy had their hands on her. It was no longer as if she were out of sight by the Pike Rock when, even if in no more than eight or nine feet of water, she had seemed forty fathoms deep and gone for ever. There was hope in all hearts and a more cheerful ring in every voice.

'Tally on to the rope, you two. Give my mate a hand,' cried Captain Nancy, who simply could not help giving orders. 'Susan and I'll keep her from bumping this side, if Captain John'll look out for any rocks under her bows.'

'Are you ready?' said Peggy.

'Steady. Steady. Not too fast,' called John.

'Heave *ho!*' cried Nancy.

'She's coming! She's coming!'

'Not too fast,' said John again. 'Go slow. The bottom's awfully rough. . . .' He ended in a gurgle, for on the outer side of the wreck he was on the very edge of the deep water, and as he spoke he slipped and went head under.

It was easier going and better footing as soon as they were round the headland and inside the cove, and presently they were towing her along a smoothly shelving bottom.

'I say, Nancy,' said John, 'what about lifting her?'

'Steady there, you on the warp,' called Nancy. 'Now then, Skipper. Are you ready, Mister Mate?'

She, Susan and John together, lifted the empty hull of the *Swallow*, which weighed very little while it was under water, and walked her into the shallows.

'She'll do here,' said Nancy. 'If we can get her out. Now then, on the warp. Haul away. Way hay, up she rises. Way hay, up she rises.'

The bows of the *Swallow* showed, and much of her gunwale, though her stern was still covered.

'Steady,' said John. 'Don't try to pull her up too fast. The water's got to run out. Now then.'

'Oh, poor dear,' said Titty.

As *Swallow*'s forefoot came up out of the water, Titty had seen the dreadful hole in the planking out of which the water was now pouring as fast as it had poured in.

They rested a moment, and then hauled again, all pulling together, and brought her half out of the water. The bottom boards had shifted but had jammed under the thwarts and had not floated out. John pulled them out now. The baler was still in her, and Roger hopped in and began to bale the water out over her stern. Susan found the milk-bottle and emptied out of it a little cloudy grey liquid that was all that was left of the thick fresh milk she had put into it before they started. She found the lid of the kettle. Then, all working together, they turned *Swallow* on her beam ends to empty out the last of the water, and at last turned her over altogether to see what could be done in the way of repairs.

This was careening that really mattered, and no pirates ever looked more anxiously over the bottom of their ship, beached on gold sand on some Pacific island, than the explorers searched now to find what damage had come to *Swallow*. There were a good many scratches in her paint, but, so far as they could see, no serious hurt except the gaping hole in her bows, where two planks had been stove in by the Pike Rock.

'Well,' said Nancy, 'you've got her up, and that's the main thing.'

'It's only the beginning,' said Captain John.

At this moment, just when they had the wrecked *Swallow* bottom upwards on the beach, and were looking at the broken planking, a shout from the mouth of the cove made them all turn round. A rowing boat was shooting in between the heads. There was nobody in her but a big man who had hitched his oars under his knees while he took off his broad-brimmed hat and mopped his head with a large red-and-green handkerchief.

'Hullo, Uncle Jim,' Peggy called back to him.

'It's Captain Flint at last,' said Titty.

'Hurrah,' said Roger.

'You needn't mind now,' said Nancy, looking at John. 'It isn't as if she was at the bottom of the sea.'

7

Captain Flint: Ship's Carpenter

'Gae fetch a web o' the silken claith,
Anither o' the twine,
And wap them into our ship's side,
And let nae the sea come in.'
The Ballad of Sir Patrick Spens

'HULLO,' said Captain Flint. 'What's happened? Lost a mast?'

He had just seen the sail spread on the rocks at the point, and the broken mast beside it.

'Much worse than that,' said Roger cheerfully. 'We had to swim ashore.'

This was not at all the way in which the Swallows had hoped to meet Captain Flint. They had not seen him since the Christmas holidays and the making up of the story in the cabin of the wherry. They had hoped to find him aboard his houseboat, flying the elephant flag at the masthead, ready once more to fire his cannon, fight for his life and walk the plank into a sea crowded with the largest kinds of sharks. He had not been there to welcome them with a salvo as they sailed by on their way to Wild Cat Island, though Roger had discussed the question beforehand with Titty and decided that if he did it would not be waste of gunpowder. He was not living in his house-boat at all, but, for the time, had sunk into a mere lands-man. There was this queer native trouble about a kind of aunt. He had not even been with Nancy and Peggy yesterday and now, at last, here he was, only to find them with their ship wrecked and the future black as ink, except perhaps for Roger, who took things as they came and was content so long as things kept on coming.

Captain Flint did not bother about asking them all how they were. As soon as he saw that something serious had happened, he rowed in to the shore, stepped out, pulled his rowing boat a little way up out of the water and joined the others by the wounded ship.

'Lost a mast? Holed her too? Well, these things will happen.'

As Nancy Blackett always said, one of the best things about her Uncle Jim was that he never asked you *why* you tumbled down.

He looked carefully at the hole in *Swallow*'s planking, but asked no questions except about the parrot.

'He's quite all right,' said Titty. 'He's looking after the island. He doesn't know yet about *Swallow*.'

'And you've left old Peter Duck behind?'

Titty looked at him and for a moment was not very pleased. But, after all, everybody there knew all about Peter Duck.

'You know he's only for a story,' she said.

'I know,' said Captain Flint, bending down and working his hand through the hole to feel if the ribs had been damaged. 'I know. But has he been up to much since he steered us home from the Caribbees when the waterspout came just in time and licked up the pirate ship?'

'No,' said Titty. 'Just staying at home in his boat and doing a little fishing.'

Captain Flint stood up again.

'It's a boatbuilder's job,' he said. 'I'll row along there and tell them to send out a salvage party.'

'Couldn't we patch her up?' said John. 'I wanted to take her to Rio to find out how much the mending would cost before going to tell Mother about it. That's why we got her up.'

'Got her up?' said Captain Flint. 'Where was she?'

'I ran her on the Pike Rock and she sank right away.'

'We all had to swim,' said Roger.

'You got her up from out there?'

'Yes.'

'By yourselves? Well done. How did you manage about the ballast and the anchor?'

'I had time to throw the anchor out before she sank. That helped when we were ready to pull her up.'

'And the ballast?'

'He dived again and again and we pulled it up one pig at a time,' said Nancy.

'Good work,' said Captain Flint. 'And don't you worry about the boatbuilders. It won't cost much anyway, and I've just got another dollop of pocket money from my publishers, and you know my book* would never have been published at all if you people hadn't saved it for me, so that you've got at least as much right as I have to the money it makes. You needn't bother your Mother about that.'

Susan and John looked at each other. Roger was hardly listening. He was looking at a promising-looking box in Captain Flint's rowing boat. Titty said, 'Not really?'

---

* *Mixed Moss*. By a Rolling Stone. Pub. 1930, 8th edition 1931.

'Of course,' said Captain Flint, 'you went treasure-hunting and found my book. My book goes on turning into publisher's cheques. They're the next best thing to Spanish gold. It's as if you'd found a barrel or two of doubloons on Cormorant Island. So don't you worry about the money.'

'I've got to go and tell Mother anyway,' said John, 'to find out what we can do next. We'll probably have to go back to Holly Howe.'

'No more sailing,' said Titty.

'But we've only just begun,' said Roger, hearing something in Titty's voice that told him things were serious.

'Something's got to be done,' said Nancy desperately. 'Of course we could lend them *Amazon*.'

'No, no, no.' Neither John, Susan nor Titty would hear of that. Roger would not have minded, though he did not think much of the look-out's place in *Amazon*. There was not enough room before the mast.

Captain Flint looked from face to face. Then he had another look at *Swallow*'s broken planking.

'There's only one sensible thing to do,' he said at last. 'You *are* shipwrecked. Why not *be* shipwrecked? Stay where you are and make the best of it until your ship's been mended and is ready to put to sea.'

'Mother'll never let us. It's the wrong side of the lake for her,' said Susan.

'Why not?' said Peggy. 'It's the right side for us.'

'It's not really much farther than the island,' said Captain Flint. 'Look here. You've got to sleep somewhere. Pitch a camp here. Make it a good one. Nancy and Peggy'll help to bring your things across. The skipper and I will see what can be done with *Swallow*, and when we go to Rio we'll bring Mrs Walker back with us and I bet she'll let you stop if you've made a really good show of it. Settled. Get a move on, you pirates. Now then, Skipper, what are we going to stop this hole with? We don't want her sinking in deep water on the way to Rio.'

'In "Sir Patrick Spens",' said Titty, 'they wapped it with silk and cloth. But the sea came in all the same.'

'We must do better than that,' said Captain Flint. 'A bit of tarpaulin's what we want.'

'We could take a bit of one of the old groundsheets,' said John. 'There's a spare one in the stores tent.'

'Polly's looking after it.'

'Hi, Titty, are you coming across?' shouted Captain Nancy, who was already getting *Amazon* ready for launching.

'We're coming too,' said Captain Flint. 'We'll give you a passage, Able-seaman.'

115

A minute or two later Captain Flint in his rowing boat, with John and Titty, was pulling hard after the *Amazon*, sailed by Nancy, with Susan and Roger. Peggy alone stayed in Horseshoe Cove to keep the fire going and to turn the clothes on the stones when they had toasted enough on one side. Susan had to leave the fire to Peggy, because she knew where everything was, and so had to look after the striking of the island camp.

Striking camp on Wild Cat Island would have been a more melancholy business than it was, if everybody had not been in such a hurry. Captain Flint and John would hardly wait for a few more small bits of cargo as soon as they had taken the spare groundsheet, and the tin box that had fishing tackle and tools in it with the hammer and the box of mixed nails which was what they really wanted. Captain Nancy kept the others at it like slaves. 'Quick, quick,' she was saying. 'Jump to it. Save all you can before the ship goes to pieces.'

'But it isn't a ship,' said Roger, 'it's an island.'

'Lucky for you it's so stoutly built,' said Nancy. 'It might have broken up long ago.'

'Besides, the tide may be coming in with a rush to sweep everything away,' said Titty, hurriedly rolling up her sleeping-bag.

'That's enough for one load,' said Nancy, who was

seeing to the stowing of the cargo. 'We don't want to be swamped. Look out, Able-seaman; the boom won't clear the parrot's cage. He'll get swept overboard. Burrow his cage down between the tents and the sleeping-bags. Hi, Roger! Come along. We'll make another voyage yet. Shove her head round. Don't wet the tents more than you can help. Scramble in.'

But long before the *Amazon*, with a full cargo, returned from her first trip to the island, Captain Flint and Captain John had landed from the rowing boat and were hard at work. A big patch of waterproof canvas had been cut out of the ground-sheet. ('In time of shipwreck,' said Captain Flint, 'you don't think twice about a scrap of tarpaulin.') It had been fitted and tacked roughly in place, and Captain Flint was now hard at it with the hammer. 'Just listen to the ship's carpenter,' said Titty, as the *Amazon* sailed into the cove.

Captain Flint was putting in a neat row of small flat-headed nails round the edge of the patch and beating the canvas close down on the planking as he did so, to make as tight a fit as he could. John was picking out the smallest flat-headed nails from the mixed lot in an old tobacco tin that had been given to him by the farmer at Holly Howe, and Captain Flint was holding two or three in his lips all ready, so that there was no waiting between banging in one nail and beginning to bang in the next. 'The last time I had this job to do,' he was saying, mumbling a bit because of the nails he was holding in his lips, 'it was when I'd come a nasty bump in a ship's gig against the coast of Java. Better patch than this, though (bang). We melted some rubber to bed it in properly (bang). Didn't leak a drop (bang). Didn't have to (bang). Shouldn't be here if it had (bang). Ready for some more nails, Skipper. That's my last.'

The *Amazon* unloaded her cargo on the beach and sailed back for more. Susan stayed in the cove this time, and Peggy rejoined her ship and sailed over with the others to the island. Peggy had been a little inclined to forget the fire while watching the patching of *Swallow*. Besides that, what with all the swimming and diving that had been done that day, Mate Susan was thinking that it would be a good thing if the captain and the rest of the crew had something solid to eat. She opened a pemmican tin, and made pemmican sandwiches, good thick ones, with one of the loaves she had brought across from the island. It was no good thinking of making any use of the loaf that had gone down to the bottom with *Swallow*, though Roger and Peggy still thought they would be able to do something with the seed-cake.

By the time *Amazon* returned with her second cargo, and Captain Nancy reported the island all clear, Mate Susan was ready with her sandwiches. Captain Flint had finished putting the patch on, too, and was calling for all hands to help turn *Swallow* over again. She was turned over, her bottom boards were put in place and then she was run down into the water. The water came in pretty fast from under the patch, but Captain Flint shouted for ballast to put in her stern. John, Peggy, Nancy and Susan ran out along the rocky headland to the place where the pigs of lead had been piled together by Nancy after she had hauled them up from the lake. One at a time they brought them and waded out and put them in *Swallow*'s stern. Each pig of lead in her stern lifted her nose a little higher out of the water until the whole patch showed above water, and the leak almost stopped. Then Roger was lifted into her to bale her out as well as he could. Then she was anchored by the stern, and after that Captain Flint said they had better knock off and have some grub and see how much she had leaked by the time they had done.

'I haven't made any tea,' said Susan.

'Tea?' said Captain Flint. 'Who wants tea? I was forgetting. That box (he pointed to the box that had seemed promising to Roger when first he saw it in the rowing boat) is full of bottles of ginger beer. I brought them along, thinking they might come in handy. Cook told me she'd had to let the pirates go off without their grog.'

Anybody would have known there had been a shipwreck now if they had seen the beach in Horseshoe Cove with all the stuff from the island camp piled on it in heaps, tin boxes of stores, tents loosely rolled up, rugs, parrot-cage, sleeping-bags, fishing rods, Susan's great fire, and the clothes of the shipwrecked hanging to dry and spread about the rocks. The Amazons' clothes were the only really dry ones, and theirs were in a heap on the beach where they had thrown them out of their ship when she had been pressed into use as a salvage vessel. But no one would have known who had been shipwrecked and who had not. All the Swallows and Amazons had rushed down into the water and out again for a last dip before eating. Captain Flint, sitting among them in his flannel trousers and white shirt, with his shirt sleeves rolled to the elbow, drinking ginger beer out of the bottle and taking big bites out of enormous sandwiches, looked like the solitary shipwrecked sailor in the middle of a lot of piebald, pigmy savages.

Bit by bit, listening to the talk round the fire, asking a question now and then, but not very often, Captain

Flint came to hear the whole story. He heard how Roger had been hauled ashore through the raging surf. He heard how Nancy and Peggy had watched *Swallow* come racing down wind from the island. He heard of the rescue of oars and other flotsam. He heard how Titty had made sure of the telescope, and how John had been seen to throw the anchor shorewards at the last moment and had then got clear as the ship sank beneath him. He heard of diving operations, of the salving of kettle and frying-pan and pigs of ballast. He heard how, in the end, they had brought *Swallow* round into the cove and careened her where she now was. The bits of the story were all in the wrong order, but Captain Flint fitted them together in his own mind and in the end knew pretty well what had happened.

'There's one thing,' he said at last. 'You've got the most sensible mate that ever I saw in a ship. There are plenty of mates to go howling round banging poor young chaps on the head with belaying-pins, but there's not one mate in a thousand who'd have the sense to start a fire and stretch a warp for a clothes-line and set about getting a dry rig-out for the whole crew. How are the skipper's clothes now, Mister Mate?'

'They're nothing like as wet as they were,' said

Susan. 'But they still steam a bit if you hold them to the fire.'

'Well, short of burning them, hurry them up. He and I'll be off in a few minutes now, and he'll want a shore-going kit. Now then, Skipper, let's see how much water there is in the hold.'

John waded out and found there was a good deal, even though the patch had been lifted out of water.

'Bound to be a little,' said Captain Flint, 'but there'd be much more than that if she was badly strained. If you want to take her to Rio under her own sail, I don't see why you shouldn't. You'll have the wind with you, now it's gone round to the south. Bring her nose ashore, and we'll see what we can do in the way of a jury rig for her.'

John brought *Swallow*'s nose well up on the beach while Nancy and Peggy hurried off to the point to fetch the mast and the sail, which was still pretty wet, though not quite so soggy as it had been. Captain Flint cut away the worst splinters and stepped the broken mast in its place. John reefed the sail and carried it down to the ship. As soon as they tried to hoist it, they found it was still too big. The broken mast was now so short that even when the yard was hoisted as far as it would go, the boom still rested on the gunwale.

'We'll cure that,' said Captain Flint.

The boom had jaws that fitted round the mast. Captain Flint pulled them clear so that he could turn the boom round and round. He turned it again and again, rolling up the sail round it as he turned. As the sail was narrower at the top than at the bottom this meant that there was a long bit of boom with sail rolled round it, sticking out beyond the sail that they were going to use. By the time the boom had been twisted and twisted until so much of the sail had been rolled up that the boom was nearly touching the lower end of the yard, the little three-cornered sail that was left was a very small sail indeed.

'It'll take you to Rio,' said Captain Flint. 'We'll take a few turns of rope just here at the foot of the leach, and a few turns at the foot of the luff. The jaws round the mast'll stop it from untwisting anyhow. It won't unroll, and you've got a sail snug enough for a hurricane.'

They hoisted the sail, and this time the boom cleared the gunwale with a foot to spare.

'What about getting some clothes on?'

Mate Susan had been fairly toasting the skipper's clothes. He quickly got out of his bathing things and into his shirt and shorts. He took his sandshoes, but put them on the middle thwart of the *Swallow*, to go on drying in the sun.

'What about the flag?' said Titty, who had rescued it the moment the broken mast and sail had been brought ashore.

'We'll jolly well hoist it,' said Captain John.

The sail was lowered once more, for the flag halyard to be reeved through the little ring at the masthead. As soon as the mast was stepped again, Titty herself hauled up the swallow flag and made it fast. The sail was hoisted, and all was ready for the start.

'Hop in, Skipper,' said Captain Flint. 'Now the mast's in her, it'll take your weight in the stern beside the ballast to keep her bows well up. No, no. Keep the anchor in the stern, too. You want all the weight there you can get.' He ran *Swallow* down into the water. 'Hi! Nancy. You're still a South Sea Islander. . . . Take her out to the headland to give her a chance.' He turned to his own boat.

Nancy waded along the shore, towing *Swallow* by hand until she reached the headland, when the little dark brown scrap of sail on the stump of a mast was no longer sheltered from the wind.

'All right,' said John. 'She's trying to sail. Let her go.'

He put his helm up, let the boom out square, and the *Swallow*, sitting on her tail, her nose high up out of the water, her scrap of sail bagging in the wind, slipped away from Horseshoe Cove. The only thing about her that was as it should be was Titty's swallow flag, which fluttered proudly from the top of the jury mast, as if it had never known the bottom of the lake.

'So long, Nancy, give them a hand with the camp,' called Captain Flint as his rowing boat shot out from between the headlands.

'We're coming too,' called Nancy, and she hurried back into the cove. The others were already launching *Amazon*. Titty, Susan and Roger were aboard. Peggy was pushing her off. Her captain scrambled into her at the last moment. There was wild work with the oars till she was at the mouth of the cove, when Nancy ran the sail up, and *Amazon* gathered speed as she hurried up the lake to overhaul the convoy. She was soon alongside the others, for *Swallow*, cocked up on end under her jury rig, sailed more like a buoy than a boat.

'This is all very well,' said Captain Flint at last. 'We're delighted to have you with us, but that camp ought to be in apple-pie order before we bring Mrs Walker back to see it.'

'There's no milk for tea either,' said Susan. 'And we don't know the way to the farm.'

For just a little longer the *Amazon* circled round the rowing boat and the gallant, wounded *Swallow*, and then with shouts of 'Good luck!' from all who were aboard her, she turned up into the wind to beat down the lake again to Horseshoe Cove, while Captain John steered a straight course for Rio, and Captain Flint just taking a stroke or two now and then to keep his rowing boat within comfortable talking distance, followed Captain John.

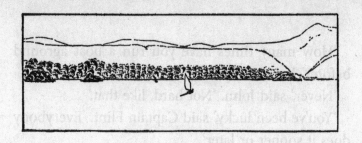

8

Rio and Holly Howe

'THEY look happy enough,' said Captain Flint, watching the *Amazon* slapping across the ripples on her way to Horseshoe Cove.

'They aren't,' said Captain John.

'I know they aren't, but the next best thing to being happy is to look it.'

Captain John knew that he did not even look happy, and he certainly did not feel it.

'It wasn't their fault, anyway,' he said at last. 'Every bit of it was mine.'

Captain Flint pulled a hard stroke, to bring his rowing boat level with the little crippled *Swallow*.

'How many times have you run a boat aground before?' he asked quietly.

'Never,' said John. 'Not hard, like that.'

'You've been lucky,' said Captain Flint. 'Everybody does it sooner or later.'

'It wouldn't have happened if I'd been reefed,' said John, steadily keeping his eye on the entrance to Rio Bay. 'If I'd been reefed I wouldn't have thought twice about jibing. And I ought to have reefed before starting with the wind there was, and I ought to have known it was no good hanging on after the sail wanted to come over. I ought to have known it would jibe whether I wanted it to or not. I ought to have jibed myself in plenty of time. I ought . . .'

'Anyhow,' said Captain Flint, 'you didn't lose a man, and you salved nearly all your cargo, and you raised your ship and are bringing her into port under sail. Things might have been a lot worse. Don't you worry about it overmuch. When a thing's done, it's done, and if it's not done right, do it differently next time. Worrying never made a sailor.'

'It isn't worrying,' said John. 'It's just that I hate myself for being such a duffer.'

'Um,' said Captain Flint, 'I wouldn't mind betting you've been just as much of a duffer lots of times before when nothing's happened. We're all duffers sometimes, but it's only now and then that we get found out.'

John remembered sailing in the dark last summer, and the noise of the water on that rock as the *Swallow* rushed past it just before she found shelter in the lee of an island. Much worse things might have happened then. He had been at least as big a duffer then as he had been this morning, only then nothing had happened, and today poor *Swallow* had had her bows stove in and had gone to the bottom of the lake. For some time he said nothing. Things might have been worse even now. After all, *Swallow* was no longer at the bottom of the lake. What if she had been run down by a steamer and gone down in deep water? What if Roger or Titty had gone down with her?

'I wish I knew what Mother will think about it,' he said.

'I shouldn't be surprised if she wasn't quite pleased to have the lot of you on dry land for a few days, even if you are at the other side of the lake.'

That was very much what John was afraid of, that Mother should think they were duffers and disagree with Daddy, who thought duffers better drowned. What if she forbade sailing altogether for the rest of the holidays?

He looked away to the right. Already the Peak of

Darien was abeam and they were opening up Holly Howe Bay. They were too far out for him to be sure if that was Mother herself, sitting outside the farm. John wished he was farther out still. He did not like to think of Mother seeing trim, neat little *Swallow* limping in to Rio after shipwreck. He was very glad when they had passed the point on the other side of the bay.

Holly Howe was hidden now, and *Swallow* and her convoy were moving in between Long Island and the shore towards the little town of Rio, with its cloud of blue smoke drifting from it in the sunlight. All along this nearer side of Rio Bay were the building yards, where rowing boats were built, and little ships like *Swallow*, and racing yachts, besides motor boats for the people who did not know how to manage sails. There were boathouses and little docks. There were sheds a few yards back from the water, with railway lines running down into the lake, and wheeled carriages resting on the railway lines to carry boats down into the water and to bring them up out of it. On one of these carriages was a racing yacht, with its mast high above the roofs of the sheds, and its sails neatly furled under its sail covers, its varnishing and painting bright in the sun, ready at any moment to go sliding down into the water and become a thing alive as all ships are when they are afloat.

The boathouses and sheds cut off a good deal of what wind there was in the bay, and Captain Flint rowed on ahead of *Swallow*, looking in between the little wooden jetties, to most of which motor boats or yachts were tied up. He was looking for the best place to bring a wounded ship ashore. He found what he wanted and called out as *Swallow* came nearer, 'Bring her in here, Skipper.'

John unfastened the halyard from the middle thwart to which it had been made fast, and hurried forward to free the yard from the traveller and to lay it in the boat with the sail. As he brought his weight forward the bows of *Swallow* came down, bringing the patch under water. The water spouted in round the edges of it. A good deal had somehow found its way in on the voyage. He scrambled back again to the stern where the water was now well over the ballast.

'Lucky I put my sandshoes on the thwart to go on drying,' he said. 'They'd be wet enough now if I had them on.'

He paddled *Swallow* in with an oar and beached her between two of the wooden jetties below a big green shed. The rowing boat grounded beside her, and Captain Flint stepped out.

'So far so good,' he said, 'and very good. I'll be back in a minute.' Leaving Captain John in charge of both boats he went up a narrow alleyway between two of the sheds.

In this place John felt more like a ship's boy than a captain. He tidied poor *Swallow*, hauled down her flag, rolled it round its stick and put it in the bows of the rowing boat. He pulled the rowing boat up another foot or two, when he saw that she was a little flustered by the wash of a passing steamer. When he had done all he could for his two charges, he began to use his eyes and nose and ears. There was something pleasant here for all of them. There was a smell of tarred rope, for one thing, one of the most heartening of all good smells. Then for his ears there was the sound of hammering, two quick taps and a good one to make sure, coming again and again from inside the green shed where a man and a boy hardly older than himself were busy putting in the copper fastenings in the planking of a little dinghy. Nor was hammering the only noise. There was the steady swish, swish of a plane taking long curling shavings off an oar that was being made. Further up the shed there was the noise of a saw cutting planks. In the next shed, into which John could see without moving more than a yard or two from the *Swallow*, there was a long wooden box with steam oozing out of it. It was not very deep or very wide, but it was more than half as long as the shed. That box, as John knew, was being used for steaming planks so that they could be bent to the right shape for the boats that were being built.

A long time in this place would have seemed short, but Captain Flint was gone only a few minutes. He came back with the chief boatbuilder, a short square man with a cheerful ruddy face and a pleasant eye, who told John it was a grand day, which, considering what had happened, John thought most untrue. He looked at the patch on the outside of *Swallow*, prodded at the planking round the patch, felt the ribs inside, and lifted out the broken mast, as if he thought it much more natural for boats to be shipwrecked than otherwise. No one would have known, while he was looking at *Swallow*, that she was the most important ship on the lake and that the holidays of at least six people partly depended on getting her put right at once.

'Well, Mr Turner,' he said, 'we're very busy just now, and I don't like taking men off other jobs . . .'

And then Captain Flint just took him by the arm and walked off up the alleyway and out of sight. When they came back a few minutes later, the boatbuilder was smiling, and things suddenly seemed less hopeless than for those few minutes John had thought them.

'You did well to get her off the bottom at all without sending for us,' the boatbuilder said to John. 'That's saved a day or two at least with us so busy here. We'll have to take those planks out and put in fresh and see what else there is to be done, but I promise we won't lose any time at all.'

'And will she really be all right again?' asked John.

'Better than a new ship,' said the boatbuilder. 'Better than a new ship she'll be, eh, Robert?' This last he said to another boatbuilder who came out from the shed in his shirtsleeves, dusting the sawdust from his trousers. This second boatbuilder shook hands with Captain Flint, nodded to John, prodded the broken planking and peered inside and out, just as the first had done.

'Bit of a bump she's had,' he said at last.

'She has that,' said the first, 'but we'll make her better than a new ship, eh?'

'And why not?' said the second.

'That's all right then,' said Captain Flint. 'And you won't forget that we're counting on you to put the job through as quick as you can.'

'That's right,' said the chief boatbuilder. 'There'll be no time lost.'

Captain Flint stepped into his rowing boat, John followed, and the boatbuilder, with one push, sent her shooting out between the jetties without touching the motor boats moored on either side.

'We'll row four oars,' said Captain Flint, and then, while they were getting the oars out, he went on: 'Um! Shipbuilders always say that, but I think old James means it for once. I told him that every day without *Swallow* is a day wasted. I think it sank in. Well, now for Holly Howe.'

John thought Holly Howe was likely to be much worse than Rio. He hardly knew what Mother would say when she heard that all four of them had had to swim from a sinking ship, even if it had only been for a few yards. But Captain Flint laid to his oars and set so fast a stroke that John, who, whatever else he did, was not going to let himself get out of time, had enough to do without worrying about what was still to come.

'Easy with the right. Pull left,' sang out Captain Flint, as they turned sharply round the point into the bay and headed for the Holly Howe boathouse from which, only two days before, *Swallow* and her crew had sailed so happily away.

*

Presently Captain Flint slackened his stroke, and John was able to take a quick glance over his shoulder. They were nearing the jetty, and looking up the field to the old farm he saw someone in a blue frock sitting on a chair outside it. That must be Mother, and the small lump of blue beside her must be Bridget playing about on the grass.

'Easy,' said Captain Flint.

A moment later, John was scrambling up on the jetty.

'Hang on to the painter,' said Captain Flint. 'I'm just going up to talk to your mother. If you give her the news you'll tell her about *Swallow* first and then she'll think that half the crew are drowned. Better let me tell her, and then she'll begin by knowing that she hasn't had the luck to lose any of you.'

He had vaulted up on the jetty and was through the gate and striding up the field before John had time to answer.

John wondered. Would he have begun by telling Mother he had wrecked *Swallow*? Why, of course he would. What else was there to say? How on earth would Captain Flint begin in any other way?

He looked up the long, steep field, up which Roger had tacked like a sailing ship that day, a year ago now, when Daddy's telegram had come to say they might sail in *Swallow* and camp on the island. He saw Captain Flint wave his hat, mop his bald head with his big red-and-green handkerchief, and shake hands, first with Mother and then with little Bridget. Then he saw him sit down on the grass. Everything looked

UNDER JURY RIG

peaceful and happy, as if there could be no news of shipwrecks in the air. Suddenly Mother jumped up out of her chair.

'He's told her,' said John to himself.

But she sat down again, not quite so comfortably this time, leaning forward as if she were asking questions. She threw her head back. 'He's made her laugh,' said John. The next thing was that Bridget went off through the gate into the farm, and Mr Jackson, the farmer, came round the corner from the barn, and Captain Flint went to talk to him and they shook hands. 'He's telling him about *Swallow*.' Then there was Bridget, running out again with a blue sunbonnet on and waving another in her hand. Then Nurse came out to the little wicket gate of the garden. Then Mother was putting on the blue sunbonnet Bridget gave her. 'Bridgie's tying the strings. She always does,' said John to himself. Then he saw that Nurse was waving from the gate, and Bridget waving back. Then Mother and Captain Flint came walking down the field towards the boathouse, and Bridget danced about beside them.

Mother was laughing. There was no doubt about it. She was laughing almost as if nothing was the matter. Everything was going to be all right.

*

'Hullo, Bridgie,' said John, as she trotted up to him for a hug. But his eyes were on Mother and Captain Flint as they came round the corner of the boathouse to the jetty.

'It's the least I can do for them,' Captain Flint was saying. 'They salvaged *Mixed Moss* for me. The least I can do is to salvage *Swallow* for them. And they'd done a good deal of the salvaging already. It won't be a big job to put her right. But it would make rather a mess of their holiday if they had to wait till it was done. You know it's bad enough, anyhow. We'd planned to do a lot of things that we can't while my aunt's staying with us.'

'How far is it to this Horseshoe Bay?'

'Not much further than the island.'

'But the other side of the lake.'

'Mary Swainson from the farm there rows to the town with milk every day, and I'd be delighted to carry mails and cargo for them. Passengers too,' he added.

'I don't like to think of their being a nuisance,' said Mother.

'They don't know how to be that, ma'am,' said Captain Flint.

*

John looked at Mother and Mother looked at John. They kissed each other. Mother looked at him again with just the faintest smile in her eyes.

'Well,' she said, 'so you've all turned into Robinson Crusoes. You've been very quick about it.'

'We didn't get shipwrecked on purpose,' said John. 'It was my fault. I thought I could just get into the cove without jibing, and then there was an extra gust and it all happened in a moment.'

'I thought just the same,' said Mother, 'when I capsized my cousin's dinghy in Sydney Harbour. A few yards less to go and I'd have done it. But I always thought there was bad temper in the wind that day, and that even if I hadn't tried to hang on too long, the wind would have hurried itself and capsized us just the same.'

John cheered up.

'Did it happen to you?' he said. 'I wonder,' he added hopefully, 'I wonder if it ever happened to Daddy. I don't suppose it ever did, though.'

'I shouldn't be surprised,' said Mother.

'It happens to most people sooner or later,' said Captain Flint, 'unless they stick to wheelbarrows.'

'The main thing is,' said Mother, 'to see that nobody gets drowned. Are you sure none of you did get drowned?'

'Mother,' said John with reproach.

'I counted the lot, ma'am,' said Captain Flint. 'Six. Four of yours and my own two nieces.'

'All the same,' said Mother, 'I think you're right. If you really don't mind dropping us on your way back, Bridget and I should be happier in our minds if we had counted them for ourselves.'

'I can count far more than six,' said Bridget.

'I dare say you can,' said Mother, dropping down into the rowing boat and holding out her arms. 'Count three now, and then jump. I'll catch you.'

A minute or two later John and Captain Flint were again at the oars. They were rowing out of Holly Howe Bay under the Peak of Darien. But they were not rowing so fast as they had been. There was no hurry now. Rather the other way, for they wanted to give the others time to have everything shipshape. Besides, they had passengers, the best of all natives and the ship's baby sitting side by side in the stern, and nobody can talk comfortably while they are rowing hard.

9

Swainson's Farm

IT WAS difficult to believe that the enormous pile
of things on the beach at Horseshoe Cove could
ever disappear into five tents and leave room for four
explorers.

'We shall never get straight if we don't set to at
once,' said Susan.

'It'll go like smoke with Peggy and me to help stow
it,' said Nancy.

'We were jolly lucky to be able to save so much
from the wreck,' said Roger.

'Why, that's nothing,' said Titty. 'Robinson
Crusoe saved rafts and rafts full. He brought chests

of drawers ashore. And barrels full of gunpowder.'

'But he lost some things,' said Roger, 'and we've got everything we had.'

Mate Susan looked about her, to make up her mind where best to pitch the tents. There was not really much choice. The thick jungle of trees came right down to the narrow beach of the cove, leaving no open space for a camp except on the wide pebbly flat where the stream left the trees to run out into the lake.

'It's a fine place to lurk in,' said Captain Nancy, 'but it's not much good for a camp. It's not going to rain today, but when it does the beck comes rushing down in a brown spate and all this dry bit is under water. But there's nowhere else to put all four sleeping-tents. Of course, you could have them separately, here and there in the jungle.'

'We can't do that,' said Susan, 'because of the crew. We can't have the able-seaman and the boy sleeping all alone.'

'Specially on the mainland,' said Titty. 'There might be anything prowling round. On an island it's different. Let's not stop here at all. Let's go on. Let's go on to our valley, Roger's and mine, the one we were going to show you if the shipwreck hadn't stopped us.'

'Let's go there at once,' said Roger.

'Rubbish,' said Susan. 'We've got to get the camp made quickly. To show Mother we really are all right. Captain Flint's going to bring her. There's no time to lose. This'll have to do. We'll find a better place tomorrow, if Mother lets us stop. But when she comes it's got to look as if we'd been here ages. And just look at it!'

There was no more discussion. It certainly did look hopeless, that great pile of bundles and tin boxes, with the parrot-cage on the top of it and the green parrot inside chattering about pieces of eight and calling himself pretty. Susan threatened to put his cover over the parrot if he didn't keep quiet, but she let Titty shut his noisy beak with a lump of sugar instead.

There was no doubt about it; the Amazons knew all about pitching tents. They had the stores tent slung between two trees in no time, and then, while Susan and Peggy stowed the things away in it, Nancy helped Titty with the little sleeping-tents, and Roger lent a hand now here now there, handing out the pegs one by one as Nancy and Titty needed them, or galloping from the beach to the store tent with a biscuit box or something else important. Horseshoe Cove began to look less like the scene of a shipwreck and more like an explorers' camp. Pretty soon it was altogether like a camp, and all that had to be done was to turn it from an untidy camp to a tidy one. No one was better than Susan at doing that, but while Susan was tidying she did not like having too many people about. People had to be tidied away too, only the worst of tidying people away was that they wouldn't keep still, and as soon as you had tidied them away from one place you found yourself falling over them somewhere else. So Susan gratefully remembered that they had not yet got any milk and that one of the Amazons would have to show them the way to the farm.

Roger had been tidied out of a tent because he had come into it all dripping after doing a little swimming. After that he went into the water again and did some more. He felt he had been rescued rather too quickly after the wreck, so he had had himself rescued two or three times over, swimming across the cove and being hauled ashore by Peggy, who was also losing interest in mere tidiness. Then Roger tried what it would be like to be the only one saved from the wreck. He swam until his feet touched bottom, crawled on through the shallow water, dragged himself just beyond the reach of the breakers (this was easy, because there were none) and lay exhausted on the beach, until he heard Susan say something about the farm, and Peggy say she would show Titty the way, when he jumped up at once and said he wanted to go too.

Susan, feeling their clothes carefully, pulled them down from the clothes-line and said they were dry enough to put on.

'It's a jolly good thing,' said Nancy, 'that you chose the tropics to be wrecked in. The stones themselves are almost too hot to touch today, and things dry at once. But just think what it would have been like if you had had to swim ashore in the Arctic, in winter, with no sun and no wood to make a fire, and nothing but snow and seals and Polar bears. There'd have been some proper shivering of timbers. You'd never have got dry at all.'

'That wouldn't have mattered to the bears,' said Roger. 'They'd have liked us better wet.'

Mate Susan gave them the milk-can and in this way got rid of everybody except Captain Nancy and the ship's parrot. That was better. After all, she could ask Captain Nancy to take the telescope and go out on one of the headlands to see if Captain Flint's rowing boat was in sight. And the parrot was in his cage, and the cage, at least, could be counted on to stay where she put it. She settled down now, while the kettle was boiling, to see that all the right things were in the right tents, that each sleeping-bag was properly unrolled in the tent to which it belonged, that the flaps of the tent doors were neatly tied back, and that everything else was exactly as it ought to be.

*

Mate Peggy took the boy and the able-seaman a little way up the beck and then struck across to the left by a fallen tree to a green cart track through the wood, the same cart track that Titty and Roger had found when they were exploring. They followed the cart track till they came to the road, and then, crossing the road (for going to get milk was a sort of native business, not at all like exploring), they went through a gap in the stone wall on the other side. The cart track did the same. It climbed away to the left and came out of the wood by an old whitewashed farmhouse with a spring beside it and a stone trough, and a lot of ducks noisily enjoying the overflow from the trough. They could hear someone singing in a creaky, small voice an old hunting song that young folks sing in a great shout:

'One morning last winter to Holmbank there came
A brave, noble sportsman, Squire Sandys was his name.
    Came a-hunting the fox. Bold reynard must die.
    And he flung out his train and began for to cry,
    "Tally-ho! Tally-ho! Hark, forward away!
        Tally-ho!"'

'That's old Mr Swainson,' said Peggy Blackett. 'He's ninety years old.'

'What's that other noise?' said Roger.

'Someone's making butter,' said Peggy.

She went into the cool white porch and knocked at the open door.

The song stopped suddenly.

'Come in, then,' said two voices at once.

Peggy and Titty and Roger went in. There was a fire burning in the low-beamed farm kitchen, though it was such a hot day outside. On each side of the fire were two old people, an old man leaning forward on his stick, sitting in a high-backed chair doing nothing, except that he had been singing, and an old woman in a chair on rockers, working at a patchwork quilt which was spread over her knees and over a good deal of the floor. Close beside her on the floor was a big shallow apple-basket full of scraps and rags of all colours, which were some day going to be part of the quilt.

'Why, my dear,' said Mrs Swainson, looking at them over her spectacles, 'it's one of Mrs Blackett's lasses. And who are these others? I thought there were only two of you. My word, and you are coming on. Why it seems no time since your mother's mother came in at that door no bigger than you are now, and I was a grown woman then and married, too.'

'Sixty years. Sixty-five,' said old Mr Swainson. 'It'll be nearer seventy since I brought her up here from the church down by Bigland, and she sat her down in that chair for the first time.'

'But who are the others, my dear?' said Mrs Swainson. 'They don't look to me like Blacketts, nor yet like Turners.'

'They're friends,' said Peggy, 'and they've been shipwrecked.'

'Shipwrecked?' said old Mr Swainson. 'Now that reminds me of a song . . .'

'Now then, Neddy,' said Mrs Swainson, 'keep your song a minute or two, and let me be hearing. . . . What was it you said, my dear?'

'Shipwrecked,' said Peggy. 'And we want some milk if you can let us have any. We've brought our can.'

'We had plenty of milk,' said Roger, 'only it went down with the ship and got away in the water.'

Titty said nothing. She was looking all round the low-beamed farm kitchen. There was a grandfather clock in the corner with a moon showing in a circle at the top, and a wreath of flowers all round the clock face. Then there was a curled hunting horn on the black chimney-shelf, and above that, on pegs jutting out from the wall, an old gun, and a very long coach horn, nearly as long as a man. There were white lace curtains to the low windows, and in the deep window-seats there were fuchsias in pots, and big spotted shells. Each shell had its own thick knitted mat, and the pots were in saucers, and each saucer had its knitted mat, just as if it were a spotted shell. Titty looked back to the chimney-shelf to see if the curly hunting horn was standing on a knitted mat. But it was too high for her to see. Close beside it on the chimney-shelf were some pewter mugs, and china candlesticks, and a copper kettle that Titty thought would be just the thing to please Susan.

As soon as old Mrs Swainson understood that they wanted milk, she shouted in a much louder voice than anyone would have thought possible:

'Mary. Mareee. *Mareee*.'

The noise of the butter-churn stopped, and clogs clattered on a stone floor, and through the passage leading from the dairy came a tall young woman, with her sleeves rolled to her elbows, and her cheeks very pink from turning the handle of the churn.

'And how are you, Miss Peggy?' she said.

'Very well, thank you,' said Peggy. 'These are our friends. This is Titty. This is Roger. They've both been shipwrecked.'

'In the same ship,' said Roger. 'We swam ashore.'

'Well, my dear,' said Mrs Swainson to Titty, 'what do you think of my youngest grandchild?'

Mary Swainson laughed.

'That's the question she always asks,' she said.

'I think she's very nice,' said Titty.

'That shows you've got good taste,' said old Mr Swainson. 'And that reminds me. There's a rare good song about that. . . .'

'Never mind the song,' said Mrs Swainson. 'Have you got any of this morning's milk, Mary? The cows won't be in for a while yet.'

'You come along with me,' said Mary, 'while I get you some. Nothing'll stop Grandad from singing if there's strangers about.'

'But I liked his song,' said Roger.

The old man slapped his knee and laughed till there were tears on his red cheeks.

'You and me would get on champion together,' he said, and laughed and laughed again.

But Mary Swainson swept them all out of the kitchen, across the passage and into the dairy.

'One of you keep turning that handle,' she said, 'while I rinse the can out for you. You mustn't stop the churn when the butter's in the way of coming. If we were to stay and let Grandad start singing it would be black night and the milk would be sour before ever you got away.'

So they took turns at the butter churn while Mary Swainson washed out the can and filled it from a huge brown earthenware bowl.

'You come and see us again, my dears,' said old Mrs Swainson, as Mary hurried them through the kitchen on the way out.

'We'd like to, very much,' said Titty.

'And you and me'll sing songs,' said the old man, winking at Roger, and screwing up one eye so that it disappeared altogether under his white bushy eyebrow.

'I'll be saying goodbye to you,' said Mary Swainson, 'or I'll have that butter spoiled yet.' And she clattered back into the farmhouse after getting Peggy, Titty and Roger safely beyond the porch.

'I wish he'd sung more songs,' said Roger, as they

went off. But they were not more than a few yards on their way before they heard the high creaky old voice singing again:

'Of such a fox chase there niver was known,
The huntsmen and followers were instantly thrown.
To keep within sound didn't lie in their power,
For hounds chased the fox eighty mile in five hour.'

'He's always like that,' said Peggy. 'And Mrs Swainson is always making quilts. She must have made hundreds and hundreds.'

'Did you see the copper kettle?' said Titty.

'I'd have liked to hear him blow the horn, the long one,' said Roger. 'May I carry the milk? I didn't have a chance of carrying it this morning.'

'Properly,' said Titty, after walking silently for some way along the cart track down through the trees – 'properly, we couldn't get milk at a farmhouse. We were cast ashore. There weren't any houses along that desolate coast. But, of course, we could have caught some of the wild goats and milked them. That's what we must have done.'

'Yes,' said Roger, 'and didn't they butt? It took two of us to hold a goat while the other one milked.'

That explained the milk well enough. Then the

153

road had to be dealt with. There it was, between the wood along the shore of the lake and the wood that climbed the side of the hill, a broad road with motor cars on it, and motor bicycles and even butchers' vans. It was a nuisance to have a road like that in newly discovered country. Columbus was never bothered with anything like that when he discovered America.

'What do you do about the road?' Titty asked after they had crossed it and were finding their way to the stream from the cart track on the other side.

'How?' said Peggy.

'Its being so noisy and native. And not the right kind of native.'

'We just don't count it,' said Peggy, 'not when we come to Horseshoe Cove. It's the edge of our country. We never bother about it at all. It's a good long way from the lake.'

'Yesterday,' said Titty, 'it was a road of the Aztecs. They were trumpeting to each other along it – the guards, I mean.'

'That was a fine idea,' said Peggy. 'I don't believe even Nancy would have thought of that. But you had to cross it, if you went up on the moor. I suppose you watched for a chance and made a dash for it when they weren't looking.'

'We didn't,' said Roger, and was just going to tell how they had found a way under the road instead of across it when they heard Nancy's voice, loud and clear, though some distance away, through the trees.

'A sail! A sail!'

All three of them started forward at a gallop, but Roger pulled up quickly, as the milk was slopping from the can. The others stopped, and Peggy took the can from him.

'Hurry up,' she said. 'I'll take the milk. It doesn't spill if you run without bobbing.' And, indeed, though she ran nearly as fast as the others, even in scrambling through the bushes, she spilt very little.

She left the milk-can at the mouth of the stores tent. Titty and Roger raced on out of the trees to the beach, where the parrot in his cage was alone looking after the fire. At the very end of the northern of the two headlands that made the narrow entrance to the cove, a large towel was waving on the top of an oar fixed in the rocks. Under it stood Nancy and Susan, taking turns with the telescope. The others joined them.

'It isn't exactly a sail,' said Roger.

It was, in fact, a rowing boat. And even eyes without telescopes could see that Captain Flint and Captain

John were rowing and that Mother and Bridget were sitting in the stern.

'You got the milk all right?' asked Susan, as the others clambered out over the rocks. 'Good. Everything's all ready for them. But only just. . . .'

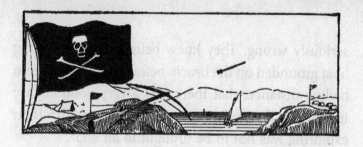

10

Making the best of it

A T THE bottom of their hearts, even Susan and Titty and Roger, all of whom knew Mother very well, had been a little afraid that when she came it would be to tell them that they must come back to Holly Howe. Nancy and Peggy had been sure, secretly, that this was what would happen, and had wondered how it was that in spite of this the shipwrecked explorers had been looking forward to her coming. But the explorers, after all, had a great deal they wanted to tell her, and, too, they had a sort of a half-feeling that when she saw the camp they had made, she would find it hard to believe that anything had gone very seriously wrong. They knew before ever the rowing boat grounded on the beach, before ever it was within hailing distance, that there was a very good chance indeed that the worst was not to happen and that their exploring was not to be brought to an end.

'It's all right, Susan,' cried Titty, the moment she saw the rowing boat. 'It's all right. Bridgie's come too. Everything's going to be all right.'

Peggy stared at her, but Nancy and Susan knew at once what Titty meant. It certainly was very unlikely that Bridget would have been allowed to come if the day was to end with a sad packing up of everything and a return of the explorers to ordinary native life. None of these thoughts came into the head of Roger, who was in a tremendous hurry to tell Mother about swimming ashore. Roger never looked very far ahead, but for the others, the sight of Bridget in the boat meant a lot.

The meeting on the beach in the cove, when the boat had turned in between the heads, and the explorers and their allies had scrambled back over the rocks, was much more joyful than it might have been. It was very noisy, because everybody was trying to talk at once, though at first nobody mentioned the question that was in everybody's mind. Mother was counting the shipwrecked and feeling their clothes and wanting to know exactly how it had all happened. The shipwrecked were telling all about it and at the same time wanting to hear from John and Captain Flint what had been said in Rio about poor *Swallow*. But no one asked whether they were to be allowed to go on being explorers. Mother said nothing about their having to come home. John seemed much happier. Bridget seemed to have no idea that anything might have gone wrong. And Captain Flint pleased Susan by saying that she had made a first-rate camp.

The talk on the beach was all of shipwreck, but no one who could not hear what was being said would have guessed that only a few hours before Horseshoe Cove had been a desert place. No one looking at that cheerful scene would have guessed that a ship had that very morning been wrecked on a rock at the mouth of this peaceful little bay, or that the camp there, so trim and tidy, had been set up in a hurry that afternoon by mariners who, only a few hours earlier, had had to swim for their lives.

There were the four sleeping-tents, two on each side of the stream, facing towards it, with running water for drinking and washing flowing conveniently past their doors. Behind them, partly hidden among the trees, could be seen the old tent that was now to be used for stores. The huge fire had been allowed to die down, and a kettle was simmering on the neat stone fireplace on the beach where this morning there had been the sort of tremendous blaze on which savages might roast long pig. Hanging out to dry were not the wet clothes of the shipwrecked but a row of bathing things and towels. It was true that the big towel flying from an oar out on the point had showed clearly enough that here were seamen in distress, but now that the best of all natives had arrived, it was taken down for fear that it might seem to be inviting help from other people. Of course, to anyone who knew them it would have seemed odd to see *Amazon* and Captain Flint's rowing boat and yet not a sign of *Swallow*, though her whole ship's company, from the captain to the parrot, were on the beach.

'What about *Swallow*?' Titty had asked, the moment she had had a chance of saying a quiet word to Captain John.

But Captain Flint heard her and answered, 'It'll be a week or ten days,' he said, 'before she can be afloat again. One of her timbers will have to come out, and then there'll be at least two new planks to go in. And then they can't launch her till she's painted, and they can't put paint on planks wet from steaming. A week or ten days it'll be, at least.'

'But she really is going to be all right?'

'She'll be as good as new.'

'Then I don't mind being shipwrecked a bit.'

'I thought you wouldn't,' said Captain Flint. 'Who would?'

John and Titty and Captain Flint looked at each other, and Titty knew that she had been right when she had guessed that they were to be allowed to stay on.

And indeed, the best of all natives, after one look round that neat camp, felt a good deal happier. She had counted the shipwrecked even before she had stepped ashore. She had felt their clothes. She had seen with her own eyes that none of the Swallows were missing. She had known already that John was all right, because there he had been, in the boat before her, helping Captain Flint to row her down the lake. But, as for the others, she had only been told that nothing was wrong with them. Telling was hardly enough to make her quite content. After all, she knew that their ship had sunk and that they had had to swim ashore, and in spite of being the best and most sensible native anyone ever knew, she was very pleased to be here and to make sure for herself (by kissing and rubbing noses, for example) that not a single one of the ship's company had been quite enough of a duffer to be drowned.

IN HORSESHOE COVE

'It's a good thing you hadn't got the ship's baby aboard when you were wrecked,' she said at last.

Able-seaman Titty was playing with the ship's baby. She looked up at once.

'I expect she was on board. It wouldn't be fair if she wasn't. You were, weren't you, Bridgie? And when the ship went down she was put on a raft, and the raft floated away in a current like the Gulf Stream, and we should never have seen her again if you hadn't happened to be coming along in your canoe and found the ship's baby sailing away on a raft by herself.'

'That must have been it,' said the best of all natives. 'She was sailing away on the raft and had nothing with her to eat but one doughnut, and even that she was sharing with a gull who had perched on her raft and looked hungry.'

'Well, I'm glad you found her,' said the able-seaman.

It was chiefly Roger, among the shipwrecked, who wanted to take Mother out on the point to see where *Swallow* had gone down and to look at the Pike Rock, now looking innocent enough. Not a word had been said about it by Captain John or Captain Flint as they rowed past it on the way into the cove. But the best of all natives seemed, after all, to want to see even that for herself. Roger showed her the way out over the rocks to the end of the headland, and the others followed her, all except Susan, who, for reasons of her own, was glad to have a minute or two without them, and Bridget, who stayed to help Susan.

'And where, exactly, did *Swallow* sink?' Mother asked.

'Close by the rock,' said Roger. 'Wasn't it lucky I learned to swim last summer?'

'I suppose it was,' said Mother.

'Well if I hadn't, I wouldn't have been able to get far enough to catch hold of the rope and be hauled out,' said Roger.

Then, by questioning, she learned something of how they had all got ashore, and of how the kettle and saucepan and ballast, and at last *Swallow* herself, had been brought up. Roger was ready with answers to most of her questions. Titty answered some. John said very little. On the whole, perhaps, she learnt most from Nancy and Peggy Blackett.

'And in the end you got her up and out of the water by yourselves?'

'Nancy and Peggy helped like anything,' said John.

'I'm sure they would,' said Mother. 'I think all of you did very well. And now I don't want to think about it any more. Things might have been so very much worse.'

'If they had been a different crew, ma'am,' said Captain Flint, who had been listening and saying nothing – 'if they had been a different crew, things might have been a great deal worse. But I gather there was no sort of panic, except, perhaps, among the spectators on shore.'

'I only squeaked once,' said Peggy indignantly, 'and anybody might have squeaked.'

'You see, ma'am,' said Captain Flint, 'there was no panic, even on shore. Taking it all round it seems to have been a shipwreck to be proud of.'

'Well, I'd rather they didn't do it again,' said the best of all natives.

'We aren't going to,' said John.

Just then there was the cheerful note of the mate's whistle, and they heard Bridget calling from the camp that tea was ready.

Susan had had everything nearly ready before ever Nancy had sighted the rowing boat in the distance. The kettle had been on the very edge of boiling, and everything else was being kept cool and out of the way until the last minute, in the store tent. Now the kettle had boiled, tea had been made, and while the others were talking shipwreck at the point, Susan had folded the old groundsheet in two (the one from which they had cut a patch to put on *Swallow*'s

165

wound) for a table-cloth, so that when they came back after hearing the whistle and Bridget's calling, they found a tea worth looking at, with the lids of biscuit tins piled high with slices of fried seed-cake (it had been dried by Peggy and it really did seem to taste all right) and sandwiches of bunloaf, marmalade and butter. Usually on the island it had been found best to carve one very thick slice for each explorer and to put the butter on at the last minute to avoid the sort of accident that so easily happens to anything when one side of it is buttered, and it is not eaten at once. But today, thin, buttered slices, and small sandwiches neatly arranged in pyramids, suggested an orderly quiet world in which nothing could ever go wrong.

'I've said it before, and I say it again,' said Captain Flint, when he saw what Susan had done, 'there never was an expedition that had a better mate.'

Everything was working out just as he had thought it might. Nobody could be much worried about shipwrecks that were already over when the shipwrecked mariners asked them to sit down to such a tea as that. Still, not even Roger thought it quite safe to ask if they were to be allowed to stay. But when tea was over, Mother, after saying what a good tea Susan and Bridget had made, let them know what the answer was to the question that had been in everybody's mind.

'And now,' she said, 'if you really don't want to come back to Holly Howe and get on with the holiday tasks, I suppose I must go and talk to this Mary Swainson.'

'We can do holiday tasks anywhere,' said John.

'If you do a holiday task indoors,' said Titty, 'it isn't really a holiday task. It might just as well be a school one.'

Captain Flint carried Bridget on his shoulder, and they showed the best of all natives the way up the stream and so to the cart track, and out through the trees to the road, and there they saw Mary Swainson herself talking to a young man sitting on a big roan cart-horse.

'It's the woodman,' said Titty, 'the one we saw leading the three horses and the log when Roger and I were exploring.'

Just then the woodman turned his great horse and rode off, clumpetty clump, down the road, waving his hand to Mary, who waved her hand to him.

'You stay here,' said Mother, 'and Mr Turner and I will go across the road to talk to Mary.'

'I'm coming too,' said Bridget.

'Less trouble to carry you than to put you down,' said Captain Flint.

The four explorers and their two allies waited in the wood while Mother and Captain Flint, with Bridget on his shoulder, crossed the road to talk to Mary Swainson. They talked to Mary for a minute or two at the other side of the road, and then went off with her along the cart track that led through the wood to Swainson's farm. They were gone a long time, while Nancy and Peggy, remembering the plans that had been upset by the shipwreck, and how they had meant to go up to the moor to see the secret valley, were asking Titty and Roger all about it, and just where it was. Titty and Roger answered their questions as well as they could, but were very careful to say nothing about Peter Duck's cave.

'Let's go up there the first day we can get away,' said Nancy.

When Mother and Captain Flint and Bridget came back, anybody could tell that Mother was very pleased with what she had seen. Captain Flint was carrying a basket of eggs, and Bridget was eating an apple.

'She's a very nice, sensible, kind girl,' said Mother, 'and I liked the farm, too, and the old people.'

'Did he sing to you?' asked Roger.

'Yes, he did, until Mrs Swainson and Mary made him stop.'

'He's a fine, musical old chap, is old Neddy,' said Captain Flint.

'So it's settled,' said John. 'We can stay where we are?'

'Yes,' said Mother, 'I think you can. Only do please remember what your father said.'

'Hurrah,' said Roger.

And then, when they had got back to the cove, Captain Flint said, 'There's just one thing. They'll have to find another place for the camp, or they'll be washed away with the first rain.'

'Why, I ought to have thought of that,' said Mother.

'But there are plenty of better places close along the shore,' said Captain Flint. 'Dry, anyhow.'

'Not so secret,' said Peggy.

'We'll find them a place,' said Nancy.

'We'll go to our valley,' said Titty. 'Next to the island, it's the finest place in the world.'

'What valley is that?' asked Mother.

Titty and Roger explained as well as they could.

'I know it,' said Captain Flint. 'But I haven't been up there these twenty years. It's a good place for a camp, if it's the place I'm thinking of. It's got a . . .'

'Oh,' shouted Roger.

'Don't tell. Don't tell. . . . It's a secret. . . . If it's . . .'

Titty was only just in time to stop him. He looked down, puzzled.

'If it's what?'

'Whisper it,' said Titty. . . . 'Oh, that's all right. It's something else that's a secret.'

'Then I can go on?' asked Captain Flint. 'What I was going to say was that it's got a good trout tarn up above it. I'll show you how to catch trout there.'

'We saw lots in the beck,' said Roger.

'How far is it from Swainson's farm?' asked Mother.

'Not much farther than we are here,' said Captain Flint.

'We haven't been up to see it yet,' said John. 'We were going today. But it would be much better to be near the lake.'

Titty's hopes that had risen high for a moment fell once more, though not very far. After all, the main thing was that exploring was not to come to an end.

'I don't mind where you are,' said Mother, 'so long as you are within reach of Mary Swainson. She's going to keep me in touch with you when she brings the milk across to the village.'

'And you and Bridgie'll come to see us,' said Susan.

'And Captain Flint, too,' said Titty.

'I'd like to see if you can make as good a job of being shipwrecked as you did of last year's war,' said Captain Flint.

'The shipwreck's real enough,' said John grimly.

170

'Bother the great-aunt,' said Nancy. 'If it wasn't for her we'd come and be shipwrecked too.' She looked almost resentfully at *Amazon*, snugly beached beside the rowing boat. 'You can do all sorts of things. You can discover the sources of the Amazon River. You can discover us. There's nothing you can't do. But we can't do anything worth doing, not until the great-aunt's gone.'

'By Jove,' said Captain Flint, 'I'm glad you reminded me. We had all to be back for tea, and now we're going to be late for supper if we don't hurry. So if Mrs Walker doesn't mind.'

'But you can tell her there's been a shipwreck,' said Roger.

'It's no good talking of shipwrecks to Aunt Maria,' said Captain Flint.

'Bridget and I ought to be getting back, too,' said Mother. 'Bridget's bedtime isn't far off.'

There was a general embarking. John and Susan pushed off the rowing boat, when Mother, Bridget and Captain Flint were aboard. Titty and Roger helped to push off *Amazon*. Then the four explorers ran out to the northern headland to wave goodbye. It felt queer and wrong to be the ones left on land and to know that even if they wanted, they had no boat in which to put to sea.

'Don't sit up late tonight,' Mother called. 'After a shipwreck it's best to get early to bed.'

The shipwrecked explorers watched the little white sail of *Amazon* disappear among the islands off Rio. Then the rowing boat moved under the Peak of Darien. It, too, was gone. They felt suddenly very tired. Nobody minded when Susan said they would get supper over at once. They had a good bread-and-milk supper, and when it was done there did not seem to be much that anybody wanted to say, even when it was found that not a flash could be got from any one of the three torches that, in the pocket of a knapsack, had gone down with the ship. Candle-lanterns were all you needed to go to bed by. There was no chattering in the tents while they were wriggling down into their sleeping-bags, and though the noise of the beck hurrying past the tent doors was different from the noise of the lake lapping on the rocks of the island, two minutes after John called 'Lights out' there was nobody awake to listen to it.

11

The Able-Seaman in Command

THERE were no trees between the tents and the sun as it rose over the eastern hills on the other side of the lake. The sunlight and the noise of the beck hurrying through the middle of the camp woke Captain John early in the morning. He woke to thoughts so sad that he turned over inside his sleeping-bag and did his best to go instantly to sleep again. Last night he had thought that the worst part of being shipwrecked was over. He knew now that it had only just begun.

Making that silly mistake about hanging on too long and trying not to jibe until at last the wind flung the sail over for him when he least wanted it . . . all that was being shipwrecked. But after the wreck there had been the diving and the salvage work, getting *Swallow* to the beach. Then there had been the mending of the ship, and the perilous voyage to Rio in her under her jury rig, with water creeping in. All the time there had been something to do in a hurry. All the time there had been something to do with boats. Just for one moment last night he had felt queer, seeing the rowing boat and the *Amazon* go away and knowing that he could not follow them. But even then there had been other things to think of. This morning he was face to face with the truth.

He had waked, thinking of taking *Swallow* over to the Dixon farm landing in Shark Bay to fetch the morning milk, and then, suddenly, he had remembered that there was no *Swallow*. There was no boat at all. There they were on the shore of the lake, as if on the shore of a great sea, but they were prisoners on land. The water was no good to them, except to bathe in. Seafaring, for the present, was at an end.

When he found that he could not go to sleep again and forget these melancholy truths, John wriggled out of his sleeping-bag. A minute later he was swimming in the cove. He swam the whole way to the entrance, and then out between the headlands. It was a still, windless morning, and there was hardly a ripple on the lake. Only, just where the Pike Rock lurked below the surface, every now and then there was a little stir in the water, almost as if a trout were coming slowly to the top and quietly sucking down a fly without really breaking the surface with his nose. John swam on and was presently resting on the rock like a wet pink seal in the morning sunlight. He rested there, and looked across and up the lake to Wild Cat Island. He remembered how pleasant it had been to feel that they lived on an island with water all round them, and that there was a little ship snug in harbour, so that they could sail wherever they wished. He remembered the time they had spent on the Peak of Darien and at Holly Howe last year, waiting day by day for their father's telegram to say they might take *Swallow* and sail to the island. This waiting was going to be much worse. They had had an island, they had had a ship, and now they had lost them both.

Presently, looking back towards the cove, John saw a wisp of blue smoke floating up against the background of the trees.

'Susan,' he called.

'Hullo!'

Almost at the same moment he heard a squeak. That must be Roger trying the cold water with his toe. The water was cold even in August, just there, where the beck ran out into the cove. Then there were two loud splashes. That must be the able-seaman and the boy flopping in one after the other. John, his mind made up, rolled, seal-like, off the rock, dived under without making a splash, came up again, had a last look towards Wild Cat Island and then swam in between the headlands.

He swam in towards the white tents at the head of the cove, where the stream from the hills ran down into the lake. Here there was a tremendous splashing going on. Roger was lying on his back with his hands on the bottom, beating the water with his legs. Titty, with one arm stretched out so as to cut the water, was whirling round and round, being a maelstrom.

'Titty,' called John, as soon as he came near enough to make himself heard through all that splashing.

The maelstrom calmed down.

'Hullo,' it said.

'Look here, Titty,' John went on, 'how far do you really think it is from that valley of yours to the farm where we have to get milk?'

'It can't be very far,' said Titty.

'Farther than from here?'

'Not much, anyhow. Perhaps not so far. We'd probably find a short cut through the woods on that side of the road. Are we going there? Do let's.' The maelstrom had become an explorer for the rest of the day.

'Who's going to fetch the milk for breakfast?' called Susan from beside the fire.

'We'll all go,' said John. 'But we won't bring it back here. Why not have breakfast higher up? We'll get the milk and then go on to look at their valley.'

'Hurrah!' said Roger.

'I've been thinking that perhaps we ought to move the camp a bit away from the shore. Floods for one thing. Swamp fever for another. You never know, between the jungle and the sea.'

'There might be alligators,' said Titty, splashing up out of the water, 'or hippopotamuses. It would never do to have a hippopotamus coming blundering through our new tents.'

'It'll be beastly being on the edge of the lake and having no boat,' said John.

'All right,' said Susan. 'But after bathing, you must have something to eat. I'll boil some eggs to take with us. It would be a pity to waste the fire now it's lit.'

'Chocolate wouldn't be bad for now,' said Roger, 'and then we can have proper breakfast afterwards.'

'Do you think it'll be all right to leave the tents?' said Susan.

'Nobody ever comes here but the Amazons, and they can't be coming today. The great-aunt wanted them.'

It was settled. While the eggs were boiling, food for the day was divided up among the four knapsacks. There was bunloaf, pemmican, butter, a pot of marmalade, four apples and two tins of sardines. John took the compass, Titty the telescope and the borrowed egg-basket, Roger the empty milk-can, and Susan the kettle, though it was agreed, of course, that this was to be carried in turns.

'Lead away, Able-seaman,' said Captain John, when all was ready and they had eaten the bit of chocolate and the hunk of bunloaf that Susan handed out to each of them as a sort of bathing ration.

'Aye, aye, sir,' said Titty, who had just given the parrot a good supply of food and water and three lumps of sugar as his day's pay. 'Come on, Roger.'

Mate Susan looked carefully round the camp before they left, to see that all was as it should be. John was in a hurry to be on the way. He wanted as soon as possible to stop being reminded every other minute that he had not got a boat.

The able-seaman was in command of the expedition, but when she led them past the place where they had turned off to the cart track in showing

Mother the way to Swainson's farm, John could not help saying, 'Oughtn't we to turn off here?'

The able-seaman stopped short.

'You can get that way,' she said. 'That's the way if you're going to cross the road. It's all right for going to get milk. But Roger and I found a better way. We can get to the other side of the road so that even if savages were watching for us all along it they would never see us.'

'Oh, look here, Titty,' said Susan, 'that's a Peter Duck story.'

'It isn't a story at all,' said Roger.

'Of course Peter Duck thought it was a good way,' said Titty.

'Is it much farther than crossing the road?' said John.

'Nearer. It's close here.'

The able-seaman led them on round a bend in the little stream, and there before them, thickly covered with ivy and overhung with trees, was the low arch of the bridge.

'We go through that,' said the able-seaman, 'and even if there were scouts from one end of the road to the other they wouldn't know how we got past them.'

'It's a jolly good way of getting across,' said John.

'Roger and I took our shoes off,' said Titty, 'but we could almost have got through without.'

'Better not try,' said the mate. 'There's no point in getting shoes wet and having to dry them.'

'The next bit would be awfully tickly barefoot,' said Roger, remembering the larch needles that made a carpet to the wood at the other side of the road.

They took their shoes off and, stooping low, waded upstream under the bridge.

'You couldn't get through if there was much more water,' said the mate.

'If there was a spate, you'd have to swim for it,' said John.

'You could float through, clinging to a log, with only your nose above water,' said Titty, 'even if the enemy were watching the river itself.'

'If you were going downstream,' said John.

'You would be,' said Titty, 'escaping to your boats.'

'But we haven't got any boats,' said Roger.

There was a grim silence. Once more everybody had been reminded of the shipwreck.

But they forgot it again when they came out from under the bridge into the larch wood on the other side, and waded ashore to dry their feet and put their shoes on. Then it was decided that two were enough to fetch the milk. Susan and the boy, with the milk-can and the egg-basket, went off close along the wall at the bottom to get to the cart track and so to Swainson's farm. After getting the milk they were to join the rest of the party higher up the stream. Meanwhile the able-seaman and Captain John followed the stream up through the steep green larch wood, up and up past one little waterfall after another, until they were out of sight of the road. There is no undergrowth worth speaking of in a larch wood, nothing under the bright green trees but the copper-coloured carpet of last year's fallen needles, so that it is much harder to hide in that sort of wood than in any other. As soon as they could no longer be seen from the road, John was ready to stop, but the able-seaman was all for pressing on. 'It's not much farther to the top of the larch wood,' she said. 'Besides, we're awfully near the road to begin whistling. Somebody else might hear us instead of Susan and Roger.'

So they climbed on, to the place where the larch trees ended and the other sort of wood began, hazels and oaks, like the trees in the wood by the lake. At the edge of the larches they stopped, though this time John wanted to go on, and it was Titty who thought it was time for a halt.

'I don't believe this wood is a very wide one,' John

said. 'If we go on a little way we shall be out of the trees.'

'That's just it,' said the able-seaman. 'The new country's just the other side. And we ought all to come out of the trees together.'

'All right,' said Captain John. 'You're in command. It's your discovery, anyhow.'

'And Roger's. We'd have turned back if he hadn't begun climbing by the waterfall. And really, it was the stream most of all. We had to go on to see where the noise was coming from. You'll hear it as soon as we're up on the moor.'

So the captain and the able-seaman lay on their backs on a smooth slope of copper larch needles, and looked up through the clear green larches to the blue sky high overhead. A squirrel hurrying through the feathery branches was startled at the sight of them lying there, and chattered at them, pretending he was more angry than afraid. They heard him, and lay still, and moved nothing but their eyes until they saw his bushy red tail and then his tufted ears lifted high above his face.

'He must hurry up,' said the able-seaman. 'I'll have to be blowing the mate's whistle in a minute, and he won't like it. She'll have got the milk by now and they'll have started up from the farm if the old man didn't keep them to sing. We ought to begin whistling to let them know which way to go.'

'Well, give her another minute or two. She can't lose the way, because of the stream. It doesn't really matter where she comes to it.' But he stirred as he spoke, and the squirrel fled away through the tops of the larches, running out on a branch that dropped with his weight and then leaping from it to a branch in another tree, when the branch he had left swung up again behind him as if trying to hurry him on his way.

'It won't matter now,' said Titty, and she sat up and blew the mate's whistle.

An owl called not far away in the woods.

'There they are,' said Titty. 'They're higher than we are.' She whistled again.

The owl answered. John jumped to his feet. So did the able-seaman.

'Come on,' she said. 'They *are* higher up. They may get to the edge of the wood first.'

But the captain and the able-seaman had not climbed more than another twenty yards or so along the banks of the stream before they heard the talking of the mate and the boy, and presently saw them, not far away among the trees.

'There's a path here,' called the mate.

'Is it coming this way?' called the able-seaman.

'Yes, and it's going up all the time.'

'Much used?' called Captain John.

'I thought it was when we were coming through the larches, but here it looks as if nobody used it at all.'

'Sheep, perhaps,' said Roger.

'Keep along it,' called John. 'It looks as if we were going to meet, anyhow.'

So John and Titty went on up the banks of the stream, and a few yards away, coming nearer and nearer, Susan and Roger pushed their way up under the branches that had grown over the path.

They came out of the trees at the same moment and close together. To right and left, as far as they could see, was wide rolling moor, and straight before them the beck hurried down over the moorland to meet them, singing its way through the heather.

'Don't lose sight of the path,' called John. 'Which way does it go?'

The mate stood still and looked at the ground ahead of her.

'It's more like a rabbit track here,' she said, 'but you can see where it goes quite plainly.'

'It doesn't go up the beck, does it?' asked Titty anxiously.

'It goes down to the beck just in front of you.'

'Half a minute,' called John. He slipped along the edge of the trees to where the mate and the boy were standing. Then he began trotting forward, stooping low as he trotted.

'People use it,' he called out. 'Here's the mark of a heel.'

'Oh, no, no!' said the able-seaman.

'Yes,' said John. 'It goes down to the beck, just here. There are stepping-stones. And yes, there it goes, up the other side and along the edge of the wood.'

'That's all right,' said the able-seaman. 'So long as it doesn't go up the beck into our valley.'

'How much farther is it to your valley?' asked the mate.

'Not very far,' said the able-seaman.

'If you were to begin eating a doughnut now,' said Roger, 'and ate it very slowly, it would be about done before you got there.'

'Roger wants his breakfast,' said Titty.

'We all want our breakfasts,' said Susan. 'We'll have it here, so that we shan't have to go so far to get wood for a fire.'

Even the able-seaman, who was in a hurry to get to her valley, thought this a good idea. After all, it was just as if the expedition had been travelling all night and were stopping to breakfast now at the beginning of a new day. There was nothing against it at all. The farther away the valley seemed the better it was. In a moment the explorers had dumped their knapsacks on the ground and were making ready for a meal.

'There is one good thing about camping near a stream,' said the mate. 'We're all right for water. And here's a good place for a fire.'

She had found a little bay of bright grey pebbles left dry by the stream during the hot weather. Close by were some bigger stones and these she made into a ring, with the three biggest stones arranged so that she could balance the kettle on them and have plenty of room to keep up a fire underneath it. She found some last year's bracken, dry as tinder, to start her fire with, and by the time she was ready for them, the other explorers were bringing in armfuls of dry sticks from the edges of the wood.

'Nobody can ever have made a fire up here,' said Titty. 'There's more wood lying on the ground than we could use if we made a bigger fire than Captain Nancy makes, and kept it going for a whole year.'

Once more John remembered the island and *Swallow* and all that he wanted to forget. But not for long. Before breakfast was ready he was back again in this new adventure on the way to the able-seaman's secret valley.

'If we want to keep your valley secret,' he said, as soon as breakfast was done, 'we'd better leave no tracks that we can help, and we'd better get on quickly before any of the natives come this way.'

So, good fireplace as it was, they pulled it to pieces and scattered the big stones, and put the charred embers from the fire into the beck to be washed away down to the lake, and buried the eggshells from the hard-boiled eggs, so that no native, unless he was looking very carefully, would have guessed that explorers had passed that way, and camped and made their breakfast there before going on into unknown country.

They hurried on along the sheep tracks that wound among the rocks and heather at the side of the stream, climbing steadily up the moor. Able-seaman Titty went first, and Captain John next. Roger had begun by going first, but he kept stopping at every pool in the beck to see if there was a trout in it, so that very soon he would have been last of all, if the mate had not waited to hurry him up, and to see that nothing that mattered got dropped by anybody and left behind.

Always before them, they could hear the noise of

the waterfall, a noise that grew more and more stirring as they came nearer. And presently they could see the white splash of the falling water, not so very far ahead.

The nearer the able-seaman came to her valley the more she hurried and the less sure she felt that it was really all that she had thought it. It had so very often happened that things which she had thought lovely had turned out to be quite dull when she had taken somebody else to see them. She began to be afraid that her valley would turn out like that. And this made her hurry all the more, partly because she wanted to make sure, and partly because, if it was going to be a disappointment, she wanted to get it over as quickly as possible.

She was out of breath when she came to the foot of the waterfall, but she scrambled up the rocks at the side of it and, for the second time, looked up into the little valley. There it was, just as she remembered it, with the other waterfall at the head of it, the steep banks of rock and bracken and heather shutting it in on either side, the broad flat floor of the valley sheltered by those high, steep sides so that from inside the valley, unless you looked back over the lower waterfall, there was nothing to be seen but the sky, and from outside the valley you could not see it was there unless you were looking down into it from its very edge. Yes, it was all that she had thought it. She turned back to wave to John, who was climbing up not far behind her, though he had not such reasons for hurrying.

'Don't look yet,' she said. 'Keep looking at the ground until you're right at the top. This way. Now, look. . . .'

John scrambled over the top beside the able-seaman and looked on up into the valley.

'It's a good enough place,' he said.

It was not much to say, but by the way he said it, Titty knew that it was all right and that the captain at least felt about her valley much as she felt herself.

12

Swallowdale

'COME on, Roger,' said Mate Susan. 'You'll be left behind.'

'It's quite safe here,' said Roger. 'It's not like being in the jungle, where there might be savages behind the trees. Here you can see as far as ever you want. Hullo, where's Titty? And where's John?'

'Out of sight,' said the mate. 'They're up at the top of the waterfall already. If we can't see them, there might be lots of other people we can't see. Come on, quick, and catch up with the rest of the expedition.'

The ship's boy hurried along. He had been held up by finding one of the big red-and-black velvet fox-moth caterpillars that feed on the heather. He turned now to more serious things and hurried along to catch up with the main body of the explorers. Susan was right. It would not do to be a straggler. Besides, Captain John and the able-seaman were already up the waterfall and in the secret valley that was his discovery as well as Titty's.

In a few minutes Susan and Roger reached the bottom of the waterfall and began climbing up the rocks. They, too, disappeared over the top. From below no one could have seen them. There was the white water pouring over, and on each side of it rock and heather. But no one looking up from the stream below the waterfall could have guessed that just up there, only a few yards away, there was a valley in which a hundred explorers could have camped unseen.

*

'Hi, hi! Wait for us!' shouted Roger, as he scrambled, breathless, up into the valley.

Titty and John looked back. They were already nearly at the upper waterfall.

'Come along,' shouted Titty.

But now it was Susan who found hurrying difficult. One glance had shown her what a perfect place for a camp the valley was, and now, looking at the steep, sheltering sides of it, and the flat spaces by the stream, she was thinking of just where she would lay out the tents, and where would be the place for the fire, and where the washing up could best be done.

'That's the place for a fire,' she said when they were half-way up the valley, 'and there couldn't be a better basin for washing up in than this pool.'

'Which pool?' said Roger.

'This one.'

'There's a trout in it,' said Roger. 'Titty and I saw him. But perhaps he wouldn't mind the washing up. He might even like it.'

'It would depend on what was left on the plates,' said Susan.

'We don't have mustard,' said Roger.

'Come along,' called the able-seaman again.

'Come along,' said Roger. 'She's waiting to show you the secret.'

'Coming, coming,' said Susan, but she had small belief in secrets, and she could not hurry much. 'There's room for all four tents on this side of the stream, and the stores tent, too, if we wanted,' she was saying half to herself and half to Roger. 'Or we could put the stores tent on the other side.'

'Do come along,' said Roger.

'Hurry up,' said Titty.

At last the mate and the boy joined the able-seaman and the captain.

'Boy!' said the able-seaman, 'did you say anything about it to the mate?'

'No,' said Roger, 'except that we were just going to show it.'

'Did you see it?' she asked Susan.

'See what?' said Susan.

'John didn't see it either. And you both walked close past it.'

'Close past what?' said John.

'Peter Duck's cave,' said Titty.

'Not a real cave?' said John.

'That's why we had to bring torches, and why it's such a good thing Susan's didn't get wet.'

'Well, where is it?'

Titty and Roger went back to the place where Susan had said she would like to put the tents.

'It's here,' said Titty.

John and Susan looked about them, but there was nothing to show where the cave was.

Titty walked up to the steep wall of grey stone with the clumps of heather growing in the cracks of it, and there, close under the heather, showed them the opening, which, unless you looked closely, might have been no more than a cleft in the rock.

'If it hadn't been for a butterfly perching on the heather no one would have seen the cave at all,' said Titty.

'Have you been into it?' said John.

'No,' said Titty.

'Not yet,' said Roger.

John twisted himself out of his knapsack straps and dropped the knapsack on the ground. Susan wriggled out of hers and rummaged in it for her torch. How lucky it was that in the hurry of starting on the day of the shipwreck she had left it behind. She gave it to John.

'Go on, John,' she said.

John, stooping and flashing the torch before him, disappeared through the opening.

'Can I come too?' asked Roger.

'Wait a bit,' said Susan. 'I say, John, have a look at the roof of it. Is it all right?'

'Solid rock,' said John, 'and high. I can only just reach it. I'm standing up. Pouf, it's awfully dusty.' For years and years the dust had been settling in the cave, and now, when John moved, it rose in clouds about his feet.

'Is there room for more of us?' asked Susan.

'Lots,' said John, from far inside, and his voice sounded as if he were shouting from the bottom of a deep, echoing tunnel. 'But look out for your heads till you're well in.'

The others crawled in, and stood up one by one, feeling with their hands in the blackness and watching the splash of light flung by the torch now here, now there, on the rough walls and roof, all cut in solid rock.

'It's not really so very big,' said John.

'But it's big enough for Peter Duck,' said Titty, 'and he would let us come in if we were attacked by savages or pirates or anything like that.'

'But why Peter Duck?' said Susan.

'Well, we haven't a tent to spare for him, for one thing, and anyhow it's just the sort of cave he ought to have.'

'It's a fine place for keeping the stores,' said Susan. 'As cool as anything. You couldn't have a better larder.'

Roger began to cough.

'Out you go,' said Susan. 'It isn't fit for you to stay in until we've got rid of the dust.'

Roger blundered out into the bright sunlight, flapped his arms and blinked his eyes. Just for the moment he was being a bat disturbed at midday, but he was an explorer again and a ship's boy before the others had noticed that he was being a bat.

Titty and Susan followed him out and John was

close behind them. All their throats were tickling from the dust.

'It wouldn't do to live in,' said John, 'but there's plenty of room in it for all our tents and everything we've got.'

'We could put Peter Duck on guard,' said Titty. 'We could live in our tents and supposing we saw an enemy coming we could hide everything in the cave and no one would ever know where our stronghold was. It's a great place.'

'It's a pity we haven't got any enemies,' said Roger.

'We may have lots,' said Titty.

'You never know on the mainland,' said John. 'And the Amazons are sure to want some sort of war or other.'

'Look at the way they attacked us last year,' said Titty, 'when they said it was their island, not ours. Anyhow, they can't say it's their valley. And no one knows about the cave. In that way it's even better than Wild Cat Island. There's not even a fireplace to show anyone's been here before. We discovered it for ourselves.'

'Somebody must have made the cave,' said John.

'It may have been here for ever. And anyway it's Peter Duck's cave.'

'But Peter Duck's only in a story,' said Susan. 'It can't be really his cave.'

'Well, anyhow, he's one of us. And if we make it his cave, then it's all right, anyway. Whose else is it?'

John agreed. Peter Duck was one of the things on which it was not safe to disagree with Titty. Anyhow, even for John, he was very nearly real. He had become very real indeed in the story they had made up in the Christmas holidays. There was no reason at all why he should not have a cave.

'Besides,' said John, 'if we call it Peter Duck's cave, then when we want to talk of it when there are natives about, or enemies, we can say, "Go to Peter Duck's," or "Fetch it from Peter Duck's," or "I left it at Peter Duck's," or "We'll meet at Peter Duck's," and no one would ever guess we meant a cave. Peter Duck's cave will do very well. But what are we going to call the valley?'

'I've got a name for that, if it'll do,' said Titty. 'Let's call it Swallowdale. Places get called after kings and princes and all kinds of people. It's much more fun to call a place after a ship. Let's call the valley after *Swallow*.'

Nobody had a word to say against that. And now, with such a valley to camp in, and such a cave to think about, even John did not mind so much hearing of the little ship. After all, she would soon be mended, and meanwhile there was all this. . . .

BREAKFAST ON THE WAY

'Does everybody agree?'

Everybody agreed.

'Right,' said John. 'Swallowdale shall be its name.'

'For ever and ever,' said Titty.

'We'll shift the camp up here tomorrow,' said John.

'There's only one bad thing about Swallowdale,' said Susan (and Titty was very pleased to hear her use the name). 'There's plenty of water, but there's no wood. We shall have to carry all our firewood from the forest below the moor.'

'Whenever we go to fetch milk, we'll bring back as much wood as we can carry,' said John.

'I don't believe it's much farther to the farm from up here than it is from Horseshoe Cove,' said Susan. 'Getting milk will be easy, but it's much harder work carrying wood than bringing it in a boat like we did last year.'

'But we're shipwrecked,' said Titty. 'We ought to have some hardships or it wouldn't be proper.'

'Well, the sooner you begin the hardships and fetch some wood, the sooner there'll be a fire for dinner.'

'Let's go at once,' said Roger.

'We must explore a bit more first,' said John. 'We must find a good look-out place. We must have somewhere to put sentinels so that they can see all round and give us warning if natives are coming down over the fells or coming up from the woods.'

'All right,' said Susan. 'I'm going to make a fireplace.'

'And as soon as the fireplace is ready, we'll go down into the forest to bring wood. We'll explore now.' John knew very well that the mate liked making fireplaces her own way and that helping her was never much use. 'Come on, you two. You can leave your knapsacks here, but bring the telescope.'

The able-seaman and the boy left their knapsacks by the door of Peter Duck's cave, and followed the captain up the northern side of the valley.

There were loose screes to avoid, where the stones slipped from under their feet, rocks to climb round, and clumps of heather to hold on by, and then at the top they came out on the open moorland, heather, bracken and grass cropped short by the black-faced fell sheep and burnt brown by the hot summer sun. Farther up they could see where the beck wound its way over the moor. And beyond the moorland in the north and west they could see the big hills.

'That one with the peak at one end of it is

Kanchenjunga,' said Titty. 'There isn't any snow on it now, but there must be lots in winter.'

'That's the hill above the valley the Amazon River comes from,' said John. 'I've seen it on the map. Its name is . . .'

'Let's have it for Kanchenjunga,' said Titty. 'And then we can explore the sources of the Amazon and climb Kanchenjunga at the same time. Real exploring. . . .'

'Kanchenjunga's a gorgeous name, anyhow,' said John.

'We'll have ropes to climb with. If only there was snow on him we'd have ice-axes.'

'Hullo, there's Rio,' said Roger.

They had been so taken up with the moorland and the big range of blue and purple hills stretching away into the distance that they had not looked back towards the lake below them. Now they turned and saw it, far away below, a blue and silver ribbon of water, with dark green wooded islands on it, and steamers, and the white sails of yachts, and the black spots that were the rowing boats of the natives, and the grey roofs of Rio town clustered about the bay. Looking down from the high moors, through gaps in the woods below them, they could see all this, though from where they were they could not see Wild

Cat Island, which was too close below them and hidden by the forest through which they had climbed.

'Where's the telescope?' said John.

Titty gave it him.

'We can see Holly Howe. I thought we could.'

'Let me see,' said Roger.

They looked in turns. Sure enough, far away on the other side of the lake, not far from Rio, there was the dark, pine-clad Peak of Darien, and beyond it a green field sloping up from a tiny bay, and at the top of the field the whitewashed, grey-roofed farm nestling among its damson trees.

'That white speck moving about there must be Nurse's apron,' said Titty, 'or perhaps it's Bridgie.'

'It's fine,' said John. 'We could even signal to Mother if we wanted anything, or she could signal to us. And that rock over there ought to make a good watch-tower, though it's a bit far from the valley.'

About a hundred yards away a big, square, flat-topped rock rose out of the heather.

But there was no time to look at the rock that day. Looking down towards the lake, they could see where the stream that ran through Swallowdale left the moor and dropped into the trees on its way down to Horse-shoe Cove. Something was moving down the beck. Roger had the telescope.

'What's the mate doing down there?' he said suddenly.

'Where?'

'There. She's just going into the forest.'

'Oh, bother!' said John. 'She's been too quick over the fireplace and now she's gone to get wood. She probably thinks we've forgotten all about it. Come on. We've got to catch her up. Anyhow, that rock'll do all right for a watch-tower. Come on. Follow the sheep tracks through the heather, and look where you're going, if you can.'

'Why?' said Roger.

'Adders,' said John.

'Loose?'

'Yes,' said Titty, 'of course loose. And very poisonous.'

'Is it safe?' said Roger.

'Not if you tread on one,' said John, 'but they get out of your way if you give them a chance. But if there's one curled up in the sun and you go and stick your hoof down on the top of him, he doesn't like it. But come on now, and show the mate how much wood you can get together before she brings her own lot back.'

'Aye, aye, sir,' said Titty.

'Aye, aye, sir,' said Roger. 'Who's going in front?'

John had already answered that question by

running full tilt along a narrow sheep track that wound down towards the woods, and looked like joining the stream some distance below the waterfall at the lower end of Swallowdale. He ran, sometimes jumping over tufts of heather, as hard as he could go. Titty hared after him. Roger hurried after her, but not so fast. Serpents were all very well in cigar-boxes belonging to old charcoal-burners who knew all about them, but there was no point in being careless and getting bitten right at the beginning of an expedition. Roger, though he lost no time, took good care to tread on no snakes.

In the forest they found all that they wanted. In the oak and hazel wood there were fallen saplings that had dried after falling and broke almost like tinder. In the larch wood just below there were thousands of old dead branches, thin, with little knobs on them, very good for starting fires. It was the mate who went down as far as the top of the larch wood. The others gathered their sticks close to the edge of the moor. John and Roger had string in their pockets, and made good bundles to carry on their backs. Titty had got a big pile together and was wondering how she was going to carry it when she saw the mate climbing up from the larch wood and staggering under a tremendous load.

'Do you want some string?' panted Susan. 'There's some in my pocket, but I haven't a hand to spare.'

Titty pulled the string out of the mate's pocket and tied up her own bundle so that she could carry it without losing more than one or two sticks by the way.

'Did you all come?' asked Susan.

'Yes,' said Titty, 'the others have just started back.'

When the mate and the able-seaman left the trees they could see two great bundles of sticks, the captain's and the boy's, moving slowly up beside the stream. They hurried after them. There was no talking. When all four of them had climbed the rocks by the waterfall and were again in Swallowdale they were pretty hot, but they had enough wood to boil the kettle two or three times over without anybody having to make a second journey to the forest.

The mate, as usual, had built a first-rate fireplace. The dry sticks lit easily, and in a very short time the explorers were eating their first meal in Swallowdale. It was already rather late. Then, while the beck was doing most of the washing up for them (for they had put the dirty mugs and spoons and the knife and the fork that did for everybody in a little whirlpool among the rocks), they stored all the wood they had not used in Peter Duck's cave. 'It's just as well to make sure of 'keeping it dry,' said Susan, thinking as mate and cook of the explorers.

'We might be besieged in Swallowdale and not able to get out for more wood,' said Titty, thinking more like an outlaw.

'Let's go and look at that rock now,' said Titty.

But Captain John was already thinking of the move and was in a hurry to go down into the woods to cut the carrying-poles on which to sling the baggage.

*

They found just the poles they wanted in the hazel wood, and John and Susan cut them, and everybody helped to round their ends. All four knives had been sharpened by the blacksmith before the explorers had left the south of England, and this was a very good chance of trying how sharp they were. As soon as the two poles were ready, the explorers slung their knapsacks on them for practice, John and Susan carrying one pole and Titty and Roger carrying the other, with the knapsacks swinging from the middle of each pole. The whole party went quickly down the steep woods, having a little trouble on the way, because the knapsacks would keep slipping forward down the poles unless the two carriers were on the same level. But they were already nearly at the bottom of the larch wood, and within sight of the road, when John, who was in front with Susan, dropped suddenly on the ground.

'Lurk!' he said, 'lurk for your lives!'

'Lucky the knapsacks are pretty empty,' said Susan, putting down her end of the pole.

''Sh! 'Sh!' said John.

All four explorers crouched low and kept perfectly still. On the road below them there was the noise of a horse's hoofs.

'Trotting or walking?' whispered Roger. Again it was hard to tell.

'Walking,' whispered Titty, but she was wrong.

A black horse was moving at a solemn trot, pulling an open carriage. Two grown-up people and two girls were sitting in the carriage.

'One of them's Mrs Blackett,' said Susan.

'The other must be the great-aunt,' said Titty, 'but those *can't* be the Amazon pirates.'

A very prim elderly lady, holding a small black parasol over her head, was sitting stiffly beside Mrs Blackett. In front of them on the little narrow seat behind the driver, facing the grown-ups, were two girls in flounced frocks, with summer hats, their hands in gloves, clasped on their knees. It was a dreadful sight. As the carriage disappeared, the explorers looked at each other with shocked eyes.

'That's much worse than being shipwrecked,' said Titty at last.

'I don't believe it was Captain Nancy,' said Roger. But there was not really any doubt about it.

13

Shifting Camp

THAT night when they came down to Horseshoe Cove, their minds full of the little secret valley of Swallowdale, and of Peter Duck's cave, more secret still, they were in a hurry to get the night over and planned to be early on the march. In the morning they hurried over their bathe, and Titty ran nearly all the way to Swainson's farm to get the morning milk. They hurried over breakfast. Their hurry lasted them through the striking of the tents and most of the packing. But when the time came for leaving the cove and marching up to the moorland, everybody had an empty feeling in the middle, though breakfast was so lately over. There is something dreadful to sailors in turning their backs on the sea, and though Captain John had yesterday been looking forward to getting away from everything that reminded him of the shipwreck, he began today to feel, like the others, that by marching inland they would somehow be putting life on Wild Cat Island farther away than it had been put by the sinking of the *Swallow*. Even Titty and Roger, the discoverers of Swallowdale, were this morning in no hurry to start. Everybody was glad when Roger sighted a rowing boat coming down the lake from the Peak of Darien, and when Titty, looking through the telescope, saw that it was Captain Flint's. The sight of Captain Flint rowing down from Darien gave them a good excuse for waiting a little longer without having to tell each other of their secret doubts. Everybody knew that he would not be rowing down towards Horseshoe Cove unless he had something to say to them.

The cove once more looked almost as it had on the day of the shipwreck. The tents had been struck, rolled up and stowed in knapsacks. The little bamboo tent poles had been taken to pieces and made into bundles. Each explorer was to carry a knapsack and, besides that, one end of a carrying-pole, on which was slung a bale of other baggage, fastened up in a rug or a groundsheet. Susan and John, who had the stouter of the two carrying-poles, had been trying how much they could manage between them. Titty's and Roger's load was to be a good deal smaller. But with everybody carrying all they could, there were still a lot of things left unpacked. It was clear that there would have to be a second journey.

This was the scene that Captain Flint found when he came rowing into the cove. And already, long before he had come so near, the explorers knew that he was bringing a great deal to add to their burdens.

'He's got an awful lot of things in the stern,' Captain John had said, after taking his turn at the telescope. 'Two sacks, as well as parcels.'

'Well I hope he's brought some bread,' said the mate. 'We've eaten nearly all the bunloaf.'

'It'll be all the more to carry,' said John, who for some time had been wishing that the expedition had a camel or two.

'We'll have to carry it sometime,' said the mate. 'We all eat such a lot.'

'What's he bringing a tree for?' said Roger.

'Hullo,' said Captain John, 'there's *Swallow*'s old mast.'

It was the tree which made them after all feel happier about going up to the camp on the moor. Captain Flint explained it at once.

'Give me a hand with the Norway pole, Skipper,' he said, as he ran his boat ashore. 'I thought you might like to be hurrying things on by making the new mast. It's a good pole this, and they've done the rough shaping. All you'll have to do is to copy the old mast.'

John took one end of a long bare pole, which showed the marks of the adze. Captain Flint took the other and brought it ashore and then *Swallow*'s old mast in two pieces. It was hard to believe that the rough pole could be made as clean and smooth as that old mast had been.

'We've only got knives,' said John.

'Shipwrecked sailors have made masts with knives before now,' said Captain Flint. 'But you won't have to. I've brought you a shaping plane and a pair of callipers. And when you're ready, we'll see about linseed oil.'

Somehow, just to have a mast to make, just to see it lying there in the rough, made it seem more certain that sooner or later *Swallow* would be back and the shipwrecked sailors free once more to live on their island and voyage as they wished.

'We'll come down here every day to work at the mast,' said Captain John.

'Aren't you moving somewhere along the shore?'

asked Captain Flint, looking at the baggage on the beach.

'No,' said Titty and Roger together. 'We're going up the moor to our valley.'

'The valley we told you about,' Titty went on, 'you know, when you said there was a trout tarn higher up.'

'By the way,' said Captain Flint, 'if it is the valley I think it is, I know why you stopped me when I was telling your mother about the tarn. I couldn't think what was the matter, but I know now. Hasn't it got a cave in it, on the left as you go up?'

Titty's face fell. Had all the discoveries in the world been made already?

'It's Peter Duck's cave,' she said.

'Thirty years ago I used to call it Ben Gunn's. It's a good place for a camp up there.'

'Do Nancy and Peggy know about it?'

'They've never been up this side of the moor, as far as I know.'

'Don't tell them about it,' said Titty.

'All right,' said Captain Flint. 'But won't you have a bit of a job carting the pole all the way up there?'

'I'll come down here to work at it,' said John.

'We all will,' said Roger.

'And you're just off, are you? The rest of my cargo,'

213

said Captain Flint, looking back at the rowing boat, 'is ship's stores. Your mother told me to hand them over to the mate. You'll want them up on the moor, whether you want the mast or not. On the whole, don't you think you'd better take me on as a porter?'

'Thank you very much,' said the mate.

'They do have native porters,' said Roger. 'All explorers do.'

'But he isn't really a native,' said Titty, 'not after the battle last year.'

'Still, I can come up the moor to carry some of the stores.'

'Please do,' said Titty.

Captain Flint might be fat but he had a broad back and the explorers loaded him thoroughly. He had a long anchor rope in his boat, and with this and one of the old groundsheets, he made an enormous bundle of all the bulkier stores, the bigger kind of pemmican tins, tins of biscuit and bread, and the two small sacks of peas and potatoes he had just brought from Holly Howe.

'Will he be able to lift it?' asked Susan doubtfully.

'Not if you put another matchbox in.'

So they roped it up as it was. Then Captain Flint bent and set his shoulder under the loose end of the rope and swung the bale on his back. He staggered under it, but he could still walk, and, as Roger said, that was the main thing.

*

'Hullo, what *are* you doing?' came a loud, cheerful voice over the water. 'What's Uncle Jim trying to run away with?'

The *Amazon* was already in the cove. Everybody looked round. The Swallows found it hard to believe that Captain Nancy Blackett and Mate Peggy Blackett, in their red knitted pirate caps, their brown shirts and blue knickers, hauling up the centreboard and lowering the sail, could be the same as those two little girls whom they had seen only yesterday, in white frocks, sitting primly side by side, being taken for a drive in a carriage with the great-aunt.

'How have you escaped?' asked Captain Flint, moving slowly round with the tremendous bale upon his back.

'As soon as she heard you'd gone, the great-aunt made up her mind it was a good day for going to the head of the lake. She said she wanted to tell the vicar how things used to be done. She's heard he's doing some things differently. Mother had to go too, of course. They won't be back till lunch-time.'

This was Peggy.

'It's a rattling good easterly wind,' said Nancy. 'A reach both ways. No need for tacking. So we jolly well took our chance.'

'We've got to be back to lunch,' said Peggy.

'Another beastly drive this afternoon,' said Nancy. 'But never mind that. What are you all doing?'

'We're shifting camp,' said John.

'To the valley Roger and I found.'

'The valley with a . . .' said Roger, but he saw Titty's face just in time.

'Well,' said Nancy, 'you're wasting Uncle Jim. You could put lots of the other things in his pockets. He's got fine pockets, really big ones.'

'Captain John,' said Captain Flint, 'you'll be wasting these pirates if you don't make them carry their share. They've plenty of time for that, and they'll get cool again, sailing home.'

'Come on, Peggy,' said Captain Nancy. 'Let's have one of the oars. We'll show them how to do it.'

So the two pirates took an oar from the *Amazon* and used it as a pole, and slung a bundle from it done up in the groundsheet from which John and Captain Flint had cut a patch for *Swallow*. There were a few small things left over, but, as Nancy had said, Captain Flint had big pockets.

The expedition was ready to start.

'What about the parrot?' said Susan. Everybody was so much in the habit of thinking of Polly as part of the crew that it had been forgotten, even by Titty, that he could not very well carry his own cage, especially if he was inside it.

'Polly and I are old shipmates,' said Captain Flint. 'You'd better let me take him.'

'Well if you could take his cage,' said Titty, 'Polly could perch on our pole and Roger and I would carry him between us.'

'Pieces of eight,' said the green parrot as he perched on Titty's hand and then on the pole and balanced there while she and Roger lifted it to their shoulders.

'If you mean my bundle,' said Captain Flint, 'it's heavier than that.'

'It can't be really,' said Roger.

'Well, it feels like it,' said Captain Flint. 'Let's get going and then perhaps it won't be so bad.'

And so the expedition moved off, but not before Titty had been able to remind John and Susan to say nothing about Peter Duck's cave. 'At least not yet,' she said. 'You never know. After all, they *are* pirates.'

Captain John and Mate Susan went first. Mate Susan had slung the milk-can on their pole, so that she could steady it with a hand if it splashed. Then came Captain Flint, bent nearly double, holding the parrot-cage in one hand and keeping his great bale on his shoulders with the other. Then came the Amazons with their bale slung on an oar. Last came Titty and Roger with the parrot perched on the pole between them, and their bundle hanging from it.

Captain Flint took one look at the bridge and said there wasn't room under it for him, let alone his bundle, and he was going through the gap in the wall and across the road and if any savages saw him, well, they would be a hard-hearted lot if they weren't sorry for him. And then John pointed out that after all if anybody did see them crossing the road they might very well mistake them for natives carrying something to the farm. So John and Susan, with all that was hung from their pole, crossed the road as if their business was of a native kind and had nothing to do with explorers or shipwrecked sailors. Even the Amazons, who at first had wanted to go through the bridge, thought better of it at the last minute. There was not much room under the bridge anyhow, and it did not seem possible to get through stooping without soaking the bundle that hung from their oar. So, though they did not look very native, they followed Captain Flint, John and Susan, and crossed the road.

But nothing would stop Titty and Roger from going through. Their bundle was smaller than those of the others, but even so, Titty thought it best to take the parrot through first, by himself, and leave him on the other side to look after her shoes. Then she came back for Roger and the baggage.

'That's the second time it's dipped,' said Roger when they were half-way through.

'Hold the pole right up against the roof,' said Titty. 'Like this.'

'I am,' said Roger. 'I've even scraped some more of the skin off my knuckles.'

The parrot welcomed them with loud screams at the other side of the bridge. Here they halted to put their shoes on again and to wash the boy's knuckles and put a bandage round them. Luckily the boy had a handkerchief a good deal of which was perfectly clean. After that was done, they went ahead at a gallop, with the bundle swinging wildly below the pole and the green parrot with flapping wings balancing himself on the top of it, as they scrambled up the steep larch wood beside the stream. They tried keeping step, but it swung worse than ever.

'Never mind about that,' said the able-seaman. 'Hang on, Polly. The main thing is to hurry.'

They caught up the others at the top of the wood, where they had camped for breakfast the day before. Here there was a short rest and a ration of chocolate all round. Even the parrot had a bit. The mate had wisely put the chocolate in the outer pocket of her knapsack, so that she could get at it on the march. Then everybody helped in heaving Captain Flint's huge bale on his back, poles were shouldered again, and the expedition went on up over the moorland along the sheep tracks that led in and out among heather and boulders at the side of the beck. This time Titty and Roger and the parrot got away first, and Nancy and Peggy came next. Susan and John came last of all, because the mate was really a little afraid that Captain Flint's pockets were so crammed that something might fall out on the way.

'This is no sort of road for a man of my age,' panted Captain Flint after a few minutes of twisting and turning up and down among the rocks and clumps of heather.

'It's a very good sheep track,' said Captain John. 'There's plenty of room in it really, if you put your feet in the right places.' Already he thought of it as the road to Swallowdale, and he would hear nothing against it, just as he would never let anyone say that anywhere at any time there was a better boat than *Swallow*.

Captain Flint said no more for a minute or two, but struggled along as well as he could.

'Why have we never been up here before?' said Peggy. 'It's not really very far. Look, there's the . . .'

She said the name of the big hill with the peak. But the able-seaman, who had heard her, was quick in putting her right.

'That one's Kanchenjunga,' she said, 'if you mean the biggest.'

Nancy stopped dead, bringing up Peggy with a jerk at the other end of the oar.

'Why not Kanchenjunga?' she said. 'Shiver my timbers, why shouldn't we climb it?'

'We're going to,' said Titty. 'Have you ever climbed it before?'

'We were taken once,' said Peggy, 'ages ago, but that's not the same thing.'

'It's an altogether different thing,' said Nancy.

'Well, let's all climb it together,' said Titty, 'with ropes.'

'If only it wasn't for the great-aunt,' said Nancy.

'We saw you yesterday,' said Roger, 'sitting in the carriage.'

'Did you?' said Nancy grimly.

They stumbled along and for some time no one spoke. It was hard to talk, carrying baggage slung on poles or on an oar along tracks so narrow and winding. And Captain Flint had no breath to spare.

The noise of the little waterfall grew louder and

louder and at last Titty and Roger, leading the expedition, came to a stop just below it.

'Are we going to climb up that?' said Nancy, 'with all these things?'

'I can't,' said Captain Flint. 'Not with a bale like this. We'd better go round and drop down into the valley from the side.'

'More fun going straight,' said Nancy. 'We can haul the baggage up from above. Our rope's more than long enough for that as soon as this bundle is undone.'

'Besides,' said the able-seaman, 'the moment you leave the bed of the stream it's all open moor and we could be seen for miles and miles.'

So all the loads were grounded at the bottom of the waterfall, and the long mooring rope from the *Amazon* which Nancy and Peggy had used for slinging their bundle from the oar was unfastened. John took one end of it up to the top of the waterfall. The other explorers and the two pirates climbed up after him, as soon as they saw that the rope was really long enough. Captain Flint stayed at the bottom to fasten the rope to each bundle in turn.

The Swallows were very glad they had moved from Horseshoe Cove when they saw how highly Nancy and Peggy thought of Swallowdale. The moment Nancy climbed up by the waterfall and was able to look up the valley she had seen what a good place it was. 'It's the best hiding place I've ever seen,' she had said. 'And to think that it's been here all these years and we never knew it.'

'You don't know yet how secret it is,' said Titty, and in her pride that Nancy thought well of her valley, was very near to saying a little more. But there was a shout from below.

'Haul away!'

Nancy turned instantly to business.

'Tally on on the rope,' she cried. 'What about piping up a tune?'

'It ought to be "Way, Hay,"' said Titty.

So she started off with:

'What shall we do with a drunken sailor?
    What shall we do with a drunken sailor?
    What shall we do with a drunken sailor?
        Early in the morning.'

Everybody joined in with:

'Way, Hay, up she raises,
Way, Hay, up she raises,
Way, Hay, up she raises,
    Early in the morning.'

LOADING CAPTAIN FLINT

The waterfall was not very high, and, with the whole lot of them pulling, Captain Flint's huge bale came rattling up and over the edge into the valley just as they got to the end of the chorus. That song, and particularly the chorus, brings a load up hand over hand so easily that you would hardly believe it, no matter how heavy the load is, when you have two captains, two mates, an able-seaman and a ship's boy all tallying on on the rope, and a parrot on a rock beside them letting loose encouraging screams. In the end, when all the bundles had been pulled up, Captain Flint hung on to the end of the rope himself and came scrambling up the rocks while the captains and the mates and the crew panted and grunted out, 'Way, Hay, up she raises.'

'It's all wrong to sing that now,' said Roger, as Captain Flint got to his feet and they were able to stop pulling. 'He isn't a she.'

'Never mind,' said Captain Flint. 'No more are anchors or bundles, if it comes to that.'

The Amazons and Captain Flint helped to shift the things from the top of the waterfall to the place where Susan meant to have the tents, close by the fireplace and the little whirlpool that was so handy for washing up. The able-seaman kept close at their heels wherever they went, afraid every minute that they would see the heather pushed into the doorway of the cave.

Roger kept pointing out trout in the little pools of the stream. Anything to keep their eyes away from the wall of grey rock with that dark shadow at the bottom of it, and the thick heather growing as if in a crack of the stone. The worst of it was that there was a track of bits of dry stick leading all the way from the fireplace to the cave, dropped, no doubt, when they were stowing the firewood away before going down to Horseshoe Cove the night before. Titty was telling herself what duffers they had been not to think of that, and how, whatever happened, they must never leave a track of anything again. You had only to see those sticks and to follow them to the rock and Peter Duck's cave would be secret no longer. But the Amazons never noticed them. They might have seen them, if they had been in less of a hurry. But Captain Flint kept reminding them that they had to be back for lunch, and they were only looking round as quick as they could before racing down again to the *Amazon* and setting sail for home.

'Remember the row there was the day before yesterday,' he said. 'And today there's no shipwreck for an excuse.'

'Even the shipwreck wasn't much good, was it?' said Nancy. 'We'll hurry. We won't get you into another mess.'

'There wasn't really a row because you stayed to help down at Horseshoe Cove?' said John.

'Wasn't there?' said Nancy. 'You don't know the great-aunt. I say, what's the valley look like from outside?'

'You simply can't see it at all,' said Titty, delighted to get the Amazons well away from the cave. 'Come and look.'

They climbed all together up the steep northern side of the valley and looked out over the moorland.

'From ten yards away you can't see there's a valley at all,' said John.

'What's that big rock?' said Nancy, pointing away to the north.

'Watch-tower,' said John. 'At least it's going to be.'

'Um,' said Nancy. 'You can see it from far enough.'

'That's why it's a good watch-tower,' said Titty.

'It'll help us to find the valley if we come over the moor,' said Nancy. 'We will. That's what we'll do. We'll make a surprise attack. The very first day we can get away. We can't come tomorrow.'

'We'll be ready for you,' said Captain John.

'You won't be able to get away at all,' said Captain Flint, 'if you don't bolt for it now.'

'Come on,' said Peggy. 'You'll be late too. We shan't. Not with this wind.'

'No. I don't come on duty until tea-time. But for goodness' sake don't you be late. I really should like to keep out of hot water for a day or two at least.'

'He's as much afraid of the G.A. as we are,' Peggy explained to Susan.

'He's much more afraid,' said Nancy. 'So's Mother, poor dear.'

'He even puts on townish clothes,' said Peggy.

'Phew!' said Nancy. 'What about our best frocks? Come on. We've only just got time. I forgot we'd slipped out in comfortables.'

They hared down into the valley, grabbed their oar, coiled their rope, raced for the waterfall, and a few minutes later the Swallows and Captain Flint, looking after them, saw their red caps disappear into the trees.

'They didn't spot the cave,' said Roger.

'No,' said Titty.

'By Gum,' said Captain John, 'just wait until they make their attack.'

'Don't count on their making one,' said Captain Flint. 'It really is a bit difficult for them to get away.'

'I think the great-aunt must be horrid,' said Titty.

Captain Flint said neither 'Yes' nor 'No' to that, but reminded them that he would be going by Holly Howe and would take a mail if they liked to make one ready. So while the baggage was still lying about the fireplace and the tents not pitched, they dug out Titty's writing things and made a despatch, dated from Swallowdale, and signed by everybody, to say that the move had been made, that there was no longer fear of fevers or floods, and that they hoped that Mother and the ship's baby would come as soon as possible to tea.

'But how will she find the way?' said Susan.

'I'll be working at the mast,' said John. 'So it'll be all right if she comes to the cove.'

This was added, and the despatch was folded up and put in an envelope and addressed to Mother at Holly Howe. Roger wrote 'Pirate Post' in the top left-hand corner.

Captain Flint had been quietly smoking his pipe during the making of the despatch. 'By the way,' he said, when it was finished, as if he had just remembered something, 'I'd like to have a look in your cave if I may. I suppose it's all right now those two have gone?'

Susan lent him her torch and he squeezed in. The explorers crowded after him.

'It's smaller than I thought it was,' he said when he was inside and able once more to stand up. He turned to the right inside the doorway and there, carved with a knife on the rock, he found the name 'Ben Gunn' in big sprawling letters.

'We'll put Peter Duck's name there too,' said Titty.

'Ben Gunn'll be glad to meet him,' said Captain Flint.

'Did you carve it?' asked John.

'More than thirty years ago,' said Captain Flint.

Soon after that he went off down the moor. He said he'd like to stop with them but after carrying that huge bale he was afraid if he didn't keep moving he might get stiff. Anyway he'd be at the cove in the morning to show John how to use the shaping plane and the callipers. They went with him to the edge of the waterfall, told him he had been very useful as a porter, and said goodbye to him when he had safely climbed down beside the stream. When he had gone a little way towards the top of the woods, he turned to wave to any of the explorers who might still be looking down from above the waterfall. But none were there. They were busy putting up the tents in the new camp.

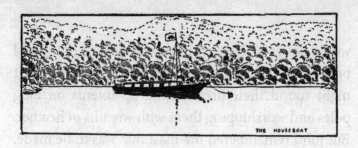

THE HOUSEBOAT

14

Settling In

THERE was a great deal to be done and, privately,
the shipwrecked sailors were glad to be left by
themselves for the doing of it. Natives and pirates
(even Captain Flint and the Amazons) were all very
well when they were wanted, useful to carry things,
for example, sometimes full of information and, of
course, very good for taking part in an adventure.
But no one wanted them about when there was a
new camp to make in a new place and there were
half a hundred things to be decided. There were some
minutes that day when it was almost settled that until
Swallow came back mended, her captain and crew

would not go on being shipwrecked sailors, but would be a savage tribe instead, cave-dwellers, dancing at night round their fires, setting up totems on long poles and worshipping them with wreaths of heather. But John remembered the mast that was to be made, and Susan said the cave was not really fit to live in, and Roger didn't see the good of having a new tent of his own if he didn't sleep in it, and Titty knew that savages never made maps, and so they made up their minds to go on being explorers and sailors, even if they had been shipwrecked. But there had been discussion about it and, when it was over, they were glad that no outsiders had overheard it. They themselves could forget it at once, but if other people had been there it would have been much harder to go on as if there had never been any doubt about what they were to be.

Titty summed up what everybody felt when she said, 'So long as we're explorers, anything can happen. Think of last year. But if we're savages there wouldn't be any point even in climbing Kanchenjunga. We'd just have to sit on our hunkers and eat raw meat.'

'Besides,' said Susan, 'we've got our holiday tasks to do. It's all right for explorers to read books.'

It did just occur to Titty that one good point of being a savage was that you did not have to learn

French verbs, but she did not say so. The French verbs had to be learnt, anyhow.

'Mine's all algebra, and sailors have to know it,' said John.

'We've been wrecked,' said Titty, 'and now to get out of the way of tidal waves and giant crabs and things like that . . .'

'Alligators, too,' said Roger.

'We've moved up into the hill country. It was the only sensible thing to do. We might all have got fever chills where we were.'

'Good,' said Susan. 'Now it's settled. Let's get on with putting up the tents.'

'It's a jolly good thing Daddy gave us these tents,' said Captain John. 'We couldn't have managed up here with the tents we had to sling between trees.'

'No trees for one thing,' said Roger.

'What about the stores tent?' said Titty.

'We'll use the cave,' said Susan.

'And Peter Duck'll be storekeeper,' said Titty.

There was a very good bit of flat ground, big enough for all four sleeping-tents on the southern side of the little valley, between the stream and the cave. The explorers made all the tents open towards the stream. They were well protected from the strong southerly winds by the steep side of the valley that rose behind them, and they could not be seen by anyone who was not near enough to the valley to look down into it from the moor. Between the tents and the stream was the mate's fireplace, one of her very best, and in the stream, close below the fireplace, was the little whirlpool that might have been specially made for washing up.

'It's far the best camp we've ever had,' said Mate Susan, looking round when the last tent had been set up.

'Not counting Wild Cat Island, of course,' said Titty.

'It isn't an island,' said Susan, 'so it can't be as good as that. It's the best of all our other camps. But there's a lot to do to it yet.'

'I'm going to dam the top pool for one thing,' said John, 'to make a bathing-place.'

'Let's go and start at once,' said Roger.

'We must get rid of the stores first,' said Susan, 'and we can't do that until we've got some of the dust out of the cave.'

'Peter Duck won't mind,' said Titty.

'Of course he won't,' said Susan. 'He's got to be spring-cleaned like everybody else. Somebody go and cut some good big bunches of heather. Go on, you two, while I'm getting dinner.'

'What about adders?' said Roger.

'All right, Roger,' said Titty, 'I'm coming too. It's a good thing we hadn't remembered the adders the other day, or we'd never have discovered Swallowdale.'

'Don't pick one up or tread on one. That's all,' said the mate.

'If Roger makes half his usual noise,' said the captain, 'they won't have a chance to do either, unless the adder's asleep.'

'Come on,' said Titty. 'Let's see whose knife is sharpest? And, I say, Roger, there's something else to do at the same time.'

The able-seaman and the boy scrambled up the northern side of the valley and, talking very loudly and stamping very hard, to give the adders a good chance to get away, they set about cutting a bundle of heather to make a broom for the mate. They cut a bit here and a bit there, but moved steadily in one direction towards the flat-topped rock that John had said would do as a watch-tower. They had been the first to discover the valley. Why should they not be the first to climb the Watch Tower Rock?

While the mate was taking some of the stored wood from Peter Duck's cave and making a fire on which to cook a dinner for the expedition, the captain was doing a bit of building. He was getting together large flat stones, of which there were plenty among the loose screes on the sides of the valley, and putting the biggest outside and filling in the middle with the smaller ones, he was making a square pillar, not very high, nor yet very big.

'What's it for?' asked the mate.

'The parrot,' said the captain. 'I want to get it done before Titty comes back.'

He cut one of the two long carrying-poles in half. One half was to be the handle of the mate's heather broom. The other half he built crosswise into the top of his pillar, so that it stuck out on either side like the arms of a scarecrow. Susan helped him to lift a big flat slab of limestone or slate and lay it on the top of the pillar. On that he put the parrot's cage and opened the door. He put in his hand and the parrot gripped a finger with its feet. A moment later and it had been lifted out and had taken a firm hold of one of the ends of the pole. It stretched its wings and flapped.

'Pretty Polly,' it said.

'He looks just right like that,' said the captain. 'I wonder if he can get back into his cage.'

'Try him with a lump of sugar,' said Susan.

John showed the parrot a lump of sugar and then put it in the cage. The parrot shuffled sideways along the pole until he could just reach the cage with his beak. He then took hold of a bar and pulled himself up, scrabbling with his feet until he found a hold. He then climbed round the outside of his cage until he came to the door and went in.

'He'll find it more of a job getting back,' said John. But no, the parrot was not a ship's parrot for nothing. He could climb like anything, and very soon had found a way of clinging to the cage with his beak and one foot, while he felt for the pole with the other.

Heather is tough stuff to cut, and the able-seaman and the boy had their exploring to do as well, so by the time they came scrambling back down the steep side of the valley with an armful of heather apiece, the parrot was perched once more on the pole, the fire was burning well, the kettle was nearly boiling and the mate had set the captain to shelling green peas.

'Well,' said the mate cheerfully, 'you've been taking your time.'

'We've been up the Watch Tower Rock. Hullo! What a gorgeous place for Polly. When did you make it? It wasn't here before.'

'While you two were cutting heather.'

'We've been up on the rock, too. You can see a hundred miles from it all ways.'

'North, south, east and west,' said Roger.

'And there's a bit of a hollow in the top of the rock so that if you lie down, nobody can see you except with a telescope from the tops of the mountains.'

'Come and look at it,' said Roger.

'Dinner first,' said the mate. 'Come here, Able-seaman, and you too, Boy, and shell peas, so that the captain can be making the broom. Then you can all go to look at the rock after dinner while I'm sweeping out the larder.'

'Peter Duck's,' said Titty.

The able-seaman and the boy set to work on the rest of the peas. They gave a pod to the parrot, and he shelled the peas beautifully, and tore the pod to bits and threw them away, but he dropped the peas and anyhow Susan said they would not be clean enough to put in with the rest. As soon as the peas were shelled, Susan was able to hurry on with the dinner: a good one, hotted pemmican and green peas with a lot of butter on them, and after that the usual bunloaf and marmalade, chocolate and apples. Meanwhile, John took the other half of the carrying-pole, left after making the perch for the parrot, and bound a huge bundle of heather to the end of it with stout string, whipping it round and round the black woody stems of the heather and finishing it off so that you could not see where the string began, as if he were putting a whipping on the end of a rope. He made a really good job of it, and when the mate saw her broom she was almost as eager to use it as the others were to go up to the Watch Tower Rock. But by that time dinner was ready, and no cook likes to let a cooked dinner wait, so the broom was propped against a rock until the meal was over and the dirty things were at the bottom of the little whirlpool being washed by clean beck water.

For one moment the able-seaman and the boy thought they would like to help in cleaning out the cave. But the mate stopped all thought of that.

'It'll be very dirty,' she said, 'and there won't be room to turn round in it if we are all crowding in there. Let me get it swept out and clean so that we know where we are, and then you can come in as much as you like.'

'Come along,' said the captain. 'No camp's much good without a proper look-out place. We must have a good place for looking out over the moor. Remember what the Amazons said about a surprise attack. They'll make it too, but they'll be the ones to get the surprise.'

'There couldn't be a better place than the rock,' said Titty.

'Well, leave the mate to her job and let's go to the rock to make sure.'

The rock was all that Titty and Roger had promised. It was more, for the best way of climbing it, up or down, was on the side of it nearest to Swallowdale.

'It'll do,' said Captain John, after he had tried it by leaving Titty and Roger on the top of it and going off himself a long way over the moor, waving his hand to show them when to start and finding that they were already down and creeping to meet him along a sheep track in the heather while, watching the rock as hard as he could, he was still thinking that they hadn't stirred.

'Good scouts!' he said. 'Nothing could be better. Someone must keep watch up here every day, and then slip back to Swallowdale to give warning the moment the enemy are in sight.'

They went rejoicing back to Swallowdale to find the mate standing by the tents and looking at the side of the valley above the entrance to Peter Duck's cave.

'What's the matter?' said John, as he rushed down the steep slope on the other side and cleared the stream with a jump.

'Look,' said the mate.

'What is it?'

'Look.' The mate pointed to the rounded end of a stout stick poking out through a clump of heather above the way into the cave and a bit to one side. 'That's the broom handle. I pushed it through from inside. I had a candle-lantern in there and knocked it over while I was brushing. And then I saw just a glimmer higher up in the roof, and I poked at it with the broom handle and it went right through. That's why the air in the cave is not bad, except for the dust. I expect people lived in it once.'

'Well done, Susan,' said John. 'Then it'll be all right for us all to hide inside the cave in case of an attack. It's exactly what we wanted. I was bothered about it a bit. I'll go up and clear the hole.'

'It means it'll be all right to let the parrot sleep there at night,' said Susan. 'We can't put up the stores tent for him, and there isn't room for him in Titty's, and it wouldn't have done for him to get stifled.'

'It was probably Peter Duck who knocked the lantern over so that you would see the hole,' said Titty. 'He knew the parrot was coming to stay with him.'

'Well, it may have been,' said Susan, who was very pleased indeed to find that her larder was properly aired, and did not mind Peter Duck making any use of it he liked.

John climbed up the rocky side of the valley, pushed the broom handle in again, so that the broom fell on the floor of the cave, and cut away a little of the heather, enough to let more air through the hole, but not enough to make anyone notice it.

Then everybody went into the cave. Susan had made a different place of it. The dust was gone. She had brought water from the beck and slopped it on the ground before brushing. 'Another time, I'm going to use tea-leaves,' she said. 'Today I'd thrown them away before thinking of it.' The biscuit tins and all the other loose bits of luggage were already neatly packed along the walls. The biscuit tins would do for seats, as Titty and Roger found at once. Along the side of one wall there was a deep fault in the stone which made a shelf, not quite level, but level enough in places for a candle-lantern to stand there, well out of the way. 'Just right,' said John. 'Except in the dark, no one would see a glimmer of it from the doorway.' The air-hole up above gave very little light, even after John had cut the heather.

'Now,' said the mate, when everybody had admired enough, 'we've used all the wood for today's dinner. The camp's ready. Let's settle down to work. All hands to gather fuel. And after that what about holiday tasks?'

'There's the bathing-pool to make,' said John.

'A dam to build,' said Roger.

'We must do that, or we shan't be able to bathe tomorrow,' said Titty.

'Well, I suppose we ought to have a proper bath,' said the mate. 'But we must pile up a store of wood first.'

By tea-time there was a woodstack in the cave as good as the stack the Amazons had made for them on Wild Cat Island. By supper-time the explorers, splashed from head to foot, were resting from their labours, and watching the water lapping over the edge of a dam firmly built of large stones, with small ones between them, smaller stones scraped up from the bottom of the pool to fill in the gaps, flat turfs laid against all this and yet another layer of big stones to keep all firm. The dam raised the water more than a foot, and the waterfall at the head of the valley fell now with a new note into a pool not perhaps big enough to swim in, but far better than any ordinary bath. The explorers wriggled down in their tents that night with the knowledge of a good day's work behind them. Life in Swallowdale had begun.

THE CAMP IN SWALLOWDALE

15

Life in Swallowdale

THE explorers slept rather late in the morning. When they waked there was a rush to the head of the valley to see if the dam had been washed away. It had not. Not a stone of it had stirred, and everybody had a dip in the new bathing-pool. They had come back and Susan was just reminding them that it was a long way down to Swainson's farm, and that somebody must fetch the milk before they could have breakfast, when a cheerful voice said, 'Well, you have made yourselves comfortable. Did you have a good night?' and they saw Mary Swainson looking down on them from the top of the slope above the cave. She had a milk-can in one hand and a big market basket in the other.

'Rice pudding,' she said, 'from Holly Howe. And Mrs Walker's coming to tea with you tomorrow and bringing another pudding with her, so you've to eat this today.'

'Don't try to get down there,' said John. 'It's slippery.'

But Mary Swainson seemed to know the valley very well. She went a few yards farther on along the edge of it and then came down by a sheep track that ended close by the bathing-pool.

'That's a good weir you've made,' she said, as John and Susan met her and took the milk-can and the basket. 'Slippery you may well say that rock is. Many's the pair of breeches my brothers wore out on that rock sliding from top to bottom of it.'

Roger had not thought of the side of the valley from this point of view. He went off to try it, first from half-way up, and then from the top. It was a very good slide.

'There's a better over here,' said Mary a few minutes later, pointing up the other side of the valley. 'Not so steep,' she added, 'and not so hard on cloth.'

'Skin,' said Roger, feeling the damage already done by two or three slides down the steep rock that hid Peter Duck's.

THE KNICKERBOCKERBREAKER

'You come down to the farm,' said Mary, 'and I'll darn that. It won't be the first by a long count. And you've found the way into the cave, have you? I thought you would have, when Mr Turner looked in yesterday to say where you were. Have you been in?'

'Come and look,' said Susan. Nobody could mind Mary Swainson, and even Titty thought it did not matter that she had known about the cave. John told her it was a secret now, and she promised to say nothing about it.

From that moment Mary Swainson, though she lived at the farm down below the moor and was busy from morning to night, seemed to the explorers more like an ally than a native. You could always be sure of Mary. She took a cup of tea with them that first morning, and after breakfast Roger, Susan, and Titty went down with her to the farm when John went down to meet Captain Flint to begin work on the mast. Roger was down at the farm next day to be darned again. Mary darned him about twice a day until at last he was tired of the 'Knickerbockerbreaker', which, Titty said, was much the best name for it.

Soon after John had left the cart track in the wood by the lake and was making his way through the trees to Horseshoe Cove, he heard the noise of a hand-saw. Captain Flint was there before him and was hard at work shaping the foot of the mast, making it exactly like the foot of the mast that had been broken, so that it would fit cleanly into the socket in the kelson. That was soon done. John had brought the shaping plane down from the camp in his knapsack, and now Captain Flint showed him how to use it. The plane was curved, so that it would take shavings off a rounded surface as evenly as an ordinary plane takes shavings off a plank. He had also brought down the callipers, big pincers that opened and shut and had a small screw to keep them just as much open or as much shut as you wanted. Captain Flint showed John how to measure the same distance along both masts, and then how to fix the callipers just so much open that both curved points touched the wood when they were used to measure the thickness of the old mast. Then he set to work planing down the new mast evenly, all round, until it too exactly fitted between the points of the callipers.

'Remember one thing,' he said. 'Never take off too much. If you take off too little you can always take off a bit more, but if you take off too much you can never put it back.'

They worked hard at the mast all that morning until nearly dinner-time, when the others came from the farm and told of how they had been singing choruses with old Mr Swainson, and sewing a patch into Mrs Swainson's new patchwork quilt, and seeing pigs and calves and a foal, and the biggest tabby cat that ever was seen in the world. 'He follows Mary about, but she isn't going to let him come near Swallowdale. But she says he's frightened of parrots, so it wouldn't matter if he did come.' And, of course, the mate invited Captain Flint to stop for dinner, and he said he would be delighted and had indeed brought five pork pies from Rio and five fruit pies to match, which he hoped would not come amiss. He brought the parcel with these good things in it out of the shade of a bush where he had put it to keep cool, and took a fishing rod, a fishing-basket and a landing-net out of his boat. He put the parcel in the basket for easy carrying.

'I thought of going up to Trout Tarn after dinner,' he said, 'and I'll show you how to cast a fly.'

'Let's all fish,' said Roger.

'You won't do much in the tarn except with fly,' said Captain Flint, 'but if you had a good worm or two you would soon get trout out of the beck.'

'We've got our fishing rods,' said Roger.

'Well, see what you can do in the way of worms.'

It was during that dinner in Swallowdale that Roger asked Captain Flint the question that for one reason or another he had not asked before, though it had been in his mind since the first day.

'Captain Flint,' he began.

'Hullo!'

'Why did you cover up your cannon with a black sheet?'

'To keep strangers and dust off it.'

'A cannon's better than a sheet to keep strangers off.'

'It didn't keep you off, did it, when you captured the houseboat and made me walk the plank? Why, I wake in the night even now thinking of the sharks.'

'Well, we wanted you to fire it this year.'

'But I'm not living in the houseboat just now.'

'Why not?'

Captain Flint said nothing just for a moment. Everybody was listening. At last he said, 'Look here, Roger, the very first minute I can I'll be back there with a barrel of gunpowder and you shall come and fire the thing yourself.'

'Let's go and do it now.'

'He can't,' said Titty. 'It's the great-aunt. Captain Nancy said so.'

'She isn't going to stop for ever,' said Captain Flint.

Trout Tarn was nearly a mile beyond Swallowdale, high on the top of the moor, a little lake lying in a hollow of rock and heather. When the Swallows saw it, they wished almost that they had made their camp on its rocky shores. But Titty said that it had no cave, and Susan said that if it was a bother bringing wood to Swallowdale it would be miles more bother bringing it to Trout Tarn. 'Two miles more bother. One each way,' said Roger. 'And besides,' said Susan, 'it would be that much farther from Swainson's farm. We'd have had to spend all our time fetching wood and milk.' John and Captain Flint were talking of something quite different, and that was the catching of trout, and when Captain Flint sat down and began to put his tackle together, the others stopped talking to look. This was not at all like the perch-fishing down on the big lake. There was no float for one thing, no minnow, and no worm. Instead, Captain Flint opened a little tin box, took three flies from it, and gave them to Roger to hold.

'What are they made of?' asked John.

'Feathers and silk. All small flies,' said Captain Flint. 'It's no good fishing big ones up here. That's woodcock and orange silk. That's dark snipe and purple, and this is a black spider – brown silk and one of the black, shiny burnished feathers from the neck of a cock pheasant. Best fly of the lot on a hot day up here, and the easiest to tie.'

'Did you make them yourself?' asked John.

'Of course I did,' said Captain Flint.

'Can we have a fly to fish with?' asked Titty. 'Roger's got his rod.'

'No good, Able-seaman, you can't throw a fly with a perch rod, and you'll frighten the trout away if you chuck a big red float at them. If you've got a good lot of worms you could catch some in the beck.'

'We've only got one worm,' said Roger, 'but he's a beauty.'

'Well, see what you can do with him in the beck,' said Captain Flint, who was himself impatient to be fishing while the wind rippled the surface of the tarn. 'Come on, John. Keep well out of the way, Mister Mate, and keep the others clear. We don't want to hook an explorer instead of a trout.'

He began moving slowly up the southern side of the tarn, the side from which the wind was coming, swishing his rod backwards and forwards, letting out line, and then letting the flies drop on the water far out along the edge of the ripples, waiting a moment, and then slowly, slowly, inch by inch, lifting the point of the rod, bringing the flies in again until with a steady upward lift he picked the line from the water, sent it flying up in the air behind him, paused a half-second for it to straighten and then, switching the

DARNING ROGER

point of the rod forward again, sent the flies out to fall light as scraps of down one behind the other, a yard farther up the tarn. The third or fourth time his flies dropped on the water there was a splash at the woodcock and orange, the rod bent, and a moment later a fat little trout was being drawn over the net that John was holding ready for him quite still and well below the surface. Roger and Titty wanted to rush in to look at the trout, but Susan knew that trout fishing is serious business, and that a crowd of explorers haring along the bank is not likely to encourage the fish to rise. So she stopped them in time, and they watched the fishing from a distance. Then Captain Flint gave John the rod, and for a minute or two John tried to make the line straighten high in air behind him and then shoot forward, unrolling itself until once more it straightened out, this time in front of him and well above the water, so that the flies should drop like snowflakes. 'Up, now. . . . Pause. . . . Forward again,' Captain Flint was saying. 'Aim about two feet above the water. . . . Don't take the rod too far back. . . . No need for force. . . . Make the tip of the rod do the work. . . . Look here. Let me hold your hand and show you the way to do it. Now then.' It was not a very good cast, for two hands on a rod are not better than one if they belong to different people. Still, the flies did, at last, go out instead of landing in a mess only a yard or two from the shore. There was a splash, John struck, the flies flew back over his head and caught in the heather behind him. Captain Flint crawled back and freed them.

'I say, that *was* a trout, wasn't it?' said John.

'Of course it was. Try again in the same place. Steady. Remember not to hurry when the line is behind you. It'll be all right if the point of your rod didn't go too far back. There he is. Got him. Well done!' and presently Captain Flint was holding the net while John pulled his first trout over it, when Captain Flint lifted it out.

This was too much for Roger.

'Let's go and fish, too,' he said, opening the tobacco tin in which he had his worm. 'The tarn is crammed with fish. Look at the way they're pulling them out. Two already.'

'We haven't got any flies,' said Titty.

'Yes, but what a worm!' said Roger. 'He's the best worm I ever caught.'

'Captain Flint said we'd better try him in the beck,' said Titty.

'The beck's not big enough,' said Roger.

They left Susan and turned back towards the place

at which the beck flowed out of the tarn. Susan slowly followed the fly-fishers. 'We'll fish here,' said Roger. 'It's a lovely place for a float.' He and Titty were crawling round the edge of a little bay, where the rock fell steeply into dark water. Together they put up Roger's perch rod. Together, not without some awful difficulties, they put the giant worm on the perch hook. They pulled the float up the line so that the worm should be deep in the water. Then Roger swung the worm and float out from the rock. They tugged a lot more line off the reel. The red float, moved by wind or the slight current, moved away from the shore and stopped when the line would let it go no farther. Roger held the rod and Titty stood beside him watching it. But the red float moved no more. They sat down to it. Then Roger gave the rod to Titty. After a bit Titty gave the rod to Roger. Then they propped the rod across a clump of heather with its butt wedged under a rock. That was better. They watched it for some time, and began talking of other things. Then they decided that it would be all right by itself, and they went scouting over the rocks till they could see far up the tarn. There were John and Captain Flint and Susan. They saw the splashing as John caught a fish. They saw it put into Captain Flint's basket. Then they saw John give the rod to Susan and take the basket, while Susan learnt to cast. For a long time they watched, and at last they saw Susan catch a fish. 'Perhaps he'd have let us fish too, if we'd gone on,' said Roger.

They looked back down into their little bay.

'I can't see our float,' said Titty.

'There it is,' shouted Roger. 'It's moving. Titty! Titty! Something's pulling like anything. Look at the rod.'

There was a frantic race back to the rod which was jerking angrily up and down.

The others had made between them a nice basket of plump little trout, a dozen, perhaps, all about a quarter of a pound apiece, and all very much the same size. 'You don't often get them bigger than this up here,' said Captain Flint, as they walked back together, 'but they're very sweet. Sometimes in the evening you may see a monster moving, but nobody ever catches one of them. A half-pound fish is a very good one, and the quarter-pounders are good enough. The really big ones never seem to come up.'

'What's the matter with Roger?' cried Susan suddenly.

They heard Titty's voice, shrill and desperate, 'Help, help!'

'They're all right,' said John. 'They're both there. But what on earth are they doing?'

ROGER FELL ON IT

'Help, help!' shrilled Titty.

'They've got a fish,' shouted Captain Flint. 'Hang on to the rod, John. Let's have the net.' And in a moment he was leaping over rocks and heather as hard as he could go, forgetting altogether how much he weighed and how many years had passed since first he fished.

'Hang on to it,' he shouted.

'Roger's fallen in,' said Susan. 'Oh, oh! I ought never to have left them.'

There was a fearful splashing away by the foot of the tarn. Titty was holding the rod now, and they had moved round the point of the little bay where they had left their float, and were at the edge of the shallows close above the place where the beck left the tarn. Into these shallows Roger had splashed, and a few moments later, splashing worse than ever, he scrambled ashore with a big trout clasped in his arms. He slipped as he was getting out. The trout fell, but Roger fell on it, and by the time Captain Flint arrived with the net Roger, Titty and the trout were a safe dozen yards from the water.

'He's two pounds if he's an ounce,' said Captain Flint. 'You've got one of the grandfathers. Beaten the lot of us. Float-tackle and all.'

*

Titty's and Roger's big fish was far too big to go in the basket. They carried it between them in Captain Flint's landing-net.

'Isn't it a pity Mother isn't coming to tea today?' said Titty.

'She ought to see it,' said Captain Flint, and in the end they sent it to Holly Howe. Captain Flint was to leave it there on his way up the lake. Very soon after tea he was off.

'I don't want to be late,' he said. 'Those two pirates were twenty minutes late for lunch yesterday. They ran into a calm. Not their fault, but their mother hadn't heard the last of it when I ran away this morning.'

'Ran away?' said Titty.

'Well, hurried,' said Captain Flint. 'I had to be down here early if we were to get going with the new mast.'

'Will the Amazons be coming tomorrow?' asked Susan.

'Don't tell us, if they're going to make their surprise attack,' said John.

'From what I heard I don't think they'll be able to get away. No, I'm sure they won't be here tomorrow. But I'll do my very best for them the day after that.'

'Perhaps it's a good thing they can't come tomorrow,' said John. 'There's a lot to do on the mast.'

'They don't think it's a good thing,' said Captain Flint.

'I think it's horrid that they can't come,' said Titty.

'So do I,' said Captain Flint, 'but it can't be helped.'

The big trout was wrapped in bracken, together with a bit of paper on which Titty had written, 'Mother. With love from Titty and Roger'; and Roger had written, 'We caught it ourselves.' For a moment, indeed, he found it hard to say goodbye to the fish and to see its rounded, spotted sides for the last time, but, after all, Mother was going to have it for supper, probably, and Captain Flint could not wait. Roger took a last look, and then held the bracken leaves together while Captain Flint made a neat lacing round them with string so that the big trout made a very handsome parcel.

Captain Flint left the rod and flies, a cast or two and the net and basket for John and Susan to look after, and they were carefully stored in Peter Duck's. 'Don't waste time fishing the tarn unless there's a good southerly wind like today's,' he said as he went off. 'You'll do much better in the beck.'

There was a little gloom that evening at the thought of the native trouble that was bothering the Amazons, but it was difficult to think of fish and trouble at the same time, and Susan had more helpers than she needed when she was cleaning the little trout for supper. Each fish was admired, though no one could be sure which was John's first fish and which Susan's. 'I wish we'd caught some of them,' said Roger, but John said he was a greedy little beast, seeing that he and Titty between them had caught a trout nearly as big as all the others put together. The sizzling and spitting of the boiling butter as Susan fried the trout in batches over the camp fire reminded them of last year's perch-fishing.

For the next two days Roger could think of very little but trout. He spent that evening, between supper and bed, partly in sliding down the Knickerbocker-breaker and partly in turning over the loose stones at the side of the beck, looking for worms and mostly finding ants. Next morning, after going down with Susan for the milk and being darned, he went up again to Trout Tarn, and tried to tempt another monster, but caught nothing, and gave it up when he found that Titty, fishing the little pools of the beck just below the tarn, and using the less important worms, had caught four little trout in a way John had shown her before going down to work on the mast. After dinner he too began fishing the pools without a float, and by the time John came up from the cove, at the end of a hard day's work on the mast, bringing with him Mother and the ship's baby, who had rowed into the cove in time to come up to Swallowdale for tea, Roger had himself caught two, and there was a good deal of hurry in getting them cleaned and cooked in time for Mother to try with the bunloaf and butter.

Yesterday's big trout had been boiled at Holly Howe, and had made a supper for Mother and Nurse, and Mr and Mrs Jackson had had some too, and there had been some for Bridget to have after her porridge at breakfast. Mother said it was the biggest trout she had ever seen in England, though she had seen much bigger in Australia and New Zealand. The ship's baby was delighted with the ship's parrot's private perch. Mother liked the bathing-pool. She had been all up the valley before, at last, they showed her its secret and pulled aside the heather from the doorway and gave her Susan's torch and told her to go in to see Peter Duck's cave. What she said about that pleased everybody.

'Any explorer would be glad if he'd found a cave like that.' This pleased Titty and Roger. 'It's a very neat and well-kept larder.' This pleased Susan. 'It wants nothing but a stone table.' (John at once decided he would make one.) 'And what a place to hide in.' This pleased all of them. 'But no sleeping in it.' Susan explained that nobody was going to sleep in it except the parrot. 'And Peter Duck,' said Titty.

'Of course,' said Mother. 'Hullo. What's this? Ben Gunn?'

She was looking at a patch of wall lit by Susan's torch, the very patch on which Captain Flint had carved the name 'Ben Gunn', so many years before. Another name had been added underneath the first and a bracket joined the two.

'You see, Ben Gunn belongs to Captain Flint, and Peter Duck is ours,' said Titty.

The others peered at the wall. This is what they read:

BEN GUNN
} PARTNERS
PETER DUCK

The letters were not all of the same size. Nor were they very straight. But it would have been hard to do better, working with a knife by the light of a candle-lantern.

'But when did you do it?' asked Susan.

'When you and Roger went for the milk this morning,' said Titty, 'and John had gone up to the Watch Tower Rock.'

'The Watch Tower Rock?' said Mother. 'What's

that?' and they took her up there and she lifted the ship's baby up to John and then climbed up herself and looked back over the lake to Holly Howe far away down below, and up over the moor to the big hills. They told her which of them was Kanchenjunga and how some day they were going to join the Amazons and climb that mountain together.

'Poor dears,' said Mother, 'from what I hear they're having rather a poor time.'

'Horrible,' said John. 'We saw them out driving.'

'With gloves on,' said Titty.

'What's the great-aunt really like?' asked Susan.

'Didn't she come to tea to make friends the day after we sailed away to Wild Cat Island?' said Titty.

'I wouldn't say she came to make friends,' said Mother. 'It was a curiosity call. She made Mrs Blackett bring her because she wanted to know what we were like.'

'But didn't she make friends when she saw how nice you are?'

Mother laughed.

'Perhaps she didn't think so.' She would say no more about the great-aunt, and all the rest of the time she was up on the Watch Tower Rock and at tea in Swallowdale and on the way down to the cove, when all the explorers went with her to see her safely through the jungle, she talked about fishing and about caves and about camping in the Australian bush, where there were much worse snakes than adders.

All the same, as they climbed through the woods on the way back to the camp that evening, Titty said to John, 'Mother doesn't like her either.'

'No,' said John. 'I'm sure she doesn't. Anyway, perhaps the Amazons'll manage to get away from her tomorrow and make the attack on Swallowdale.'

Next day, almost sure that the attack would come, John waited most of the morning in Swallowdale or on the Watch Tower Rock. Titty and Roger were sent for the milk by themselves and told not to be a minute longer than they could help, for fear the attack should come while they were away. Later on, Susan said she must have some more wood, and while three of the explorers were gathering wood one was waiting on the Watch Tower Rock to signal to them in case of need, and the wood-gatherers kept near the edge of the forest and kept looking every few minutes to see that the look-out away on the rock above Swallowdale was making no sign. But the whole morning passed, and in the afternoon when John went down to the cove, sure that the Amazons would not think it worth while to cross the moor so late, he found that Captain Flint had been in the cove all morning working on the mast. John worked hard all the afternoon and as Captain Flint had left a note pinned to the mast to say he would not be coming next day, John decided that something ought to be done about the holiday tasks. When he came up to Swallowdale in the evening he said so to Susan, and Susan agreed that with a whole week of the holidays gone and the holiday tasks not yet begun, it was high time that everybody settled down to them.

'I don't believe the Amazons are really going to attack,' he said. 'Not now, anyway. It isn't as if they were free, like last year.'

'They probably can't get away,' said Susan.

'Even Captain Flint can't,' said John.

But on the fourth day after the move to Swallowdale, when nobody was really expecting it, the attack came.

WILD CAT ISLAND FROM THE SOUTH

16

Surprise Attack

TITTY on that morning had taken the telescope and a French grammar up to the top of Watch Tower Rock to be getting on with her holiday task. Sometimes she swept the horizon with the telescope and then, as nothing was moving but the sheep, put the telescope down and had another go at the book. She had a pretty firm hold on *J'ai, tu as, il a* but was still muddled with *avais* and *aviez* and *avaient* and lost hope altogether when it came to *eus, eut, eûmes,* and *eurent.* Roger, who had no holiday task to bother about and had wanted Titty to come fishing with him, was looking, very carefully, for adders. Presently he

WATCH TOWER ROCK

tired of that, climbed to the top of the watch-tower and threw himself down beside Titty. He picked up the telescope and looked away over the moor to the north, and then away to the north-east over the woods and across the lake to Rio and Holly Howe. He watched a steamer until he could see it no more, and then, slowly, swung the telescope back towards the north, looking at the farther edge of the moorland where it dropped down towards the invisible valley of the Amazon River.

'Hullo,' he said.

'Shut up,' said Titty. 'There's nothing there. *J'eus, tu eus, il eut . .* '

'But there is,' said Roger.

'*Nous eûmes, vous . . . vous . . . vous. . . .* Botheration, Roger, now I've lost the page.'

'It's a red cap,' said Roger, 'like a red spider . . . moving very fast.'

Titty took the telescope, and a moment later French verbs had lost their chance for that day.

'It's Nancy,' she said, 'or Peggy. Yes. There's another. Two red caps. They're a long way apart. They must be crawling, too . . . keeping low in the bracken. What donkeys not to take their red caps off. Come on, Roger. Don't stand up. Wriggle backwards to the edge and then let yourself down. I'll go first. They'll be watching. Don't let them see we've spotted them. Lucky we've not got red caps.'

'One more look,' said Roger.

Titty gave him the telescope, took the edge of the French grammar between her lips, so as to have both hands free, and slid feet foremost over the edge of the rock on the side nearest to the camp, where there were ledges in the rock that made good steps.

'Come on, Roger. Hand down the telescope. Take care.'

Roger, lying flat on the rock, handed down the telescope and then slewed round. His feet showed over the edge. They wriggled. His knees showed. He hung by his middle, scrabbling for the top step with one foot. Titty, risking getting kicked, grabbed the foot and put it in the right place. A moment later, Roger was safely on the ground.

'Keep the rock between us and them,' said Titty, 'and be quick. We must catch John before he goes up to the tarn to do algebra. And Susan was going too.'

They dodged through the heather and in a minute or two were over the edge and scrambling and sliding down into Swallowdale. Then they picked themselves up and ran towards the tents. John, with an algebra lying open on the ground beside him, was just knotting three flies on a cast. The rod was ready, propped up against the rocks by the door of Peter Duck's cave. Susan, with an exercise book and a pencil, was busy with geography and at the same time keeping half an eye on the saucepan. John had suggested that it would be a good thing to serve out rations of hard-boiled eggs, and the water in the saucepan was very slow in boiling.

'Quick, quick,' called Titty. 'They're coming. Over the moor.'

'We've seen them,' squeaked Roger. 'Both of them. I saw their red caps. They're trying not to be seen.'

'How far away are they?' John quickly wound up his cast on his hand and put it back in the basket with the rest of the fishing tackle.

'Right away on the edge of the moor.'

'I wonder if there's really time. It would be silly to let them catch us half in and half out.'

'They're a long way off,' said Titty. 'I'm sure we can do it.'

'Well, you two, start away with your tents, and the mate and I'll scout. Then if there isn't time, we can easily put your tents up again in a minute or two.'

'Come on, Roger, I'll race you,' said Titty. 'You say, "Strike tents" when you're ready to begin, and then we'll both start together.'

Susan and John hurried up the steep side of

Swallowdale and disappeared, while Roger and Titty flung themselves upon their tents, loosened guy-ropes, jerked up tent pegs, took the little bamboo poles to pieces and folded up the pale, cream-coloured canvas. They rolled up their sleeping-bags and then, folding their groundsheets once across, wrapped tent and sleeping-bags and poles together, put each set of tent pegs in its little canvas sack, and stuffed each little sack into the middle of the bundle to which it belonged.

Titty would have been ready first, but she left a peg out and had to dig for the little sack to put it in. They were both sitting breathless on the top of their bundles when John and Susan came crawling over the edge of the valley, and hurried down to the camp.

'We'll do it all right,' said Captain John, quickly taking the fishing rod to pieces, 'but there's not much time to spare. All right, Mister Mate. I'll do both tents if you can deal with the cooking things. What about that parrot, A.B.?'

'He'll not say a word,' said the able-seaman. 'We'll put his cover on his cage to make sure. You won't mind, will you, Polly?'

Ten minutes later the camp in Swallowdale was as if it had never been, or, at least, as if it had been long ago deserted. Nothing but the blackened stones of Susan's fireplace showed that human beings had at one time or another had a fire there. Susan had been chosen to have a last look round. The others could count on her to notice anything that had been forgotten. She found a bathing-towel spread over a clump of heather to dry. She picked it up, but could find nothing else.

A loudish whisper came from behind her.

'Hurry up!'

The mate looked once more up and down the deserted valley and then joined the others in Peter Duck's. The moment she was inside, John pulled into place the last of the big clumps of heather that disguised the doorway.

In the cave a candle-lantern had been lit and was standing on the narrow uneven shelf that ran across one of the rocky walls. Titty and Roger, already holding their breath, were sitting on their bundles close under the lantern. The tin boxes with the stores were neatly piled beside the woodstack, and on the top of the woodstack was the parrot's cage, covered with its dark blue cloth. As the mate's eyes grew accustomed to the dim, flickering candlelight she saw that Titty had arranged the cooking things in a neat row, and that the fishing rods, which had been propped against the woodstack when she went out, were standing up in a corner, out of everybody's way.

IN PETER DUCK'S CAVE

'Peter Duck's enjoying this like anything,' said Titty. 'He says it's just what his cave is meant for.'

'Mister Mate,' said Captain John, turning round from the low and narrow slit of a doorway, 'that was good work all round. You've got a very smart crew. Serve out a ration of chocolate.'

'No need, Roger,' said the mate. 'Don't move. Don't touch the lantern. I put a lot of chocolate out on purpose. It's on the top of the tins.'

Voices sounded somehow hollow in the cave. 'Thank you,' whispered by one or other as the chocolate went round, seemed even to the one who whispered it as if it had been whispered by someone else. And when a half-empty biscuit box slipped and fell on the stone floor of the cave it startled everybody like an explosion.

''Sh! 'Sh!' said John. 'They may be quite near by now. They were coming fast, though they were keeping as low down in the heather and bracken as ever they could. They didn't know we'd seen them.'

'Listen,' said Susan.

In the cave it seemed almost as if nothing outside could be heard except the noise of the stream. John lay down on the ground with his head on the threshold, hidden by the heather in the doorway. The others saw his hand signalling back to them for silence. For some minutes there was not a sound, except that once the parrot scraped his beak on his perch.

Then, suddenly, outside, there was a long shrill whistle that was heard not only by John but by everybody else. It sounded as if it came from just overhead. Then another whistle shrilled, this time from the other side of the valley. Then there were yells of 'Amazons for ever!' from two different directions, the noise of stones slipping, the noise of scrambling feet, and then once more a long silence, broken at last by the voice of Captain Nancy, quite close to the mouth of the cave.

'Shiver my timbers, but where are they?'

'They must have gone,' came the voice of Peggy.

Both voices were puzzled and doubtful.

'Didn't you say you saw someone on their watch-tower?'

'I thought I did.'

'But the whole camp's gone. They've shifted.'

'P'raps they've got in a row, too.'

Inside the cave nobody breathed, except the parrot.

Nancy's voice came again, with the noise of a stone dropping on stones.

'Hullo! They can't have been gone long. These stones are hot. Susan's had a fire here, and cleared it away in a hurry. There's a burnt stick in the beck. No ashes in the fireplace and yet the stones are too hot to touch. They've thrown the embers in the beck. Yes. There's another burnt stick. They must have seen us, put the fire out, and sloped.'

'I'd have seen them if they tried to get down to Horseshoe Cove. I couldn't have helped seeing them, unless they went long ago, because all the time I was working round I could see the place where the beck drops into the woods.'

'Well,' said Nancy's voice again, 'they must have gone up to Trout Tarn, where Uncle Jim said they caught the big fish. They could have done that without being seen if they crept along the beck. But with all their tents and everything! It's a rum go. Shiver my timbers if it isn't.'

John had been scribbling on a bit of paper. Without moving from his place, lying close to the very mouth of the cave, he passed the scrap of paper back and waved it behind him. Susan took it quietly and read it in the light of the candle.

'Can you make the parrot say something?'

Susan showed it to Titty, and Titty, moving on tiptoe, lifted the parrot's cage off the woodstack and took it to the mouth of the cave. She tapped John's shoulder, and he glanced back, saw the cage, wriggled to one side and made room for it, and Titty put it close to the doorway so that all the light that came through the doorway fell on the blue cover that was keeping the parrot quiet.

Outside there was the voice of Peggy. 'We're very late already.'

'Come on,' said Nancy's voice, 'at the trot. They can't be gone farther than the tarn.'

There was the noise of hurried steps going up the side of the stream towards the bathing-pool.

'Now,' whispered John.

Titty pulled off the blue cover from the parrot's cage.

'Pieces of eight!' yelled the startled parrot, and then, as Titty hurriedly pulled the cover on again, he gave a long, angry scream, more like a wild forest parrot in a rage than like a tame and learned one who knew how to talk and even a small bit of the multiplication table.

'*Where* are they?' came the voice of Nancy outside, coming nearer again down the valley.

'The parrot sounded close here,' said Peggy's voice.

'I know that, you tame galoot. Of course it's close here. But *where*? They've hidden the parrot some-where in the heather. Anybody can see they can't be here themselves.'

'Let's go and climb the watch-tower and look round from there.'

'That's the best idea you've had yet. We'll spot them then wherever they are.'

There was a splash as someone slipped in crossing the stream, and then the clattering of the loose screes as the Amazons ran up the farther side of the valley.

Just for a moment John waited. Then he cautiously moved the heather and peeped out.

'All clear,' he said. 'Come on. Quick.'

A moment later everybody was blinking in the sunshine outside.

'Half a minute,' said Susan, 'I've forgotten the sticks.'

She dived into the cave again and came out with a handful of firewood and a bundle of the dry leaves she used for kindling. John put the clumps of heather back into place behind her.

'I've got the matches,' he said.

Susan hurried across to the fireplace and in a moment had her fire ready for lighting.

The others settled round the fireplace as if they had been lying there all day. Susan lit the dry leaves. Smoke poured up. Titty pulled the cover once more off the parrot's cage, and the parrot made up for lost time by a long series of shrieks and all the words it could remember. 'Pretty Polly, Pretty Polly. Pieces of eight. Two. Twice. Polly. Two. Two. Two,' and then shrieked again.

The puzzled faces of the Amazons looked down into Swallowdale from the edge of the valley.

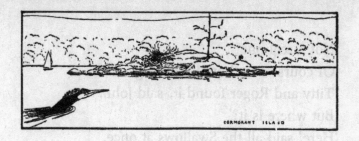

CORMORANT ISLAND

17

Later and Later and Later

'BARBECUED billygoats!' said Captain Nancy, 'but however did you do it?'

'Where were you?' said Peggy.

'You had us all right,' said Captain Nancy. 'One up to you. But where are all your things? What have you done with the tents?'

'Let's tell them,' said Roger.

Susan looked at John.

'Go ahead,' he said.

'We were in Peter Duck's cave,' said Titty.

'Peter Duck's?'

'His cave.'

'Not a real one?'

'Of course a real one,' said Roger.

'Titty and Roger found it,' said John.

'But where is it?'

'Here,' said all the Swallows at once.

The Amazons stared about them.

John pulled aside the loose clumps of heather that partly hid the doorway.

'Go in and look at it,' he said.

'No tricks. No capturing?' said Nancy. 'We've got to hurry back.'

'No, no. Peace,' said John. 'Just go in and have a look. There's a light inside.'

Nancy first, followed by Peggy, stooped and went in through the hole in the rock. The others crowded in after them. The Amazons were as surprised as even Titty could have wished when they saw the candle-lantern burning on its shelf, and by its yellow, flickering light saw the rough walls of the cave, the woodstack, and the piled boxes, the bundles, the fishing rods, and the cooking things. Then John pulled some of the heather back into place and showed how they had laid in wait, able to hear all that went on outside. Then they went out again, blinking in the sunlight, and John covered the entrance with the big heather clumps, when really, unless you knew, you were hardly likely to guess that the doorway of the cave was there.

'No wonder you wanted to come up here instead of staying down by the lake,' said Nancy. 'Barring Wild Cat Island, it's the best place for miles round.'

'You could almost live in a cave like that.'

'Nobody'd ever find you there,' said Nancy.

'Well,' said John, 'you saw how it was when the Amazon pirates attacked the camp.'

Nancy laughed.

'If you hadn't come out, and if the parrot hadn't shouted, we'd have gone home and told Uncle Jim you'd gone away.'

They went into the cave again.

'Let's come and hide here from the great-aunt,' said Peggy.

'No good,' said Nancy, 'because of Mother.'

'I wish we had a cave on the island,' said Titty.

'Let's make one when we get back there.'

'Why not?'

'I wish we could get the great-aunt into a cave like this and shut her up and forget about her,' said Nancy. 'We could write "Leave Hope Behind" over the doorway, and shove her in and wall her up.'

'Now, then, you fo'c'sle hands,' said Mate Susan to

the able-seaman and the boy, 'let's see how long it takes you to get the tents up again.'

'We'll help,' said Nancy.

'And then we'll see about dinner,' said Susan.

'We haven't brought much,' said Peggy. 'We ought to be getting back.'

'Iron rations,' said Nancy. 'Just things to be eaten on the march.'

'That's all right,' said Susan, 'we've got lots. The potatoes are in the sack in the far corner. And we're not sick of pemmican if you aren't.'

'We're homesick for pemmican,' said Nancy. 'We've been sitting up and saying please and thank you till we didn't want to come to meals at all.'

Swallowdale was soon full of bustle. Susan was hurrying on the fire, boiling water in kettle and saucepan at the same time, and opening a large-sized pemmican tin. Peggy was peeling potatoes. John and Nancy and Titty were putting up tents, bringing things out of the cave, and sorting them out, some for one tent and some for another. They wanted to help Roger, but Roger would not be helped. He was working slowly but making no mistakes, putting up his own tent by himself for the first time. This was a good deal more difficult than taking it down.

*

When the camp was itself again, with the tents up and the parrot-cage once more on its stone pedestal ('Oh, that's what it's for,' said Nancy. 'We couldn't think.'), and they were watching Roger carefully tightening his guy-ropes, Titty asked Nancy, 'Has the great-aunt been getting worse? Is that why you want to wall her up? But it ought to be in a new bridge or a castle or something like that. It would be waste to do it with a cave.'

'Anything would be too good for her,' said Nancy. 'It isn't as if it was only us. We can stand it. But she *will* go for Mother. There was an awful row again just because we ran into a calm the day we helped you to move camp. And, anyway, who can help being late in summer? But the moment she looks at her watch and thinks there ought to be a meal she doesn't wait decently till the gong's been banged once or twice in the house and then taken out in the garden and banged good and proper in case we're up on the fell. She just goes into the dining room and waits. And ten to one Cook isn't ready. And the old gong doesn't go until she is. And Mother doesn't know what to do between the great-aunt and poor old Cook. And even when her food's shoved under her nose the great-aunt won't begin until we've been rounded up. And when Uncle Jim isn't there she's even worse. Last night she made Mother cry.'

Titty stared and her mouth stayed open. She tried

to think what she would do if anybody ever tried to make the best of all natives cry.

'It was about us, of course. She dragged Father in. We knew because after we'd gone to bed we couldn't help hearing Uncle Jim talking to Mother just outside our window, and he said, "Bob would have liked them as they are." And he called Mother "Mops", which he only does sometimes. Then we made a noise and Mother said, "Go to sleep, you donkeys," and pretended to laugh. But she couldn't.'

Nancy walked suddenly away, but she came back in a moment with her face very red.

'If only we could get the G.A. to go,' she said. 'I thought of putting little stones in her bed between the mattress and the sheet. And Peggy thought of putting drops of codliver oil in her morning tea. But it's no good. It would only be worse for Mother.'

'In some places,' said Titty, 'the natives do this sort of thing when they have an enemy. I found it in a book. They make a doll and call it the name of the person. Then they stick pins in it, and every pin they stick in the doll is felt by the person, and if they stick the pins right through, the person dies. You could do that, and stick the pins in just a little way every night until she was so uncomfortable she would go of her own accord.'

Nancy laughed bitterly. 'You could fill a doll cram full of pins. You could use it as a pin-cushion and it wouldn't hurt the great-aunt. She wouldn't notice it. Pins would blunt on her.'

'Perhaps they ought to be silver,' said Titty. 'It said that in the same book about shooting witches and were-wolves. They always had to use a silver bullet.'

'Susan's pins look like silver ones,' said Roger, who was listening now that his tent was properly pitched.

'They might do,' said Titty. 'How could the great-aunt find out they weren't really silver? She wouldn't see you sticking the pins in.'

'All that's rubbish,' said Susan. 'Nobody believes in it now.'

'It must have worked or people wouldn't have gone on doing it,' said Titty.

'Anyway it's a bad sort of magic,' said Susan.

'But it would be good magic if it made the great-aunt go away and stop being beastly to Mrs Blackett.'

'Well, nobody's going to try it,' said Susan.

'She'll go sooner or later,' said Nancy. 'She doesn't usually stay more than a week. I believe she's only stopping now because she knows Mother would let us come and camp with you if she wasn't here.'

*

The potatoes, unluckily, were in one of their bad moods. Peggy and Susan kept on prodding them, almost as if each potato was a Voodoo doll being prodded to make a great-aunt uncomfortable, but for one reason or another they would not get soft. And the two mates had set themselves to make a really good dinner, with the hotted pemmican and the potatoes coming along at the same moment instead of letting the potatoes lag behind and come dawdling in when the meat course was over, so that they spoilt the taste of chocolate or apples that might be meant for dessert.

The result of this was that dinner started very late and took a very long time. People were making the pemmican last out in hopes that the potatoes would be ready before the last mouthful of pemmican had gone down. It was very late in beginning, and lasted indeed so long that, by the time it was done and Captain Nancy threw the core of her apple into the camp fire and asked Captain John to look at his chronometer, it was already past eight bells, and it was clear that even if Captain Nancy and Mate Peggy ran the whole way home, they had not the smallest chance of being back for tea.

They looked at each other in dismay, and were on the point of bolting home over the moor when Nancy remembered that drawing room teas did not wait, so that they would do no good by running home now and putting on best frocks when everything was over. 'We're late now whatever happens,' she said. 'It can't be helped. Besides, if we do go now there'll be no tea.'

'There mustn't be any mistake about supper,' said Peggy.

'There'll be a dreadful shivering of timbers if there is,' said Nancy.

So they stayed on, and, to lose no time, Susan kept the fire going strongly and had water boiling for tea almost as soon as washing up was done after dinner. Dinner had been late and tea came very soon after it, but the hot August day made it a good one. The pirates and explorers were just finishing their second mugs, when they heard a big stone crash down among the rocks by the upper waterfall.

They looked up. A native was just dropping down into the valley. Hot, tired, panting, he came trotting down the beck-side dragging a bundle of dusty sacking after him at the end of a rope. He stumbled as he ran, and was in the middle of the camp before he saw what it was. He pulled up short.

'You'll be having the hounds through here, but don't you mind them.'

'Hullo!' Nancy had jumped eagerly up. 'Is it a hound-trail?'

'Aye,' said the man. 'Practice-like. Maybe a score of hounds from Low End and round about.'

'What is a hound-trail?' asked John.

'You'll see it,' said Nancy. 'When'll they be off?'

'Happen before I get down to Low End.'

'Will you have some tea?' asked Susan, who had quickly washed out her mug.

'I will that, and thank you,' said the native. 'It's a hot day and all.' He drank the whole mug in one gulp, and went trotting on his way.

'Never you mind the dogs and dogs won't mind you,' he called back as he disappeared down the beck.

'What is it?' asked Roger. 'Is someone coming after him?'

'Bloodhounds?' said Titty.

'No, no. It's the loveliest thing,' said Nancy. 'That sack he was lugging round is full of some smelly stuff. And they let all the hounds go together, no one with them, and they race over the trail made by the sack, right round over the fells and back again into the bottom. And when they're coming in, you'll hear all the men shouting to their own hounds, and each man has his own noise and each hound knows the noise that belongs to him. Listen! Listen! You can hear the hounds away at Low End, down by the steamer pier, wanting to start.'

They listened, and far away in the valley below,

down by the foot of the lake, they could hear gusts of hound noises.

'Won't they tear the tents to pieces?' said Susan.

'Not they,' said Nancy. 'They'll run right through the camp. They'll stop for nothing. We'll go up to your watch-tower and see them coming far away, and then we'll come back here and see them come leaping down by the waterfall.'

She told the Swallows of the great hound-trails of the district, of the guides races where the young men row in boats across the lake, race up to the top of a big hill and down again each to his boat, and so back. She told them of the wrestling and the pole-jumping. She told them of the sheep-dog trials, where the sheep-dogs gather sheep, pen them in a field, take one sheep from among the others, and all at no more than a sign or a whistle from the shepherd. Then she was back again talking of the hound-trails, of the white specks flying through the heather, dropping down through the bracken on the steep hillside, getting larger and larger, until at last with the whole world yelling itself hoarse the winning hounds come loping into the sports field and the hound-trail is over. The missed meals at Beckfoot, the great-aunt, and everything else was forgotten.

Nancy was still in full cry, when the chorus of hound noises far away in the valley swelled out very loud and urgent and then came suddenly to an end.

'They're off,' she shouted. 'Come on.'

'What about the telescope?' said Titty.

'Bring it. Bring it,' said Nancy, who was already scrambling up the side of Swallowdale.

For some time after they had all climbed up on the Watch Tower Rock, there was nothing to be seen. Then, suddenly, Nancy, who had borrowed the telescope and was searching the hills with it, called out, 'There they are!'

'Where? Where?'

'Coming up out of Longfell Wood. Look! They're all pouring up out of the trees into the heather.'

'Close together,' said Peggy.

'No. There's another lot.'

'Where? Where?' said Roger. 'Longfell Wood' meant nothing to him because he did not know where it was. Nancy gave him the telescope, let him see where they were, but presently took it again, looked through it, and gave it back. It passed from hand to hand. Everybody had a look through it.

'They're spreading out now,' said John, who could see the white specks even without the telescope now that he knew where to look for them. 'One white speck's a long way ahead of the others.'

'They're going up Brockstones,' said Nancy. 'We

can't see the front ones now. . . . There they are again. Going it like anything.'

The white spots far away, slipping into sight and out again among the screes and heather, dropping away into a dip, showing again now startlingly nearer on the moorland slopes, disappeared. Farther away one or two white spots, hounds wavering and at fault, could still be seen. Then these, too, vanished, and it was as if all the hounds had fallen over a precipice or been swallowed up in some hidden chasm in the fells. 'We shan't see them any more,' said Titty. But Nancy knew better.

'We shall see them again in a minute,' she said. 'They must come through here, because the man with the drag did. They'll be working up through the woods on the other side of the fell. We'll see them again. Somewhere over there. They must come that way.'

'There's one,' said Susan. 'All by himself. By Trout Tarn. No. There's another.'

Nancy grabbed the telescope. 'Yes. There they are. Still together. Quick, quick! They'll be here in a minute. Let's go down and see them come over by the waterfall.'

'And put the parrot out of the way,' said Titty. 'He'd never understand them.'

They hurried down from the rock and back to the camp, and for the second time that day, the ship's parrot was banished into Peter Duck's. They were only just in time.

'Look, look!' said Nancy.

A lean white hound with patches of yellow and black on his shoulders and flanks showed on the skyline at the side of the waterfall, and came leaping down over the rocks.

'Well done! Well done!' shouted Peggy.

'Be quiet! Be quiet!' said Nancy. 'Don't talk to him.'

The hound stopped by the bathing-pool, looked about him, and lapped the cool water.

'He ought not to have done that,' said Nancy.

He had hardly moved forward again before half a dozen more hounds came pouring down the rocks like the white water when the beck is in spate after rain. The leading hound was not more than a dozen yards ahead of them. 'He must have lost forty or fifty yards by taking that drink,' said Peggy.

All these hounds took no notice whatever of the camp, but ran straight through it, down Swallowdale, and over the waterfall at the low end. It was only the later comers who stopped to look about them and hardly seemed to be taking the race seriously.

'You're no good,' said Nancy to them. 'Go on.'

'The others are miles ahead,' said Titty. 'You'll never catch them if you don't hurry.'

These hounds, too, went on after the others and disappeared.

And then, suddenly, from far away below the moor, from the foot of the lake, came a new noise, a noise of yells and rattles and shrill whistles and screams and howls.

'It's like parrots and monkeys all yelling together,' said Titty.

'Worse,' said Roger.

'That's the owners of the hounds,' said Nancy. 'They must have seen the first one in the distance. Listen! Oh, I wish we could see the finish.'

The noise rose higher and higher. There was a burst of cheering and then the shouts died away into silence.

'It's over. Now all the owners are patting their hounds and giving them lumps of sugar and telling them how good they are.'

*

Nancy's cheerful voice changed suddenly. 'The great-aunt won't be saying how good we are if we're a minute late for supper. Come on, Peggy. What's the time, John?'

John looked at his watch, but did not put the time into bells. It was far too serious for that.

'All three meals,' said Peggy.

'We've fairly done it this time,' said Nancy. 'Come

on. We'll go by the road. It's quicker, really. And someone may give us a lift. But we're done, anyhow.'

The Swallows looked at each other. If Captain Nancy Blackett talked of using the road and even hoped for a lift from a native, things must be very bad indeed.

'It'll be all right when you tell her about the hound-trail,' said John. 'She'd understand you had to wait for that.'

'It's no good talking to the great-aunt about hound-trails,' said Nancy. 'Even the shipwreck made no difference to her.'

'And we really did mean to be back for dinner,' said Peggy.

'But you can tell her so,' said Titty.

'She'd only look at Mother,' said Nancy.

'We'll go with them as far as the road,' said Susan, jumping up.

'Yes,' said John. 'Come along, Roger.'

'Never mind,' called Peggy over her shoulder. 'Don't bother.'

'We want some milk at the farm,' said Susan.

'And I want to give a rub to the mast,' said John.

Really, they wanted to be with their allies as long as they could. They would have liked to go with them all the way to Beckfoot to face the great-aunt herself.

'Aren't you coming, Titty?' said John.

'Someone's got to look after the fire unless we put it out,' said Susan, picking up the milk-can.

'I'll stop,' said Titty. 'I want to. Good night, Captain Nancy. Good night, Peggy.'

Nancy and Peggy were already hurrying down Swallowdale to go through the woods to the road that would take them along the shore of the lake back to Beckfoot and to all kinds of trouble. They went off at such a pace that the others had hard work to keep up with them.

As soon as they were all out of Swallowdale, Titty went straight to Peter Duck's cave. She found it in darkness. The candle was out. She got a box of matches from her tent and went into the cave again. Yes, she had been quite right. The lantern had got very hot and had melted the candle too fast, and all round it on the ledge of rock that made a shelf was a mass of thick white candle-grease.

'It isn't wax,' she said to herself, 'but it's good enough for the great-aunt. Anyway, it'll have to do.'

299

18

Candle-Grease

IT WAS not that Able-seaman Titty knew very much of the mother of the Amazons. She had seen her only twice, once last year after the great storm on Wild Cat Island, when she had been full of chatter and jollity, and once this year sitting sadly in the carriage side by side with the great-aunt, while Nancy and Peggy sat on the other seat facing them, and looking not at all like pirates. It was not really of Mrs Blackett she was thinking. She was thinking of her own mother. When Nancy told of how the great-aunt had made Mrs Blackett cry, Titty thought of what she would feel if someone were to do that to Mother, and in a moment she was feeling as if the great-aunt had made Mother cry, so that there was nothing Titty would not have been ready to do to the great-aunt if only it would stop her. She did not know if the wax image would work, but it was worth trying, even with candle-grease, because there was nothing else that she could do.

She picked up the little lantern from the shelf of rock and the candle-grease that had oozed out and hardened all round it came away like a thick whitish plate stuck to the bottom of the lantern. Her match went out. But a little light came through the doorway, and after waiting a minute till her eyes had grown accustomed to the dark, she stooped low, and carefully shielding the lantern for fear of knocking it on something, she came out with the slab of candle-grease unbroken.

Outside in Swallowdale, sitting by the fire with the sticks crackling cheerfully, the clean blue smoke climbing up into the evening sky, and the parrot out of his cage and preening his breast feathers, she very nearly gave the thing up. Looking at the smooth, hard, oily slab of candle-grease which she had now broken off the lantern, she began to doubt if she could do it. What was the great-aunt like? She remembered the stiff, upright figure in the carriage, but could not see her face, try as she would. Then she remembered the native images she had seen in a museum. After all, they weren't very much like anything.

'It's the name that matters,' she said to herself, 'and the magic.'

The name would be easy. She would simply call the thing 'great-aunt'. The magic would be more difficult. Just making a candle-grease doll and calling it 'great-aunt' would hardly be enough. There would have to be a spell. Why, of course she knew the way to do it. She remembered the African and Jamaican stories told by her mother in the evenings, and how when the king's wife died in the heat of the weather and the king he was real vexed, he sent for the Obeah woman who was the witch and had wrinkles deep as ditches on her brown face and told her to cast a spell so that nobody should use his queen's name again, because his queen she was so beautiful. 'And de Obeah woman, dat was de witch, she walk roun' de room an' roun' de room an' roun' de room, castin' one spell dat anybody who use dat name again dey dwop down dead dat minute. . . .'

'Roun' de room an' roun' de room an' roun' de room,' said Titty to herself, counting with a finger as she said it. 'Three times round. That's easy enough. And the cave ought to be a good enough room to do it in.'

She had trouble over the making of the image, even though she did not try to make a very good one.

302

Candle-grease is not wax and the able-seaman soon found that she could do nothing with it unless it was warm and almost liquid. She had nothing to warm it in except the mate's cooking pans. She did not much like using them, but decided that to save anybody's mother from a great-aunt of this kind it would be right to use anything, and anyhow it would soon be over and she would be able to get the frying-pan (which seemed to be the best shape for melting candle-grease) clean and shiny again before Susan came back from Swainson's farm.

She remembered that before frying anything the mate always put a little butter in the pan, so that nothing should stick to it. It was a good thing she remembered that, she thought, and by the time she had put the butter in the frying-pan and was warming it over the fire she felt she had been doing this kind of cooking all her life. As soon as the butter was properly melted and sizzling on the bottom of the pan she broke up the slab of candle-grease and dropped the bits in and tilted the pan first one way and then the other until the bits all melted and ran together again. There seemed to be very little candle-grease to make an image of. She got the other three lanterns out of the tents. There was only a stub of a candle-end in each, and there were plenty of new candles in one of the tin boxes. So she put the three candle-ends into the frying-pan with the stuff that was there already, added a little more butter and warmed it up again until, as she tilted the pan, the candle-grease poured round like thick sauce. Then, of course, the trouble was that it was too hot. She had to wait for it to cool. But the moment it was cool enough, she began scraping it up with a spoon, and presently had a good big lump of candle-grease, not quite too hot to touch, and was kneading it between her hands and keeping it moving from one hand to the other as if it were a hot potato.

She turned it quickly into a great-aunt. There was a small round blob for a head ('It's no good trying to do snakey hair') stuck on a long straight body, rolled between her hands, plumped down on a stone and made to stand upright, and then pinched in a little at the middle. The arms, too, were made separately and then stuck on. She scraped a little more candle-grease from round the edge of the frying-pan and used it to make two feet. They were not a success, so she squashed them together and made them into a hat instead, pressing it down on the blob that was meant for a head. There was no time to do much modelling. The candle-grease hardened too quickly as it cooled. Anyhow it was horrid to touch, but that, perhaps, was partly the fault of the butter. She gave the thing eyes, marking them in with a charred and blackened stick from the edge of the fire, and she scratched a slit of a mouth somewhere below the place where she would have liked to make a nose if the candle-grease head had still been soft enough.

The frying-pan smelt as nasty as it looked. There was no time to lose if it was to be cleaned and polished before the others came back. So Titty borrowed Susan's torch out of her tent and hurried into the cave to get on with the spell. She did not think of it as Peter Duck's. Nor did she think of asking Peter Duck to help. Peter Duck had nothing to do with magic. It was not the sort of thing in which he could be of any use.

She set the torch on the ground in the middle of the cave, pointing upwards so that it lit the roof, and then, holding the candle-grease doll before her, she walked three times round the cave, talking to the image as she walked.

'*Be* the great-aunt! *Be* the great-aunt! *Be* the great-aunt!'

Then, catching her breath, she ran hurriedly out into the sunlight. It was a comfort, after that, to see that the parrot had gone back into his cage and was eating a lump of sugar as if nothing special was going on.

The great-aunt, smelling horribly, now felt somehow different to her fingers. Had she really found the right spell? She almost wished the others would come back before anything else happened. Then she remembered what Nancy had said about Mrs Blackett crying and she bit her teeth tightly together. She was not going to stop now.

But the question was, what, exactly, ought she to do? It would be no good just pushing pins into the great-aunt's legs and arms, or into her body, because if something went wrong with a leg or an arm, or if she were seriously ill, the great-aunt would be sure to stay at Beckfoot and be horrible to everybody until she felt better. Besides, perhaps it was true that only a real silver pin would be any good. What she wanted was just to make the great-aunt thoroughly uncomfortable, so that she would want to go away. Titty looked doubtfully at the image. If she rolled the image in the dust would it mean that the real great-aunt, away at Beckfoot, would suddenly throw herself on the ground and begin rolling about? That would be most worrying for Mrs Blackett.

Then she remembered reading in the book how the native wizards when they make the wax image of an enemy melt it slowly over a fire, and believe that as the image melts away so does their enemy lose strength until at last, when the whole image is melted, he dies.

Of course, the thing would be to melt the image

just a very little, not enough to make the great-aunt ill, but just enough to make her feel not quite herself, and that she would be better in a more bracing air. Then she would pack her boxes and go away and everybody would be perfectly happy.

She held the candle-grease doll out over the fire. Nothing happened except that the hand in which she was holding it grew very hot long before the doll seemed to feel the heat at all. She changed hands until that hand too was very hot. Then she changed hands again and this time, perhaps because she took hold of a part of the image that had been nearest to the heat, perhaps the wood shifted and a little flame licked up and burnt her fingers, perhaps just because the candle-grease was melting and slippery (how it was she never could explain to herself) the thing was gone, her fingers closed on nothing, there was a dreadful spluttering in the fire, yellow smoky flames shot up and a moment later, though Titty scattered the sticks in all directions trying to save her, no one could have told that a great-aunt had ever been there at all.

Titty's first thought was that there would never be time to make another. But the next moment she had thought of something else, and, no longer an able-seaman, no longer even a negro witch, she burst into horrified tears.

CANDLE-GREASE AUNT

'I didn't mean to kill her,' she wailed. 'I really didn't.'

She saw the great-aunt, at Beckfoot, stricken suddenly, gasping for breath, dead. She saw Nancy and Peggy running along the lake road not knowing that when they came home they would find the blinds down in the windows of the house. Would they guess at once what she had done? What would they think? Even Nancy would think it was too much. It was all very well for the scuppers of a pirate ship to run with blood. This was different. The great-aunt dead, and dead in such a manner, was worse than the great-aunt alive even if she made Mrs Blackett miserable and was spoiling the Amazons' holidays. And she had done it. She felt as if she had tried to ring the bell quietly at the door of a big house and the bell was going on pealing and pealing as if it would never stop.

'I wish I'd never thought of it. But I didn't mean to kill her. I didn't. All I wanted was for her to want to go to the seaside.'

'Pretty Polly. Pretty Polly,' said the ship's parrot, who had come to the end of his bit of sugar and was wondering if he had any chance of getting another.

Titty looked at him through her tears, and wondered suddenly if she had truly done anything at all. Had she just planned to make a great-aunt and to cast a spell . . . ? She had often planned things until they seemed quite as real. But when she wiped her face with her hands she felt the smudge of sooty candle-grease. She saw the frying-pan waiting to be cleaned . . . the empty lanterns. . . . No. There was no doubt about it. The thing had really happened.

Just then the others came climbing up into Swallowdale.

'A farmer's cart gave them a lift,' shouted the ship's boy.

'They're going to be awfully late just the same,' said John grimly. 'I wish they hadn't waited for the hound-trail. Hullo, Titty, whatever's the matter?'

'What have you been doing to the fire?' said Susan, 'and the frying-pan? And the lanterns? And what have you got on your face?'

'Roger, go and get some more wood out of Peter Duck's,' said Captain John. 'There's some just inside the door.'

The moment the boy had gone into the cave, Titty poured out the dreadful truth.

'I've done it,' she said, 'but I didn't mean to kill her. She slipped in my fingers and got melted and burnt up.'

'Who did?' asked John.

'The great-aunt,' said Titty. 'I made her out of

candle-grease and I meant to melt her just a very little, but she slipped.'

'Well, you can easily make another,' said John.

'But she's dead,' said Titty. 'They'll find she's dead when they get back to Beckfoot and they'll know it's my fault.'

'Rubbish, Titty,' said Susan. 'She's perfectly all right and scolding them like anything. All you've done is to make a dirty mess of a clean frying-pan. Go and wash your face and clean the frying-pan while I crack the eggs into a mug. I promised Roger I'd scramble them.'

'Look here, Titty,' said John. 'It isn't as if you'd had the proper wax, and even if you had you'd have had to burn it on purpose if you were going to do any good. Just dropping it in the fire by accident means nothing at all.'

Roger came out of the cave with an armful of wood and Susan's torch.

'I found it in the middle of the floor,' he said. 'It's gone very dim.'

'I'm most awfully sorry,' said Titty. 'I forgot it when I was casting the spell.'

'What spell?' asked John.

'Going round and round three times,' said Titty.

'Go and clean the frying-pan,' said Susan, 'and let's have supper.'

Susan built up the scattered fire and soon there was once more a cheerful blaze. Scrubbing the frying-pan made Titty feel rather better, and though at supper the scrambled eggs did taste a little of candle-grease, just eating her share of them by the fire with the others was enough to make black magic seem unreal.

But late that night Susan heard Titty stir uneasily in her tent. Susan wriggled a hand out from under her tent and into Titty's which was close beside it. Titty found the hand and held it tight.

'I didn't mean to kill her,' she whispered.

'Of course you didn't and you haven't,' said Susan.

'We'll know in the morning.'

'We know now,' said Susan. 'Go to sleep.'

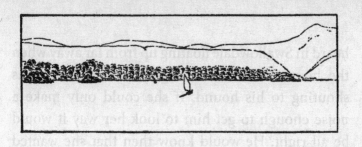

19

No News

TITTY woke in the morning from a muddled dream in which she was trying to save the great-aunt, who was being hunted by all the hounds of the hound-trail with Peter Duck urging them on. All she had to do was to tell Peter Duck that it was a mistake and that he must call the hounds off. Just to call 'Peter' or 'Mr Duck' would be enough. But she opened her mouth and no sound came. She could not make any noise at all. And there was the great-aunt walking slowly along, not knowing that the hounds were on her track, and there was Peter cheering them on with yells like the yells they had heard in Swallowdale floating up from far away when the hound-trail was ending and each owner was shouting to his hound. If she could only make a noise enough to get him to look her way it would be all right. He would know then that she wanted the great-aunt to escape. But she could not get even a whisper out from between her lips. She woke almost choking and was very glad to hear nothing but the beck flowing by and to see nothing but the cool clean walls of her little tent.

She wriggled out of her sleeping-bag and went up to the bathing-pool, and plunged into the cold water and put her head under the waterfall. What a donkey she had been the day before. Nothing could really have happened except that she had wasted three good candle-ends and used up the battery of the last of the torches. Susan and John were quite right. They always were, especially Susan. And yet she dreadfully wanted to be sure. She was in a hurry to be off down to Swainson's farm for the morning milk. Roger came too, and was surprised that Titty did not hurry him away, but waited while old Mr Swainson sang one song after another. Old Mrs Swainson asked her advice about what patch of colour to sew next into her patchwork quilt. Mary Swainson bustled in and out with the milk-can and told them the name of the hound that had won the hound-trail yesterday. (Melody was its name.) It was clear that nobody at Swainson's farm had heard of any sudden illness of the great-aunt at Beckfoot.

But before she was back in Swallowdale with the milk, Titty remembered that it was still early and that even if anything had gone wrong at Beckfoot last night the news might not have reached this end of the lake. She pleased John very much by saying she would like to come down to the cove if he was going to work at the mast.

'Captain Flint may be coming too?' she asked.

'He said he would as soon as he could get away.'

Roger went fishing. Susan went with him and took her geography book as well, but kept on finding she was reading a bit that she had read before.

Unluckily Captain Flint did not come. Work on the mast was going on well, so Captain Flint was not really needed; but Titty spent a good deal of the morning among the rocks on the northern side of the cove, looking up the lake and hoping that every distant rowing boat was bringing the retired pirate with news from Beckfoot. Of course it was all right, but until news came she could not be properly sure.

When the captain and the able-seaman went up to Swallowdale for dinner the mate asked them at once, 'Did he come?' and John said 'No', and, by the way both of them spoke, Titty knew that they, too, wanted news from Beckfoot. The captain and the mate felt that they were partly to blame for the lateness of the Amazons, though really it was the fault of the hound-trail, and they were wanting to know whether Nancy and Peggy had been able to get home so late without even worse trouble than they had feared. Roger alone was free from this kind of worry. His was of a different kind. He had not been able to catch any fish and he thought it was probably the fault of the worms. He remembered the bright red worms with yellow rings that John had brought for perch-fishing from Dixon's Farm last year and he wanted to ask Mary Swainson if there were any worms as good as that to be found in her farmyard.

Everybody except the parrot went down to Horse-shoe Cove that afternoon. A great deal of work was done on the mast, which was now almost everywhere about the same size as the old mast that John was copying, though not so smooth. Roger went to Swainson's farm and Mary gave him a fork and left him in the farmyard and washed him up afterwards when he had half filled a tin with the best of all kinds of worms, 'the friskiest,' as he said, 'he ever saw.' He was a long time at the farm, because there was no one to hurry him away, and he and old Mr Swainson took their chance and did a lot of singing together.

'Did they say anything about Beckfoot?' asked Titty, when Roger came back with his worms.

'No,' said Roger, 'but Mr Swainson said it was no wonder I was catching no fish because rain was coming and the fish knew it.'

John, Susan and Titty looked anxiously up at the sky. It was certainly looking rather thick, and there was a heaviness in the air which all of them had thought was in their own minds. Perhaps it only meant that it was going to rain. They cheered up at once.

'We'll want some more wood in Peter Duck's,' said Susan, 'so as not to have to dry it.'

'We haven't tried the new tents in the rain,' said John. 'Let's go and get the wood, and have all snug before the storm.'

John put the shaping plane and callipers in his knapsack to take them up to Swallowdale, and presently the whole party were loading themselves with dry sticks near the top of the woods. Already, as they trudged home beside the stream they could see over the moor dark purple sky behind the hard edges of the hills.

It rained heavily that night. The first drops fell as they were tidying up after supper, but that was no more than a shower. It was not until after 'Lights out' that it settled down to rain in earnest. There was very little wind with it, just steady, tremendous downpour.

'Take care not to touch the walls of your tents,' called John.

'I'm not,' said Roger.

'It's trickling down the tent pole by my head,' said Titty.

'Don't let it trickle into your sleeping-bag,' said the mate.

'How's your tent, Susan?'

'None come in yet.'

For some time the four explorers lay still listening to the rain drumming on the thin tent walls within a few inches of their faces. Then John remembered the guy-ropes, wriggled out of his sleeping-bag and nightclothes and slipped, a naked savage, into the rain.

'What are you doing?' asked the mate.

'Loosening the guy-ropes,' said the savage, 'and tumbling over them in the dark,' he added suddenly as he fell to the ground with a bump.

'You'll get your pyjamas wet.'

'No, I won't,' said John. 'It's a good thing I thought of it. The ropes are as stiff as wires already.'

The rain made a different noise on the slackened tents. John crawled into his own, dried himself as well as he could, and settled down again to try to sleep.

'Listen to the beck,' said Titty.

The beck was sounding a new note, hurried, impatient, not stopping for anybody, quite different from the quiet music of the little waterfalls to which, in Swallowdale, the explorers had grown used.

'If it rains like this tomorrow, the Amazons won't come anyway,' said Susan.

'And there won't be any work on the mast,' said John.

Titty shivered. That would mean another day without knowing what had happened at Beckfoot. With the others, in sunlight, she was almost ready to be sure that the great-aunt had gone on scolding and being horrible in spite of the burning of the candle-grease image. At night, alone in her tent, in darkness, she remembered the casting of the spell and the feeling of the image in her hands as she ran out of the cave. Something must have happened.

'Mr Swainson says they'll bite like anything when the rain comes,' said Roger. He was still thinking of trout.

For a long time the explorers lay awake listening to the rain on their tents and the rushing noise of the stream and the new roaring of the waterfalls. But the rain was softer now. The noise was a steady noise and in the end even Titty fell asleep. In the morning they crawled out into a sodden world. The rain had stopped, but every stone was shining. The pale sunlight was glittering in thousands of drops that clung to every sprig of heather. The wet bracken was bowing to the ground. There was brown in the white foam of the waterfall, and the stream that flowed through Swallowdale was dark and coppery and had risen so much that it lapped the stones of Susan's fireplace, and was within a yard or two of the tents.

'It's a good thing we weren't still camped in Horse-shoe Cove,' said Susan.

'The dam's gone,' called John, who had gone up to look at it. 'At least one side of it has.'

'May I go for the milk?' asked Titty, but at that moment Mary Swainson herself climbed up into Swallowdale bringing her own can.

'Well,' she said, 'I thought I might find you washed

away. I see you're not, and that'll be good news for Mrs Walker. How are you for dry wood?'

'We've got lots in the cave,' said Susan.

'That's good. Dad says the rain's given over now, and weather's going to pick up again.'

Susan had brought out the explorers' milk-can. Mary Swainson filled it from her own, and turned to go back down the valley.

'Do stop and have some tea like you did the other day,' said Titty, but Mary was in a hurry. She was rowing across to the village, and, besides that, was going to Holly Howe to report that all was well.

Titty ran after her and went with her as far as the lower waterfall.

'Have you had any news from Beckfoot?' she asked nervously.

'News? Nay. What news?'

'Not about anyone being ill there, or anything like that?'

'Not a word,' said Mary.

'Not about Miss Turner?'

'Nay. I'm sure I'd have heard if folk knew of anyone ailing there. I saw Jack last night. He's loading logs round from over yonder, and working late, and he comes right by Beckfoot. He'd heard nothing of it or he'd have said.'

321

With that Titty had to be content.

Again Captain Flint did not come to Horseshoe Cove. Again there was no news of any kind from the Amazons. But in the afternoon, Mother came rowing into the cove just as John was putting his tools away and Titty was going out on the rocks to have a last look in hopes of seeing Captain Flint.

Mother came up to Swallowdale, felt the sleeping-bags and found them all dry, and praised Susan for making a good fire and making use of the sunshine as well for a thorough airing of anything that might seem a little damp.

But she, too, had no news from Beckfoot.

'I expect they got in an awful row,' said Susan, telling how one thing after another had helped to make Nancy and Peggy late in spite of running home by the road.

'I know they got into trouble over the shipwreck,' said Mother. 'They were late then, poor dears, anybody would have been.'

'I wish we could find out,' said Susan.

'They're probably locked up on bread and water,' said John.

'Much more likely made to stay with their grown-ups and have afternoon tea,' said Mother. 'Why, Titty, what's the matter?'

Titty and Mother walked up Swallowdale together, to look at the water pouring through the gap at one side of the dam. Roger was going with them, but John grabbed him just in time. Titty told Mother the whole dreadful story of the candle-grease, and how the great-aunt had made Mrs Blackett cry, and how Titty had wanted to make the great-aunt feel weak and tired so that she would think of going away to the seaside and leaving the Blacketts to be happy, and how, somehow, the candle-grease image had slipped and been melted and burnt up in the fire, and did Mother think the great-aunt could be all right, because really Titty had not meant it to be burnt up but only melted just a very little.

Mother did not think it was a good thing to make candle-grease images even of great-aunts in order to do magic with them, but when she and Titty walked back together to the camp, where Susan had a kettle on the boil, and a groundsheet spread for tea, Titty was looking happier than she had looked for two days.

Later in the evening when they went down to the cove to see Mother off with half a dozen little trout Roger had caught in the stream during the day, John said, 'I say, Mother, if you do hear anything about what happened to the Amazons the other night, could you put it in a letter and send it us by native post?'

Titty said, 'Let's all go there at once and ask to see them, and then we'll know.'

But Mother said that this would only make things worse for Mrs Blackett.

Again, on the third day after the surprise attack, there was no direct news. Captain Flint did not come. The morning was spent in mending the dam, now that the beck had gone down again after the rain. The afternoon and evening were spent in the cove, where Susan made a fire and they had their tea, going up to Swallowdale only in time for supper. There was still too much water coming down to let them go through under the bridge at all comfortably, and anyhow, they were feeling too glum about the fate of the Amazons to mind just crossing the road. After all Nancy and Peggy had even gone home by it. And as they crossed the road they saw Mary's woodman going off with his three horses and load of great trees, and were in time to call to Mary, who had been talking to him, when they saw her hurrying along the cart track towards the farm. She came back at once.

'I saw Jack this morning,' she said. 'He happened

to be coming by, and I asked him to find out if anything was gone wrong at Beckfoot, and he's just been telling me, though how you should know it beats me.'

Titty stiffened. But it was not what she feared.

'He saw the cook there, who's second cousin to Tom's wife, that's Jack's brother, and she was in a fair taking about Miss Turner. Knows her own mind, Miss Turner does, so Jack says, and there's no pleasing her. And it's not as if the Blackett lasses aren't as good-hearted a couple as any. But she's always on to their mother about them, and there was a fair to-do when they came in late two nights gone by, and there's to be no more of their being out all day, and if Miss Turner doesn't leave soon Mrs Blackett'll be losing her cook. Jack says she was boiling properly with what old Miss Turner had said about plates not being hot to meals.'

It was comfort to Titty at least to hear all this. Miss Turner could hardly be dead if she were complaining of cold plates. But for the others it showed that they had been right. Nancy and Peggy had been late once too often.

'Everything's gone wrong this time,' said John. 'First I go and wreck *Swallow*, and now the Amazons are done for.'

'I wish Captain Flint would come,' said Susan. 'They'd probably send a message by him.'

The day after that the message came, but not through Captain Flint.

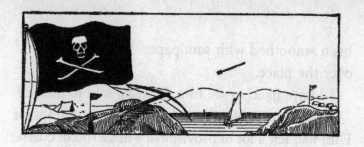

20

Welcome Arrow

THE day began badly. They were late with breakfast, and after that there had been a wooding party, and then when at last John had gone down to work at the mast he found that Captain Flint had been and gone. He had done a lot of work on the mast. He had indeed done two things that John had wanted to see done. A round hardwood cap with an eye for the flag halyards had been neatly fitted to the top of the mast, and the sheave for the main halyard had been fitted in below it, a piece of neat work with the chisel. The pin on which it moved was flush with the mast which had, at this point, been smoothed with sandpaper. John ran his hand over the place.

'I'd have liked to see him do it,' he said to himself.

This was not all. Close beside the mast Captain Flint had left a lot of provisions, a huge roll of coarse sandpaper, and a big can of linseed oil. Tied to the roll of sandpaper was a page from a notebook, on which was written, 'Hurry up. Get it good and smooth and then don't stint the oil.'

John packed the provisions into his knapsack, which was empty except for the plane, which he had thought might perhaps be needed. He then settled down to hard work with the sandpaper to give the whole mast as smooth a finish as Captain Flint had given to the masthead.

In doing this he soon forgot all worries about what had happened to the Amazons. The smoothing of the mast left no room for any other thoughts. The wood changed colour and grew pale under the rubbing of the sandpaper, so that it was easy to see just how far the final smoothing had gone. Each foot of the paler colour seemed to bring *Swallow* nearer to coming back. It was about half done when John suddenly remembered the time, looked at his chronometer, slung his stuffed knapsack on his back, and hurried off up the beck to Swallowdale.

In Swallowdale he found Susan, Titty, and Roger, more disappointed at his missing Captain Flint than pleased to hear that the mast was nearly done.

'Why didn't he come up to Swallowdale?' said Susan.

'Perhaps he's gone native, too,' said Roger.

'Oh, no, he wouldn't,' said Titty. 'Not this year. Not unless he had to.'

'He's done the masthead most beautifully,' said John. 'If he'd gone native he wouldn't have bothered.'

There was something in that, but not enough to raise the spirits of the explorers very much. After dinner Roger said he wanted to fish. Titty said she would come too. Susan said that she was busy, with all that wood to stack in Peter Duck's. Roger and Titty said they would help for a bit. Susan said they needn't bother. John said he was going down to the cove to go on rubbing down the mast.

Down in the cove he forgot about tea, and went on rubbing away with the sandpaper until the whole mast felt like soft velvet. He tried it with his fingers, looked at it sideways, to see if there was the slightest roughness, and decided at last that it would do. It seemed almost a pity to put the oil on. But he soon found that the oil made the mast look even better. He rubbed it with a handful of cotton waste that he had found pushed into the handle of the can, and the mast shone under the oil like a gleaming pebble from the lake before it has had time to dry. The clean Norway pole was thirsty for oil, and John rubbed away and rubbed away, turning the mast a quarter of a turn every now and then on the chocks of wood on which it lay.

'It's a better mast than the old one, I do believe,' said John to himself. 'I wonder what Captain Nancy would think of it now?'

And with that he remembered that, except for Mary Swainson's gossip, there was still no news from the Amazon River.

Just then, while he was resting and looking at the shining yellow mast, he heard the chug, chug of a motor launch. It was coming down the lake, and it sounded as if it were coming much nearer along the shore than most of the launches and steamers he had heard during the day. Or perhaps it was that he had been too busy to listen to the others. Now the whole mast was done and oiled and he had to give it a little time to let this first coat of oil soak in. So his ears were awake to noises, and this chug, chug sounded to him so near the shore that he slipped out on the rocks on the northern side of the cove to see just what it was.

Yes, it was a motor launch, and he was right, it was very near the shore.

'They'll have to turn out again before they get here,' Captain John was saying to himself, 'or they'll be running on the Pike Rock, just like we did.'

He was watching for the launch to alter course, when he began to think that there was something familiar about it. Suddenly, he knew. It was the Blacketts' motor launch, from Beckfoot, the launch that he had seen first by the light of a torch in the boathouse in the Amazon River, and seen again when Mrs Blackett came down to Wild Cat Island in it on the morning after the great storm nearly a year ago.

'Hurrah,' he said aloud, 'it's all right. They're forgiven. They're coming here.' He jumped up and was going to wave to them when he thought that perhaps he had better not. There were several people in the open forepart of the launch, and, after all, he might be mistaken. Better wait till he was sure. There would be plenty of time to wave later. So he dropped into hiding, and wriggled his way like a snake towards the mouth of the cove. The chug, chug of the launch came rapidly nearer and nearer. When, at last, John cautiously lifted his head among the heather and rocks of the northern of the two headlands the launch was hardly a dozen yards away.

He was right. It was the launch from the boathouse up the Amazon. But he was glad he had not waved.

The forward part of the launch was open, with seats running round it, and here were seated Mrs Blackett and that same grim, elderly lady whom the Swallows had seen driving that afternoon when they had looked down on the road from among the trees. They were both sitting with their backs towards Horseshoe Cove, and Peggy Blackett, looking not at all like a pirate mate, but like an ordinary little girl at a school speech day or a garden party, was pointing towards Wild Cat Island or the woods on the far side of the lake, so that all their attention was drawn that way.

Nancy Blackett was nowhere to be seen, and John wondered whether she was in such awful disgrace that she had been left behind. He was thinking that perhaps she would have liked best to be left behind when, suddenly, he saw her.

The launch was passing close by the mouth of the cove. John could even see the remains of a tea spread on the table in the little cabin amidships. Aft of the cabin was an open well, and there was Captain Flint, dreadfully smartly dressed, steering the launch. And there, too, was Nancy Blackett. She was crouching low so that nobody in the forepart of the launch should see what she was doing. Captain Flint, somehow, seemed to be too much taken up with the steering to notice her. She was in a best frock, as unnatural as Peggy's. But, as she crouched there, John saw that she had a crossbow in her hand. He saw her take one look forward through the glass-windowed cabin. Everybody seemed to be following Peggy's finger and watching something far away on the other side of the lake. Just as the launch had passed the entrance to the cove Nancy loosed her arrow. John thought he heard the twang of the bowstring even through the noise of the motor, but perhaps he didn't. The arrow flew over the water and stuck in a heather bush among the rocks of the southern headland, where they had landed after the shipwreck.

Again, for a moment, John thought of jumping up and waving, this time to show that he had seen. But, after loosing her arrow, Captain Nancy was no longer looking towards the shore. In a moment she had pushed her crossbow out of sight, under a seat in the steerage, slipped through the cabin and was already looking as proper as Peggy, talking to the natives in the forepart of the launch. Not even Captain Flint was looking towards Horseshoe Cove. A moment later the launch was hidden behind the southern headland and John could not see it, though he could hear it chug, chugging away towards the foot of the lake.

He heard a shout from among the trees where the beck ran out into the cove. 'Hullo!'

'Hullo!' he called back, hurrying over the rocks on his way round the cove to look for the arrow.

Roger came out of the wood, smelling his hand after touching the newly oiled mast.

'Titty's close behind,' he said, 'and Susan says we're to tell you you've had no tea and she's cooking supper early. She's cooking it now. And she says, Don't be late. And you mustn't. Titty and I caught two trout each, fat ones, one for each of us, and Susan's cooking them, and . . .'

'Did you see the launch?' asked John.

'I can hear one,' said Roger, just as Titty joined them on the beach.

'It was the Amazons' launch from the Amazon River. The one we saw in the boathouse last year. And Captain Nancy was in it, and she shot an arrow from it. It's on the south cape. Mrs Blackett was there too, and Peggy, and Captain Flint and . . .'

'Was the great-aunt all right?' asked Titty.

'She was there,' said John. 'Come and get the arrow. It's sticking in the heather out there.'

'Did Nancy really shoot at you?' said Roger. 'Is it war?'

'I don't think she saw me,' said John. 'But of course she knew I'd be down here finishing the mast. Come on and let's get the arrow.'

Titty was already scrambling out over the rocks. If

the great-aunt was going for picnics in launches, the candle-grease couldn't have done much harm. John and Roger hurried after her.

She found the arrow easily enough, sticking in the heather with its feathered end high in air.

'It's a new arrow,' said John. 'It's not a good one like the arrows they had last year. It's not half so well made.'

Titty was looking at its green feathers.

'They must have just made it,' she said. 'This is one of the feathers I brought them this year. I know it, because it got clipped with the scissors when I was cutting something else.'

'The ship's parrot wouldn't like it if he knew they were using his feathers to shoot at us,' said Roger.

'It didn't look exactly as if she was,' said John. 'It was too secret from the others.'

He looked carefully at the arrow. There was a curious wide band on it, near the green feathers. It had been neatly spliced with red string. In a moment John had his knife out and had cut the end of the splice and begun unwinding the string.

'Don't spoil their arrow,' said Titty.

'Well, they shot it at us,' said Roger.

John unwound the red string and almost at once they could see the end of a narrow, folded strip of paper that had been wound round the arrow and fastened to it by the very splice that hid it.

'It's a message,' said Titty. 'Be quick. Now we shall know.'

The little strip of paper that had been wound round the arrow and then hidden by the splicing of red string curled up tightly the moment it was taken off. John straightened it out. They looked at it together.

On it was written in capital letters and the usual red pencil of the Amazon pirates:

'SHOW THE PARROT HIS FEATHERS.'

There was no signature, but only a skull and cross-bones drawn in black ink.

'It's a very silly message,' said Roger.

'I don't see what it means,' said Titty.

'It doesn't explain anything,' said John. 'You can't call it even a declaration of war.'

They went slowly back into the cove to the old camp, and John gave another dose of linseed oil to the mast, and the others helped to rub it in.

'There they are,' said John suddenly, pointing out through the trees and between the headlands of the little cove. Far away on the other side of the lake the Beckfoot launch was moving along the farther shore. The Swallows ran out of the trees, climbed up among the rocks, and watched the launch disappear behind Wild Cat Island.

'They're going to land there without us,' said Titty bitterly.

But they did not. The launch soon showed again beyond the island, and they watched it going fast up the lake, not stopping even in Houseboat Bay, and vanishing at last behind the Peak of Darien.

'The thing that's so funny about it,' said John, 'is that Nancy did it as if it really mattered.'

'Perhaps it does,' said Titty, 'and we can't see how. I wish Captain Nancy wasn't so awfully clever.'

'She isn't cleverer than John,' said Roger.

John said nothing. 'Show the parrot his feathers.' It did not seem to him to mean anything at all.

At last Roger reminded them that Susan had said supper was to be early, and, after giving one more rub down to the mast, the captain, the able-seaman, and the boy set off on their way back to Swallowdale. There were the four trout to think of, as well as Susan. Roger at least was not likely to forget them, though the others might. They hurried up the side of the beck, crossed by the road instead of under the bridge, and climbed the steep woods to the moor, carrying the arrow with them.

21

Showing the Parrot his Feathers

THEY found the mate in a very native mood, due
to the cleaning and cooking of the four trout. Fried
trout ought to be eaten the moment they are cooked.
You can't go on hotting them up for people. If you
keep them frying too long they dry up and you might
as well throw them away. It was enough to turn
anybody native to have cleaned them and salted them
and got the fire just right and the butter melted in the
frying-pan and the four little trout sizzling noisily as
if in a hurry to be eaten, and then not a sign of the
crew in spite of all the trouble taken. Susan had made
the frying spread out as long as she possibly could,

and really it was a little too much when the others came up into Swallowdale at least twenty minutes after the trout were at their best, and Roger sniffing the good smell of them said, very happily, 'Just in time.'

'You aren't,' said Susan. 'You ought to have been here half an hour ago. I told you to come back straight away. Another time you'd better cook your own fish and I'll be the one to play round and to come back "just in time".'

Roger was going to say that perhaps there wouldn't be any fish left if she did that, when he caught John's eye, and saw that the captain thought it would be just as well to take no risks with the mate.

'I've seen the Amazons,' said John.

'They're not coming to supper are they?' said the mate. 'We've only got the four fish.'

'I didn't see them to talk to,' said John. 'They were in the launch. Nancy shot an arrow at the point by the Pike Rock. An arrow with a message on it.'

'It's all right about the great-aunt,' said Titty. 'John saw her.'

'Let's get supper done,' said the mate.

'We've got the arrow,' said Roger. 'Here it is.'

'That's your bit of bread and butter,' said the mate.

'These are jolly good fish,' said John. 'They couldn't be better cooked. They're better even than the ones we had the day we went fishing with Captain Flint.'

After that for some time nobody talked of anything but the trout and the supper. Titty and Roger told how the trout had been caught, one in the bathing-pool and the other three in the small pools between the top of Swallowdale and Trout Tarn. Roger told of the bigger ones there would have been if only they had not dropped off. Everybody said how good they were to eat. When the bones of the last trout had been emptied into the camp fire, Susan showed them just how lucky they were to have so good a cook as mate to the expedition. She had baked four apples to go with the rice pudding, burying them in a biscuit tin under the hot ashes. They liked their supper so much that when it was over Susan herself brought the talk back to the arrow. She had no sooner mentioned it than Roger handed it across to her and everybody began to talk at once of the launch and of the shooting of the arrow which John alone had seen.

'It had a message fastened to it,' said John, 'but it doesn't seem to mean much. . . . "Show the parrot his feathers." . . . Look at it.' He gave the mate the little curled slip of paper.

She unrolled it and looked at it.

'It doesn't look as if it meant anything at all,' she said. 'But when Nancy shot the arrow, she hid behind the cabin and looked as if it was something that mattered very much.'

'It isn't like the arrows they had last year,' said Roger. 'It isn't shiny.'

This was true. The arrow they were looking at in the camp was very rough, as if it had been made in a hurry. It was blunt at the end and the wood had never been varnished.

'I suppose those *are* the parrot's feathers,' said Susan.

'Yes,' said Titty. 'This one is the first that came out after we went home last year. I'd been saving it ever since the winter. I know it because it got snipped in the scissors by mistake. The other one came out just before we came here. They were both in the lot I gave Nancy when they came to the island the day Roger and I discovered Swallowdale.'

'So it must be a new arrow.'

'It looks as if they'd only just made it,' said John, 'with nobody to help.'

'Let's do just what the message says,' said Titty.

'What?'

'Show the feathers to Polly. He's awfully clever.'

'He isn't as clever as all that,' said John. 'If we don't know what it all means, he won't.'

'Anyhow, let's do what Nancy said. She'll probably ask whether we did it or not.'

'HI! HI! STOP HIM!'

Titty took the arrow with the green feathers and walked across with it to the ship's parrot, who was on his perch making the most of the evening sunshine.

Instantly the parrot screamed aloud and seized the arrow with its beak and one of its claws.

'Take care,' said John. 'Stop him. He'll pull the feathers out. There's only a narrow splice at each end to hold the thing together. He'll smash it up and then what'll Nancy say?'

But he was too late.

There was a noise of splitting wood, and in a moment the ship's parrot had not only torn his own old feathers out of the arrow but had broken the arrow itself at the splice just below the place where the feathers had been fastened in.

'Hi! Hi! Stop him! Look at that!' shouted John, jumping up.

'No, Polly, no,' said Titty. 'Give it me. You don't want it.'

Something beside the feathers had been torn from the split and now broken arrow. Titty rescued it just in time.

'Well done, Polly,' she said. 'Of course Nancy knew you'd do it, because she's seen you do it before.'

The ship's parrot took no notice. It did not want the

scrap of closely folded paper that Titty had in her hand.

'Pretty Polly, Pretty Polly,' it said contentedly, tearing shreds of wood off the arrow and dropping them round its perch.

Nobody bothered about the arrow now. Titty with trembling fingers unfolded the paper. She saw the skull and crossbones at the top of it and a lot of writing in red pencil underneath, and she gave the paper to Captain John.

'Read it aloud,' she said.

'It's meant for all of us,' said John, and began to read.

'TO THE CAPTAIN AND CREW OF THE SHIP "SWALLOW". GREETING. FROM FELLOW MARINERS IN SORE DISTRESS. WE ARE NOT SUPPOSED TO GO ANYWHERE OUT OF SIGHT OF THE NATIVES. THE GREAT-AUNT LIKES TO SEE US ALL THE TIME. WE WERE LATE THAT DAY WE KNEW WE WOULD BE AND WE ARE LIVING IT DOWN. BUT CLOUDS HAVE SILVER LININGS (THIS IS A QUOTATION) AND EVEN LESSONBOOKS HAVE LAST PAGES. IT'S NEARLY OVER NOW. IMPORTANT. START EARLY TOMORROW BY THE WAY WE CAME. KEEP ON THE TOP OF THE MOOR HEADING DUE NORTH UNTIL YOU SEE FOUR

FIRS IN WHAT USED TO BE A WOOD. FOLLOW THE
WAY THEY POINT AND KEEP TO THE STONE WALL
TILL YOU COME TO THE ROAD. THE RIVER IS TWO
FIELDS AWAY ON THE OTHER SIDE OF THE ROAD.
LOOK FOR A STONE BARN. ABOUT A CABLE'S
LENGTH ABOVE THE BARN IS AN OAK TREE CLOSE
TO THE RIVER. HERE YOU WILL FIND A NATIVE
WAR CANOE. BECKFOOT IS THE NAME ON ITS
TRANSOM. . . .'

'It can't really be a canoe,' said John, interrupting
his reading. 'It's a rowing boat. Canoes haven't got
transoms. They're pointed at each end.'

'Their natives may have their own kind of canoes,'
said Titty. 'Not all natives have the same.'

John went on reading.

'EMBARK WITHOUT FEAR AND DROP DOWN
THE RIVER TO THE LAGOON. YOU KNOW IT. THE
ONE WHERE ROGER THOUGHT THERE WERE
OCTOPUSES.'

'I knew they were flowers afterwards,' said Roger.
'Water lilies.'

'Don't interrupt the captain,' said Titty. 'Do go on.'

John read on.

345

'CROSS THE LAGOON. RUN THE WAR CANOE INTO THE RUSHES ON THE RIGHT BANK OF THE RIVER. LAND ONE SCOUT IN THE WOOD. LET HIM CREEP THROUGH THE WOOD, GIVE THE OWL CALL AND WAIT. TRAVEL LIGHT BUT WITH TWO DAYS' FOOD AND BAGS FOR SLEEPING AT NIGHT. KANCHEN-JUNGA BECKONS. WE'VE GOT A ROPE. WE'RE HIDING THE WAR CANOE FOR YOU TONIGHT: BY THE OAK. YOU CAN'T MISS IT. DON'T BE SEEN BY THE NATIVES. PRETTY GOOD THE PARROT. HE ALWAYS CHEWS UP ARROWS IF THEY HAVE HIS FEATHERS IN THEM. DO NOT FAIL US.

CAPTAIN NANCY BLACKETT
MATE PEGGY BLACKETT
PRISONERS OF WAR. BUT NOT FOR LONG.
SWALLOWS AND AMAZONS FOR EVER!'

'Is that the end?' said Roger.

'That's all,' said John.

The explorers looked at each other.

'Do you think it's all right?' said Susan at last.

'Well, what could be wrong?' said John. 'It's all on dry land. There won't be any night sailing. It doesn't make any difference where we sleep so long as the able-seaman and the boy get to bed in proper time.'

346

He knew at once what were the sort of questions that were bothering Susan.

The able-seaman and the boy listened breathlessly.

'Then there's the milk,' said Susan. 'It's no good carrying two days' milk with us, especially if it's as hot as it's been today.'

'There must be lots of farms in the valley of the Amazon,' said John, 'and Nancy and Peggy are sure to know them. We can get milk anywhere, only we may have to take our own can.'

'But what about leaving the camp for a whole night.'

'We won't,' said Titty. 'Peter Duck'll look after it. We'll stow everything in Peter Duck's cave. It'll be safe enough there.'

'What about the parrot?'

'He'll keep Peter Duck company. I'll leave him a tremendous lot of food and water and put him in the cave, too. He won't mind having a little extra sleep, just for once. Or he'll keep watch and watch about with Peter Duck. I expect he's lived in lots of caves before, real pirate ones.'

'And you know we've never tried sleeping in the bags without any tents. What if it pours?'

'So long as it doesn't rain, it'll be all right. If it looks like rain, we won't go.' John dived into his tent and came out again at once. 'The barometer's as steady as it can be. And there's another thing. Captain Flint would never have finished the mast up and left a message for me to hurry with the polishing and oiling if *Swallow* wasn't nearly ready. Painted, I should think. And in weather as hot as this she'll dry fast. We may have her any day. And we can't climb mountains and sail at the same time. If we're going to climb Kanchenjunga at all it would be a good thing to do it while we're up here.'

'Mother did say she didn't see why we shouldn't climb it if we wanted to,' said Susan, and the others knew that she was coming round.

Just before settling down for the night they went to the Watch Tower Rock, climbed its steepest side, just for practice, and stood on the top of it, all four of them, looking over the moorland towards the distant hills. The sun was dropping behind them. Already the peak of Kanchenjunga began to look as if it had been cut out of dark purple cardboard. To the right and to the left of it were other hills, and somewhere over the edge of the moor the explorers knew they would find the valley of the Amazon River. Farther round to the right they could see the edges of the forest, and far beyond them glimpses of the lake and the hills behind Rio.

'When the Amazons came over the moor, we saw them first over there, beyond that rock,' said Titty, pointing to a jagged rock about half a mile away in the heather.

'But not so near,' said Roger.

'That's the way we'll go,' said John. 'It's just about in a line between here and the northern side of Kanchenjunga.' He laid the compass on the rock and waited till the needle steadied. 'North-north-west's about it. We'll go to the rock and then strike north.'

High overhead there was a creaking noise, like someone very quickly swinging a big door that needs oil in its hinges. They looked up.

'Swans,' said John at once.

There were five of them, great white birds with their long necks outstretched before them, flying fast with steady, powerful wing-flaps towards the setting sun.

'Where are they going?' said Roger.

'There's another lake somewhere over there,' said John.

Over there to the west there were far dim hills beyond the rim of heather that shut them in like the horizon at sea. Beyond the heather was the unknown.

'Perhaps the swans can see the water,' said Titty, 'flying as high as that.'

'I expect they can,' said John.

The swans seemed to fall into the distance, and when they could be seen no more, the explorers climbed down from the Watch Tower Rock and walked gravely back to the camp in Swallowdale, thinking of what was before them.

They sat talking round the fire much later than usual. As Susan said, it was always the way on the night before an early start. There was so much to think of that it would have been useless to try to sleep. The stars were clear in the sky before they went to bed.

Long after the lantern in each tent had been blown out, John sat up, took his knapsack and crawled out again into the open. He pulled his sleeping-bag after him. Rummaging under the clothes in his knapsack he found the thin waterproof covering of the sleeping-bag which, in the tent, he did not use. He put the sleeping-bag into it, so that he would not need a groundsheet. He got back into his sleeping-bag, wriggled about in it till he had found a comfortable place for his bones, and settled down once more. His knapsack, which was still pretty well stuffed, made his pillow.

'What are you doing?' This was Susan's voice in the dark.

'Trying what it's going to be like without tents.'

'Let's all try,' said Roger.

'Why aren't you asleep?' said Susan.

'Can you see the stars?' asked Titty.

'Yes,' said John.

'I wonder if the prisoners of war can see them from their cells.'

'They aren't in cells at all,' said John.

'If they can't get out when they want, I expect it feels as if they were.'

'Good night,' said John.

'Good night, good night, good night,' came from the three tents in which there were still explorers. The fourth tent was empty, and John, lying comfortably stretched in his sleeping-bag, with his head on his knapsack, was looking up at the stars and feeling less like sleep than ever. At least he thought he did not feel like sleep.

After a bit he wondered whether counting stars would work as well as counting sheep going through a gap in a hedge. That was what Mother used to tell him to do when he was a little boy. He snuggled down in the sleeping-bag, so that only his nose was over the edge of it and began to count the stars in the

Milky Way. But he had not time, really, to count the bigger stars in more than a few inches of it. It may have been the counting that closed his eyes for him, or it may have been the hard day's work on the new mast with the sandpaper and the linseed oil.

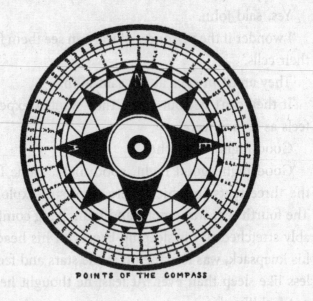

POINTS OF THE COMPASS

22

Before the March

THE camp was astir early in the morning. Susan began at once making ready for the march. Titty had waked with a plan in her head which she had told to Roger, and the two of them had taken their knapsacks and rushed off to the woods, promising to come back at once. John passed them there, filling their knapsacks with small pine-cones, when, after sleeping very well in the open, he was hurrying down to Swainson's farm with the milk-can. They were back in Swallowdale long before he was, for he had to go first to Horseshoe Cove to give a last dressing of oil to the mast, and then round by the farm to get the milk for breakfast and to tell Mary Swainson that they would not be wanting any more milk until the evening of the next day because they were going to be away for the night.

'I'm just rowing over to the village,' said Mary, using the native name for Rio. 'Is there anything you're wanting there?'

'I suppose you won't be going to Holly Howe?' said John. 'I'd like to tell Mother not to come here today or tomorrow because of our being away.'

'Why, of course I can and welcome,' said Mary Swainson. 'You bide a minute while I get you a bit of paper and you can tell her what you like.'

But old Mr Swainson shouted from the kitchen and called to John to come in.

'Maree,' he shouted, 'what are you letting him stand out there for? Come in, young man, and sit you down at the table. That's the place if you want to do a bit of writing.'

John went in and said 'Good morning' to the two old people. Mary got a pencil and a sheet of paper out of a drawer and set him to the kitchen table. Then she clattered off for the milk, while old Mrs Swainson went on with her patchwork quilt, and the old man watched John at his writing and half hummed, half sang bits of a song about a young man saying 'Fare thee well' to someone he was leaving behind.

John wrote:

'Don't come to Swallowdale today or tomorrow because we are going to the Amazon River for the climbing of Kanchenjunga. We are taking our sleeping-bags. The crew will go to sleep at the proper bedtime. We are coming back tomorrow. Everything is quite all right. The mast is finished. *Swallow* will soon be back, so it's a good thing we are going to climb Kanchenjunga now. With love from all of us.   John.'

He folded it up and wrote, 'Mrs Walker, Holly Howe,' on the outside.

Old Mr Swainson watched him all the time he was writing.

'Eh, but you can make that pencil move,' said the old man. 'In my young days they didn't teach us to write as fast as all that. But you're not such a one for singing as that young brother of yours. He's the lad for a song, so he is. But perhaps he isn't as quick with a pencil. And there's me. Can't write at all. Never wrote a letter these fifty years. But sing. Now, if it comes to singing . . .'

John did not know what to do. There were the others waiting for the breakfast milk, and there was the camp to be struck and the whole expedition to get on its way, and if songs began who could tell how long it would be before he could stir. But luckily Mary Swainson came bustling in at that moment, and took his note and gave him the milk and got him outside, and all in such a rush that it was almost as if she had swept him out of the farmhouse door. He never knew quite how it was done, but he thanked her very much and hurried away through the forest by the short cut up to Swallowdale. As he went he could hear for some time the voice of the old man singing in the house.

*

When he climbed up beside the waterfall and looked up Swallowdale he could hardly believe it was the place he had left so short a time before. The four little cream-coloured tents were gone. The others had taken down his tent as well as their own, and the valley did not look like a camp any more. Tents make all the difference to a place. Now, once more, it was a wild, rocky valley as it had been when first they came there. It did not look like anybody's home, and John knew that when they had gone back to Wild Cat Island, Swallowdale would look as if they had never been there. The first real flood would wash the dam at the bathing-pool away for ever. Everything would be as it had been, and their own Swallowdale, with its neat tents and cheerful fire, would be no more than a memory or something he had read about in a book. It was a queer thought, not comfortable. Still, at the moment the cheerful fire was still burning and all the signs showed that breakfast was waiting only for the milk.

'Here's the milk,' said John, 'and I've sent a despatch to Holly Howe to tell Mother where we're going.'

'Well, that's a good thing,' said Susan.

'Did you tell her not to tell any of the other natives?' asked Titty.

'I forgot about that.'

'She probably won't, anyway,' said Titty. 'At least, not unless she'd made certain it was all right.'

'Did Mr Swainson sing?' asked Roger.

'Yes. He wanted you to be there to sing with him.'

'I will, when we come back,' said the boy.

'Porridge today,' said the mate. 'We've got a long way to go. I've made enough for second helps all round. It's no good trying to make the milk last out. We'll finish it.'

'Everything stowed?' said John.

'In Peter Duck's,' said Titty.

'Breakfast first,' said the mate. 'Have a look at the cave afterwards. There was plenty of room for everything. It's better than when the Amazons came.'

'It looks almost like a shop,' said Titty.

'Only everything in it is ours,' said Roger.

They made a tremendous breakfast, the sort of breakfast explorers ought to make before marching into unknown country. There was much more porridge than ever Susan had made them before, and then bacon, fried till it crackled, and lots of it, and after that the usual bunloaf and marmalade and big mugs of tea. And while they were getting through the bunloaf and marmalade Susan had eight eggs in the saucepan being turned into hard-boiled ones, to take on their journey.

'I shan't want any more till the day after tomorrow,' said Roger, when breakfast was done and Susan was giving them all two eggs apiece to put in the outer pockets of their knapsacks.

'Well, put these eggs in, anyhow,' said Susan.

'I shan't want them,' said Roger.

'Perhaps you'd better leave your chocolate behind too,' said Susan, and Roger thought better of it, and packed his eggs away like everybody else.

Then the last of the things that were to be left behind were stowed away in Peter Duck's cave. Really very little was being taken, just a sleeping-bag and a waterproof covering for it in each knapsack, one mug for the party, one cake of soap for the party, a tooth-brush apiece and the food, which had been parcelled out, some taking one thing and some another. There were four bunloaves, two tins of pemmican, the hard-boiled eggs, a good lot of chocolate and some apples. The mate scrubbed the kettle with a bundle of heather till there was no more black on it that would come off. She put the lid in the outer pocket of her knapsack and strapped the kettle on the outside with the flap that came down over the neck of the knapsack when its string had been pulled tight. John was to carry the empty milk-can in the same way, and under the mate's orders was rinsing it out in the beck. The other two were let off easily, and this was just as well, because they wanted to cram their knapsacks full of pine-cones. 'For patterans,' Titty explained.

'But a patteran is to show other people how to follow us.'

'These are for finding the way back,' said Titty. 'You see, on the moor there are no trees to blaze, and we couldn't leave bits of paper. But there are no pine-cones on the moor, so if we mark our trail with them we shan't miss it when we are finding our way home from Kanchenjunga.'

Susan and John knew very well when it was no use arguing with Titty, so, once their sleeping-bags were inside, they were allowed to fill their knapsacks to the brim with the pine-cones they had brought up from the forest.

They crowded into Peter Duck's for a last look round by the light of one of the candle-lanterns that the mate had lit and put in its old place on the shelf with the other three beside it. She had made a first-rate job of the stowage. At one side of the cave there was a deep bed of firewood, already cut and broken to a useful length. On the firewood in four rolls side by side were the four sleeping-tents, each with its own bundle of tent poles and little sack of tent pegs. There they were well out of harm's way. The old groundsheets from last year's camp had been spread on the floor opposite the woodpile, and on them were the stores tent, rolled up, the tin boxes with the main stores in them, and the spare clothes, and three other tin boxes, one of fishing tackle, one with Titty's writing things in it, and one with books, the ship's papers of the *Swallow*, and the barometer.

'I say, Mister Mate,' said Captain John, noticing this box, 'I don't much like leaving those behind.'

'It's no good taking them,' said the mate. 'It isn't as

if we were sailing. And you've got the compass to take, anyhow, and the telescope. And, anyway, it's only for one night.'

'Peter Duck'll look after them,' said Titty. 'He knows how important they are. He'll take watch and watch with the ship's parrot.'

'You'd better bring the parrot in now,' said Susan.

Everything that could be done to make the parrot comfortable had been done. He had been given a lovely piece of bacon rind to tear at, and three days' allowance of seed and a lot of fresh water. Also Titty had explained to him carefully how much they were trusting to him, and that he was to be on guard too, so that Peter Duck could take a rest now and then. There was a good deal she would have liked to say to Peter Duck himself, if only he had not happened to be out at the time. So she made things very clear to the parrot. The parrot had been noisier than usual in the camp, saying, 'Twice, twice, two, two, pretty Polly, pieces of eight,' besides several times giving the wild shriek that showed he knew everybody else was agog about something. But as soon as he was put in the cave, though his cage was in a very good place, on the top of the pile of tin boxes, he stopped saying anything at all and it was only too clear that he did not think he was being fairly treated.

ON THE MARCH

'We're coming back tomorrow,' said Titty, 'and you know you wouldn't like it on the top of a mountain.'

But the ship's parrot said nothing and there was a look in its eye that was worse than a lot of things it might have said.

'We can't possibly take him with us,' said Susan.

For one dreadful moment the able-seaman began to think that perhaps she ought to stay behind to look after both Peter Duck and Polly, but she thought better of it.

'It's much darker than this in a tropical forest,' she said, 'even at midday. So you'd better be sensible.' She gave the parrot three lumps of sugar which she had been keeping for him till the last minute and then hurried out of the cave into the sunlight. She slung her knapsack on her back, stuffed her pocket with some of the small pine-cones left over, and was ready to start.

Susan blew out the lantern and followed her. She arranged the big tufts of heather at the mouth of the cave so that no one who did not know of it would guess it was there. On the rocky ground there were no footmarks leading to and from the cave as there would have been in soft turf, and John and Roger had already seen that the bits of broken stick that might have betrayed it had been cleared away. When the four explorers climbed the northern side of Swallowdale and looked back into the empty valley, there was really nothing but the charred stones of the fireplace and the paler patches where the tents had been to show that it had been a camp.

23

Overland to the Amazon

CAPTAIN John once more looked carefully through the Amazons' message. '"About north" is what they say, but really it's north-north-west till we get to that rock.' He looked at the compass. 'North-north-west is what I made it last night, but we'll just have one more look from the watch-tower.'

From the top of the watch-tower everybody turned the telescope towards Rio and Holly Howe, but today there seemed to be no one about. Then they looked the other way at the peak of Kanchenjunga towering into the morning sunlight. It was hard to believe that they were going to the top of it.

'North-north-west it is,' said John, taking the bearing of the jagged rock past which the Amazons had come when they made their attempt to surprise the camp.

'But we needn't go straight across the heather,' said Susan.

'Not if we can find a sheep track,' said the captain.

There seemed to be two or three going in the right direction. John chose a likely one, and in a few minutes the expedition had left the watch-tower and was fairly on its way, walking in Indian file along a narrow sheep track in the heather, John first, then Roger, then Titty, and Susan last of all.

This order was not kept for very long.

'Don't waste pine-cones,' said the able-seaman. 'It's silly when we're still close to our own watch-tower. We shall want all we've got when we're in really unknown country beyond the other rock.'

But Roger's pockets were bursting with pine-cones, and every dozen yards or so he stopped and put two pine-cones in the middle of the sheep track, one crosswise and one pointing along the track. Then, of course, he had to stop to see that Titty and Susan did not tread on them by mistake. Again and again the mate found herself brought up short by Roger crouching in the track to make his patteran and by

Titty who, though she urged him not to waste pine-cones, stood on guard all the same to see that the mate walked over them without moving them. So the mate let the able-seaman and the boy have the track to themselves while she walked in front of them immediately after the captain.

Long before they came to the jagged rock Roger's pockets were empty and he wanted to get a new supply out of his knapsack. This Titty would not allow.

'You see now,' she said, 'if you go on putting them down like that there won't be enough to last and then we shall have no patteran just when we want them most, in the most difficult part of the trail.'

Empty pockets brought the boy to reason and it was agreed that only one pine-cone should be laid at a time, because they knew, anyhow, which way they were going, and that they should be laid a long way apart.

'We don't want a regular string of them,' said Titty. 'We want to be able to find one every now and then so as to be sure that we are in the right way.'

At the jagged rock they caught up the others and looked back.

'We needn't have used a single one so far,' said Titty. 'You can see the watch-tower from here. Where we shall want the patterans is where we can't be sure of the way without them.'

Now, however, unknown country opened before them.

From the rock at which they had first aimed, they moved as nearly as possible due north. The captain kept looking at his compass, choosing a rock or a clump of bracken or heather that bore due north, walking straight to it, and then choosing another in the same way.

They were on a wide ridge of rolling moorland, so that often they could see not more than two or three hundred yards ahead of them and sometimes even less. Sometimes, though, when they were on the top of one of the waves that seemed to cross the moor they could see how the ridge sloped towards the right where, far away, they could see the green tops of larches and pines. Somewhere below those woods must be the lake. Sometimes they could see where the moor began to drop on the other side of the ridge, where also there were the tops of trees showing beyond the heather. Once they caught a glimpse of water on that side very far away, but even with the telescope could see no boats upon it.

'Perhaps it hasn't yet been discovered,' said Titty.

'That's where the swans were going,' said John.

Not all the moorland was covered with heather. There were wide stretches of tall green bracken, and short-cropped grass burnt brown by the sun. Grey rocks rose up out of the grass and heather alike. It was as if an old ragged counterpane of deep purple, patched with scraps of faded green and rusty brown, had been thrown over the earth's skeleton and the bones were showing through the threadbare places. Peewits circled overhead, swooping down towards them, and tumbling and swinging up and away again, shrieking at them as if to say they had no business to be there. Twice a curlew with his long, curved, thin beak stretched before him, screamed shrilly as he passed overhead from one valley to another. Grouse rose suddenly out of the heather, with a loud whirring of wings and a shout of 'Go back! Go back! Go back!'

'No, we won't,' said Roger.

'They wouldn't tell us to go back if they knew what we were going to do,' said Titty. 'They think it has something to do with them. That's why they shout at us.'

Always before them, away to the west of their course, though not much, on the port bow as they would have said if they had been afloat in *Swallow*, rose the great mass of the hill they had agreed to call

Kanchenjunga. It changed its shape a little as they moved northwards. It looked less of a solitary peak, and they could see a deep gully running up into it just above the woods that covered its lower slopes.

By the time the first halt was called all the pine-cones from Roger's knapsack had been used up and Titty's knapsack was not as full as it had been. They had long ago lost sight of the watch-tower. To east of them they could see nothing but the rolling waves of heather. To the west there was less heather and the moorland seemed to come suddenly to an end. Before them the ground seemed to be still rising, though they knew it must sooner or later drop into the valley of the Amazon River. Nor could the end of the ridge be very far away. Going due north over the moor they were steering a straighter course than if they had been sailing to the Amazon from Wild Cat Island, when there was always Rio Bay to allow for and the islands, to say nothing of the wind. The line of their march over the moorland was as straight as a crow's flight, thanks to the captain's careful use of his compass.

He had explained this to Roger.

'It's easier for crows,' said Roger. 'Crows keep their wings still and go on and on without stopping, but if we keep our legs still for a minute nothing happens. We just stick.'

'This is a good place for sticking,' said the mate. 'There's a flat rock for a table. And we must be much more than half-way. Off with the knapsacks. Apples all round.'

'Yes,' said the captain. 'It's no good getting there with any of us tired. We don't know what we may have to do when we come to the river.'

Knapsacks were dumped on the flat rock. Apples were taken out and a moment later only the peewits circling overhead could have known that the explorers were there. All four of them were lying flat on their backs on the dry turf beside the rock (the mate had felt it carefully and said it was not damp) eating their apples and shading their eyes while they blinked up between their fingers into the blue sky.

When they set off again, another half-hour's walking brought them to the edge of the high ground. They looked down into the valley of the Amazon. A spur of the ridge along which they had come reached forward and hid the place where the river flowed out into the lake, but they could see the flash of water here and there in the green meadows far below them, and away to the right, under the foot of a wooded ridge, they could see a long ribbon of pale reeds that widened suddenly on either side of a little glittering tarn.

'That must be the lagoon,' said John. 'Beckfoot must be just round the corner of those woods.'

Though they could not see where the river ran out into the lake, they could see the lake itself, the wide sheet of the northern end of it where they had never been, the Arctic of their maps, and the big hills above it.

'I wonder if any of these hills are as high as Kanchenjunga,' said John.

'They haven't got a peak like his,' said Titty.

'More hummocky,' said John, who felt already towards Kanchenjunga much what he felt towards *Swallow* and Swallowdale and Wild Cat Island.

Looking the other way towards Kanchenjunga himself, they could see that the valley of the Amazon wound round beneath the high ground on which they were standing, so that the mountain was on the farther side of it. Below them woods dropped steeply down toward the meadows in the bottom.

'Let's aim straight for the lagoon,' said Roger. 'We know the Amazons live just the other side of it.'

'Duffer,' said John. 'Coming down that way we could be seen for miles while we were getting across the fields. Besides, if that was the best way they'd have said so.'

'Perhaps nobody would be looking,' said Roger.

'The natives have probably got sentinels posted all round,' said Titty, 'and anyhow we've got to get the canoe.'

Captain John once more opened the message that had been hidden in Nancy Blackett's arrow. He read it all through to himself and then looked down into the valley towards the woods that covered the slopes between the moorland and the meadows.

'Four firs in what used to be a wood,' he said aloud.

Titty had the telescope and handed it to him.

'Over there,' she said, 'it looks as if it might have been a wood some time or other.' She pointed a little to the left where close below the open moor there were short stumpy bushes and patches of rock and bracken and fern, with a few solitary oaks and ashes.

'There are the firs,' shouted John. 'Come on. I thought there were only two, but that was because they're all in a straight line. Come on.'

Titty had only three pine-cones left. She gave them, one at a time, to Roger, and the ship's boy laid them carefully on the ground in clear open spaces, where they could easily be seen.

'The trees'll show us how to find them,' said Titty. 'We can't miss them with the four trees being in a line.'

When the last patteran had been put in its place

the able-seaman and the boy galloped downhill after the captain and the mate, their knapsacks bumping on their backs.

They went a little slower through a broad belt of heather, and after that were picking their way among stumpy little bushes, fresh saplings, fern and moss-covered rocks, and huge old tree stumps still left in the ground.

'Don't go so fast,' panted Roger.

John and Susan were already far ahead of them.

But the captain stopped when he came to the four big fir trees that they had seen from the moor. He pulled out the message again.

'These are the trees all right,' he was saying as Roger and Titty came galumphing down. '"Follow the way they point," it says, and they point down the hill. "Keep to the stone wall." . . . There it is. They're pointing to it.'

It was a tumble-down old wall, built, like all the walls of these parts, of rough stones with no mortar. There were big gaps in it made by the sheep, who always pull down walls sooner or later, but even where no more was left of it than a lot of loose stones lying on the ground where they had fallen, anybody could see that it had at one time been a stone wall running straight up the fell from the valley below.

'Come on,' said John, 'but go quietly. There's the road somewhere in front of us.'

They followed the old wall down from the partly cleared ground into thick bushy forest like the woods round Horseshoe Cove.

'That's why they chose this way,' said John. 'Nobody could see us here. Hullo! Listen! Halt!'

There was the sound of a motor horn only a little way ahead of them. The explorers stiffened like startled hares. The sound died away, and at a signal from John they crept on, pushing their way through the hazel bushes, with the remains of the old wall close on their right.

'Steady, Mister Mate!' whispered John. 'I'll see if the coast is clear.'

'Steady, Able-seaman!' whispered Susan, stopping short.

'Steady, Ship's Boy!' whispered Titty.

'Steady, Roger!' said the ship's boy to himself.

''Sh!' said Titty.

John had seen, close in front of him, a different wall. It was in much better repair than the old wall, and higher, and he guessed at once that the road must lie on the other side of it. At a place where a big copper beech spread its branches over the wall John climbed carefully up and lay at full length along the top, covered by the dark coppery leaves. He lifted a thin spray of leaves so that he could see out. There was nothing on the road. On the other side of the road there was another wall. Beyond it there were grass meadows not long since cut. But the meadows ended only a few yards farther to the left, where another wood began.

'That's the thing to do,' said John to himself. 'We'll cross the road and get into that wood and keep in it along the edge of the fields until we come to the river. Two fields away, they said it was.'

He whistled softly, and a moment later a hand touched his foot. The mate was there.

'Get the others,' he whispered. 'We've got to cross the road.'

He heard the crack of a twig, no more, and then 'All right,' said rather firmly by Roger. His foot was touched again. Another twig cracked. The mate and the crew were just below the wall, ready for orders.

At that moment they heard the quick clumpety clump of horses' feet and the rattle of heavy wheels, and clear above all that noise the loud and cheerful whistling of a tune.

Whispering seemed useless.

'What is it?' said the mate.

Three horses, trotting heavily along with the two

pairs of great wheels on which the big logs are carried from the woods, and Mary Swainson's woodman sitting on the shafts at one side and whistling like the very loudest of all blackbirds, made such a noise that it was quite safe to talk. There was no great log being carried, and the road just here was a little downhill, and the three huge horses, one before the other, were trotting like overgrown colts, with the heavy, red-painted wheels clattering and rattling behind them. They passed in a towering wave of noise, and a moment or two later were out of sight round the next bend in the road, though for some time the explorers could hear their hoofs and wheels, and sometimes the shriller notes of the woodman's whistling.

'I saw them,' said Roger, 'through the hole in the wall. Meant for rabbits, I should think. You can see quite well. It's Mary Swainson's woodman.'

'I thought it must be when I heard the whistling,' said Titty. 'Of course, this must be the same road we cross, going down to Horseshoe Cove. Mary Swainson said they come round by Beckfoot with the big trees from the next valley. I wish I'd seen them too. Was it the same three horses?'

'Shut up, you two, for a minute,' said Susan. 'John says, be quiet and listen. We've got to slip across the road.'

There was a soft thud as John dropped on the grass at the other side of the wall. Susan climbed up where John had been. John was already across the road and looking for a good place at which to cross the other wall. He found a stone jutting out and was up in a moment.

'This is the place,' he called softly. 'Easy climbing. Come one at a time. Send the boy first.'

'Goodbye,' said Roger to Susan, when he had climbed up beside her among the beech leaves.

'We're coming too,' said Titty.

But Roger was scampering across the road. He was already at the foot of the other wall when the horn of a motor sounded beyond the bend.

'Quick!' said John, and reached down to help him. There was a tremendous scrabbling at the wall. Moss flew in all directions, but somehow or other, with John pulling and Roger climbing, he came to the top and rolled over and dropped into the wood on the other side. A motor car, full of natives, shot past down the deserted, empty road.

'Now then, Titty,' said Susan, the moment the motor car was out of sight. 'Your turn. Quick, before something else comes along.'

Titty slithered down out of the dark beech leaves.

'One minute,' she said. 'The last patteran of all.

Just so that we shall know where to get over on the way back. There may be lots of other trees like this one.'

She pulled a tuft of grass and stuffed it firmly in between two stones half-way up the wall.

'If we climb just there on the way back,' she said, 'we'll find a good step on the other side.'

'Buck up, Titty,' called John, and the able-seaman ran across the road, and was soon over the wall and in the wood beyond it where she found the boy, still a little shaken and out of breath.

'I wonder if they had scouts in that motor car,' he said.

'They didn't see anything, anyhow,' said John from the wall just above. 'Hi, Susan. This is much the easiest place.'

There was nothing to stop them now, and they hurried through the trees towards the river. They could see where it was by looking out across the meadows. 'Two fields away,' said John, 'and a stone barn, and then an oak.'

'There's the stone barn,' said Susan. 'It's straight ahead, at the corner of the field, almost touching the wood.'

The trees were already not so thick, and when they came to the barn there was but a strip of green grass between them and the rushes at the river's edge.

'And there's the oak,' said John. 'Stop a minute while I scout.'

He crawled carefully out from among the trees, looking this way and that.

'All clear,' he said, and the four explorers rushed headlong towards the great tree with low, wide-spreading branches that grew at the very edge of the river.

'The Amazon,' said Titty solemnly. 'We ought to lie full length beside it and dip water with our hands to cool our parching throats.'

'Why,' said Susan, 'it's no time since you had an apple.'

But Titty dipped some water for herself and got a little of it into her mouth.

'It's fresh,' she said to Roger. 'It really is the great river of the continent.'

'Is it?' said Roger. 'Where's the boat?'

John and Susan were looking for the war canoe in the rushes on either side of the big tree.

'Perhaps they weren't able to get out to bring it,' said John.

'I see it,' shouted Roger.

He had crawled right in under the branches of

the oak till he could touch its huge trunk. On the other side its branches hung out over the river, the tips of them sweeping the water, and there, under these branches and tied to one of them, hidden so that it could hardly be seen from the river or from the shore except by someone who had crept in under the tree, was a long, narrow, native rowing boat.

'Nobody can beat the Amazons at things like this,' said John.

'But it isn't a war canoe,' said Roger. 'It's the same as Captain Flint's boat, or the one at Holly Howe.'

'It's probably the rowing boat we saw in the boat-house last year,' said John. 'Anyhow, it's beautifully hidden.'

He climbed out on a branch of the oak, untied the painter from it, climbed back, and hauled the boat ashore.

'It's their boat all right,' he said. 'There's "Beckfoot" painted on the stern. Tumble in. You go to the stern, Mister Mate. We'll drift down with the current. I'll take the oars in the bows.'

In another minute the four explorers were crouching in the boat and pulling her out by catching at the oak branches that brushed over them with rustling leaves.

'It's lucky we don't wear hats,' said Roger.

THE HIDDEN BOAT

Inch by inch they worked her out from under the branches. As soon as they were clear, John put the bow oars out. He pulled a stroke now and then to keep her in the current, and they drifted silently downstream between the swaying walls of pale green reeds.

24

The Noon-Tide Owl

THE able-seaman was afloat on the Amazon River for the first time. The other three had been there once before, last year, when they had rowed up to the lagoon in the dark while Nancy and Peggy were sailing down to Wild Cat Island where Titty had been left alone in charge. But you cannot see much of a river in the dark and they were glad to see it by daylight. Besides that, it was pleasant to be in a boat again, even if it was not a sailing boat, but only a war canoe that was very much like one of the ordinary rowing boats of the natives. They soon tired of drifting, and John pulled the boat round, shifted to the middle thwart, and began to row properly, while Roger went to his place in the bows, and Susan called 'Pull right!' or 'Pull left!' so that John could row without looking over his shoulder and yet without running the nose of the war canoe into the reeds.

'We haven't been long, coming over the moor,' said John.

'The desert uplands,' said Titty, almost to herself, as she sat beside the mate in the stern, looking up to the ridge of moorland along which they had marched from Swallowdale, and seeing all she could of the scraps of meadow that showed through the gaps between the reed-beds.

'We've not been long, really,' said John. 'But they want us to be as quick as we can.'

'Here's the lagoon,' said Susan, and the boat shot out into a small lake almost covered by big patches of broad-leaved water lilies. Even in daylight it was hard not to catch them with the oars.

'We were lucky ever to get out of this place that night,' said John.

They crossed the lagoon, keeping to the river channel that made a lane between the patches of water lilies. Then the reed-beds on either side closed in on them again and once more they were in the narrow river. On the right bank, trees came down to the water's edge.

'Steady,' said the mate. 'We shall be in sight of the house in half a minute. I can see its roof already. This must be the wood they meant.'

John glanced over his shoulder, shipped his right oar, and backwatered gently with his left. The war canoe swung round and slid with a low swishing noise into the reeds, on and on until even Susan and Titty, sitting in the stern, had reeds all round them. It lost way. John stood up and used an oar as a pole. Another yard through the reeds, another foot, and 'Can you jump it, Roger?'

There was a jerk astern as the ship's boy jumped. Then with another jerk the painter drew taut, and he hauled the boat's nose up against the soft shelving bank.

For the last time Captain John read carefully through the message from the Amazons. Then he gave it to the mate.

'I might be captured,' he said, 'and it would be a pity to have to swallow it.'

He stepped ashore.

'Be ready to cast off in a moment,' he said. 'And if you're attacked pull across to the other side of the river. Don't leave the boat. Stay in it or close to it. You'll hear the owl calls, I should think. But whatever other noises there are, don't come. That's right, Roger, don't make the painter fast. Be ready to slip and bolt for it.'

He was gone.

*

Mate Susan laid the oars ready, but inside the boat, so that if she had to shove off in a hurry they would not catch in the reeds. She went ashore to see if the ship's boy was in a dry place or getting his feet wet, for the reeds were so thick that she could see nothing from the boat. She listened for the noise of breaking twigs or the rustle of last year's leaves that would show where the captain was. But there was not a sound. The trees in the wood were close together and very thick. It would be possible for natives to creep through them until they were so near the bank that they could dash out and seize the boat. The mate thought it better to have everybody aboard. Roger found that the painter was just long enough to go round a tussock of grass and back into the bows of the boat, so that he could sit in the boat and hold the end of it and be ready to let go in a second. A ration of chocolate was served out.

'He's been gone ten minutes at least,' said the mate.

'Nearly an hour,' said Roger.

Then came the owl call. 'Tu whoooooooooooo.

Tu whoooooooooooooo.' It sounded a long way from the river.

'He's done it beautifully,' said the mate. 'I've never heard him do it so well.'

'Anybody might think it was a real one,' said Titty.

'Some real ones aren't half so good,' said Roger.

There was silence for about a minute. Then again they heard the owl call, far away, but not, they thought, in quite the same place. Then silence for a very long time.

'Perhaps he's fallen into an ambush,' said Titty. 'Hadn't we better go and help?'

'He said we were to stick to the boat. He may have had to go a long way round to get back.'

They sat still, listening, hardly breathing. For a long time there was no noise at all. Then they heard a branch creak and steps on the bank, and a moment later the reeds parted and there was John.

'Hullo!' he said. 'Aren't they here?'

'No,' said Roger.

'They're coming. At least I think they are.'

'Did you see them?' asked Susan.

'Were they behind bars?' asked Titty, 'or had they already got out? Were they in disguise? And, oh, John, did you see anybody else?'

''Sh!' said John. 'Listen!'

They listened but could hear nothing.

'It was awful. The first thing I saw on the lawn in front of the house, just the other side of the wood, was Captain Flint and Mrs Blackett and the great-aunt herself. . . .'

'Did she look all right?' asked Titty.

'Of course she did. She was walking about with a stick pointing at things on the lawn. I couldn't see what she was pointing at. So I slunk on in the wood till I had got right round behind the house. Then I gave the owl call.'

'We heard it,' said Roger.

'Nancy Blackett was at one of the upstairs windows at once. She put her hand to her lips as if she meant me to shut up. Then I saw Nancy and Peggy creeping out of a back door and going off the wrong way. So I had to do the owl call again, just to show them where I was. But it only made them bolt like anything.'

'If they've seen you and heard the owl call, we needn't do anything more,' said the mate. 'They know where we are, because we've done just what they told us to do.'

'Well, I hope it's all right,' said John. 'Everybody else must have heard the owl calls too.'

'They were both beauties,' said Roger.

'What's that?' said John, sharply.

Steps were coming nearer through the wood.

'Here they are.'

Suddenly there was the noise of heavier steps. Someone was running hard, and then close to them, behind the screen of pale reeds and dark green leaves, they heard a sort of squeak cut off short.

"Sh! You tame galoot.' This was Nancy's voice and it went on in an altogether different tone. 'Friends or enemies, Uncle Jim?'

'Betwixt and between,' came the answer of Captain Flint.

'Lurk, lurk,' whispered John, and the four explorers crouched in the boat. The voices were only a yard or two away.

'Betwixt and between,' Captain Flint was saying. 'I don't know what you're up to, and I won't ask. But you're up to something, and all I want to say is that it won't be fair on your mother and me if you don't get back by five thirty. Remember it's the last day. I'll hold the fort for you till then, driving her round. But if you fail to show up when we come back, it'll be more than I can manage to put things straight.'

'Honest pirate! We'll be back.'

'That's all right,' said Captain Flint. 'Now then, I haven't seen your allies and I'd rather not, but just you tell them from me, if you *should* happen to meet them, that if they want to give a signal right bang in the middle of the day, it wouldn't be so hard on their friends if they'd choose blackbirds or jays instead of owls. Your Aunt Maria wants to write to the Natural History Museum about it. She says she's never heard one at midday before. You tell them to be jays next time. Easier for me.'

'Come on and see them.' This was Nancy's voice again. 'They must be close here.'

'I don't care where they are. I haven't seen them and I'd rather not know anything about them. The midday owl's put a weight on my conscience already, to say nothing of "Casabianca".'

There was a laugh, quiet for Nancy's, and the noise of Captain Flint's footsteps going away.

*

John jumped ashore again, through the rushes. The boughs parted, and Captain Nancy, with a big fishing-creel slung on her back, and Mate Peggy, carrying a big white bedroom jug, pushed their way out from among the trees.

'Well done, Skipper,' cried Nancy, on seeing John. 'You've hit the very place. Others all here? Hullo, Mister Mate. Did you hear my mate squeak just now? A galoot she is, a tame galoot. Anybody might have heard her. Hullo, Roger. How are you, Able-seaman? Let's get aboard. There isn't a minute to lose. You heard what Captain Flint said?'

'What was it he said about "Casabianca"?' asked Titty.

'Not that. I mean about our having to be back by half-past five. We really must, and there's only just time to show you the way. Come on, Peggy. Easy there with the grog.'

'Well, you take it,' said Peggy. 'It's an awful weight. And you needn't talk about my squeaking. Anybody would have squeaked just then. I thought we were done for.'

'All the more reason for not squeaking,' said Nancy. 'The trouble with you is, you never know when not to squeak.'

'Yes, I do.'

'No, you don't. You very nearly went and squeaked over the "Casabianca" business, and then you'd have got Uncle Jim and Mother into trouble too.'

'Well, who's making a noise now?'

'True for you,' said Nancy under her breath. 'Let's be moving, Captain John. It would be too awful if the G.A. found out you were here.'

'Sit down everybody,' said John quietly.

Susan, Titty, Roger, Nancy, and Peggy, sat down,

where they were, in the stern and amidships. John pushed off with an oar over the bows. The war canoe, now heavily laden and more like a rowing boat than ever, brushed out through the reeds and, the moment it was clear of them, began to drift downstream. It was now Nancy's turn to squeak.

'Shiver my timbers,' she said. 'Out with those oars. Quick! Quick! Another ten yards and we'll be below the wood and in full view of the lawn.'

There was a desperate scrabble to get the oars out, and one of them hit the water with a splash. That very instant Peggy quacked like a duck, indeed, so very like a duck that Roger looked about him expecting to see a duck rise out of the reeds.

'Well done,' said Captain Nancy. 'She really is good at ducks. And they often come in handy.'

John had the oars in the bow rowlocks by now and had pulled a hard stroke or two. The war canoe moved upstream again along the wooded bank.

'That was a narrow shave,' said Nancy. 'They'd have been bound to see us from the lawn.'

'What are they doing on the lawn?' asked John. 'The great-aunt was poking at things and showing them to Mrs Blackett.'

'Daisies, probably,' said Nancy. 'Ragging Mother about them. She says there never used to be any on the lawn and now there are lots, and every time she gets Mother into the garden she tells her about the daisies all over again.'

'Daisies?' said Roger, with wide open eyes.

'She's never missed a day,' said Peggy. 'It's always the same. As if Mother could help it.'

'Straight up the river, Captain John,' said Nancy. 'Keep her moving.'

'But what was it Captain Flint said about "Casabianca"?' asked Titty again.

'It was very sporting of him,' said Nancy. 'If it hadn't been for him we shouldn't be here now, and you would have made your march for nothing, and everything would have gone wrong. You don't know what it's been like the last few days. . . .'

'Was it very bad when you got back that night after watching those hounds?' asked Susan.

'Dreadful,' said Nancy. 'All leave stopped. Boathouse out of bounds. . . .'

'We wanted to bale out *Amazon*, and had to get out of bed and creep out and do it in the middle of the night,' said Peggy.

'We weren't allowed to come and see you any more,' said Nancy. 'That's why the message had to be so secret. . . .'

'And on the way back from the boathouse there

was an awful moment,' said Peggy. 'We were pretending she was a heathen goddess, and she looked out when we thought she was asleep and saw us bowing our heads to the ground in the moonlight under her bedroom window.'

Titty interrupted them both.

'Was the great-aunt ill when you came back that night after being in Swallowdale?'

'Ill?' said Nancy. 'Ill? Never in better form. She made the worst row that night she's made ever since she came to stay. What are you looking so pleased about?'

'Oh, nothing,' said Titty. 'But do go on about "Casabianca".'

'Coming to that,' said Nancy. 'Do shut up, Peggy, just for a minute. You see, the whole thing is, she's going away tomorrow. . . .'

'Not really?' said John, suddenly resting on his oars.

'Yes. But do keep on rowing. We've got a long way to go before we're safe. She's going tomorrow. We shan't see her again till next year. Perhaps not then, if only she comes in term-time.'

'Hurrah!' shouted Roger.

'Sh!' said Susan.

'She wanted us to be made to drive round with her this afternoon to pay her farewell calls. Just when everything was working out beautifully. We'd sent the message with the arrow, and got out last night and hid the boat under the oak, and we'd told Cook about your coming, and she'd made us enough grog to drown an admiral and crammed this basket full of grub and hung it up behind the back door so that we could swipe it without her having to know. Somehow or other the G.A. guessed that we were up to something. That's why she asked us to come out with her this afternoon. And we were expecting your owl call any minute. We couldn't tell her that, so we simply had to say we'd rather not, and she was very snuffy indeed and said that all the time she's been here she'd never once heard us recite any poetry, and that as this was her last day we could learn a bit during the afternoon and let her hear it when she came back from leaving cards on people and giving them the good news that she was clearing out.'

'Things looked very black and beastly,' said Peggy.

'She said Mother and Uncle Jim used to learn a poem every week, and we knew they did, because they'd told us how awful it was, and then, luckily, she asked Uncle Jim what would be a good bit of poetry for us to learn. And he saved us, and said "Casabianca", and Mother went out of the room in a hurry.'

'But how did that save you?' asked Titty. 'It's a pretty long poem.'

'Because we knew it already, and Uncle Jim knew that we knew it. We had to learn it at school.'

'Theboystoodontheburningdeckwhenceallbuthehad *fled*,' rattled Peggy.

'So her dark plot was jolly well dished,' said Nancy, 'and here we are.'

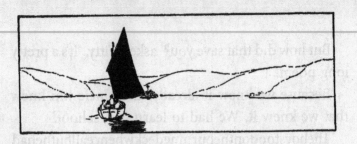

25

Up River

ABOVE the lagoon the current seemed to be faster, and John began to wish that the war canoe were not so deep in the water. He could see Nancy looking at the reeds at the side of the river, and he knew that she was thinking how slowly they were moving past. But presently Nancy said, 'We're not safe yet, you know. Let's get the other pair of oars out and make her hum. The G.A.'ll be driving round to the head of the lake and crossing the river at Udal Bridge, and we'd better get above it and out of sight, or Mother and Uncle Jim will be dished as well as all of us if the G.A. happens to see us with you while she's driving round.' After that, with John and Nancy rowing and Peggy telling them which side to pull hardest, they went up the river at such a pace that there might have been no current at all.

'What are we going to do now?' asked Roger, and Peggy was just going to say something, when Nancy stopped her.

'Wait till we get to the first cataract,' she panted. 'No talking about plans while we're rowing. It isn't fair.'

The war canoe swung upstream, past the great oak tree.

'We wouldn't have found the boat if I hadn't crawled in under the branches,' said Roger.

'It's the best hiding place on the river,' said Peggy. 'Once when we were little and Nurse was looking for us, we got into the river underneath it, and crouched there like hippopotamuses with the water up to our necks, and she passed close by the tree and never saw us. But you've no idea what a job it was getting the boat there last night, and tying it under the tree in the dark.'

'Did you do it at night?' said Roger.

'Of course,' said Peggy. 'Pull right, pull right.'

Above the oak there was a bend in the river and then a straight stretch with little bushes on the banks and no reeds, and at the top of this stretch there was a wide arched stone bridge carrying the road that went round to the head of the lake.

'Are we going through the bridge?' asked Titty.

'In the boat?' asked Roger.

Nancy took a quick look over her shoulder, and then, still rowing hard, spoke to John.

'We can't quite shoot it against the stream,' she panted. 'We go for it full tilt, ship our oars, and scrabble through with our hands. Then as soon as there's room you get your oars out again and pull for all you're worth. Peggy'll sing out when to ship. She knows. We've done it again and again by ourselves. It's easier with someone to sing out. Now then, put your back into it.'

She had been rowing a hard, fast stroke before, but now she rowed faster still. Luckily John had done this sort of thing before, and was able to keep time. There was a good deal of splash, but that hardly mattered. What did matter was speed.

Roger half stood up with excitement, but the next stroke of the two captains sent the boat forward with such a jerk that he sat down hard and there was really no need for Mate Susan to tell him to sit still.

'Right! Right! . . . As you are. . . . Left. . . . A wee bit more. You're going straight for it. . . .' Peggy shouted her orders. 'Two more strokes. . . . Ship your oars!'

As he heard the last word John was already in the shadow of the bridge. There was a rattle and crash as all four oars were lifted from the rowlocks and brought inboard.

'Quick! Quick!' shouted Nancy. 'Keep her going.' She was standing in the boat, stooping a little and grabbing at one stone after another under the curved arch of the bridge.

John did the same.

'Heave her along,' shouted Nancy. 'Don't let her slip back.' Foot by foot the nose of the rowing boat came out above the bridge. John was through.

'Out with your oars the moment you can,' cried Nancy. 'Quick! She'll swing. Don't let her. Never mind. (The blade of an oar hit the stonework.) Pull! Good! Oh, good! She's through now.' Nancy had her oars out in half a second and watched for John's blades going forward, brought her own after them and with the next stroke was pulling as well as he. 'It's pretty hard work with so much water coming down. That's all that rain we had the other night.'

'You've got a lot of blood on your hand,' said Susan.

'So I have,' said Nancy. 'I usually do. Some of these stones are pretty sharp. We're nearly there, and then

I'll give it a wash. Can't stop till we're round that corner.'

Again the river twisted. The bridge was hidden by trees. There was a loud noise of splashing waters. Not very far ahead of them the smooth water ended in foam-covered rocks and a line of low waterfalls that marked the place where the mountain stream changed into the placid little river that wound through the meadows to the lake.

'First Cataract,' said Peggy.

'Nobody can row up that,' said Roger.

'Nobody's going to try. We land there. By that splashing. There's an eddy on this side.'

Nancy glanced over her shoulder.

'Safe now,' she said. 'Ship your oars, Captain John. I know the place. You'd better let me take her in.'

John shipped his oars, while Nancy rowed on, nearer and nearer to the line of falling, splashing water above them. Suddenly she pulled two strokes as hard as she could and then lifted her blades high out of the water, as the boat shot forward between two rocks. Again Nancy pulled a couple of strokes, and a moment later, so close to the falls that John in the bows felt the cold spray blowing on his face, the boat slipped across a patch of dead water and came to rest beside a shelving rock on the left bank of the river.

UP THE AMAZON RIVER

'Hop out, Skipper,' called Nancy loudly, so as to be heard in spite of the noise of foaming waters. 'Hop out. Make fast to that little rowan. Hang on to the rock, somebody in the stern, or she'll swing round under the falls. She did once, and got swamped.'

John was already ashore with the painter. Susan grabbed the rock just in time and hung on to it till Nancy had followed John ashore, when Peggy flung her a rope and made it fast to a ring-bolt in the stern. In a few minutes the Beckfoot war canoe was moored alongside the rock, the painter tied to the little rowan, and the long warp from the stern fastened round a big stone.

'Now for the cargo,' called Nancy cheerfully, and Susan, Roger, Titty, and Peggy passed up the knapsacks of the Swallows and the big fishing-creel and bedroom jug that belonged to the Amazons.

John and Susan were very glad that this stage of the expedition was safely over. There was something about these Amazons hard for them to understand. It was clear that they had been forbidden to have anything to do with the Swallows, that they had been forbidden to touch their own boats, since the boathouse was out of bounds, that they were supposed at that very minute to be sitting somewhere solemnly learning poetry by heart. Yet, they had got into touch with the Swallows by sending that arrow with its message from the very launch in which their enemy was being taken for a picnic; they had visited the boathouse at dead of night, once just for baling, and once more seriously, to bring the rowing boat up the river and hide it under the oak; and here they were, doing the very thing that it seemed the great-aunt was most determined that they should not do. Of course, there was this to be remembered, that it almost seemed as if Captain Flint and Mrs Blackett were privately on the same side as Nancy and Peggy. At the same time it was a very good thing that they had got through the bridge and out of sight round the bend above it before the great-aunt came driving by and saw the Allies all rowing up the river together. If she had seen them, the whole thing would have been very difficult to explain, and whatever Mrs Blackett might think about it, it was just the sort of trouble in which Mother, away at Holly Howe, would not like them to be mixed. Susan almost wished they had not come. Why couldn't Nancy have waited a day if the great-aunt was leaving? John, of course, knew that Nancy would not have been Nancy if she had. Titty did not consider this side of the affair. One thing was quite clear, and that was that the burning of the candle-grease, just as Mother and Susan had said, had done no serious harm to the great-aunt. At the same time, the great-aunt had made up her mind to leave. Was it possible that candle-grease had something to do with it after all? She would very much have liked to ask whether the great-aunt was going to the seaside or just to some ordinary place. As for Roger, after the excitement of going down to Beckfoot and bringing the Amazons away, and shooting the bridge, and mooring close by the cataract, he was thinking that it must be long past dinner-time. He said so.

'We've had ours,' said Peggy.

'We haven't,' said Roger.

'We didn't eat much,' said Peggy. 'We meant to start again.'

There was not much talk while Nancy was unpacking the big fishing-basket. The Swallows had had an early breakfast. They had marched from Swallowdale to the Amazon River and had eaten on the way only an apple apiece and some chocolate. Instead of stopping to eat by the big oak tree, they had pushed off and gone down to Beckfoot at once, for fear there might be some urgent reason for hurry. The moment they began to think about food and to see food unpacked, they wanted it badly, and for a time could think of little else.

Mate Susan wanted to open one of the two pemmican tins, but Nancy would not let her.

'You'll want it tonight, where you're going to sleep,' she said. 'And you'll want the other for the top of Kanchenjunga.'

'Besides,' said Peggy, 'it's no good taking things back to Cook. She doesn't like it and she only gives you less next time. And she's fairly stuffed the old fishing-basket.'

She certainly had. John and Susan saw at once that one person at least at Beckfoot had nothing against the goings-on of Captain Nancy and her mate. Cook had given them a fat beef roll, like a bigger and better kind of sausage. There were enough apple dumplings to go round. There were lettuces and radishes and salt in a little tin box. There was a lot of cut brown bread and butter. There was a hunk, the sort of hunk that really is a hunk, a hunk big enough for twelve indoor people and just right for six sailors, of the blackest and juiciest and stickiest fruit cake. And then to wash these good things down, there was the bedroom jug full of pirate grog, which some people might have thought was lemonade. Lemonade or grog, whatever it was, it suited thirsty throats. Altogether this dinner among the rocks, close to the leaping splashing water of the First Cataract, was one of those after which everybody feels a little sleepy but ready for anything when the sleepiness has worn off.

'Where did you say we were going to sleep?' said Susan at last.

'Half-way up the mountain,' said Nancy, tipping the last dregs of her lemonade down her throat. (She and Peggy shared one of the two glasses Cook had put in their basket. John and Susan shared the other. Titty and Roger shared the mug that the expedition had brought with it from Swallowdale.)

'Half-way up?' said Titty, looking up at the woods that hid the mountain from them.

'Half-way up,' said Nancy. 'It's a fine place for a camp, just above the tree level. You see the whole thing is this. The great-aunt is going tomorrow, so we can come and join the camp at Swallowdale. . . .'

'Good,' said John.

'Wait a minute,' said Nancy. 'There's something else. *Swallow* is nearly finished. Uncle Jim said nothing left to do but a lick of paint.'

'Not really,' said Titty, jumping to her feet.

'That's why he sent the message for me to hurry up with the mast,' said John.

'Well, the thing is that as soon as you've got *Swallow* again you'll be moving back to Wild Cat Island.'

'Rather,' said John.

'And you're coming too, and we'll make a cave there, like Peter Duck's,' said Titty.

'Anyway,' said Nancy, 'we'll all be wanting to sail. And you can't both sail and climb Kanchenjunga. And we can't camp in Swallowdale and Wild Cat Island at the same time. So we're coming to Swallowdale tomorrow night. And we'll climb Kanchenjunga first. That's why it was so important to get the message to you. We've saved a whole day.'

'But you can't climb Kanchenjunga now,' said Susan. 'You've got to be back by half-past five.'

'That's why you're going to sleep half-way up the mountain. It's proper to have a half-way camp, anyway. You see, the G.A. goes at eight o'clock tomorrow morning.'

'Five minutes to eight,' said Peggy. 'I heard them making up their minds how long it would take to get to Rio and then up to the station, and they said they must start at five minutes to, if there wasn't to be a rush at the last minute.'

'They don't want her to miss the train,' said Nancy. 'Anyway, two minutes after they've gone (it'll take us that long to get into pirate rig), we'll row up the river like smoke, leave the boat here, climb up the way we'll show you, and join you at the Half-Way Camp. By nine we'll be with you, bringing the rope, and then, all together, we'll make the last dash for the peak.'

'You'll have to go back to Beckfoot again to get your tent and things.'

'We'll get the tent all stowed in *Amazon* tomorrow morning early. Then, when we've conquered Kanchenjunga, we can all sail down to Horseshoe Cove together.'

'Don't forget about the race,' said Peggy.

'Oh, yes. Uncle Jim says *Swallow*'s going to be as good as ever, and he wants us to race to see how much *Amazon* can beat her by. And Mother's agreed about our going to Swallowdale, and she wants you to come to Beckfoot. She wanted you to come before, but she couldn't ask you because of the G.A. And Mrs Walker is coming too, and Vicky. . . .'

'Bridgie,' said Titty.

'And that's to be as soon as ever *Swallow* comes back. We'll race you right up the lake. Uncle Jim says he'll start us. Finish at Beckfoot for the feast.'

'Right,' said John. 'Fair sailing. No oars to be used.'

'Shall we give you some start?' said Roger.

'Humph!' said Captain Nancy. 'If you were in my crew. . . .'

'Lucky for you, you aren't,' said Mate Peggy.

'Look here,' said Nancy, 'there really isn't much

time. We've got to show you the way. Don't bother about the jug and the basket. We'll pick them up on the way back. Let's have that knapsack of yours, A.B., and my mate'll carry the boy's. You've had a fair day's march already.'

'Our knapsacks were heavier when we started,' said Roger. 'Full of pine-cones.'

'Whatever for?' said Peggy.

'Patterans,' said Titty. 'Good ones. We laid a trail of them across the moor for finding our way back.'

'Well, you won't want them tomorrow,' said Nancy. 'When we come down from Kanchenjunga, we'll all sail down in *Amazon* so there won't be any marching.'

'Roger and I are going back over our trail,' said Titty. 'That's what we put the pine-cones for.'

'Yes,' said Roger, rather doubtfully, and then, with more firmness, 'There's no room for anyone before the mast in *Amazon*. I looked last year, and I'm bigger now.'

'Oughtn't we to get some milk before we start up?' said Susan.

'We'll get milk at Watersmeet. That's where Peggy and I'll have to turn back.'

They hurried along the rocky bank between the woods and the river, a little river now so noisy that it was hard to believe it was the same quiet stream that flowed under the great oak and through the meadows of the lower valley. Here there was no room for a boat, and even a small canoe would have been battered to bits among the stones. There were woods on both banks, though here and there, through the trees, the explorers saw green fields and feeding cattle. Sometimes, at bends of the river, they caught just a glimpse of the mountain they had come to climb.

'Is it true there are wild goats up there?' asked Roger.

'Not lots,' said Peggy, 'but there are some.'

Nancy, who led the way at such a pace that nobody had much breath to spare, stopped at last where a stream, too wide to cross without paddling, poured down out of the woods to join the little river, which, as the Swallows now saw, flowed down the valley between Kanchenjunga and the great ridge of moorland along the top of which they had walked from Swallowdale.

'The farm's just through these trees,' said Nancy, dumping the able-seaman's knapsack on the ground. 'Let's have that milk-can of yours, Captain John. Come too, if you like.'

She and John hurried off with the milk-can and disappeared among the trees. They were soon back, but the milk-can was only a quarter full.

'They haven't milked yet,' said Nancy. 'I was a galoot not to think of it. But there's enough for some tea, and they'll fill the can for you as soon as the cows come in. You'll have to wait here. Anyway, there wouldn't be time for us to come right up to the place where you'll sleep. But you can't miss it. Follow the beck right up till you come out of the trees and you'll find yourself in a gorge half-way up the mountain. That's the place. There's a path, of course, but naturally you wouldn't use it. You can get up by following the beck. We'll be with you at nine o'clock tomorrow morning, with the rope. Come on, Peggy. Right about turn. We've got to stir our stumps and then row fit to bust the oars. Come on. Back to best frocks and "Casabianca"! Tomorrow Kanchenjunga and the roof of the world!'

'Won't you have some tea, too?' asked Susan.

'No time.' Peggy was wriggling out of the straps of the boy's knapsack. 'So long, Swallows,' she said, and hurried after Nancy, who was already on her way back down the valley to the place where they had left the Beckfoot war canoe. For a few moments the Swallows watched the two red knitted caps bobbing up, now here, now there, along the rocky wooded bank until they were hidden by a bend in the river.

'What time is it?' asked Susan.

John showed her his watch.

'They haven't much time to lose,' she said.

'The rowing's all downstream,' said John. 'They ought to do it all right.'

The explorers rested where they were. The Amazons, Nancy particularly, always left them a little out of breath. When she was there, things seemed to move so fast. Now that she was gone, it was a few minutes before things settled. For these few minutes everything seemed in a whirl like the dust and bits of paper in a railway station when an express train has roared through.

But presently Roger wriggled down the rocks till he could see into a small pool of clear water in the little stream that came rushing down through the trees from somewhere high on Kanchenjunga. He wanted to know if the trout he had frightened under a stone was going to show himself again. 'Don't move, Roger,' called Titty. 'There's a dipper, bobbing . . . there. . . . Farther up. . . . On the other side. . . .' John looked at his watch and then tried to find a place where the trees did not get in the way, so that he could see the top of the mountain. 'It's not a bad thing that we've got to wait for the milk,' he said. 'We can't be very far from the camping place, and it'd be a pity to get there too early.'

'Hi,' called Susan, 'don't you go and tumble in, Roger. Let's find a place for a fire, and then all hands to gather wood.'

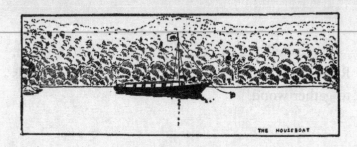

THE HOUSEBOAT

26

The Half-Way Camp

THEY had had tea. They had bathed. They had scouted through the trees to see what sort of a farmhouse it was that John had visited with Nancy. They had decided that it was more like Dixon's Farm than Swainson's, although, as Roger pointed out, there were no geese. They had returned to the place where the waters met, where they had left their knapsacks, and were already thinking that it must be time to fetch the milk, when a small boy, not bigger than Roger, carrying a huge milk-can, came out of the trees.

'Where's your can?' he said. 'Mother says you're to have it filled for you.'

Susan had washed out the can and now gave it to the small boy. He put it on the ground, filled it to the very brim out of his big can, ran his finger round the edge where some milk had slopped over, licked his finger and was just starting back when he seemed to change his mind. He put his can down, turned round and put both hands in his pockets.

'Where be you going?' he asked. 'Up the beck?'

'Yes,' said Susan.

'Foxes up there,' he said. 'Bite you. I'm not afraid of them.'

'Neither are we,' said Roger.

'Eight lambs they took, and eighteen fat pullets. Ask my Dad.'

'Jacky,' a loud call sounded through the trees, followed by a louder, 'JACKEE!'

The small boy winked, picked up his can, said, 'Happen I'd best be going,' and went slowly off again into the wood.

'Oh, bother,' said Roger a minute later, 'I never asked him about the goats.'

'Never mind about the goats,' said John. 'Shoulder

packs. We can be getting on. All right, Susan, I'll take the milk.'

Two minutes later the explorers were once more on the march.

*

Almost at once they began to climb. This stream hurrying down from Kanchenjunga fell far more steeply than the little beck that had led the able-seaman and the boy to the discovery of Swallowdale. It dropped sometimes ten, twenty feet at a time into pools from which the white foam spirted high in air to meet it. The explorers were glad they had no sticks to hamper them. They were glad to use their hands to cling to rock or tree as they pulled their way up. Careful as he was, John spilt a little of the milk, not more than a drop or two, but enough to show that anybody else would have spilt a lot. Sometimes they caught a glimpse of a path not far away, but remembering what Nancy Blackett expected of them, they took no notice of it whatever.

The evening sun shone down through the trees above them. It would soon be hidden behind the shoulder of the mountain, but when they looked back from high in the wood, they looked through the tops of pine and dark fir to broad sunlit country already far away. The hills beyond Rio now showed over the

Swallowdale moors, and beyond those hills they could see hills more distant still, faint and blue, like clouds that had borrowed colour from the sky.

On and on they climbed, and came suddenly out of the trees into a ravine of naked stone and heather. They stopped short. The sun had that moment sunk behind the mountain above them, but it still lit the tops of the pine trees they had left. Presently these, too, were in shadow, though for some time yet the explorers, looking back, could see bright sunshine on the distant hills. To the left the peak of Kanchenjunga rose above the lesser crags that curved about the head of the ravine. Far up among those crags they could see thin white lines where the becks were still carrying off the water collected on the tops. To right and left of them were rough fells through which it seemed that the little stream at their feet had carved a channel fit for a river a thousand times bigger than itself.

'Isn't he a beauty?' said Titty.

'Who?' said Roger.

'Kanchenjunga, of course. He's the finest mountain in the world. I say, Susan, let's put our things down, and run up just this little bit so that we can look out over the trees.'

'Go ahead,' said Susan. 'I suppose this *is* the place for the camp?'

'It must be,' said John, and putting down milk-can and knapsacks they climbed the side of the ravine and then, resting, looked back once more, out of the shadow, over the sunlit country far away.

'You can't see Rio,' said Titty. 'I thought perhaps you could. But we'll be able to see it from the top.'

'Hullo,' said John. 'Let's have the telescope.' Titty had brought it up in hopes of seeing Holly Howe. She gave it to John, who looked through it, not at the distant country but at the Swallowdale moors. He had seen, even without the telescope, the grey blob of the watch-tower. Everybody looked at it in turn. There was the rock, and the dark patch of water in the middle of the heather that they knew was Trout Tarn. Just beyond the rock must be Swallowdale itself. Titty thought of the parrot and Peter Duck taking care of the cave. 'I expect they'll be quite all right,' she said.

'Who?' said John.

'Polly and Peter Duck. They'll be keeping each other company, just like Mother and Bridget. Bridget'll be in bed. It's a pity we aren't a little bit higher, so that Mother could see our fire.'

'We'd better be making it,' said Susan, 'and getting bracken or heather for beds before it's dark.'

They gathered fallen branches in the top of the wood and cut a lot of bracken to make a soft place for their sleeping-bags. Then, while Susan was boiling some water over the camp fire, John opened a tin of pemmican, and the explorers had a simple and well-earned supper, just a scrap of pemmican for each of them, and some bunloaf after it, and a bit of chocolate, while the expedition's one mug was refilled again and again with milk and a little tea and went round and round like a loving-cup.

Very soon after supper Susan blew her mate's whistle, two short puffs and a long one, which means, 'You are standing into danger, so look out.' Titty and Roger, who had been doing a little exploring in the dusk, knew what it meant and came running back to the camp where the fire was already beginning to look like a night fire, more flame than smoke, instead of like a day fire, which, in bright sunlight, often looks as if it has no flames at all.

'What danger?' asked Roger eagerly.

'Getting into trouble for going late to bed,' said Susan 'Hop in and go under.'

Titty was in her sleeping-bag in a moment. It was the first time in her life that she had ever slept half-way up a mountain and she did not want to waste a minute of it.

'It feels very naked going to bed without a tent,' said Roger.

NIGHT ON THE MOUNTAIN

'It's all right,' said John. 'I tried it last night.'

'Do I go under clothes and all?'

'Clothes and all,' said the mate, 'and hurry up.'

'Where are you going to be? And John?'

'Close to you.'

'Near enough to touch?'

'Yes. But don't do any touching when we've got to sleep.'

'Not even if the foxes come nosing round, like that boy said.'

'Not for anything short of bears,' said John, 'and there are no bears. Remember you're going to climb the peak tomorrow.'

'What am I to think about to get to sleep quickly?'

'Count the feathers in the ship's parrot,' said Titty. 'It's much worse for him, poor dear, in the cave. It's as if he'd had his cover on all day.'

Roger snuggled down in his bag. The stuffing in the bags was better than nothing, and with the bracken underneath he was comfortable enough.

'Who's going to keep watch?' said Titty hopefully.

'Not you,' said the mate. 'Go under and see if you can get to sleep before Roger. . . . If anybody wants a hot bottle,' she added presently, 'I could put a hot stone from the fire at the foot of their sleeping-bag.'

'I'm as hot as anything,' said Titty.

There was no answer from Roger.

'Lucky there's no wind,' said the mate.

'It's almost stuffy,' said John.

For some time he and the mate sat by the camp fire.

'So long as they're warm I suppose it's all right,' said the mate at last.

'Of course it is,' said the captain.

The shapes of the tree-tops grew harder and harder to see against the darkening western sky. Only, far above them, there was still light behind the mountain. The mate carefully built in her fire with clods of earth that she had cut with a knife and pulled up with her fingers. Like that, it would last till morning.

'We're here, anyway,' she said. 'So even if it is all wrong it can't be helped now.'

'But it isn't all wrong,' said John.

*

Ten minutes later four bundles lay side by side in the dusk. For a long time now the two middle bundles had stirred so little that they might have had nothing in them but old clothes. The two outer bundles were still wriggling to find positions in which bones and stones did not press too hard on each other.

There was quiet except for the stream and the waterfalls in the steep woods below the camp.

One of the outer bundles whispered across the two inner ones, 'Are you all right, Susan?'

'Yes.'

'Good night.'

'Good night.'

Far away, down in the valley, an owl called.

John heard it, and thinking with a chuckle of that other owl that had been awake at midday, fell happily asleep.

*

Not one of the explorers slept all night without waking. But they woke at different times. Roger was wide awake for a minute or two, thinking he heard wild goats. He listened as hard as he could, but there was no other noise than the breathing of the others, and of course the stream and the waterfalls in the woods. He put out a hand to touch Susan's sleeping-bag. It was still there and she was in it. He made sure of that, but did not wake her, and when she woke herself a little later, he was already asleep again.

Susan sat up when she woke, sniffing the wood smoke from her smothered fire. Very carefully she wriggled out of her bag and covered up a place where the fire was trying to find its way through its blanket of earth. She damped the earth with a little water from the kettle. A drop of water hissed on a hot ember, sounding to her so loud that she thought the others would be sure to wake. It felt queer to stand up there, half-way up a mountain in the dark, and to know that the three dim bundles at her feet were the captain and the crew. But she felt warm and the others were fast asleep, and in their bags must be warmer still. She wriggled in again without waking them and went to sleep again a good deal happier.

John was awake for a minute or two before he knew that he was not in Swallowdale. Then he felt for his chronometer, wondering what time it was, and forgetting that he had no torch. . . . Lighting a match would be bound to wake the others. He tried to guess what time it was by looking at the sky and wondering if he could see any signs of the coming dawn. There did not seem to be quite so many stars as he had seen last night, looking up out of Swallowdale. Well, he would not try to count them. The boy and the able-seaman had gone to bed in good time, just as he had said they should. *Swallow* was coming back. The great-aunt was going. There was to be a race. Haul in the sheet. Keep her full, though. Keep her sailing. . . . Luff now. . . . Luff. Into the wind. . . . And he was asleep once more.

Titty was waked by feeling the tip of her nose cold.

She brought a warm hand up out of the sleeping-bag and rubbed it. Then she remembered that she was half-way up Kanchenjunga. This was real exploring. The smell of wood smoke made it more real still. It was already not so dark as it had been, and looking east, away from the mountain, she saw the sheltering tops of the pines already black against a paler sky. She thought that now nobody would mind if she were to stay awake and keep watch over the camp. But there would be no harm in putting her nose down into the sleeping-bag just for a minute or two to warm its cold tip. By the time she looked out again it was already broad daylight.

*

The sun set a golden cap on the head of Kanchenjunga, and the morning glow, creeping down, found out the creases and wrinkles of his old face almost as well as it does in winter when the sunshine makes every crevice and gully a blue shadow in the gleaming snow. The light crept lower and lower down the mountain sides and lit the tops of the pine trees in the woods below the camp. The shadows of the trees, which at first had been flung far over the four bundles of the expedition, grew shorter. Roger suddenly turned over, bag and all, in one angry movement, as if he felt that the sun had shone on his face on purpose. John yawned and sat up and looked straight into the eyes of Titty.

'I've been watching it,' she said.

'It's too early to get up,' said John.

'Well, let's go on not getting up. Susan's hard asleep. Roger's been dreaming about something. He said, "Of course I can," out loud.'

For a while they lay, propped up on their elbows but not for very long. The sun rose higher and grew hotter, and presently the able-seaman said, 'What about getting her some more wood?'

'She'll want some,' said the captain, looking first at the smouldering fire, an earthy mound from which a thin trickle of pale smoke climbed up into the sky and disappeared, and then at the still sleeping mate. 'She'll want some. We may as well get some. But don't wake Roger when you wriggle out.'

Half an hour later Roger reached out towards Titty's sleeping-bag, and finding it empty, sat up suddenly and looked about him. He prodded the mate, who was still asleep.

'What's the matter?' said the muffled voice of the mate.

'Titty and John are gone.'

'What?'

'Gone,' said Roger, and added hopefully, 'Probably eaten by bears in the night just because John went and said there weren't any.'

'Rubbish,' grunted Susan.

'Well, wolves then, or some of those foxes.'

Susan sat up and saw the empty sleeping-bags, lying desolate and flat with nothing in them, like balloons that have been blown up too hard and burst.

'They're somewhere about,' she said. 'Listen.'

They heard laughter and a noise of splashing and blowing from the wood, close at hand.

'They're washing,' said Susan. 'Go and take them the soap, and wash yourself. I'll come too, as soon as I've pulled the fire together.'

The captain and the able-seaman had gathered two good bundles of wood and then had begun to feel that perhaps their eyes were not quite so wide awake as all the rest of them. So they had gone and dipped their heads into a pool and found the water very cold, much colder than the water of the stream in Swallowdale. John had taken his shirt off and put his head under a tiny waterfall which had almost taken his breath away. By the time Roger brought them the soap they felt they had not much use for it, except to clean their hands after gathering the wood and that this was not worth while as they would have to pick the wood up again to carry it to the camp. But the mate came down just as they were deciding that it would be best to keep the soap dry until they were ready to have breakfast. In spite of being high up on the side of a mountain, after sleeping in the open, without even a tent, the mate was in her most native mood, and in about two and a half seconds the captain and the able-seaman were washing themselves all over again, using plenty of soap, and telling each other that they had meant to anyhow.

When the washing was all done and the bundles of dry sticks carried up out of the forest to the camp fire, which Susan had already coaxed to life again, there were soon leaping flames about the kettle. That was Susan's strong point. She never allowed excitements such as sleeping in the open half-way up a mountain, or a naval battle, or a dangerous bit of exploring, to interfere with the things that really matter, such as seeing that water is really boiling before making tea with it, having breakfast at the proper time, washing as usual, and drying anything that may be damp. Really, if it had not been for Susan, half the Swallows' adventures would have been impossible, but, with a mate as good as that, to see that everything went as it should, there was no need for any native to worry about what was happening.

Today, for example, she had turned all four sleeping-bags inside out and laid them on the heather to air in the sun. And up here, high on Kanchenjunga, there was a breakfast plain but satisfying, hot tea and plenty of it, hunks of pemmican improved by being held for a moment over the fire (this gives the meat just that touch of camp fire smoke that makes the difference), bunloaf and apples. What more could any explorer want? And the moment breakfast was over, she set the captain and the crew to tidying up, just as if they had been in Swallowdale and not half-way up the mountain and waiting only for the Amazons and the rope to make the final dash to the summit. The expedition's mug was washed in the beck. The sleeping-bags were turned the right side out again and rolled up in their waterproof covers.

'No, don't empty out the kettle,' she said. 'There's enough tea in it to fill the mug for the Amazons. They may want it.'

'The best thing about being on the march,' said Roger, 'is that there's only one knife and one fork to clean instead of four of each.'

'Three of each less to lose,' said the mate. 'You hand that knife and fork over here instead of sticking them in the heather, where they're bound to get lost.'

'They're stuck there to dry,' said Roger.

'Hand them over,' said the mate. 'We'll get everything except the mug packed before the others come. Hullo, what's that?'

There was a noise in the wood below them, a noise something like an owl and something like a cuckoo, ending in a gurgle of laughter that was not like a bird at all.

'Here they are,' said John.

'It's no good their trying to make the owl call,' said Roger. 'They can't do it.'

'What they're good at is ducks,' said John. 'I've never heard anybody quack so well as Peggy.'

'Nobody can be good at everything,' said Titty.

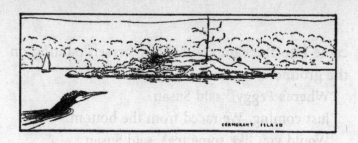

27

The Summit of Kanchenjunga

ONE reason why the Amazons found it hard to make good owl calls was that they had very little breath. They had pulled hard all the way up the river and then had had to climb the steep gorge to the top of the woods. Not even guides can run uphill and make good owl calls at the same time, and the Amazons, after all, were more pirates than guides, and knew more about sailing than about climbing mountains. Still, for the moment, they were being guides, and Captain Nancy, beside her knapsack, had a huge coil of rope slung on her shoulder for easy carrying. She took it off as she came into the camp and threw herself panting on the ground.

'Where's Peggy?' said Susan.

'Just coming. We raced from the bottom.'

'Would you like some tea?' said Susan.

'Wouldn't I?' said Nancy, rolling over. 'We had breakfast awfully early because of saying goodbye to the G.A. But it was worth it. Everybody thought so. We saw the housemaid dancing in the kitchen. And Cook said, "Now we can breathe again." And it wasn't any good Mother and Uncle Jim pretending. Anybody but the G.A. would have known how they felt.'

'Come on, Peggy,' called Titty, as the mate of the *Amazon* struggled up out of the trees.

'I couldn't come any faster,' said Peggy. 'I could hear the nectar sloshing round in the bottle in my knapsack, and hitting the top of the bottle inside, and I thought it would bust the cork out any minute. It's a weight, too.'

'Nothing to the rope,' said Captain Nancy. 'And Cook crammed my knapsack with doughnuts.'

'I'll carry the bottle now,' said John.

'Or shall we leave everything here?' said Susan.

'And just make a desperate dash to the summit,' said Titty.

'Much better have it to drink *on* the summit,' said Nancy.

So while Peggy and Nancy were using the expedition's mug to share the tea that Susan had kept for them, John shifted the big bottle of nectar from Peggy's knapsack to his own.

'We'll carry it part of the way,' said Nancy.

'How do we fasten the rope?' said Roger.

'Give them time to get their tea down,' said Susan.

'It's all right,' said Nancy, 'we can't both drink at once.'

'Has the great-aunt really gone?' asked Titty.

'She jolly well has,' said Nancy. 'If we hurry, we ought to be able to see the smoke of the train that's taking her away. The quicker the better. Swallows and Amazons for ever. Hurrah for Wild Cat Island and the Spanish Main. And *Swallow*'s nearly ready. And Uncle Jim is so sick of being a nephew that he's going to be a first-rate uncle for a change.'

'We packed our tent and stowed it in *Amazon* last night,' said Peggy.

Nancy held the mug upside down and let the last dregs of the tea hiss on the embers of the fire. 'What about going on?' she said, and was going to put the mug as it was in one of the knapsacks, but Susan took it in time to save that, and washed it out in the beck and dried it so that wet sugar should not trickle out of it into places where it was not wanted. The four sleeping-bags, neatly rolled up, were packed between two rocks with everything else that was not being taken to the top. Nothing but food was being taken, besides, of course, the telescope, the compass, and the huge bottle of lemonade, nectar or grog, that Peggy had carried up from the valley.

'How do we fasten the rope?' asked Roger again.

'We fasten it to all of us,' said Nancy.

'Then we mustn't pull different ways,' said Roger.

'Nobody exactly pulls,' said Nancy. 'It's so that nobody falls over a precipice. There are six of us. If one tumbles, the other five hang on so that the one who tumbles doesn't tumble far.'

'Are there any precipices?' asked Roger.

'Dozens,' said Titty, 'and if there aren't we can easily make some.'

'There really are plenty,' said Peggy.

'We shan't go by the path,' said Nancy. 'When we come to a rock, we'll go over it.'

'Let's begin,' said Roger. 'Who goes first? Can I?'

'No,' said John. 'The rope isn't a painter for you to jump ashore with. We must have somebody big in front. It ought to be Nancy. I'll take the other end.'

'We must make loops in it,' said Nancy. 'Six loops, big enough to stick our heads and shoulders through.'

It was done. There were about five yards between each loop. Nancy hung the first loop on herself. Mate Susan took the next, and after her came Able-seaman Titty, Boy Roger, Mate Peggy, and Captain John.

'Now then,' said Nancy, 'everybody ready?'

'We ought really to have ice-axes,' said Titty.

Nancy heard her. 'I thought of that,' she said, 'but they'd get horribly in the way. Worse than the rope. Hands and feet are better, especially on the rocks.'

The long procession moved off. Just at first the rope made it difficult to talk. This was because when anyone wanted to talk to the one in front he hurried on and tripped over loose rope, while at the same time he stretched the rope taut behind him and so gave a disturbing jerk to someone else. By the time they had learnt to talk without hurrying forward or hanging back they were climbing slopes so steep that nobody wanted to talk at all. There were things to shout, such as 'Don't touch this rock. It's a loose one,' but mostly it was grim, straight-ahead, silent climbing.

At the start they had been scrambling up beside the tiny mountain beck that was now all that was left to remind them of the river far down below them in the valley. But as soon as they had come to a place from which they had had a clear view of the summit, Nancy, the leader, had turned directly towards it, and within a minute or two everybody had learnt how useful it is on a mountain to have four legs instead of two. Sometimes Nancy turned to left or to right to avoid loose screes, but when she came to a rock that could be climbed, she climbed it, and all the rest of the explorers climbed it after her.

'The really tough bit's still to come,' she said cheerfully.

The tough bit came when nobody expected it, and the explorers were very glad they had a rope in spite of its being such a bother from the talking point of view. They had come to a steep face of rock, not really very difficult, because there were cracks running across it which made good footholds and handholds, but not a good place to tumble down, because there was nothing to stop you and there were a lot of loose stones at the bottom of it. Nancy had gone up it easily enough, and Susan after her. Titty was just crawling over the edge at the top of it and Peggy and John were waiting at the bottom ready to start, when suddenly Roger, who was about half-way up, shouted out, 'Look! Look! Wild goats!'

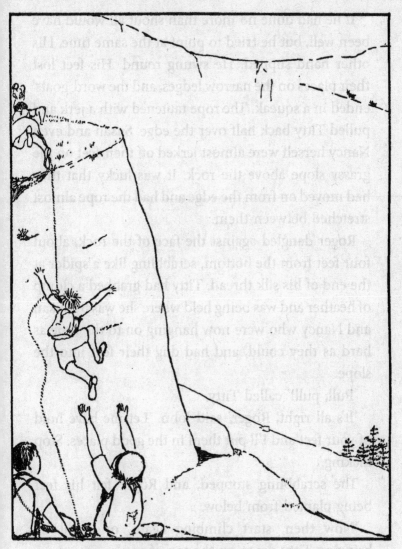

THE WORD 'GOATS' ENDED IN A SQUEAK

If he had done no more than shout all would have been well, but he tried to point at the same time. His other hand slipped. He swung round. His feet lost their places on the narrow ledges, and the word 'goats' ended in a squeak. The rope tautened with a jerk and pulled Titty back half over the edge. Susan and even Nancy herself were almost jerked off their feet on the grassy slope above the rock. It was lucky that they had moved on from the edge and had the rope almost stretched between them.

Roger dangled against the face of the rock, about four feet from the bottom, scrabbling like a spider at the end of his silk thread. Titty had grabbed a clump of heather and was being held where she was by Susan and Nancy who were now hanging on to the rope as hard as they could, and had dug their feet into the slope.

'Pull, pull!' called Titty.

'It's all right, Roger,' said John. 'Let me have hold of your feet and I'll put them in the good places. Stop kicking.'

The scrabbling stopped, and Roger felt his feet being planted from below.

'Now then, start climbing again, or you'll be bringing Titty down on the top of you.'

The moment Roger began to climb, he took his

weight off the rope and Nancy and Susan pulling together found the weight suddenly less. Titty came head first over the edge and up on the grass above the rock.

'Keep on pulling,' she panted, 'or he may go flop again. But don't pull too hard.' She crawled on as well as she could. She had had much the worst of it, and had scratched her elbows and knees slipping back over the edge of the rock.

Roger's voice came cheerfully from below.

'Did you see the goats?'

'Never mind goats,' called Susan from above. 'Is he hurt?'

'Only another scrape,' said Roger. 'But *did* you see the goats? There they are again.'

'Don't point!' shouted John, just in time.

'I must,' said Roger. But he didn't. 'There! There! You'll see them again in a minute. There they go. Right up by the top.'

The topmost peak of Kanchenjunga was directly above the explorers. But to the right of it, as they looked up, the huge shoulders of the mountain, lower than the peak itself but high in the sky above them, swept round to the north, and it was up there, almost behind the explorers, that Roger, looking over his shoulder as he climbed, had seen things moving on the grey stone slopes under the top of the crags. Up and up they were going, now close under the skyline. Just as John and Peggy caught sight of them they crossed the skyline itself, tiny, dark things, goats cut out of black cardboard against the pale blue of the morning sky.

'I see them,' called Titty.

'Five,' said John.

'There's one more,' said Roger.

A moment later they were gone.

'Well, I'm glad we've seen them,' said Roger.

'Get on up to the top of the rock,' said John. 'And don't look for any more. If it hadn't been for Titty and the others hanging on to the rope you might have broken your leg.'

'And no stretcher to carry me on.'

Roger hurried up with his climbing and was soon on the grass slope above the rock, being looked over by Susan. Neither she nor Nancy had seen the wild goats, so naturally they thought more about the accident.

'Shiver my timbers,' said Nancy, 'but that was a narrow go. We really ought to have waited at the top, taking in rope hand over hand so that he couldn't slip. But you can't allow for everything. Who would have thought of his seeing goats just at that moment? If they were goats. Probably sheep.'

'They were goats all right,' said Peggy, climbing up. 'We all saw them.'

'All right,' said Nancy. 'Goats. But not such goats as some people I know. What about you, Able-seaman? Are you hurt too?'

Titty had been trying to lick the blood off her right elbow, but had found that she could not reach it, and anyway it wasn't really bleeding enough to matter.

'Lucky it was Roger who fell and not John,' said Nancy. 'Not so heavy, for one thing, and if it had been John, what would have become of the grog?'

They were more careful after that, and there were no more accidents. The last few yards up to the top of the peak were easy going. The explorers met and crossed the rough path that they might have followed from the bottom, and then, with the cairn that marked the summit now in full view before them, they wriggled out of the loops in the rope and raced for it. John and Nancy reached the cairn almost together. Roger and Titty came next. Mate Susan had stopped to coil the rope, and Mate Peggy had waited to help her to carry it.

All this time the explorers had been climbing up the northern side of the peak of Kanchenjunga. The huge shoulder of the mountain had shut out from them everything that there was to the west. As they climbed, other hills in the distance seemed to be climbing too, and, when they looked back into the valley they had left, it seemed so small that they could hardly believe that there had been room to row a boat along that bright thread in the meadows that they knew was the river. But it was not until that last rush to the top, not until they were actually standing by the cairn that marked the highest point of Kanchenjunga, that they could see what lay beyond the mountain.

Then indeed they knew that they were on the roof of the world.

Far, far away, beyond range after range of low hills, the land ended and the sea began, the real sea, blue water stretching on and on until it met the sky. There were white specks of sailing ships, coasting schooners, probably, and little black plumes of smoke showed steamers on their way to Ireland or on their way back or working up or down between Liverpool and the Clyde. And forty miles away or more there was a short dark line on the blue field of the sea. 'Due west from here,' said John, looking at the compass in his hand. 'It's the Isle of Man.'

'Look back the other way,' said Peggy.

'You can see right into Scotland,' said Nancy. 'Those hills over there are the other side of the Solway Firth.'

'And there's Scawfell, and Skiddaw, and that's Helvellyn, and the pointed one's Ill Bell, and there's High Street, where the Ancient Britons had a road along the top of the mountains.'

'Where's Carlisle?' asked Titty. 'It must be somewhere over there.'

'How do you know?' asked Nancy.

'"And the red glare on Skiddaw woke the burghers of Carlisle." Probably in those days they didn't have blinds in bedroom windows.'

'We know that one, too,' said Peggy. 'But not all of it. It's worse than "Casabianca".'

'I like it because of the beacons,' said Titty.

John and Roger had no eyes for mountains while they could see blue water and ships, however far away.

'If we went on and on, beyond the Isle of Man, what would we come to?' asked Roger.

'Ireland, I think,' said John, 'and then probably America. . . .'

'And if we still went on?'

'Then there'd be the Pacific and China.'

'And then?'

John thought for a minute. 'There'd be all Asia and then all Europe and then there'd be the North Sea and then we'd be coming up the other side of those hills.' He looked back towards the hills beyond Rio and the hills beyond them, and the hills beyond them again, stretching away, fold upon fold, into the east.

'Then we'd have gone all round the world.'

'Of course.'

'Let's.'

'We will some day. Daddy's done it.'

'So has Uncle Jim,' said Peggy.

'Of course, you couldn't see round, however high you were,' said Roger.

'You wouldn't want to,' said Titty. 'Much better fun not knowing what was coming next.'

'Well, up here you're properly on the roof.' Nancy threw herself down on the warm ground. 'What about that nectar? Oh, I say, I've forgotten all about it and let you carry it all the way up.'

'That's all right.' John brought the big bottle out of his knapsack, and the mug began to make its rounds with lemonade rather warm after its journey, while Susan and Peggy were cutting up the bunloaf and opening the last of the pemmican tins, and Nancy emptied out the doughnuts.

'I wonder whether anybody's ever had dinner on the top of Kanchenjunga before?' said Titty, when she had eaten her share of pemmican and was finishing off with a doughnut.

'They must have done, when they built the cairn,' said Peggy. 'Think of the time it must have taken to build up all those stones.'

'Perhaps it didn't take any time,' said Titty. 'Perhaps some tribe or other had won a victory, and everybody brought one stone and put it there.'

'But they'd have a feast after that,' said Roger. 'Can I climb up the cairn?'

'No,' said Susan. 'You've had one tumble already, and there aren't thousands of us to build the cairn up again if you go and bring it down.'

'It's very well built.'

'That just shows the people who built it didn't want ship's boys to pull it down.'

'I'll be very careful.'

'Have an apple.'

'May I lean against the cairn?'

'Anything you like so long as you don't start climbing on it.'

Roger sat down with his back against the cairn, so as to be less tempted to climb it. It seemed a pity not to and so be a few feet higher even than the top of Kanchenjunga. He would climb it, he thought, next year or perhaps the year after. In the meantime . . . He looked down towards Swallowdale somewhere on the moors so far below, tried to see Wild Cat Island, but could not be sure if he had, watched a steamer moving at the low end of the lake, looked out to sea and then, when he had eaten his apple, rolled over and began feeling the stones at the foot of the cairn. Was it so very well built, after all?

The others were planning what they would do, now that the great-aunt was gone, and the Amazons were once more free to be pirates, and there seemed to be hope that *Swallow* would soon be back, when they were startled by a shout from Roger. 'Look, look! What's this?'

In his hand was a small round brass box with the head of an old lady stamped on the lid of it. Framing the head of the old lady were big printed letters: 'QUEEN OF ENGLAND EMPRESS OF INDIA DIAMOND JUBILEE 1897.' Roger had found a loose stone at the foot of the cairn, had pulled it out, and seen the little brass box hidden behind it.

'She must be Queen Victoria,' said John. 'She came before Edward the Seventh.'

'She really is awfully like Bridgie used to be,' said Titty.

'There's something inside,' said Roger, shaking the box.

'Let's open it,' said Nancy.

'I'll open it,' said Roger, and he did. Inside was a

folded bit of paper and a farthing with the head of Queen Victoria on it.

'Take care,' said Titty. 'It may be a treasure chart. It may be a deadly secret. It may crumble at a touch. They often do.'

But the paper was strong enough. Roger let Nancy unfold it. She opened it, began reading it aloud, and then stopped. Peggy took it and read it aloud, while the others looked at it over her shoulder. It was written in black pencil that had scored deeply into the paper:

> 'August the 2nd. 1901.
> We climbed the Matterhorn.
> Molly Turner.
> J. Turner.
> Bob Blackett.'

'That's Mother and Uncle Jim,' said Peggy in a queer voice.

'Who is Bob Blackett?' asked Susan.

'He was Father,' said Nancy.

Nobody said anything for a minute, and then Titty, looking at the paper, said, 'So that was what they called it. Well, it's Kanchenjunga now. It's no good changing it now we've climbed it.'

'That was thirty years ago,' said John.

'I wonder how Mother and Uncle Jim escaped from the great-aunt to come up here,' said Peggy. 'She was looking after them, you know.'

'Probably Father rescued them,' said Nancy.

'Why did they put the farthing in?' wondered Roger.

'Let's put it all back,' said Titty hurriedly. 'They meant it to stay for a thousand years.'

'Has anybody got a bit of paper?' said Nancy suddenly.

Nobody had, but Titty had the stump of a pencil. Nancy took it and wrote firmly on the back of the paper on which her father and mother and uncle had set forth their triumph of thirty years before:

'Aug. 11. 1931.
We climbed Kanchenjunga.'

'Now,' she said, 'we all sign here,' and she wrote her name. 'You next, Captain John. Then the two mates, and then the able-seaman and the ship's boy.'

Everybody signed. Then Nancy folded up the paper, put it back in the box with the farthing, and gave it to Roger.

'You found it,' she said. 'You put it back, and then perhaps in another thirty years. . . .' She broke off, but presently laughed. 'Shiver my timbers,' she said, 'but I wish we had a George the Fifth farthing.'

'I've got a new halfpenny,' said Roger.

'Can you spare it?'

'I'll give you another if you can't,' said John, 'when we get back to the camp.'

Roger dug out his halfpenny. The box was closed and pushed far back into the hole at the foot of the cairn. Roger wedged the loose stone firmly in its place.

'Nobody'd ever guess there was anything there,' said Roger. 'I wouldn't have found it if the stone hadn't worked loose.'

'And now perhaps it won't be found for ages and ages till people wear quite different sorts of clothes,' said Titty. 'Perhaps it'll be more explorers just like us. I wonder how big Captain Flint was then?'

'I wonder if they had a clear day for it,' said Peggy.

'And saw the Isle of Man,' said Roger.

They looked out to sea.

'Hullo,' said John. 'We can't see it any more.'

'I saw it a minute ago,' said Titty.

'There must be a fog out at sea,' said John. 'What luck that we came up early while it was still so clear.'

'Come along,' said Nancy suddenly. 'Remember we've got to get down to Watersmeet and then to

Beckfoot and then sail to Horseshoe Cove and carry our tent up to Swallowdale. We ought to be starting.'

'Where's the rope?' said Roger.

'I'll carry the rope,' said Nancy. 'We used it all right coming up. I don't see why we shouldn't use the path going down. It'll be lots quicker.'

A minute or two later, after a last look round from the top of the world, the six explorers who had climbed Kanchenjunga as Kanchenjunga should be climbed, were hurrying down the mountain at a good jog-trot.

28

Fog on the Moor

IT WAS early afternoon when the Beckfoot war canoe, or rowing boat, shot through the bridge into the lower reaches of the Amazon. The two captains were rowing, Roger was in the bows, and the rest of the explorers were in the stern, together with the rope and the knapsacks and the sleeping-bags, the kettle and the milk-can that they had picked up at the Half-Way Camp on their way down from the top of the mountain.

'There's our tree,' called Roger, as the boat turned a bend of the river and he saw the huge oak with its branches spreading far out over the water.

'Easy all,' called Mate Peggy.

'You're sure you really do want to go home that way instead of coming in the *Amazon*?' said Mate Susan.

'Of course we do,' said Titty. 'That's what we laid the patterans for.'

'Besides,' said Roger, 'there's hardly any wind.'

'Well, look here, Titty,' said Susan. 'There really isn't much wind, so if you do get back before us you can get the fire going and put some water on to boil. You'll find the saucepan in the larder.'

'Susan!' said Titty indignantly.

'In Peter Duck's cave, I mean,' said Susan. 'There's no point in taking the kettle. The less you have to carry the better.'

'We don't need anything but chocolate,' said Roger.

'And the compass,' said Titty. 'We'll take great care of it. We ought to have the compass, you know.'

'We shan't need it,' said Susan.

'All right,' said John.

'Backwater with your left,' cried Peggy. 'Ship your oars!'

With a loud swishing of oak leaves, the rowing boat ran itself gently into the bank beside the big tree. Roger was out in a moment and hanging on to the painter to stop the boat from slipping back until Titty had picked out their two knapsacks and worked her way past the rowers to join him on the bank. John gave her the compass. Susan handed out a double ration of chocolate for each of them. Except for the chocolate and compass there was nothing in their knapsacks, but, when exploring, they would rather have had empty knapsacks than none. They would not need their sleeping-bags which, as Nancy said, would cram in with the rest of the cargo in *Amazon*. 'Much better send things by sea than by pack-horses.'

'Pack-donkeys,' said Susan. 'They'd be much better off in *Amazon* themselves.'

For a moment the able-seaman was afraid that Susan was going to think better of it, and not let them go after all, but Peggy called out, 'Shove her off,' so Roger threw the painter aboard, and the two of them, pushing together, sent the boat shooting out into the river.

'Out oars,' called Peggy, who was enjoying giving orders to the captains. 'Backwater with your right. Pull left. Left. Pull both. Steady. Left again. All right now.'

The war canoe with the two captains and the two mates moved fast downstream and disappeared.

Roger looked after it.

'Suppose we never see them again,' he said.

The able-seaman was not going to allow that kind of talk.

'Now then, Boy,' she said, 'get your knapsack on. We mustn't hang about. It wouldn't be fair to the ship's parrot. He's waiting in the cave.'

'He's got Peter Duck,' said the boy.

'No, he hasn't. Not now. We'll have Peter Duck with us. He was waiting for us under the oak tree. It's just the sort of thing he'd like, following patterans over the moor. Besides, he'll be a help in case of natives.'

'Unfriendly ones?' said the boy, struggling into the straps of his flapping, empty knapsack.

'Savages,' said the able-seaman. 'They might go for you or me if we were by ourselves. But if Peter Duck were to give just one look at them they wouldn't dare.'

All the same, when they had slipped through the edges of the wood to the road, they listened carefully, lying on the top of the stone wall, to make sure that no natives of any kind were coming either way.

'Are you ready?' said Titty.

'Aye, aye, sir,' said the boy.

'Peter Duck says now's our chance. Drop and hare across for all you're worth.'

They dropped, and hared.

'Here's my tuft of grass. That's the first of the patterans. There's a good step on the other side. Be quick. Give me one foot. Don't kick with the other. Wriggle with the top of you. Quick!'

The able-seaman hoisted the boy up the wall. He scrambled over the top and disappeared, all but his hands, which for a moment clung on to the moss-covered stones.

'I'm feeling for the step,' his voice came in a whisper, as if he were afraid of being overheard. 'I've got it.'

His hands were gone and Titty heard him drop into the dead leaves on the other side of the wall. She found it none too easy to climb the wall herself, and would have been glad if Peter Duck had been real enough to give her a leg up as she had given Roger. Of course, he would have done if he had been there. So she had to pretend that he had already climbed over. 'He did it in one jump,' she said to herself. 'It was nothing to him after running up and down rigging all his life.' A moment later she, too, had found the step on the other side and jumped from it down into the wood. Roger was already looking for pine-cones.

'No,' said the able-seaman, 'we didn't put any here. No need. We follow the wall till we see the four firs, and then the four firs show the way to the first of our patterans. We can't go wrong here. All we've got to do is to keep along the wall and climb as fast as we can.'

They had crossed the road just at the place where the old wall came down from the moor. They could almost touch it when they dropped down into the wood. There was nothing to keep them, and they began at once scrambling up through the wood, keeping close to the old wall, and pushing aside the hazel branches. It was hard climbing, and they were glad when they came to the edge of the thick wood, to the place where the trees had been cut down and there was little left but old stumps, and foxgloves, and ferns, so that they could see where they were going and how the ruins of the old wall led on to the four dark fir trees standing one above another on the steep hillside.

'What about chocolate?' said Roger, less because he wanted chocolate than because he wanted a rest.

'Come on,' said Titty. 'We'll have our first chocolate under the four firs. That'll be the first stage. Then we'll have to look for our patterans to show us the rest of the way.'

They hurried on, climbing still, over the rough, broken ground where the old tree stumps and the few scattered young trees showed there had once been a wood. Under the four great firs, which were all that were left of that old forest of thirty or forty or fifty years ago, the able-seaman and the boy ate a ration of chocolate, and looked back into the valley of the Amazon.

Roger said, 'I wish I'd seen the great-aunt close to.'

'It's a good thing none of us did,' said Titty. 'Just think of what happened to the people who looked at the Gorgon. We might all have been turned into stone and stuck about the Beckfoot garden with bird-baths or sundials on the tops of our heads.'

'It didn't happen like that to the Amazons,' said Roger.

'Perhaps they always looked the other way,' said Titty. 'And, anyhow, she almost did turn them into stone. Look at the way they got stuck here and couldn't do any of the things they wanted to do. And remember how stiff they were when we saw them in the carriage. That was because they were sitting just in front of her. I don't believe even Captain Flint felt properly springy while she was anywhere near.'

'I wonder where he is.'

'Playing the accordion in his houseboat probably. At least I think that's what he'd do. He saw her off this morning, you know. Come on, Boy. Let's get on to Swallowdale. Remember the Amazons are going to be in the camp tonight. Come on. We must keep the four firs in a line and look for the patterans.'

'Aye, aye, sir,' said the boy, and scampered on towards the moor with his eyes on the ground, running to right and then to left and back again like a dog trying to pick up a scent.

The able-seaman moved crabwise, and not so fast, all the time looking over her shoulder to see that the four firs looked as nearly as possible like one.

They crossed the broad belt of heather and had already left the four firs far behind when Roger found the first of the pine-cones.

'Good,' said the able-seaman. 'I was beginning to think we'd missed it.' She had another look back at the firs, and then hurried forward. She was picking up the second pine-cone before the boy saw it.

'Hurrah,' shouted the boy. 'They're the best patterans that ever were. We can't miss the way now.' He galloped on over the moor and presently picked up the third.

'Shall we leave them for another time?' he said.

'No. Better throw them away. We don't want to show anybody else the way to Swallowdale.'

'Which of us can throw farthest?' said the boy, giving Titty a pine-cone and running on to pick up another for himself.

The able-seaman knew that Roger could beat her at throwing, but she threw her pine-cone none the less. Roger threw his but not quite in the same direction, so they had to measure the distances by stepping before they could be sure that his had really gone a yard or two farther than hers.

IN THE FOG

'This is waste of time,' said the able-seaman. 'Besides, Peter Duck could throw yards farther than either of us if he wanted to.'

They hurried on again, picking up the pine-cones one by one as they found them, and throwing each one away as soon as they saw the next.

They were high up on the top of the open moorland and had already long lost sight of the four firs, when Roger stopped suddenly and said, 'What's become of the hills?'

Titty looked back towards Kanchenjunga. Kanchenjunga stood out clear in the sunshine and so did the great hills beyond him to the north, but the lower hills to the south had disappeared altogether. It was as if there was nothing beyond the moorland but the sky.

'It's not so hot now,' said Roger.

It certainly did seem much cooler all of a sudden. And the sunshine was not so bright as it had been.

Titty looked back again to Kanchenjunga. A wisp of pale cloud was floating across his lower slopes. His head was somehow fading. She could no longer see the peak with the cairn that they had that morning climbed. She looked over the moorland towards Swallowdale. Something was happening. There was no doubt about it. The moorland was shrinking. It was nothing like so wide as it had been. The trees away to the left had gone. The hills away to the right had disappeared. The moorland, instead of ending sharply where it dropped into the farther valley, faded into a wall of soft white mist.

'It's coming in like the tide,' said Titty.

'We're on a cape with the sea pouring in on each side of us,' said Roger.

A high wall of mist was now rolling towards them from the south along the top of the ridge. There seemed to be no wind, but the mist moved forward, little clouds sometimes spilling ahead of it like the small waves racing up the sands in front of the breakers.

'It's cold,' said the boy.

'Let's hurry,' said the able-seaman.

And then the mist rolled over the top of them and they could see only a few yards ahead.

'It wasn't a cape,' said Roger. 'Only a sandbank. And now the sea's gone over the top of it.'

Titty sniffed and coughed.

'It's sea-fog,' she said. 'The tickling sort. Don't breathe it more than you can help.'

'There's a pine-cone somewhere close here,' said Roger. 'I saw it a minute ago.'

He ran on a yard or two and was gone in the white mist.

'Roger.'

'Hullo!'

'Where are you?'

'Here.'

'Don't move. Where are you now?'

'Here. Where are you?'

'Keep still. I'm just coming. Good. I can see you. That's all right.'

'I can't find that pine-cone.'

'Don't run on again, anyhow,' said Titty. 'We must stick together or we'll lose each other. The fog'll blow over.'

'Your hair's all over dew.'

'I wonder if they've got it like this on the lake.'

'Shall I make a fog signal?' said the boy. 'I will.'

'There's no one to hear it.'

'I will, anyway,' said the boy, and a few damp sheep up on the top of the moor were startled by hearing what they did not know was the deep hooting of an Atlantic liner feeling the way towards Plymouth in a Channel fog.

'Don't,' said Titty in a minute or two. 'I want to think.'

Roger sent one more long booming hoot into the fog, and stopped.

'Nobody's going to run us down for a minute or two,' he said.

'We ought to be able to find the next pine-cone. Keep fairly close to me and we'll look for it. We shan't be able to cover much of the ground if we're very close together, but if we try going far apart one of us'll get lost.'

'If one of us is lost both of us are,' said Roger. 'Because if the one that was lost could see the one that wasn't lost then neither of them would be lost, and if the one that was lost couldn't see the one that wasn't lost, then that one would be lost, too, as well as the one that it couldn't see.'

'Oh, shut up, Roger. Do. Just for a minute.'

'Aye, aye, sir,' said the boy; and, a moment later, 'may I say something?'

'What is it?'

'Here's the pine-cone.'

'Good,' said the able-seaman. 'Now you see the use of patterans. We'll be able to find our way to Swallowdale in spite of the fog.'

'How will they manage on the lake?'

'With the compass. Oh, we've got it. But probably Captain Nancy has one of her own.'

Titty pulled the compass out of her knapsack and opened it.

'The black end points north,' she said, 'so the white end points south. And south is where we have to go to find the next patteran.'

She held the compass before her, looking down into it and moving slowly ahead.

Roger, who had been keeping close to her, searching the ground, presently pulled at her sleeve.

'We've probably passed it,' he said.

The trouble was that Titty thought so too, but there was no way of knowing. The compass did not seem to help. This part of the moor was covered with short grass with patches of bracken and rocks and loose stones, and stones not quite so loose, bedded in the ground, with ants' nests under them, if you lifted them. Here and there were thin tufts of dark green rushes, the sort of green rushes that are white when peeled and can be made into rings and plaits and even baskets. There was no track that anyone could have seen even if there had been no fog. Here and there were the sheep runs, but they ran all ways, and mostly from side to side of the moor and not straight along the top. It was very puzzling.

'You stand still,' said Titty, 'and I'll walk round in sight of you and look for the next patteran.'

That let her look all over a circle of a dozen yards

across. But when she had worked all round it she was no better off.

'Now you stand still, and I'll hunt,' said the boy, but he was no luckier.

'The only thing to do is to go on,' said Titty at last. 'We must get home, because of Polly. And Susan said, "Get the fire going," too.'

She held the compass close in front of her and moved forward with her eyes fixed on the needle. The needle swung to and fro, no matter how steadily she held it, and the worst came to the worst when she caught her foot in a tussock of lank grass and fell on her face. The compass did not touch the ground. She saved it by letting herself fall anyhow, without trying to put out her hands. After all, the compass mattered most, so she kept it in the air, though she hit the ground herself much harder than she thought possible.

'Is it smashed?' asked Roger.

The able-seaman picked herself up.

'No, it isn't hurt,' she said. 'But I wish I knew how to use it properly. John didn't try to look at it all the time. I watched what he did. He looked at the compass to see which way was north and then he looked north and found a rock or something. And then he put the compass in his pocket and walked till he came to the rock. But it's no good us looking south, because there's nothing to see.'

'Just one blanket everywhere,' said Roger.

Titty looked at the compass again.

'South is there,' she said, pointing into the fog. 'If we walk perfectly straight we can't go wrong, and anyhow we can't help coming to the beck, and as soon as we've found the beck it'll be easy enough to find the camp.'

She had one more look at the compass, and then, putting it in her pocket, set out doggedly into the fog, looking straight before her, and doing her best to take steps with her right foot exactly the same length as those she took with her left.

'Come on, Boy,' she said.

'Aye, aye, sir,' said the boy, and followed close at her heels, scouting a yard or two to either side in hope of finding one of the pine-cones to show them that they were in the right way.

They moved slowly along the moor in a white, almost empty world, a world in which something that they thought might be a stray cow turned out to be a rock, and rocks turned out to be worried, black-faced sheep that bleated and scurried away into the whiteness all about them.

'Are we properly lost?' said Roger at last.

'Of course we aren't,' said the able-seaman. 'Besides, it isn't as if we were alone. Peter Duck says it's quite all right, so long as we keep going straight.'

'We must be nearly there.'

'I expect we are. We may hear the parrot any minute.'

'It's very squashy here. I've got water into one of my shoes.'

'It's only a bit of swamp. We'll have to go round it.'

For some time they picked their way from one tuft of green rushes to another. The able-seaman was rather bothered by this, because though they had seen plenty of these rushes, they had not crossed any really swampy ground on the way to the Amazon. Still, there were lots of small marshes up on the moor, and just a little bit to right or left would not matter much if they kept on moving straight ahead. Suddenly she stopped short, listening.

'What is it?' whispered Roger.

'Listen!'

There it was, quite clear, not very far before them, the gentle tinkle of water.

'It's the beck. Now we're all right.'

They ran forward and almost fell across a little stream trickling down the moor from one tiny pool into the next.

'We've come much too far to the right,' said Titty. 'This must be a long way above Trout Tarn for the beck to be so small. But we can't miss the way now.'

With the beck to guide them through the fog, they hurried cheerfully along.

'We'll have the rest of the chocolate when we come to Trout Tarn,' said Roger, but when they had walked a long way without coming to it, though the beck was much bigger than it had been, the able-seaman agreed that it was time for a short rest.

They took their knapsacks off to sit on, first emptying out the chocolate. Titty took the compass out of her pocket, and, while she was eating her chocolate, opened the compass on the ground beside her.

'There's something gone wrong with the compass,' she said suddenly. 'It makes the beck flow west, and of course it flows east all the way by Trout Tarn and Swallowdale down to Horseshoe Cove.'

'Did it happen when you tumbled?'

'I don't think it could have done. It didn't touch the ground at all. Perhaps it got too much shaken up on Kanchenjunga. We did come down at a good pace.'

'Well,' said Roger, 'it's lucky we found the beck.'

29

Wounded Man

'AREN'T you ever going to stop hogging?' said the able-seaman at last.

'There's only one more bit of chocolate left,' said the boy, 'and now it's gone in. Let's start. But the fog hasn't lifted like you said it would.'

'That doesn't matter now we've got the beck,' said the able-seaman. 'Come on.'

They wriggled into the straps of their empty knapsacks and set off again, cheered by the chocolate and by the little stream beside them, trickling from pool to pool, and showing them the way.

Titty, of course, was sorry about the compass, but

even if John couldn't put it right, she was sure Captain Flint could. And, anyhow, the compass going wrong wasn't half so bad as losing the way home when she was in charge of the ship's boy. Just for a little while she had known the sort of worry that kept on making Susan go native. Now she was free to be happy with the thought that the candle-grease had not done any harm and that anyhow, whether the candle-grease had helped or not, the great-aunt was gone. *Swallow* was nearly finished, too, and then on the top of these thoughts, happy in themselves, came another that would have made the able-seaman galumph, if only the fog had not been so thick and she had not been afraid of tumbling among the loose stones at the side of the stream.

'Boy,' she said, 'we'll be back on Wild Cat Island before the end of the week, and then anything can happen.'

'I'm going to be allowed to sail *Swallow*,' said the boy. 'By myself. Not like last year. John's promised not to put even one finger on the tiller.'

'And the Amazons are coming. Six tents there'll be, counting our stores tent. And we can put up the other old tent for a spare room.'

'Or a dungeon, in case of prisoners,' said Roger.

'Bridget's coming to stay. And Mother.'

'Why not Captain Flint?'

'We'll have him, too. And we'll have Mary Swainson. We'll have everybody. Come on. Peter Duck's just reminded me that the ship's parrot is all alone. And there's the fire to light. Come on.'

They hurried along the banks of the little stream.

'It can't be far to the tarn now,' said the boy some little time later.

'No,' said the able-seaman, 'and from there it's no way to the camp.'

They walked on and on, sometimes on one side of the stream, sometimes on the other, but always keeping close to it, and to each other, because they could not see more than a yard or two in the fog and neither of them liked to lose sight of the stream or to see the other one looking like a soft grey shadow instead of like a solid boy or able-seaman. The stream began to be stonier, and noisier, and less like a tiny ditch draining the swamp on the top of the moor. It was a real stream now, though they could easily jump across it. It made more noise than it had, as if it was in more of a hurry. And still there was no tarn.

'We must have gone an awful long way to the right,' said the boy.

'It can't be much farther now,' said the able-seaman.

And then, suddenly, their cheerfulness came to an end.

'Look,' said Roger, who was a yard or two ahead, 'there's a tree! On the other side. I'm going to cross.'

'There aren't any trees,' said Titty.

'I can see it. It's a big one,' said Roger, and jumped.

He landed with a short squeak of pain on the other side. His left foot slipped between two stones and twisted over. He fell forward, tried to pick himself up, squeaked again and flopped on the ground.

'Have you hurt yourself?' asked Titty, jumping across the stream.

'Rather,' said the boy.

'Badly?'

'Very badly. I can't get up. But I was right about the tree. Look at it.'

If Roger had something in his mind, nothing would stop him from talking of it. He had been thinking of the tree before he jumped. He was thinking of it still, as he lay beside the stream. Titty looked up.

Close above them a tall pine towered like a grey ghost in the white mist. Titty was almost as much troubled by the tree as by Roger.

'There are no trees on the top of the moor,' she said. 'There aren't any till down the other side of Swallowdale in the wood above Swainson's farm.'

'Well, there it is,' said Roger. 'Ouch!'

'Where does it hurt?'

'It's my best foot. Broken, I think.'

'Oh, Roger.'

'And there is no more chocolate.'

'But it can't be our wood, because the Swallowdale beck is twice as big as this when it comes out of Trout Tarn and it's bigger still by the wood. It can't be our beck at all. And we've been following it for miles and miles.'

'I can't move my foot,' said Roger.

'Oh, Roger,' said Titty again, kneeling beside him, 'try not to squeak while I get your shoe off.'

Roger sat still and stiffened himself all over, waiting for a twinge, but none came. The shoe slipped off in the able-seaman's fingers almost before he knew she had loosened the laces.

'I don't think it's broken,' she said. 'Try waggling it, just a little.'

But the first beginning of a waggle brought the pain back at once. It was as if someone were pushing a red-hot skewer through the boy's ankle. 'Ouch!' he said, 'I'm not going to waggle it any more.'

'Try putting it in the water. I wish the mate were here. She'd know what to do. Anyhow, you ought to be sitting on your knapsack.'

The boy slid himself over the stones and lowered his foot carefully into a little pool in the stream.

'Cold,' he said, 'but not half bad.'

'I wish I knew where we were,' said the able-seaman, undoing the boy's knapsack and putting it so that he could sit on it. Susan, she knew, would have thought of that at once.

'Well, it isn't anybody's fault,' said the boy. 'Bother the fog. Hullo! Look at the tree now. It's breathing.'

So it was. The drooping branches of the pine were moving very gently up and down in the mist, though the trunk of the tree did not stir.

'Listen! Listen!' said Titty. 'Wind's coming at last.'

There was a faint noise of wind in tree-tops somewhere behind the white blanket of mist that closed them in from all sides.

'There's another noise, too,' said Roger.

Titty listened. Yes. 'Plunk, plunk, plunk.' It was the noise of an axe. 'Woodcutters,' she said.

'Ouch!' squeaked the boy. 'Sorry. It's all right really. It was only when I turned round too quick. The fog's going away. More trees. Lots. A forest. Wherever are we?'

Titty licked the back of her hand and held it in the air to feel where the wind was coming from.

'It's coming from the other side of the trees. Look,

the whole fog's lifting. I told you it would. I wish we'd waited.'

The able-seaman and the boy now saw that they were in a place where they had never been before. They were on the very edge of the moorland, which stretched up behind them into the thinning mist. Before them the ground dropped so sharply that they could see over the tops of trees growing only a few yards away. The little stream that had led them to this place flung itself down into the forest. Far away below them they could see fields, and beyond them woods climbing the other side of a valley.

'Where's the lake?' cried Roger.

'There isn't a lake,' said Titty. 'It isn't our valley at all.'

'But the lake must be there somewhere.'

'It isn't. And those hills aren't the hills behind Rio or Shark Bay.'

The mist lifted up and up, so that first the low hills showed beneath it, and then other hills above them, and then a patch of sky. But at one place, higher than this, though the mist was still lifting, there was nothing to be seen but dark rock and heather. The mist rose higher and higher, and still in that place there was no sky.

'There's a mountain,' said Roger. 'It must be a

mountain, and there are really no big mountains behind Dixon's Farm.'

Still the mist lifted until at last they could see two great patches of sky on either side of the mountain, though they could not see its top. The two patches of sky grew upwards and towards each other, while wisps of mist drifted between them across the mountain-side. At last the patches of sky joined. The top of the mountain was clear of mist, and the boy and the able-seaman shouted together, 'It's Kanchenjunga!'

'The compass hasn't gone wrong after all,' said Titty. 'It was the stream that was going the wrong way.'

'And us,' said Roger.

'We must have turned right round in the fog.' She laid the compass open on the ground.

'How are we going to get back?'

For a moment the able-seaman thought of turning round and going upstream to the top of the moor where, perhaps, with the fog blowing away, she would be able to see where they had gone wrong, and find the trail of pine-cones again, and so come to Swallowdale not too late.

But the next moment she knew that this was no good. There was Roger unable to move his foot. It was no good thinking she could carry him. Besides, even if she could, she could not be sure of finding the pine-cones, and then perhaps the mist would come rolling down on them again and they would be worse lost than ever. What would Susan do if she were here? There could be no sort of doubt. Though the able-seaman found it hard to have to give in, she knew that there was only one thing to be done. Help had to be got from the natives. And who could tell what sort of natives she would find?

'Plunk, plunk, plunk.' She could hear the noise of the axe somewhere in the woods beneath them. She turned to Roger with her mind made up.

'I'm going on down,' she said.

'But I can't move.'

'You must wait here till I bring help.'

'By myself?'

'Look here, Roger, I'll lend you Peter Duck. You can have Peter Duck while I'm away. I must go down and find the woodcutters. Peter Duck says so too.'

'You stay here, and let Peter Duck find the wood-cutters.'

'Perhaps he doesn't know their language. No! There's nothing else to be done. I've got to go.'

'But I don't want to be left behind.'

'Roger,' said Titty sternly, 'just you remember, you're a ship's boy. And not the youngest any more.'

479

'Of course I'm not,' said Roger. 'There's the ship's baby.'

'Well, that's what I said. And there's no time to lose. We ought to be back already. It'll be evening soon. And it's been night for the parrot ever since yesterday morning.'

Roger pulled himself together.

'I don't mind, now the fog's gone,' he said.

'So you'll be all right? I'll be as quick as I can.'

'Aye, aye, sir,' said Roger.

'There's one lump of chocolate left in the pocket of my knapsack,' said Titty, wriggling out of the straps.

'I won't eat it unless I'm very hungry,' said Roger.

Titty dropped her knapsack beside him, and set off down into the forest.

*

The ship's boy felt suddenly a good deal less brave as the able-seaman disappeared among the trees. Almost he called after her, but stopped himself in time. He thought then of giving the owl call, to show that he was still being a ship's boy and not afraid of anything. But he remembered that Titty might not know that his owl call meant exactly that. She might think he wanted her to come back. Then she would come and that would be no good at all, because she would have to start all over again. No, there was nothing for it but sitting still and being ready for anything that might happen. Bears, for example. It looked just that kind of forest. Or wolves. But, after all, the bears and wolves had missed their chance. The fog had lifted now. Before, a bear or a wolf could have crept close up on the able-seaman and the boy as they struggled along in the fog, and then leapt upon them without warning. 'They needn't even have growled or snarled. The first thing we'd have known would have been the snap of their jaws.' It was an unpleasant thought and though, now that the fog had lifted, surprises of that kind were impossible, Roger took three or four good stones and put them together where he could grab one up in a moment if he needed it. Then he had another look at his wounded foot, and found that somehow it did not hurt so much to move it when he was by himself as it had when someone else was there hoping it would not hurt him more than he could bear. Still, it hurt quite badly enough. Moving it at all reminded him of the mermaid who had to walk on sharp knives. He found that if he had been a mermaid he could have managed quite well without legs even on dry land. He heaved himself up on his hands and then let himself down again. It would have taken a long time to get very far, but, happily, he did not need to. He made himself a comfortable lair, arranged both knapsacks on the ground and, sliding himself along, settled down on them, with his stones within easy reach and the stream so near that he could take a drink from it in the palm of his hand. It did come into his head that dragging himself about in this way was not too good for the seat of his breeches, but, after all, it was nothing to what they had had to suffer from the Knickerbockerbreaker in Swallowdale, and Mary Swainson, when she last darned them, had used good strong stuff and had said, 'It'll take you more than a slide or two to get through that.' Then, of course, came a rather grimmer thought. He would not be able to do any more sliding on the Knickerbockerbreaker with his foot all gone wrong, even if the seat of his breeches had been made of leather instead of being mostly Mary Swainson's darning.

He had another look at the damaged foot, and when he saw how blue and green a bit of it was turning, he thought for a moment that it must be hurting him badly. But he soon found it was not, by waggling it, when it hurt at once, so that he could easily tell the difference. He remembered what he had heard in several stories about wounded men fainting from pain. He was not quite sure how they did it. He flopped backwards, but a sprig of heather tickled the back of his neck. He had to find a smoother place to faint on. He wriggled until he could lie very comfortably at full length and then set about fainting in the grand style, but just when he thought he had at last found out how to do it, breathing very slowly with his eyes tight shut, something happened that he had not expected. He had been up early the day before for the march to the Amazon River. He had waked early again today in the camp half-way up the mountain. A great deal had been happening to him ever since and now, without thinking about it at all, he fell asleep.

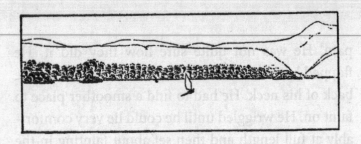

30

Medicine Man

THE noise of the axe, 'Plunk, plunk, plunk,' was
very near. Titty slackened her pace. She had come
fast down the steep wood, holding now to one tree
and now to another to steady herself. But, now that
the noise was so near, she moved a little less like
someone running for a doctor and a little more
like an explorer in an unknown country. With Roger
lying wounded at the edge of the moor, there was no
time to be lost, but Titty did not want to run straight
into the natives without knowing first what sort of
natives they were. She tried to keep her feet from
making so much noise among the dry leaves and

fallen twigs. This was difficult because the wood just here was of the noisy kind, oaks, beeches, rowans, and especially hazels, with leaves and twigs that seemed to crackle and snap on purpose. Here and there were a few old giants, but most of the trees were short, young, bushy, and so near together that even a small and careful able-seaman could not push her way through without making a noise. Close in front of her, however, the trees had been lately cleared. The green curtains of leaves were not so thick as they had been, and in another moment she would be able to see who it was so steadily chopping away down there with hardly a rest between the blows. Titty heard the 'plunk' of the axe, and then another, and then the noise of a chopped stick breaking off with a loud crack. Whoever it was, he was not cutting down a big tree, but was chopping small stuff. Almost it seemed too much to hope, and yet the noise did sound very much as if it might be charcoal-burners. Titty crept quietly to the edge of the clearing and looked out.

There beside the stream was a stretch of level ground, as it might be a platform on the side of the hill. On it there was a ring of sticks laid for the burning. The round stack was three or four feet high already, made of sticks about a yard long, all pointing towards the middle. Between the stack and the stream was a great pile of cut sods of earth. Titty knew what they were for, because last year she had seen one of the charcoal-burners' stacks already alight, and covered all over with sods of earth, so that the fire should not burn too fast. She had seen the charcoal-burners keep the fire caged inside by covering every little hole with a sod the moment smoke or flame showed that the fire was finding a way out. On the other side of the half-finished stack, so close against the trees that she would hardly have seen it unless she had been looking for it, was the charcoal-burners' hut, a wigwam built of long poles, their thick ends on the ground, their thin tops meeting high overhead. In front of it a big black kettle was hanging from a tripod over a small fire. At the other side of the flat space the wood dropped steeply again down into the valley. The sun, which had disappeared altogether during the fog, was now low over the shoulder of Kanchenjunga, and shone straight into Titty's eyes as she looked out from among the trees. For a moment she did not see the charcoal-burner, though she heard him. Then the chopping stopped and from the other side of the woodpile came an old, bent, brown man with a bundle of sticks which he put on the fire under the kettle.

Titty ran joyfully out. She did not know which of

them he was, but she knew that the old man was one of the two Billies, the charcoal-burners who had shown them their adder last year when they had been making charcoal up in the woods on the other side of the lake.

'Well, lass,' said the old man, 'we've been talking of seeing you again. And where are the rest of you?'

'There's nobody here but me,' said Titty. 'But Roger's up on the moor at the top of the wood and he's hurt his foot and I've got to get him home.'

The old man looked at Titty. She thought perhaps he had not understood.

'We got lost in the fog.'

'Aye,' said the charcoal-burner, 'I was thinking it would be that. Came on fast, didn't he? Thick, too. Older folk than you lose the road on the fells when he comes on thick as that. I was lost three days up on the tops fox-hunting one back end. Fifty year ago, it'll be. Roger's the little lad, eh? Where did you leave him? Top of the wood. By the beckside? You and I'll be going to look to him right away.'

He walked to the edge of the flat space and put one hand to his mouth, to shout down through the trees.

'Kettle's on,' he shouted, in a much louder voice than Titty had expected. 'Kettle's on. Come up, one o' ye, to see to't. I'm away.'

'Aw reet, Billy.' A shout came up from far below, and now for the first time Titty heard noises from down there, the clanking of chain over a pulley, the stamping of horses and the creak of heavy timber.

'What is it?'

'Shifting timber,' said the old man. 'There are some rare big logs to go yet. You'll have seen some of them going round to the foot of the lake. Like to run down and have a look?'

'I must go back to Roger,' said Titty.

'I'll be thinking I'm getting old next,' said the charcoal-burner. 'I was forgetting the lad already. Come on then, lass, and we'll soon see what's to do.'

The old man and the able-seaman set out to climb through the trees up to the moor.

'Aye,' he said, 'they were saying you were back and up on fellside above Swainson's. There was a rare lot of talk last year about you folk and finding Mr Turner's things for him that were taken. And this year they say you've had a bit of a sad do with your boat.'

'It wasn't John's fault,' said Titty. 'It might have happened to anybody. And *Swallow*'s nearly mended and she's coming back as good as new. And the new mast's done. And as soon as we've got her again we're going back to the island.'

'And the Blackett lasses,' said the charcoal-burner. 'There's old Miss Turner been staying at Beckfoot. You'll not have been seeing so much of the lasses, I reckon.'

'She's gone now,' said Titty. 'And Nancy and Peggy are camping with us tonight. They've sailed down the lake, with John and Susan. And we ought to have had the fire lit before they got to the camp. And then the fog came. And now Roger . . .'

'Don't take on, lass,' said the old man. 'Happen the fog bothered them a bit, too, on the water.'

That was true, she thought. Perhaps the boat party were not yet at Swallowdale. It might yet be possible to get there first. Titty looked at the old man and made up her mind to ask him a question.

'I hope you don't mind,' she said, 'but are you Young Billy or Old Billy? It was Young Billy who had the adder, wasn't it?'

The old man laughed.

'You remember that, do you? Aye, it was my adder you saw. I'm Young Billy, I am. It's my Dad's Old Billy.'

'And where is he?' asked Titty. 'Was he down there where you said they were loading trees?'

'Nay,' said Young Billy. 'It's like this. There's a hound-trail over Bigland way today, and a bit of a do, like, after it, and my old dad heard that old Jim Postlethwaite was going to be there, and thinking he'd be oldest of the lot. Now Jim Postlethwaite's nobbut eighty-nine and my Dad's seen ninety-four this last back end. "I'm not going to be beat by a young chap like that," says my Dad, and he was off to Bigland this morning, walking over the fell, and he'll be stopping there the night with a young nephew of mine that has a mort of great-grandchildren to show him.'

Young Billy himself was over seventy and had grandchildren much older than the able-seaman, but she was more out of breath than he was as they climbed up the wood.

When they came near the top, Titty gathered all the breath she had left to give the owl call so as to let Roger know that help was at hand.

There was no answer.

'It wasn't a very good one,' she said, and tried again.

This time a decidedly shrill young owl answered from close above them.

'To-whooooooooo,' called Titty again, and in another minute Roger, who had waked up suddenly in the lair by the stream where he had fallen asleep while trying what it was like to faint from pain, saw the able-seaman and the old charcoal-burner coming up out of the forest.

'Hurrah!' he shouted, 'it's the Billies.'

'Only the young one,' laughed Young Billy, who would have been called old if only his father had not been older still. 'Well, lad, don't you stir. Let's have a look at that foot of yours. Properly puffed, it is. Is it broken?'

'I can waggle it,' said Roger, 'and it doesn't hurt as much as it did. It hurts a lot all the same.'

'That's all right,' said the charcoal-burner, after holding the foot in his hands. 'A poultice is what it wants. Now then, lassie, hold that leg of his off the ground while I heave him up on t'other. Steady. Up with him.'

Roger found himself standing on one leg, with Titty and the charcoal-burner holding him up.

'You can let go that leg of his now,' said the charcoal-burner.

'Ouch!' said Roger.

'Keep it off the ground. Now then.' He stooped. 'Get you a good grip round my shoulders. So.' And the ship's boy found himself clear off the ground and on the old charcoal-burner's back.

'Heavy? Nowt to some faggots I've carried. Are you right, lad?'

The old charcoal-burner hitched the ship's boy a little higher on his back and set off by the side of the stream down once more into the forest. Titty picked up the two knapsacks, put the compass in her pocket, and hurried after him.

When they came down to the open space with the wood stacked for burning and the charcoal-burners' hut, they found two other, much younger natives, busy by the fire, filling tin mugs with hot tea from the kettle and pouring milk in out of a big green bottle.

'What's amiss?' said one of them, looking up, and Titty knew him at once for Mary Swainson's woodman. So this was the place he was bringing the logs from, and the horses she had heard stamping down below must be the three great horses they had seen the day Roger and she discovered Swallowdale, and again and again since, passing one way or the other along the road that went to the foot of the lake.

'Nothing much,' said the old charcoal-burner. 'Lad's turned his foot on wrong side. He'll be right enough with a bracken poultice. Whoa, now. Steady, lad. Stand on the one leg and keep game one off the ground. Lend a hand, Jack, to lay him down.'

The two young woodmen helped and presently Roger was comfortably lying by the fire looking at the natives and over his shoulder at the charcoal-burners' hut. What he was thinking about was, whether he had a chance of seeing the adder.

Titty was watching Young Billy, who was hunting about for old, dead bracken leaves from last year. He found the leaves he wanted and made a great bundle of them round Roger's foot, and wrapped it over with a big red handkerchief damped in hot water from the kettle.

'But there's tea in it,' said Titty.

'Water's none the worse for a drop of good tea, take it inside *or* out. And now you'd best be taking a drop inside yourselves.'

He lifted the bit of sacking that did instead of a door, went into his hut and came out with two tin mugs, one for himself and the other, which was really Old Billy's, his father's, to be shared by the able-seaman and the boy. And Mary's woodman poured them some milk in out of his green bottle and there they were all having tea together, and the woodmen were saying that it was no wonder Titty and Roger had missed their way, for you could have cut that sea-fog with a blunt knife and used the bits to build a wall with.

It was very pleasant after being lost in the fog to be sitting there in the quiet wood having tea with a medicine man and other friendly natives, and Titty would have been happy if only she had not been thinking all the time of Susan and the others up in Swallowdale wondering what had happened. Time was going on. The sun was already low, and she would have to ask one of the natives to show her the way over the moor. And then there was Roger. How was he to get along with only one foot and the other a huge red bundle that must not be allowed to touch the ground?

'How soon will Roger be able to start?' she said.

'Nay, he won't shift tonight,' said the old man. 'He'll have to bide here with me, and you can come for him in the morning. He'll bide with me. You tell the Blackett lassies that the lad's with Young Billy in the Heald Wood and they'll bring you over the fell in the morning. You won't mind biding here, will you, lad?'

'In the wigwam?' said Roger, almost jumping up, but reminded by his foot that he had better not. 'With you? May I really? I'm sure Susan wouldn't mind.'

Titty was not so sure, but after all the main thing was to let Susan and John know that Roger was all right, and of that she was sure enough. The boy had not squeaked even when the old man put the poultice on. He was being cured in the right way, by savage medicine, herbs, bracken leaves at least, and probably charms. She jumped up.

'Is it very far from here across the moor?' she asked.

The old charcoal-burner was talking to Mary's woodman.

THE RETURN OF THE ABLE-SEAMAN

'There's no two ways about it,' he was saying. 'The lad must lie and the lass must away back to tell the others not to be in a taking. And it's a poor road across the fell from this side for folk what don't know it. You'd best take her with you, Jack. It's nobbut a step for her from Swainson's farm, and you'll be stopping there likely. Bonny lass is Mary Swainson, aye, and a good wife she'll make and all.' He laughed and the woodman reddened and then laughed too.

'And welcome,' he said. 'She can ride on the log and the horses'll not know the differ. Are you ready to be starting now?' he added, turning to Titty. 'We're more than a bit late tonight.'

Almost before she had time to say 'Goodbye' to Roger, she was going down the wood with the two woodmen and the charcoal-burner. At the bottom of the wood in a clearing close to the road were the three great horses harnessed to a huge log resting on two pairs of big red wheels.

Mary's woodman lifted Titty high in air and set her on the end of the log where it stuck out far beyond the wheels.

'Are you right?' he asked.

'Yes, thank you,' said Titty.

'Hold tight while we get going.'

The other woodman was taking their nosebags off the horses.

'You'll set her down at Swainson's,' said the old charcoal-burner. 'And tell Mary I'll have the lad right by morning.'

'Thank you very much indeed,' said Titty.

'Goodnight, Billy,' said the two woodmen.

'Goodnight, Jack. Goodnight, Bob.'

'Coom up, lass!'

For a moment Titty thought that Jack was speaking to her, but the horse between the shafts threw its weight forward with a jerk, and the two leading horses pulled on the traces, and the huge log, with the able-seaman sitting high on the after end of it, as if on the poop of an old galleon, moved out of the wood and off along the road.

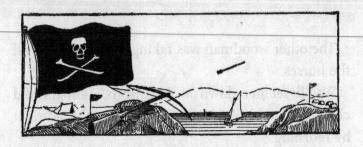

31

Wigwam Night

ROGER had been very sure that he would like to stop with the old charcoal-burner and spend the night in the wigwam. It was the sort of thing that anybody might plan for himself, like crossing a roaring torrent on a bridge made of a single tree trunk, meeting a bear half-way and somehow waggling the trunk so that the bear fell in and the hero did not. It was the sort of thing that anybody might safely plan for himself because it was not likely to happen. Never for a minute had he believed that he would be allowed to stay and at the very moment when he was saying hopefully that Susan would not mind, he was expecting that Titty, who, as able-seaman, was in command, would say that he must not. And then what with the woodmen being in a hurry to be off, and Young Billy arranging that they should give Titty a lift down the valley and along the lake road to Swainson's farm, and Titty, instead of forbidding it, being really glad to have Roger in a safe place, everything had been settled so fast that Young Billy had gone down to the road to see Titty start on her way with the woodmen before Roger realised that he was alone and already in the middle of a new adventure from which he could not possibly draw back.

Lying by the fire he looked out over the green tops of the trees below him to see Kanchenjunga heaving up into the sky on the other side of the valley. Where everything else was strange that, at least, he knew. He had been on the top of it only that morning. He tried to see the little gorge where they had made their half-way camp. It was hidden by a spur of the great hill. It had seemed natural enough to sleep in such a place, in the open air, without even a tent, but with Susan and John and Titty sleeping beside him. It was not at all the same thing as sleeping in a charcoal-burner's hut, with an old man nearly as old as Kanchenjunga, and a snake hissing in a cigar-box somewhere under the blankets. Roger knew suddenly that it would be only too easy to begin thinking of the old charcoal-burner as of a sort of ogre who might take a fancy for eating ship's boys. Of course, Young Billy was nothing of the sort. But Roger knew that it would be easy to begin thinking of him in that way. He must not do that. There could be no turning back now. For one thing he could not very well run for his life with his ankle made up into a huge bundle with bracken and a damp red handkerchief that did not belong to him. For another thing, he did not know where to run. And, for a third thing, he knew very well that the Billies were the friendliest of savages.

All the same it would not do to think too much, just in case he began to think of the old man in the wrong way, when it would be difficult to stop. He looked at the hut. It looked newly built, not like the old hut they had seen last year when they had left *Swallow* and climbed through the woods to see the charcoal-burners and their snake. But he could not be sure. The moss that had been pushed between the logs to keep out the rain was still green, but perhaps it was an old hut with new moss on it. 'It's a very good wigwam, anyway,' said Roger to himself, almost as if it was his own.

The old charcoal-burner came climbing up the wood again.

'The lass'll be all right,' he said, 'and how's the lad?'

'Very well, thank you,' said Roger.

'Bracken's rare stuff for taking the hurt out of a sprain.'

'Is this a new wigwam?' asked Roger. 'Have you just built it?'

'New what?'

'Wigwam. Log hut. No. It isn't a log hut, because all the logs stand on end instead of lying sideways. And it's round instead of square. I don't see what else you can call it.'

'It's been called a hut for long enough,' said the old man. 'Not but what your word may be right. And this hut's old and new. They've always burned charcoal here when there's been any burning done in Heald Wood. Happen some of those logs have seen a good few seasons. But huts don't last so long. They generally fall in a bit between one burning and another. It'll be a good few years like before we come back to them. And a winter storm'll easy shift them if they're not cared for. And then when we come to build them up there'll be new logs put in with the old and new moss to make all tight, and the time all's done you'd be hard put to it to say whether hut's old or new. Fire-spot's old enough. You can say that without lying.'

Roger began to feel that to the old charcoal-burner

it did not seem at all odd to be sleeping in a wigwam in the woods on the side of the fells. For him, in summer that was the natural place to sleep. And why not? Roger stopped worrying about it, and after that everything went easily.

The old man picked up his axe and went on chopping sticks to the right length for the round stack that he was building, putting sticks of the right length in one pile and letting the little odd bits lie to be picked up afterwards and used in his own fire. Roger lay watching him, sniffing the pleasant smell from the embers still smouldering away under the kettle. He felt very sleepy, but he was not going to say anything about that unless the old man said something about it first.

And as the old charcoal-burner chopped away at his sticks, he kept stopping from time to time and talking. He talked of what his old dad might be seeing at Bigland besides the hound-trail. There would likely be some wrestling, and when Roger asked what that was, Young Billy said it was high time he was taken to see some. And then he told of how long ago he was taken, when no bigger than Roger, to see his old dad wrestle for a belt with a bit of a silver buckle on it, and then of how the time came when he was wrestling in that place himself. And with that his back straightened and he swung his old arms and rubbed his old hands and clapped them together and rambled away with talk that Roger could not understand at all, about half-Nelsons and cross-buttocks and fair throws and lost handgrips. But Roger did not say that he did not understand. He just listened and the words went over his head like great poetry, only leaving him the feeling that the old man who was talking was very much stirred up by something or other that had happened a very long time ago.

And then, suddenly, the old man stooped again. 'Fifty years ago, that was,' he sighed, 'but I could show some of them a trick or two yet.'

And now the sun began to go down behind Kanchenjunga, and the old man picked up some of the small bits that had fallen from his chopping and threw them on the fire. And he wiped his axe on the palm of his hand and wiped his hand on the seat of his trousers, and asked Roger what he thought about a duck egg to his supper.

'I've never eaten one,' said Roger.

'There's no hen can lay an egg to touch them,' said the old man, 'not for meat and virtue. And with Dad being over to Bigland there'll be one for you and one for me and then we shan't be clemmed for hunger in our sleep.'

He stirred the dry sticks till they blazed up under the kettle which he had filled with fresh water from the beck after Titty and the woodmen had gone. He went into the wigwam and came out with two huge greenish-white eggs and a big spoon with which he lowered them into the kettle. Roger knew that Susan said you ought not to boil eggs in the kettle if you could help it, and he was just going to ask a question about that, but stopped himself, remembering that different tribes have different customs and that he really knew very little about this one.

Then the old man brought out a lot of blankets from the wigwam and shook them and took them back again. Then he came out with a loaf of bread and he opened his pocket knife and cut two big hunks off the loaf. Then he slapped his knee and said he was forgetting the salt and went in again and came out with an old tobacco tin full of salt. Then he took the eggs out of the kettle and put in some tea and put the kettle back on the fire with the tea in it, a thing that Susan never did.

'There's enough milk left for both of us,' he said, lifting the green bottle, 'with Dad away.'

The big eggs were almost too hot to touch, but the old charcoal-burner rolled a foxglove leaf and held his egg in that while he began peeling off the shell after battering it a little with the big spoon. He showed Roger how to do the same. By the time half the shell had been peeled off the egg was not so hot and the other half was managed without the leaf, and there were the two eggs, ready to be eaten, bluish, quivering things, like egg-shaped corn-flower moulds. The old man took a bite off the top of his egg, and there was the dark orange yolk trying to pour itself out. Roger did the same to his egg, and both the old man and Roger licked at the orange yolk of their eggs as it ran down over the edge of the white. Then the old man took a huge bite of his bread and Roger did the same.

'Rare things are duck eggs,' said the old man, dropping a pinch of salt into his.

'Jolly good,' said Roger, 'and plenty in them.'

Soon after that the old charcoal-burner began to make things ready for the night.

'You'll be wanting a pillow,' he said to Roger. 'Dad's taken his coat with him.'

'I'll put my clothes inside my knapsack,' said Roger.

'You'll be cold without them,' said the old man.

'I slept in them last night,' said Roger.

'Better sleep in them again,' said the old man, 'but I'll put some dry bracken in that bag of yours to make a pillow.'

'Now then,' he said, a few minutes later, and he

helped Roger up on one foot, and almost carried him into the hut. The door was too low for that, and Roger had to crawl through it in spite of his bad foot, which did not hurt him as much as he expected. Inside the hut a farm lantern was hanging, for it was growing dusk outside and very little light came through the doorway, even when the sacking was pulled out of the way. The hut was divided in three by two big logs that lay on the floor, cutting off the bed space on each side, and leaving a narrow passage in the middle where there was a small stone fireplace with no fire in it.

'Too hot for that these nights,' said the old man.

The bed on the left of the doorway was waiting for Roger. A blanket lay on the thickly piled bracken, and at one end of it the old man had put Roger's knapsack.

'Lie you down there,' said the old man, 'and I'll fold blanket over you and you'll be warm enough.'

Roger hesitated.

'Have you still got an adder in a box?' he asked.

'Never fear for that,' the old man laughed. 'Adder's my side of the hut and he won't get out.'

'May I see him?'

'I'll take him out in the morning,' said the old man. 'It's getting too dark for that now.'

Roger lay down on the blanket with his head on

his stuffed knapsack. The old man folded the blanket over him and then folded the other side over the first.

'Snug enough like that,' he said. 'Now don't you be waking when you hear me stirring in the morning. Good night to you.'

'You aren't going away?' said Roger.

'Nay,' said the old man, 'I'll be close outside.'

There was a bitter smell in the hut, of bracken, and burnt wood and newly cut timber, and smoke from the wood fire outside, and oil from the smoky farm lantern overhead. The lantern had been joggled a little by the old man in tucking up Roger for the night, and for a long time it went on swinging on the end of the long bit of wire on which it hung, so that splashes of light and shadow moved round the edges of the darkness on the sloping walls of the hut. Part of the way up the walls Roger could see and count the poles of which the hut was built, but above the lantern they melted together into blackness.

Outside there was a noise of chopping, not with an axe but with a knife. And the old man grunted as he worked away by the fire in the deepening dark. The old man? It might be something quite different grunting out there. Roger lifted himself on his elbow and listened. 'Chop, chop. Grunt, grunt.' Was it the old man or had something else taken his place?

'What are you doing?' he asked at last.

The grunting stopped.

'Aren't you asleep?' came back the voice of the old charcoal-burner.

'Not quite,' said Roger.

'I'm just fettling up a crutch,' said the old man. 'You'll be wanting to be getting about in the morning, and that foot of yours'll be all the better for being off the ground for a day or two. Now, get you to sleep.'

'A crutch for me?'

'Aye.'

And in the shadows dancing along the edges of the darkness overhead, Roger saw Long John Silver with his crutch and his parrot, hopping about the Bristol tavern, stumping the decks of the *Hispaniola*, and being bothered by the point of the crutch sinking in the loose sand of Treasure Island. Titty had the parrot, and now he was going to have the crutch. This was going to be worth a hurt foot and worth it a hundred times over. How soon would he be able to go across the lake to Holly Howe and stump up the field to the farm, as an old sailor back from the sea, to show his crutch to Mother and Nurse and the ship's baby? What would Titty say that Peter Duck thought about it?

Later on in the night he woke to find that all was dark. There was the noise of the old man breathing on the bracken bed at the other side of the hut. There was the noise of wind stirring the tree-tops. The sacking did not cover the whole doorway, or, maybe, a corner of it had blown aside, for looking that way, past his own feet, Roger could see a patch of dark blue sky with stars in it. He thought of the others sleeping in the camp in Swallowdale. Little they knew that a one-legged sailor . . . that Long John Silver . . . that . . . that . . . But before his thought was finished even for himself, he was again as fast asleep as the old charcoal-burner at his side.

WILD CAT ISLAND FROM THE SOUTH

32

Fog on the Lake

THE two captains laid to their oars, and it seemed no time before the war canoe crossed Octopus Lagoon and shot into the lower river, past the wood, and below the Beckfoot garden, where yesterday John had seen the great-aunt pointing with her stick at the daisies on the lawn. 'Pull right,' called Mate Peggy. 'Right. Easy. Ship your oars.' Nancy and John brought their oars in as the canoe (which was really the Beckfoot rowing boat) slid on into the dark boat-house, where the *Amazon* lay moored beside the Beckfoot motor launch. There seemed to be a good deal of cargo in the *Amazon* already, what with the tent and the tent poles, and two sleeping-bags, and some fishing rods and a lot of mixed food.

'Stow your things aboard her,' said Captain Nancy. 'There's nothing to keep us now, and if we had a Blue Peter we'd hoist it.'

'Anyhow, we'll be flying the skull and crossbones in two minutes,' said Peggy. 'It's all ready.'

John and Susan had really very little dunnage to stow. They had crammed the sleeping-bags of the boy and the able-seaman into their own knapsacks, and all the food had been eaten. Besides the knapsacks they really had nothing but the milk-can and the kettle. This was lucky, because there was a big basket and a small wooden barrel waiting on the narrow stone quay that ran round inside the boathouse.

'Well done, Cook,' cried Nancy, rolling the little barrel to the edge of the quay. 'Jolly good of her after we swiped that jugful yesterday and she filled the big bottle this morning.' Nancy began handing the things down out of the basket. 'Ginger biscuits. What's this, labelled THIS SIDE UP? Oh, apple-pie. And here's a tin of toffee fudge. I can hear it rattle. Good! And here's one of her best cakes, one of the black and sticky ones.'

'The sort the G.A. said was indigestible,' said Peggy.

'My word, she has been going it,' said Nancy. 'She's

celebrating, too. You should have seen her this morning the moment the G.A. was out of the house.'

When everything was safely stowed it seemed a good thing that the able-seaman and the boy had chosen to travel overland. There was very little room for passengers amidships, and none before the mast, for even the smallest kind of look-out man.

'All aboard?' cried Nancy at last. 'Cast off the bow warp! Give a shove at the quay, Captain John. Look out, Peggy; don't let her bump the launch.'

The *Amazon* was worked by hand and by poling out of the boathouse into the river, when Peggy hauled up the sail, and hitching the little flagstaff to the flag halyards, ran the Jolly Roger hand over hand to the masthead.

'There's precious little wind,' she said, looking up at the black flag idly dangling against the mast.

'There'll be more on the lake,' said Nancy, as the *Amazon*, broadside on, almost without steerage way, drifted down with the stream.

Even on the lake there was very little wind, not enough to let the Jolly Roger do credit to its owners. There was hardly wind to fill the sail and the little flag hung limp, but Roger was not aboard, so nobody was in a hurry to suggest that it would be better to use the oars. What wind there was came from the south or south-west, and down the lake the water in the lee of the islands was like a looking glass in which every tree and rock was reflected. The little white-sailed *Amazon* crept slowly out from the mouth of the river, so slowly that it was hard to tell that she was moving. She left no wash, and not the smallest ripple stirred under her bows.

'Let's broach the fudge,' said Captain Nancy. 'Easy there with the apple-pie, Peggy. You nearly rammed it with your starboard elbow.'

'Hang on to the pie, somebody, while I dig for the fudge,' said Peggy. She screwed herself round and pulled the apple-pie out of the way and handed it to Susan, licking her fingers because the juice from the pie had spilled over the edge of the pie-dish. Then, digging down again among the knapsacks and bundles, she pulled up a big tin that had once held coffee, but now held something better. The tart was wedged firmly back in its place and the tin was opened with the help of the marlinspike on the ship's knife (the very same knife that had been picked up by Roger and given back to its owners after the parley on Wild Cat Island a year ago). Inside the tin was the fudge, and on the top of the fudge was a bit of paper on which was written, 'Love from Cook.'

'Good old Cook,' said Nancy. 'Let's have that bit of

paper.' She pinched a tiny scrap from it and dropped it overboard. Very slowly, inch by inch, it drifted astern.

'We're moving all right,' she said, 'and there's sure to be more wind presently.'

The other three munched fudge and watched the scrap of paper. Nancy did not look at it again for a long time. She was trying to do the best she could with what wind there was, and there was so very little that she could not be sure where it was coming from. But the *Amazon* seemed to be moving slowly across the lake, though the scrap of paper, small as it was, was still in sight when they had another bit of fudge all round.

After all, there was really no hurry. Nancy and Peggy felt today, now that the great-aunt had gone, what the others had felt on the day when, for the first time this year, they sailed out from the Holly Howe bay. Holidays had at last begun. And John and Susan had been looking forward all the year to sharing new adventures with the Amazons, and now the Amazons were free, and in another day or two they would once more have *Swallow* and be able to voyage to the Arctic, the Antarctic, or anywhere else. Today, for the first time, the Amazons were not bothered by having to get home in time for some wretched meal. Everybody was well content to be afloat and, if not truly sailing, at least ready for a wind.

A long time passed and a lot of fudge was eaten before the wind came, in a steady, gentle breath that carried them across to the eastern shore of the lake, where they went about and stood out again, now on the port tack. They had almost reached the middle of the lake when the sun seemed to stop being so hot, and Peggy said it was very cold, and John and Susan sniffed the air, wondering what was this faint smell they seemed to know.

'I know,' said John. 'It's like fog in the Channel.'

'So it is,' said Susan. 'It's like that day outside Falmouth with Daddy.'

'When we had such a job to find St. Mawes.'

'And the lighthouse was lowing like a cow.'

'It isn't fog in the Channel,' said Nancy. 'It's fog here. Look at it drifting up over the islands.'

'The hills are gone already,' said Peggy.

'I can't see the islands,' said Nancy.

'Or the shore,' said John. 'Not properly. It's going. There it is again. Now I can't see it at all.'

A minute or two later the fog was so thick about them that they could hardly see the length of the boat. It was as if instead of air there was nothing but thick, damp cotton-wool and instead of water, a dull steaming plate under the wool.

'Well, this is a go,' said Nancy. 'Sing out as soon as you see anything, anybody.'

'I wonder whether those two will be all right up on the top there,' said Susan.

'It's taken us ages just to drift across and back again,' said Peggy. 'And they had a long start anyhow. And Titty was in a hurry to get back and give the parrot some sunshine to make up for yesterday. They're probably back by now.'

'Well, I hope they'll have the sense to get something to eat for themselves without waiting for us,' said Susan. 'I did tell them to get the fire lit.'

'Roger'll see that he gets something to eat,' said Nancy. 'You needn't worry about that.'

They drifted slowly on in the white fog. Away to the south somewhere by Rio they heard a steamer hooting steadily. Then the hooting stopped.

'Tied up or anchored,' said Nancy. 'They won't run the steamers while it's as thick as this. Hullo, what's that chap?'

There was the noise of a motor boat coming nearer very fast.

'I wish we had a foghorn.'

But before anybody could even think of shouting, the noise roared past them in the fog and then grew fainter and fainter as the motor boat rushed up the lake.

'That's the way,' said Nancy bitterly. 'In a hurry to get home. Idiots. They never think of anybody but themselves.'

Then they heard voices.

'Better get ashore and boil.'

'Aye. There'll be nothing doing with this fog on the water.'

There was a squeaking of oars on pin rowlocks.

'Fishermen,' said Peggy. 'Going ashore to make their tea.'

'That motor boat's left such a wave that I can't see if we're moving,' said Nancy. 'Anyhow, stand by to go about. Mind your heads.'

The others bobbed their heads down, but the boom was a very long time in coming over. Indeed they presently lifted their heads again and found that the boom was idly jerking as the *Amazon* rolled in the wash left by the motor boat. Captain Nancy impatiently brought her ship's nose round by waggling the rudder.

'It's only that there's so little wind,' she said. '*Amazon*'s a beauty at coming about, really, but of course even she can't do it in a dead calm.'

With the help of the rudder, *Amazon* was put on the starboard tack, and then, thanks, perhaps, to the will-power of two captains and two mates, she began to move again, very, very slowly back towards the Rio shore. It must have been will-power that moved her, because there was now no wind that anybody could feel on the back of a hand even if licked first. But move she did, because another scrap of the paper on which Cook had sent her love, dropped overboard by Peggy amidships, drifted slowly astern and after some time was to be seen close to the rudder.

'If only there were a lot of wind instead of a calm,' said John, 'and if only the fog was black instead of white, this would be like the sail we had in the dark last year when Rio lights went out and everything went pitch black and I tried to steer by compass but couldn't really because the compass wouldn't keep still.'

'It'd keep still enough now,' said Peggy.

'Shiver my timbers for a tame galoot,' said Captain Nancy, 'what's the good of having a compass and not using it? We've got one. It isn't a good one like yours, but it's better than nothing. It's in the pocket of my knapsack. Dig it out, Peggy, and hand it over.'

'We're going backwards now, aren't we?' said Susan, looking at that last scrap of paper which had drifted back and was now close under the bows.

'Howk up the centreboard,' said Captain Nancy, as soon as Peggy had given her the little pocket compass.

'Up it is,' said John.

'Make fast with the peg so that it doesn't slip back. You show him, Peggy. Lower away the sail. It's no good waiting about like this. We'll row, and get down to Horseshoe Cove by compass.'

'I'll row,' said Peggy, as she unhooked the yard and laid it down in the boat.

'We'll take turns,' said Nancy. 'There'll be rowing enough by the time we get down there, if the wind doesn't come first.'

Rowing was not very easy. The boom was a little in the way, for one thing. Then the space on each side of the centreboard case was stuffed with sleeping-bags and knapsacks and the long roll of the Amazons' tent, to say nothing of smaller things like the pie. The rower could not get a proper pull on the oars, but, as Captain Nancy said, that did not matter, because it wasn't as if they were wanting to behave like a motor boat and try to sink an island.

Susan went forward to balance the boat, and sat on the cargo aft of the mast. Peggy did her best with the oars. Nancy held the compass, a small scout compass, and, watching the needle, pointed in the direction in which the boat ought to be going. John took the tiller and steered, keeping his eyes on Nancy's hand.

'South-east's our course,' said Nancy. 'We must be more than half-way across the lake, and that'll bring us to the eastern shore. Then we'll know where we are for getting through the islands. It'll be easy enough to strike across when we're the other side of Rio. You'll have to keep a look-out, Susan. I've got to watch the compass and John's got to watch me.'

'Aye, aye, sir,' said Susan, as readily as if she had been the ship's boy.

For a long time Peggy pulled away at the oars, while Nancy's hand, moving a little to right or to left, signalled the course to the helmsman, and Susan stared into the thick white fog. The only noise was the tinkle of the water under *Amazon*'s bows, the faint splash of the oars in the water, the dripping of the lifted blades, and the squeak of the rowlocks.

'Trees. Trees on the port bow,' suddenly called out Susan and John together.

'Don't look round, Peggy, you goat,' said Captain Nancy. 'It'll be your turn to keep a look-out when one of us is rowing. I was thinking we must be nearly across.'

A few yards away in the fog they could see a row of ghostly blue-grey trees.

'We'll follow the shore for a bit,' said Nancy. 'We're bound to come to a tree or a boathouse that we

520

know.' She stared at the shadowy trees as they slipped slowly by.

John steered so as to keep the trees in sight, which he could do by keeping the boat about ten or a dozen yards from the shore.

'This must be a pretty deep bay,' he said at last. 'I've been giving her an awful lot of starboard helm.'

Nancy opened her hand and looked once more at the little compass.

'Easy!' she cried. 'We're heading nearly north. This must be one of the islands and we've been following the trees all round it.'

The two captains looked at each other with some shame.

'Somebody ought to have been looking at the compass,' said Peggy and, though this sounded almost like mutiny, even Captain Nancy had nothing to say.

'What's the course?' said Captain John.

'South-east again,' said Captain Nancy.

It was rather like letting go of a rope, to turn away and lose sight of the trees and be alone once more in the white fog. But there was no point in rowing round and round an island, so Nancy once more kept her eyes on the compass, and John watched Nancy's hand and steered, and Peggy rowed, and Susan tried to see through the whiteness that shut them in.

Suddenly they heard voices, close ahead of them.

'By gum, but it came on sharp.'

'It did that.'

'What's yon?'

Ghostly in the fog they saw the figures of men on a low landing stage.

'What's yon? What boat's that?'

'*Amazon*.'

'Pretty thick it's come on. Better tie up.'

But already the *Amazon* was slipping along by the shore, and the men and the landing stage had vanished.

'Couldn't have hit a better place,' said Nancy, confident again. 'There's a field here. That's why we can't see any trees. When we see trees it'll be the beginning of Rio Bay. Then we can follow the shore right round by the pier, or, yes, much better, we'll steer due south right across the mouth of the bay. That'll bring us to the boat-building shops.'

'Where they're mending *Swallow*?'

'Yes. We'll have to look out for the Hen and Chicken on the way across the bay, but we ought to see them easily enough with the lake being so low. And we'll go slow anyhow.'

'Rocks?'

'Yes. The Hen is the big one where the gulls paddle,

right out in the middle of the bay. The Chicken's just a little one.'

'Here are the trees,' said Susan.

'Now then,' said Nancy, 'don't row too hard. Keep your eyes skinned, Susan. The rocks are only just above water.' She looked at the compass and pointed south.

The trees faded astern, and once more there was nothing to be seen all round the boat but thick, white, woolly fog and a ring of steaming, oily water.

'Rock on the port bow.'

'All right, Mister Mate, we can clear it,' said John to Peggy, who had lifted her oars, waiting for orders. She rowed again and the rock was swallowed up astern in the fog.

'That was the Hen all right,' said Nancy. 'Now for the Chicken.'

But they never saw the Chicken. 'Steamer buoy right ahead,' was the next thing called by the look-out.

John put the tiller hard a-port and they passed close by the high floating framework of the steamer buoy.

'We've missed the Chicken then,' said Nancy. 'The buoy marks the fairway south of both the rocks. Listen!'

Over the water came the noise of hammerings, and the chug, chug of a small petrol engine, and the rattle of shafting, and every now and then the long 'woosh' of a circular saw slicing through a plank.

'The boatyards,' said John, 'where I was with Captain Flint. Let's go and have a look at *Swallow*.'

'We simply mustn't,' said Susan, 'with those two waiting up at Swallowdale.'

Peggy rowed on.

The tall mast of a racing yacht at her moorings towered above them.

'The *Polly Ann*,' said Nancy. 'She's moored close by the point. We ought to see it in a minute now. There it is. Done it. We're across. It's easy enough now. Come on, Peggy, swop places. I'm going to row.'

John took the compass now, while Peggy steered. They kept close along the shore by the point, and then rowed across the mouth of the Holly Howe bay seeing nothing until the Peak of Darien loomed high and dark out of the fog.

'Now we'll row across the lake. South-west's the course.'

'Come on and take the compass, Captain Nancy,' said John. 'She's your ship. And I'd much rather row.'

Again there was a change of places, and again something known and certain was left behind as the Peak of Darien vanished astern of them while they moved out into the unknown where the only certain thing was the little needle in Nancy's pocket compass, pointing always to the north. John rowed, stroke after stroke, as regular as an engine, while Nancy watched her compass, and Peggy, at the tiller, watched Nancy's pointing hand. It was a long blind passage in the fog, south-west across the lake, but they made the farther shore at last, after which they had only to follow it until they should come to Horseshoe Cove. John rowed steadily on, and presently they were startled to find that they were already in the narrow channel between Cormorant Island and the mainland. They were close under the little rocky island before they saw it, for they were watching the shore on the other side of the boat. The cormorants were startled too. There they were on the dead tree, grey shadow birds in the fog. Neither Swallows nor Amazons had ever seen them quite so near before, but, as Peggy said, they were so dim in the fog that they might as well have been a hundred yards away.

And then, when the shadow birds had vanished with the shadow tree on the shadow island, a ripple showed on the water under the fog, and suddenly they could see the island again, and trees well back from the shore, and the headlands of Horseshoe Cove, and Wild Cat Island at the other side of the lake, and the lower part of the woods, and the hills at the foot of the lake. The fog was lifting, and John stopped rowing for a moment, and they looked back to the islands by Rio as the fog rolled away before the wind. It was hard to believe that they had come all that way from the other side of these distant islands without being able to see more than two boat's-lengths out of their own little ship.

'Let's sail the last bit,' said Nancy.

'It's so very near now,' said Susan. 'It'll be quicker to row.'

'Your mate's thinking of her crew,' said Nancy. 'But never mind.'

John rowed on. He, too, was thinking now of the able-seaman and the boy, who must be wondering up there in Swallowdale how they had managed in the *Amazon* with the fog so thick on the lake. In a few more minutes he was pulling in between the headlands, and this strange voyage was done.

There was a lot of baggage, even for four, when *Amazon* had discharged her cargo on the beach. There was the big tent and its poles, and then there were Nancy's and Peggy's sleeping-bags, which were bigger and heavier than those which were stuffed into the knapsacks of the Swallows. There was the kettle and the milk-can, and the little barrel that had to be slung from an oar. Then there was that pie, too, a kind thought of Cook's, and very good to eat, but a dreadful thing to carry.

'It's no good,' said Captain Nancy. 'We'll have to make two journeys. Just take what you can manage comfortably.'

'We'll have tea and then we'll run down and bring up the rest,' said John.

'It's late for tea now,' said Susan. 'We'll have tea and supper both together, as soon as we get up to Swallowdale. Titty's sure to have some water boiling.'

33

The Empty Camp

SUSAN for a long time had been worried by thinking of the able-seaman and the boy alone in Swallowdale. They would be wondering what had happened to the *Amazon*. Titty would be imagining her run down by a steamer in the fog. Roger would be hungry. Would Titty think of making a meal for him, or would she go and think it was the proper thing to wait for the captain and the mate? You never knew. And then, when Nancy and Peggy, with their tent rolled up and carried on its tent poles, climbed up out of the wood, there came the first hint that things might be far worse than even her most native fears.

'There's no smoke,' said Captain Nancy.

'Those two young donkeys haven't lit the fire,' said Peggy.

Susan and John, heavily laden, hurried up out of the trees. It was true. Not the faintest wisp of smoke was blowing from Swallowdale.

'Had they any matches?' said Captain John.

'No,' said Susan, 'but there were plenty in Peter Duck's cave. Titty was there when I stowed the things. She must know where they were put. If they've gone and waited for us all this time, they must be nearly starving.'

'Yes,' said Peggy, 'they must be. We are, in spite of the fudge.'

'They had nothing with them but some chocolate,' said Susan. 'I thought we'd all be back and have tea together.'

'Is there anyone on the watch-tower?' said John. 'Just half a minute while I get out the telescope.'

But Susan hurried on. This was no time for waiting. Nor did Nancy and Peggy want to stand still with the weight of the tent on their shoulders as well as their crammed knapsacks. They wanted to hurry on to Swallowdale and unload.

'Duffers,' said John, a little uneasily, shutting up the telescope with a click, and running after the others.

'They haven't lit the fire and they haven't even got anybody looking out.'

'Perhaps they're busy putting up your tents,' said Peggy.

'That doesn't take two minutes,' said Susan, 'and we've been ages, because of that fog.'

'What about giving them one of your owl calls?' said Captain Nancy.

John took a deep breath and let it out in one of the best owl calls he had ever made. The long 'Tu whooooooooooooooo' was enough to frighten every mouse on the moor. But it brought no answer out of Swallowdale.

He tried again, but his owl call was not such a good one. He caught sight of Susan's face, just while he was making it. He knew at once that she was feeling much too native for owl calls.

Again there was no answer.

'They're probably making an ambush for us,' said Nancy.

'Scouting along in the heather,' said Peggy. 'They'll probably come charging down on us in a minute.'

'We never ought to have let them go off by themselves,' said Susan.

'We're all ready for you,' shouted Captain Nancy to

the open moorland. 'Make your attack and get it over. We want our tea.'

But nobody leapt up in the heather or dashed out from behind a rock.

'They wouldn't hear anything if they were in Peter Duck's,' said John.

'I told Titty to light the fire if we weren't there,' said Susan.

A few minutes later they were climbing up the side of the waterfall into Swallowdale, Susan first, John next, the Amazons last. The Amazons were bothered by the difficulty of hoisting up their tent, and John and Susan would have stopped to help them if they had not been in such a hurry to know the worst.

'They haven't even put their own tents up,' said John.

'They aren't here at all,' said Susan.

A covey of grouse flew up out of the little valley with their startled cry, 'Go back! Go back!'

'Nobody's been here for a long time,' said Nancy as she and Peggy struggled up over the edge, 'or the grouse would have been far away.'

Susan and John raced up the valley to the old camp. It was just as they had left it the day before. The heather still covered Peter Duck's doorway. They pulled it aside and went in, to be met by an angry scream from the parrot. John lit a match and then one of the candle-lanterns that were waiting in a row on the stone ledge. Nothing in the cave had been touched.

Susan looked at John, and he saw that this was worse than the worst that she had feared. He picked up the parrot's cage and carried it out into the evening light.

'They haven't been here at all,' he said grimly to Nancy and Peggy, who were just dumping their tent by the fireplace.

'They've probably just been held up a bit by the fog, like us,' said Nancy.

'Or Roger's got interested in something,' said Peggy.

'They've got lost,' said Susan.

'Pretty Polly, Pretty Polly,' said the parrot.

'I bet they'll show up before we get the tents pitched,' said Nancy. 'Let's get on with it. It's got to be done, anyhow.'

'I'm just going up to the watch-tower,' said John. 'They may be in sight from there.'

'Good idea. We'll have the tents up in no time. What about starting the fire, Mister Mate?'

'Make a good pillar of smoke so that they can see it from wherever they are,' said John, and climbed up the side of the valley to see what could be seen from the top of the Watch Tower Rock.

Susan did not feel at all like being Mister Mate. Her thoughts were all native thoughts, as she built her fire and lit it and then piled it higher than she ever did when all was well and she wanted a fire just for cooking. One dreadful scene after another came into mind. The able-seaman and the boy were lost, had fallen down a precipice, had been swallowed up in a bog. She had hardly a word to say as she brought the four tent bundles out of the cave and began putting the tents up, while Nancy and Peggy were busy marking out the place for theirs and making holes for their tent pegs. And with these pictures of horror came others, of Mother and Bridgie and Nurse. At Holly Howe they were probably giving the ship's baby her supper. Mother and Nurse were happy and at peace, quite sure that nothing could be wrong with Titty and Roger so long as Susan was there to look after them. And there was Susan putting up tents for the able-seaman and the boy, and not even sure that there was anyone to sleep in them. And it made things even worse, somehow, to hear Nancy whistling cheerfully through her teeth, as she shoved the tent poles into the long canvas tubes at either side of her tent door, and hove the whole tent up into its place, and took in the slack in the long guy-ropes.

'Cheer up, Mister Mate,' said Nancy suddenly. 'It's

all right. I know what's happened to those two galoots. They went straight down to Swainson's for milk, and Mary Swainson's given them tea, and then the old man's started singing at them and they haven't had a chance to get away.'

'Of course that's it,' said Peggy. 'And Mary Swainson's stuffing Roger with cake.'

Susan looked almost hopefully at Nancy. That really did sound possible. Quite wise, too. Titty had known the milk would be wanted and had not liked to light a fire and leave it burning, and so had gone down to the farm first of all, and then, well, she knew how hard it was to get away from the old people.

'It's just what I ought to have thought of myself. We haven't any milk, anyway. Only I was so bothered about us being late.'

John came back into Swallowdale to say that nothing was moving on the moor, and now it was Susan herself who comforted him.

'Nancy thinks they're down at the farm,' she said, 'and they probably are.'

'Milk,' said Peggy, 'and listening to the old man's songs.'

'Lend a hand here, Captain John,' said Nancy, 'and then we'll go down and bring them up.'

In a few minutes Swallowdale looked itself again,

and better than it had looked before, now there was the Amazons' big tent as well as the Swallows' four little ones. Susan had built a huge fire and then put a lot of bracken on it, so that a thick curling column of bitter grey smoke climbed up into the evening sky. In the smoke hung the kettle, so that there would be boiling water by the time they came back. Susan damped the sods of earth that she kept by the fireplace and built them in round the edge of her fire.

'It's safe enough really,' she said, 'but perhaps someone ought to wait here, in case they miss us.'

Nobody wanted to stay, and besides there were still the things to fetch up from Horseshoe Cove. Susan got out a bit of paper from Titty's box, and Nancy wrote on it in big letters, 'STOP HERE TILL WE COME BACK.'

'Where shall I put it so that they'll be sure to see it?'

'On the parrot's cage,' said John. 'Titty always says "Howdy" to him, even if she's only been away ten minutes.'

Susan's hopes suddenly fell again. It was very unlike Titty to leave the parrot a moment longer than she could help. Not even the old man's singing was likely to hold her when the parrot had been shut up for two days.

THE MEDICINE MAN AND HIS PATIENT

The two captains and the two mates hurried down the beck on the way to Swainson's farm. Just as they dropped into the wood John looked back towards the last of the sunset over the moor, and saw the high cold column of smoke from the Swallowdale fire swaying in the quiet evening.

'Mother'll be able to see that from Holly Howe,' he said. 'She'll know we've got back.'

Susan said nothing, but hurried on with the milk-can down into the wood.

The farm seemed very quiet as they came down the path towards it.

'The old man isn't singing,' said Susan.

'Out of breath,' said Nancy.

'I don't believe they're here,' said Susan. 'We'd hear Roger's laugh if they were.'

'Not if he's stuffing,' said Nancy.

But before they came to the farm gate they saw Mary Swainson coming from the dairy with a bucket.

'Ah, you're back, are you?' she said.

'Have the others been here long?' asked Susan anxiously.

'What others?'

'Titty and Roger.'

'Nay, they've not been here. Weren't you all away together? I was up this afternoon with the letter, before the fog came on, and there was none of you about then and the cave all shut up.'

'What letter?'

'It's for you,' said Mary, and she put down her bucket and took an envelope from the pocket of her apron. 'I didn't leave it. I knew one of you'd be down for the milk as soon as you got back.'

On the envelope 'Native Post' was written in very small writing in one corner, and then, in large writing that she knew at a glance was Mother's, Susan read the address, 'Mate Susan, The Camp, Swallowdale.' She tore it open and read:

'My dear Mate and Cook,
I'm coming over tomorrow morning with Bridgie to hear all about Kanchenjunga. Don't do too much cooking. We'll bring our own rations. This is just in case you might all be exploring if you didn't know we were coming. Expect us about eight bells of the forenoon watch (John knows when).
                Love to the Captain and the Crew,
                        The Mother of the Ship's Baby.'

Tears filled her eyes and she could hardly read the last words. Mother was so sure that everything was as it should be. And she, Susan, who should have been taking care of the others, did not even know where they were. . . . Blindly she pushed the letter at John. The others looked at her gravely.

'What's ado?' said Mary. 'Don't take on.'

'They're lost. They're lost,' sobbed Susan, 'and Mother's coming tomorrow and Bridgie. . . . She doesn't know.'

'Nay, don't take on,' said Mary. 'They'll not be far.'

'It was in the fog,' said John.

Susan made up her mind.

'We must go and tell Mother at once. We must go and tell her now.' She started off down the cart track to the road.

'Susan's right,' said Nancy. 'The sooner we do it the better. The sun's gone down and it'll be getting dark. Something's got to be done.'

Mary Swainson agreed with Nancy. She plumped her bucket down by the gate, and hurried after Susan. 'I'll row you over,' she called. 'There's no wind for sailing and our boat's quicker for rowing.'

The others caught them up just before they came to the road.

'Nay,' said Mary, 'there's no call for all to go. Some of you'd best bide in your camp. It'll be bad for them, poor lambs, if they find their way in and nobody to give them something hot and put them to bed.'

Just then they heard the noise of horses' hoofs coming nearer in the dusk.

'Lurk,' said John, from habit, but added at once, almost as if he were ashamed, 'What's the good of lurking?' The whole party walked out into the road, in full view of any natives, friends or enemies – who cared which? – who might be coming along.

'Carting trees,' said Peggy.

Three great horses were coming round the bend in the road under the steep woods, and after them the enormous tree chained firmly down on its two pairs of big red wheels. Dusk was falling, and for a moment nobody saw anything but the horses, the log, and a woodman walking beside the leading horse.

Mary Swainson half stopped.

'Whoa, Neddy,' came the voice of the woodman. 'Whoa, there! Steady now.' The three horses came to a standstill.

'Evening, Mary.'

'Evening, Jack.'

'We've a friend o' yours here,' he said, and then they saw Titty slip down from the high-tilted end of the great log into the arms of the other woodman, who was standing below her in the road. They ran towards her.

'Thank you very much indeed,' Titty was saying, and then, 'Hullo, Susan! Roger's hurt his foot, but everything's *quite* all right.'

34

Stretcher-Party

'WHERE is he?'
And then everybody was talking at once.
The woodmen talked to Mary and Mary talked to
Titty. Titty was trying to explain what had happened,
but answers that did very well for Nancy and Peggy
were not quite enough for John and not nearly enough
for Susan. Roger was sleeping in a wigwam. Oh, well,
a charcoal-burner's hut, and a native medicine man
had poulticed his leg and said that nothing was
broken. Was it Old Billy? No, said the woodmen, it
was Young Billy. But where was he? Titty only knew
that he was somewhere on the other side of the moor

and that she had come back down the valley and all along the side of the lake. The woodmen told Mary the Billies were working in the Heald Wood. Yes, of course, that was the name Young Billy had told Titty to tell Nancy and Peggy. And then Nancy and Peggy and Mary all tried at the same time to explain to Susan that it was too far to go there at once. And then Titty was trying to tell her that Roger couldn't be better off than he was, and to tell John how she had tumbled with the compass and how they had thought it had gone wrong but it hadn't, and how they had gone round in a circle without meaning to, and followed a beck going the wrong way, and how Roger couldn't come back that night anyhow, because his foot was all bound up with brackens and the medicine man said he had to keep it still.

'We must have a stretcher-party,' said Nancy. 'We'll fetch him across first thing tomorrow.'

'Can we do it before Mother comes?'

'Of course we can. It's not far to the Heald Wood, going over the moor. Come on, John, let's get the things from the cove.'

'We'll have to start jolly early,' said John.

'Stretcher-party on the road soon after dawn,' said Nancy.

'So long as we're back before Mother comes,' said

Susan. 'It'd be awful if she found the camp empty, like we did.'

'She shan't. Come along.'

'Well, you needn't worry Mrs Walker about him tonight,' said Mary. 'No need to take on now you know where he is. And that's a good thing. And now I've the pigs to see to. Good night, Jack. Good night, Bob. There's no call for you lads to wait.'

'Good night, Mary,' said the woodmen, rather sheepishly, and told their horses to come up. The great log on which Titty had travelled round from the valley beyond the moor moved on along the road.

'You'd think those lads had nothing else to do,' said Mary, looking after them, 'loitering about.' But she waved her hand as they passed out of sight. 'Now,' she said, 'you folk had better take up enough milk for your breakfasts now, and then I'll be bringing you the morning's milk before Mrs Walker comes, so that you'll be off over the fell without wasting time coming down here for it.'

Susan and Titty went with Mary back to the farm, and waited by the orchard gate while she went in with the milk-can and brought it back brimming over with new milk. John, Nancy, and Peggy went down to Horseshoe Cove for the last of *Amazon*'s cargo. By the time they climbed up again into Swallowdale, Susan had supper ready.

Supper of weak tea and hot bread and milk was quickly over. Susan was thinking already far into the next morning, and wondering how bad Roger's foot really was, and what could be done if she found it too bad for Roger to be moved. Peggy or John asked a question sometimes and Titty tried to tell them about the beck, and those other woods, and how startling it had been to see Kanchenjunga come up out of the fog when she had been thinking she was looking at the hills the other side of Rio. Sometimes a question of Titty's set Nancy or Peggy talking of the fog on the lake and of how they had groped their way through it with the compass. But these little gusts of talk died very quickly. It had been a long day and everybody was thoroughly tired out.

They were too tired to be surprised when Susan said there would be no washing up, and that the cups and spoons and things could be rinsing in the beck all night.

Their eyes were already more than half closed as they crawled into their sleeping-bags.

'Whoever wakes first in the morning wakes the others,' said Nancy, yawning. But nobody was awake to answer her.

*

It was a good thing that the great-aunt had kept the Amazons at home so long that this was the first night these holidays that they had spent in a tent instead of in a mere bed. The morning sun woke them early, but had no effect on the Swallows, who might have slept for twenty-four hours on end if Captain Nancy had not roused them with loud shouts while galloping off to plunge into the bathing-pool.

An hour later the stretcher-party was on the move. This time it did not seem worth while to hide everything in Peter Duck's. They wanted the camp to look like a camp just in case Mother should get there before they were back with the wounded Roger. So the four tents of the Swallows were left standing, and the parrot's cage was on its stone pedestal. The Amazons had taken down their tent, because they wanted two of its poles to make a stretcher. It was the only tent with poles stout enough to bear anybody's weight. Nancy rigged up a regular cat's cradle of rope between the two poles, and then folded up the tent for a mattress, and laid it lengthwise between the poles on the top of the cat's cradle.

'It won't be very comfortable,' she said, 'but it wouldn't be real if it was.'

Nobody wanted to stay and look after the camp, and nobody was left behind, except the parrot, and even he was very angry about it and screamed, 'Twice, twice. Two, two,' from the multiplication table.

'He's telling us we left him behind once already, so it isn't his turn,' said Titty. 'We shan't be so long this time, Polly. Going to fetch Roger. Back very soon. And besides it isn't as if you were being left in Peter Duck's.'

But the parrot refused to be comforted.

'I think I'd better go back and fetch him,' said Titty, as they heard him still screaming furiously after they had climbed out of Swallowdale and were already going up along the beck to Trout Tarn.

'All right,' said Susan, 'but we shan't wait for you. You must catch us up. Do remember Mother's coming in the middle of the day, and she's much more likely to be early than late.'

Titty ran back and took the parrot out of his cage and climbed up again and went tearing along the side of the beck after the others, while the parrot, comforted now and screaming on quite a different note, balanced himself on her arm and flapped his short green wings.

'It's all right,' she panted, as she caught up the rest of the expedition. 'You know that notice there was on Polly's cage last night, the one saying "STOP HERE TILL WE COME BACK." I put it in the empty cage so that Mother won't be able to help seeing it if she does get there a minute or two too soon.'

'Jolly,' said Nancy, 'if lots of other people see it, and we come back to find the camp cram full of great-aunts all thinking they're invited.'

'I never thought of that,' said Titty. 'Shall I run back?'

Nancy laughed.

'There's only one great-aunt in the world,' she said, 'and she's gone.'

They climbed on past Trout Tarn, and Titty showed Peggy where she and Roger had caught their big trout. They followed the little beck from the high end of the tarn up over the moor until they came to a wide marsh with tufts of those rushes that Titty and Roger had seen yesterday growing out of moss that squashed down into water when they trod on it. They bore away to the north round the marsh, and were presently over the top of the moor and looking down towards the valley on the other side.

'We've been here before,' said Peggy. 'We know all this side of the fell. I don't believe we could lose our way on it even in a fog.'

'Oh, couldn't we?' said Nancy. 'In a fog anybody can lose his way anywhere. Even the huntsmen get stuck up here sometimes.'

Peggy was looking eagerly before her.

'We ought to be coming to High Street in a minute,' she said. 'There it is.'

'Now we'll get along,' said Nancy. Peggy was already running forward along a clearly marked path, a narrow lane through the purple heather and a track trodden firm across the grassy spaces. Nancy and John, with the stretcher, trotted after Peggy, followed by Susan and Titty with the ship's parrot. There was only room in High Street for one sheep or person, so that the expedition had to march in Indian file.

'If it hadn't been for High Street,' said Nancy, 'we'd probably have discovered Swallowdale. But we've always come up this side of the fell, and High Street is such a good track that we've always used it and never crossed over the watershed.'

'Watershed,' said Titty, as if she had been waiting for the word. 'I ought to have thought of that at once, instead of thinking it was the compass getting bumped.'

On and on they walked along High Street, which, though it twisted sometimes, round a boulder stone or a bit of swampy ground, was in the main a straight track. At last Nancy said, 'We ought to be turning away to the left now, if we're to come down by the Heald Wood,' and soon after that Peggy pointed away down the moor.

'There's your pine tree,' she said. 'There's a little bit of a beck under it, and waterfalls in the woods below, going down to the place where the charcoal-burners have an old hut.'

'If that's the tree,' said Titty, 'that's where Roger hurt his foot. But where's the beck?'

'You can't see it from here,' said Peggy.

'Come on,' said Susan.

They left the regular track and made straight for the pine tree. In a few minutes they caught sight of the beck coming down the moor on their right. They met it by the tree.

'This is the place,' cried Titty. 'Look. There's a scrap of silver paper off the last bit of chocolate. That's where Roger waited while I went down to find the medicine man.'

Susan plunged on down into the wood. The others hurried after her.

Somewhere below them they heard whistling, rather blowy whistling. Someone was trying to whistle 'Spanish Ladies'.

'Roger,' called Susan, and the whistling stopped short.

'Hullo,' came from below them, and the next moment, as they pushed their way out through the bushes they saw Roger himself hopping across the open space by the charcoal-burner's hut, swinging himself along on one foot and a crutch, the other foot just a big bundle in a red handkerchief kept carefully off the ground.

'Fifteen men on the dead man's chest,' shouted Roger, who was enjoying himself very much indeed. 'Yeo ho, ho, and a bottle of rum. Hullo! I am glad you've brought Polly. Hullo, Polly. Say "Pieces of eight", Polly. Do say "Pieces of eight".'

Susan rushed at him. 'Are you all right?' she said. 'Going and hurting your foot.'

'Yeo ho, ho,' said Roger, spinning round on the point of his crutch.

'Who made that lovely crutch for you?' asked Titty.

'Young Billy did,' said Roger. 'He says it's all right to call him that.'

'It's a grand morning,' said the old charcoal-burner coming out of his hut. 'Aye, and he's a grand lad. There's not much amiss. He'll be right enough if he doesn't work his foot overmuch.'

'We've brought a stretcher for him,' said Nancy.

'That's right,' said the old man. 'If he keeps his foot off the ground for a day he'll never know he harmed it. And how are you, Miss Ruth, and you, Miss Peggy? Haven't seen you this long while. Eh! and isn't that Mr Turner's parrot?'

551

'He used to be,' said Titty.

It was always a shock to the Swallows to hear Captain Nancy, the Terror of the Seas, called Ruth. But today Nancy did not seem to mind.

'How are you?' she asked. 'And how's the adder? Do let's see it now we're here.'

'It was in the wigwam all last night, but I slept just the same,' said Roger. 'And he had it out this morning. . . . Hissing like anything.'

'We really ought to be getting back at once,' said Susan; but after all, there was nothing much wrong with Roger, and there was the adder in the hut, and it would be a little hard if Nancy and Peggy were not to see it if they wanted to. So the old man went back into the hut and came out with his box, told Titty not to let the parrot come too near, and lifted the lid at one side, when the adder poured out like a stream of some quick, dark liquid, and was picked up on a stick and hung there, hissing, with his forked tongue darting out between his narrow, bony lips. Susan herself, with all her native worries about being late, was glad to have a chance of looking at the snake again, but oh, how dreadfully easily these Amazons did seem to forget about the time.

At last the adder was dropped back into its box, and the lid closed. Nancy turned to the ship's boy.

'Now then, let's see how you fit into the stretcher.'

'I can get along like anything with a crutch,' said Roger.

'Get into the stretcher at once,' said Susan. 'Mother's on her way to Swallowdale, and we've got to get you back before she comes.'

The stretcher was laid on the ground, Roger lay down on it between the two tent poles, with his crutch beside him. John and Nancy lifted the ends of the poles. The old man came with them to show them the best way up out of the wood.

'Thank you very much indeed for looking after him,' said Susan.

'And I had a lovely ride round on the big tree,' said Titty.

'That's all right,' said Young Billy. 'Be seeing you again one of these days.'

'Goodbye, and thank you very much,' said Roger.

'Goodbye,' called the old man from the edge of the wood.

'Lie down, you little donkey,' said Captain Nancy, as Roger suddenly tried to sit up on the stretcher and wave his crutch.

'If you get tumbled out, you'll go and hurt the other foot and then you'll be no good for anything,' said John.

The stretcher-party hurried up the moor until they

found the track the Amazons called High Street, when they went along it at a good pace.

'I shall get pins and needles in both my legs if I don't do some hopping,' said Roger after a bit.

Light as he was, the stretcher-bearers were glad to have a rest from him, and so, though most of the way Roger travelled as a badly wounded man, he was allowed sometimes to caper along on one foot and his crutch as a very active kind of Long John Silver. Of all the party, perhaps the parrot liked the stretcher best. Its poles were just the thing for him to perch on, so he was ready to travel all the way on the stretcher whether Roger was in it or not.

*

Mother and the ship's baby were a little disappointed when they found no one to meet them in Horseshoe Cove. 'Perhaps we are a bit early,' Mother said. 'No. There's no need to wait, thank you very much.' Mr Jackson, who had rowed them down from Holly Howe, rowed out of the cove and away, and Mother and the ship's baby looked at the *Amazon* pulled up on the beach, with her painter tied to a tree, and then at the new mast for *Swallow*, thinking every minute that they would hear the shouts of the explorers hurrying down through the wood.

For a moment Mother thought she might have mistaken the day, and that they were not yet back from Kanchenjunga; but no, she had seen Captain Flint that morning and he had told her that Miss Turner was gone, and that Nancy and Peggy had joined the camp in Swallowdale. Well, perhaps John's watch had gone wrong again. It often did. It was a pity that none of them were there to help her with the big basket of good things from Holly Howe, but it couldn't be helped. She would probably meet them before she got to the top of the wood. And she would not be going very fast, because of Bridget. 'Come along, Bridgie,' she said, 'let's see how far we can get before they meet us.'

They got the whole way. They crossed the road, not being in the least afraid of natives, since after all, Mother was a native herself. They climbed up through the wood on the other side. They rested at the top of it, looking up to Swallowdale, and wondering why there was no smoke. 'Of course, it's a long way to carry wood, and Susan probably doesn't light the fire unless to boil a kettle.' They went on up the beck, and then, carefully, Bridget going first on all fours, and Mother close behind, lest the ship's baby should slip, they climbed up by the waterfall. And there were the four tents and the empty parrot cage and the empty fireplace, and no sight or sound of a human being.

'Ah, ha,' thought Mother. 'Hiding in that cave of theirs.' And she and Bridget waited outside it, very quiet, with fingers on their lips, to surprise the first explorer who should come crawling out; but none came, and Mother at last went in and found nobody there, and a can of milk, left by Mary, keeping cool in the shade of the doorway.

It was not till then that, coming back into the sunlight, she noticed the scrap of paper inside the parrot's cage. She looked at it.

'STOP HERE TILL WE COME BACK.'

'Hm,' said Mother, 'short and sweet. It sounds more like Captain Nancy than Captain John. Not John's writing. And Susan would certainly have said "Please". "Stop here till we come back." We won't, will we, Bridgie?' And she walked on up Swallowdale to the bathing-pool, and then she and Bridgie climbed up out of Swallowdale and looked up towards Trout Tarn. And there, in the distance, hurrying towards them, they saw the stretcher-party.

Susan was in front and seemed to be hurrying the others. And then came John and Nancy, carrying something between them, something white and long.

And then came Peggy and Titty. But where was Roger? And then Mother saw the parrot, clinging to the thing that John and Nancy were carrying. And suddenly something moved on that thing, and in a moment Mother was running to meet them. What had happened to Roger? It wasn't safe, after all, to let them do things by themselves. Broken arm? Broken leg? Both legs broken?

But there was a sudden cheer from the stretcher-party. It stopped. There were wild jerks of something on the stretcher . . . she knew now only too well what it was . . . and in another moment there was Roger, hopping towards her with tremendous hops, swinging first on his crutch, then on one foot, and shouting 'Yeo ho, ho' at the top of his voice.

*

'Oh, Mother, I'm so sorry we're late,' said Susan. 'We did try to be in time.' But somehow lateness did not seem to matter. Mother was thinking of nothing but Roger's foot, and at the same time was laughing with happiness to find things were so much less terrible than for one dreadful moment she had feared. Titty had run on to poor Bridgie who had not much liked being left suddenly behind. Roger was trying to explain how it was that his foot was bound up in a ball of bracken as big as his head. Nancy was trying to persuade him to get back on the stretcher and be carried into camp properly. The parrot was complaining because the stretcher had been dumped on the ground and nobody was taking any notice of him. Susan ran on and down into Swallowdale to get the fire lit at once. All talking together, Mother, Bridgie, Roger and the rest of the stretcher-party came down into the camp.

'Shiver my timbers,' said Nancy, looking about her. 'It isn't half a camp without our tent. Come on, Peggy. It isn't wanted as a stretcher any longer.'

By the time Mother's basket had been unpacked, and Susan was ready with the kettle, Nancy and Peggy had their tent pitched again and Mother had unrolled all the brackens that the old charcoal-burner had put round Roger's foot, and had a good look at the foot for herself.

'I don't suppose the brackens have done it any harm,' she said.

'It's nearly all right today,' said Roger. 'I can waggle it and it doesn't hurt a bit, at least hardly at all.'

'Well,' said Mother, 'you shall have them all back again if you want them,' and Roger, who wanted to keep his bandaged foot for at least one more day, said he did.

STRETCHER-PARTY

And then, during the feast, the whole story of the climbing of Kanchenjunga had to be told, and the two stories of the fog, and of sleeping on the side of the mountain, and of how Roger tried to hold on to a rock and to point at wild goats with the same hand, and of the night in the wigwam, and of the glories of duck's eggs. . . . It was not until late in the afternoon that Mother said, 'And I'm nearly forgetting one of the things I came to do . . . now is the chance while Bridgie is with Peggy in the big tent. . . . You know it'll be Bridgie's birthday in a few days, and I want to see just how your tents are made. I want to make a little one for her just like them. . . . And then I thought we'd have her birthday party on the island, like we did last year.'

'But shall we be back there?' said Susan.

'What about *Swallow*?' said John.

'Mother knows something about *Swallow*,' said Titty, looking at her mother's face.

'Ask your Captain Flint about her,' laughed Mother. 'He's coming to row us home. And here he is.'

Captain Flint walked into the camp. He was going to shake hands with Mother, but didn't.

'My hands are all oil,' he said, and wiped them on a tuft of grass, but found that no use, and had to borrow the soap from Susan and wash them in the beck.

'He's been working on the mast,' said John. 'Have you?'

'You've made a good job of that mast,' said Captain Flint.

'How soon do you think *Swallow* will be back?'

Captain Flint hardly seemed to hear this question.

'Hullo!' he said, 'what on earth has the ship's boy been doing to himself?' Roger had just come out from Peter Duck's after trying how well he could get through the doorway without letting his bandaged foot touch the ground. And then, of course, he had to be told of all that had happened. And long before he had heard the whole story there was tea. And Mother found a cake at the bottom of her basket.

They were still talking of the Kanchenjunga adventure when Mother said, 'It's getting rather late for Bridget,' and Captain Flint jumped up.

All the explorers came down to Horseshoe Cove to see them off, even Roger, who had already found, privately, that when he put his foot on the ground it did not really hurt.

'I shall be seeing you all tomorrow at Beckfoot,' said Mother, as they crossed the road.

'But that isn't till *Swallow* comes back,' said John.

Mother caught Captain Flint's eye and laughed.

'She isn't back, is she?' said Titty.

'She wasn't last night,' said John.

Mother, Captain Flint, and Bridget were left behind in a moment, as all six explorers rushed ahead through the trees, Roger almost forgetting to use his crutch in his efforts to keep up with the others.

'The mast's gone,' shouted John, and a moment later, bursting out from the trees into the little cove, he saw where it had gone to. *Amazon* was no longer the only sailing boat in the cove. Drawn up on the beach beside her was another little boat, very like *Swallow*, but in such a glory of new paint that at first sight they could hardly believe she was the same dinghy, beloved old *Swallow* they had known. The new mast had already been stepped in her, pale gold with sandpapering and linseed oil, and hung with new buff halyards for sail and flag. Spread on the beach, the damage done in the wreck already neatly mended, lay the old brown sail, and beside it lay the boom and the yard, new-scraped and varnished, together with a coil of fine rope for the lacings.

Not one of the four Swallows could say a single word. They rushed at her, and tenderly touched the new paint and found it dry. They looked at the place where, when they saw her last, there had been a patch of old stained groundsheet over gaping broken planks. They could not have told, if they had not known, where that dreadful hole had been. She was a new ship, better than new, for she had renewed her youth and kept her memories and was still at heart the same old *Swallow* – more, far more, to them than any other vessel could be, anywhere, in all the world.

When Captain Flint had explained yet again in answer to the chorus of thanks that they had nothing to thank him for, because it was only a tiny bit of what he owed them, he helped Mother and Bridget into his rowing boat and pushed off.

'And tomorrow,' he said, 'we'll see which is the faster ship. Start at the houseboat. Finish at Beckfoot. I'll be aboard the houseboat pretty early in the morning. Come along with your fleet as soon as you're ready.'

'Good nights' were shouted, and the rowing boat was just going out between the headlands, and John's fingers were already unfastening the end of the coil of fine rope to begin the bending of the sail, when Captain Flint stopped rowing.

'By the way, Roger,' he called over the water, 'I've got that barrel of gunpowder.' And his oars dipped again and the rowing boat had left the cove.

'Three cheers,' shouted Roger.

'What did he mean?' asked Susan.

'He's going to let me fire the cannon,' shouted Roger, and waved his crutch in the air.

35

The Race

THE two little ships were swinging astern of the houseboat. Their captains and crews were up on the after-deck drinking fizzy lemonade with Captain Flint, who had called at Rio on his way down the lake from Beckfoot and had brought a whole case of it, just the stuff for tropical days, in the Beckfoot motor launch which was moored alongside. Everybody was a little deaf, because not only had Captain Flint welcomed them with a salute of guns as they sailed into Houseboat Bay, but he had kept his promise and loaded and reloaded the little cannon, while Roger, still playing Long John Silver

564

and leaning on his crutch, fired it with a long taper, not once only, but again and again. The smell of gunpowder hung about the houseboat as it had during the battle of last year.

'With the wind like this,' Captain Flint was saying, 'northerly, pretty well straight down the lake, you'll be beating all the way to the Amazon River, and that's where the race must finish because they're expecting you to a feast ashore at Beckfoot.'

'And we had one feast yesterday, when Mother came to Swallowdale,' said Titty.

'By the time you get to Beckfoot today, you'll be ready for another,' said Captain Flint. 'I heard something about strawberry ices.'

'Anybody can eat a strawberry ice, any time,' said Roger. 'They don't take any room like other sorts of food.'

'That's true,' said Captain Flint. 'But about this race. All beat and no run is no test of a ship. You'd better start here, sail down the lake, round Wild Cat Island, and then finish in the Amazon River, the first ship past the boathouse to win.'

'Which side of Wild Cat Island on the way down?' asked Nancy.

'Whichever you like, so long as you sail all round it, and go down one side and up the other.'

'And which way through the islands at Rio?' asked John.

'Take your choice. Each skipper uses his own judgment. Now, I'll give you two guns for a start. The first gun means you've two minutes to go. At one minute to go, I'll wave my handkerchief. At the second gun, you're off, and may the best ship win. Until the second gun goes neither ship must cross a line drawn between the houseboat's mast and the northern point of this bay. Anybody who does has to come and cross it again after the gun goes. Understand?'

The two captains nodded.

'Are you coming, too, in the launch?' asked Roger.

'Too much to do here,' said Captain Flint. 'Shore life ends for me tomorrow, and I'm coming back to live aboard.'

'And we're going back to Wild Cat Island,' said Roger.

'And everything's going to be even better than last year.'

'By the way, Able-seaman,' said Captain Flint, 'what have you done with the parrot?'

'He's taking care of the camp. We took him with us yesterday.'

'We couldn't have him with us, racing,' said Susan.

'Think if he fell overboard and we had to pick him up and lose the race,' said John.

'All aboard!' said Nancy.

'Muster your crew, Mister Mate,' said John.

Two minutes later everybody was aboard his own ship except Roger, who, with his crutch slung about his neck was allowed to come down the rope ladder from the houseboat into the *Swallow*, as if he was a pilot leaving a liner at sea.

'That's that,' said Captain Flint, as Roger let go. 'Now then. I'll fire the first gun as soon as you've both got sail set and look like being ready.'

*

'How do you think the sail's setting?' asked John. 'What about getting the peak a wee bit higher?'

'Will it go?' asked Susan, looking up at the brown sail through half-closed eyes. In that sunshine she was glad that *Swallow*'s sail was brown and not glaring white like *Amazon*'s.

'Another half-inch,' said John, swigging on the halyard. 'Ease off that tackle a moment till I get the peak right up. Now bring the boom down. Handsomely. Stop. So. The wind'll flatten out those wrinkles as soon as she's out of the bay. . . .'

BANG!

A cloud of grey smoke blew away from the foredeck of the houseboat, and they saw Captain Flint reload the little cannon and stand beside it waiting, looking at the watch in his hand.

Nancy and Peggy in *Amazon* were also ready, and the two little ships were sailing to and fro in the bay, their skippers watching each other, each skipper hoping to be sailing for the line when the second gun should go, and near enough to it to be over it and away without losing a second.

'You watch for the handkerchief, Titty,' said Susan. 'And, Roger, we shan't want you forward until we've rounded the island. Stow yourself down there by the middle thwart and keep your hurt foot well out of the way.'

'Aye, aye, sir,' said Roger.

'He's waved his handkerchief,' said Titty.

'One more minute to go,' said John. 'I do wish I hadn't lost the seconds-hand off my watch. Listen! They've got theirs all right. They'll know to a second when the gun's coming.'

Amazon came gliding down towards them in the smooth, sheltered water, and they saw Peggy's head bent, looking at something in her hand, and heard her voice, loud and eager, counting the seconds. 'Forty . . . thirty-five . . . thirty . . . twenty-five.'

Then they heard Nancy, 'Shut up, you tame galoot. Don't count so loud.' They heard no more.

'There can't be more than five seconds now,' said John. 'Nancy's going for the line. Come on.' He swung the little ship round and headed for the mouth of the bay, between the houseboat and the northern promontory. *Amazon*, too, was reaching out. Both vessels were on the starboard tack and not more than a dozen yards apart, but *Amazon* was just a little astern of *Swallow*.

'We're nearly on the line now,' said John, glancing to and fro between the houseboat and the point. 'We'll have to stop her or she'll be across it before the gun goes.'

'He's bending over the gun,' said Titty.

'Can't help it. We're too soon. I've got to luff,' said John, and he brought *Swallow* up into the wind with her sail all ashake.

BANG!

The gun went, and the smoke had not blown away before *Amazon*, already sailing hard, was over the line and away. John put his helm up, brought his ship on the wind again, and was soon after her, but precious seconds had been lost, and *Amazon* was a dozen yards ahead as the two little ships left the bay, and the mates paid out the mainsheets, and, with booms out on the port side, the run down to the island began.

'My fault,' said John. 'Bother that seconds-hand.'

'Never mind,' said Susan. 'It's a long race. We'll make up that little bit.'

'There'll be more than that to make up,' said John. 'Look at her. She's creeping away from us now. They've got their centreboard up. They can always run faster than we can.'

There was no doubt about it. Little by little *Amazon* was adding to her lead. John and Susan hauled in the mainsheet a few inches and let it out again, trying to find just the place where the sail did most good. But it made no difference. Running before the wind and in fairly smooth water, *Amazon* was the faster boat, though not by very much.

'We'll make it up again when it comes to beating,' said Susan.

'If only there's a bit more wind,' said John. '*Swallow* likes something she can feel.'

'That's more like,' said Titty a little later, as the wind strengthened, and a murmur of water came from under *Swallow*'s forefoot. 'You can hear she's pleased with it.'

'Nancy can jolly well sail,' said John, glancing over his shoulder at the wake of the *Swallow*, after watching the wake of the *Amazon*, straight as if it had been laid down on the water with a ruler.

'Are they going to keep ahead of us all the way?' asked Roger.

'The race has hardly begun yet,' said the mate.

The *Amazon* was already close to the northern end of Wild Cat Island, heading as if to pass outside it, when, suddenly, as if Nancy had changed her mind at the last moment, she changed course and headed for the channel between the island and the Dixon's Farm landing.

Swallow's wake waggled for a moment.

'They'll get smoother water that side of the island,' said John to himself, 'and smooth water suits *Amazon* best. But there's more wind outside and *Swallow* wants all she can get.'

'We ought to make up a lot keeping down this side,' said Susan.

Swallow's wake straightened out again as John made up his mind and held her to her course. A moment later they could no longer see the *Amazon*. The island was between the racing ships.

'We must be gaining on them like fun,' said John. 'We may even get to the foot of the island first.'

'It'll be awful, beating up the other side if there's no wind,' said Titty.

John and Susan looked at each other. There was nothing to be done now. 'Down one side and up the other.' The best they could hope for was a lucky gust or two to help them in the narrows, and to make as much as they could now while they still had the wind.

'Isn't it lovely to think we'll be back on the island tomorrow,' said Titty, as they rushed along, close by the well-known shore.

'Lucky nobody has collared it while we've been away,' said John.

'Look out for the rocks off the low end,' said Susan.

'We won't try to go too close, anyway,' said John, 'or the trees'll blanket us. If we go far enough out to keep some of the wind, we'll be clear of all rocks.'

They churned past the low end of the island and *Amazon* was not yet in sight. At the foot of the island, in the lee of the trees and the big rocks that hid the harbour, was an oily patch of smooth water. John watched it carefully. At the edge of it there was not so much a ripple as a promise of one.

'That'll do us,' said John. 'Ready for a jibe. Rattle in the mainsheet, Mister Mate. Round she comes. Steady. That's enough. We'll be close-hauled the moment we're clear. Now, haul in!'

'Here's *Amazon*,' squealed Roger.

Amazon was gliding slowly towards them in the

smooth water of the inner channel. *Swallow* had reached the low end of the island first, and now, after turning round the outer rocks, was coming, close-hauled, to meet her.

'She's still running free. We're close-hauled. She's got to keep out of our way,' said John.

The *Amazon* met them and passed smoothly under their stern.

'Hurrah,' shouted Roger. 'We've caught up yards and yards.'

Nancy laughed. 'Just you wait before shouting "Hurrah" till you've been in there a minute.'

Swallow moved more and more slowly, standing across towards the Dixon's Farm landing. There was hardly a ripple on the water. The island trees and the promontory above Shark's Bay cut off most of the wind. The noise under the forefoot died away, and looking astern John saw *Amazon*, now clear of the outer rocks, come close to the wind and heel over to a puff that he wished with all his heart he could borrow to help poor *Swallow* along.

'Of course they were right to come down inside,' he said. 'Running with hardly any wind is not so bad, but beating when there's no wind to beat against is awful. And now they're clear and can make long boards in a good wind, and we can only make short ones in no wind at all. They'll have made up all we gained and more before we get out again.'

'Can't we row?' said Roger.

'Rowing's not allowed,' said John. 'Don't pinch her, Susan. Our only hope's to keep her moving.'

'She'd head much nearer to the wind.'

'But she wouldn't move so well. Get your weight a bit farther forward, you two.'

To and fro and to and fro again the *Swallow* beat in the narrow sheltered passage between the island and the eastern shore of the lake, while, outside, with a good wind, *Amazon* was making up in a single board, right across to the western shore, all she had lost by taking the inner passage on the run down.

'It's one up to Nancy,' said John. 'Two up, counting the start.'

'Shall we ever catch her?' said Roger.

'Can't tell, till we see where she is when we get clear of the island again.'

'Nobody's touched the fireplace,' said Titty, who had the telescope and was looking at the island. 'I can just see it.'

'Bother the fireplace,' said Captain John. 'Ready about. We'll clear Look-Out Point on this tack. Sing out as soon as you see them. I must watch the sail.'

'There they are,' called Roger, as *Swallow*, now on

574

the starboard tack, sailed out close under the northern headland on which he had spent so many happy hours with the telescope.

'Coming this way,' said Titty.

'They're on the port tack,' said Susan.

'They must have gone about by Cormorant Island,' said John. 'They'll fetch nearly to Houseboat Bay, the way they're heading. They're yards and yards ahead of us again.'

'Are they?'

'Of course they are. If we were to go about now we shouldn't fetch anywhere near Houseboat Bay, and if we go on as we are they'll be at the houseboat before we've gone far enough to head for it. Still, we're out of that channel now. A bit more wind is what we want.'

'Well, it's coming,' said Titty. 'Look!'

A black patch of wind-combed water was sweeping down the lake marking the track of a squall coming down from the mountains.

'They'll be getting it first,' said Susan.

'*Amazon* won't like it,' said John. 'She's not as stiff as *Swallow*. Besides, all together, we must weigh more than them. Look, she's feeling it already.'

They saw the little, white-sailed *Amazon*, far out in the middle of the lake, heel suddenly as the squall struck her. They saw her luff and come up into the wind with sail shaking for a moment. It filled a moment later, but again she heeled over and again she came up into the wind.

'They've got all they want,' said John.

'We'll be having it in a minute,' said Susan. 'Here it is.'

'Hang on, Susan. Don't ease unless you have to. She'll stand it all right. Keep her down to it. *Good little ship.*'

The squall whistled down on them. *Swallow* heeled over, picked herself up, and shot forward, the foam spirting from her bows. There was no need for her to come up into the wind. She was glad of the whole force of it to send her flying on her way.

At this point *Swallow*, on the starboard tack, was racing towards the western shore of the lake. *Amazon*, on the port tack, was scurrying towards the eastern, but was already so far ahead that when next she went about she was off Houseboat Bay, while *Swallow*, on the same tack, would, if she had gone about, have been only just able to make that point that *Amazon* had already reached. But John was taking no interest in Houseboat Bay, and held on his course, for the best wind was in the middle of the lake.

The squall passed, and once more there was only

a light wind. John and Nancy were now sailing tack for tack. When *Swallow* went about, *Amazon* did the same, as if to be sure of keeping the distance she had already gained. For some time no one in *Swallow* could tell whether they were overhauling her or not. At last both little ships were nearing the islands by Rio, both on starboard tack, heading about north-west. *Amazon*, of course, was much nearer to the islands than *Swallow*.

'She'll have to make up her mind pretty quickly,' said John.

'What about?' asked Titty.

'Whether to go through Rio Bay,' said John.

'They always do go that way,' said Susan.

'I know,' said John.

Just as he said it, they saw *Amazon*'s white sail flap as she came up into the wind and went about.

'Of course they're going by Rio,' said Susan. 'Aren't we?'

'We'll hang on a bit longer,' said John. 'We'll lose nothing by that, anyway.'

'We lost by not following them last time.'

'Yes,' said John. 'They were right at Wild Cat Island, but they may be wrong here. They went about before they could see what it was like up the western side of the islands.'

'It's narrow there,' said Susan.

'But look at the way Rio Bay is sheltered by the hills and by the trees on Long Island and by the trees on the point beyond. Well, we'll know in half a minute.'

'They've passed the point of Long Island now,' said Roger.

'Good,' said John. 'They can't turn back. And now, look at that!'

The wind was driving clear down the narrower channel between the islands and the western side of the lake. It was blowing down that narrow passage straight from the Arctic. The channel was rippled with sharp little waves from shore to shore. And already *Amazon* was slipping quietly, slowly, on even keel, into the calms and smooth water of the usual channel under the lee of Long Island.

'We'll beat them yet,' said John, and held on his course into the narrow channel along the western shore. 'Short tacks it'll be, but a good wind to make them with. We'll beat her yet.'

'She's behind the trees now, I can't see her,' said Roger.

'You don't need to,' said John. 'We'll see where she is when we come out the other side of the islands. Ready about!'

Swallow shot up into the wind and a moment later, heeled over on the other tack, was dashing back across the narrow channel. Narrow as it was, every yard of it was good sailing. From shore to island, from island to shore and back again, never for a moment was *Swallow* without a wind to send her singing on her way. 'Nancy can't have found anything like this in there behind Long Island,' said John, half aloud and half to himself.

They were nearly through the channel, heading for the most northerly of the islands on that side of the lake, when they saw *Amazon*'s white sail standing to meet them out from Rio Bay.

'We've beaten her! We've beaten her!' shouted Roger.

'It's a near thing anyhow,' said John. 'We'll know better in a minute or two. Bother this island. Ready about!'

Swallow went about just before coming under the island and headed, now, like *Amazon*, on starboard tack for the western shore. She reached it, went about again, and, on port tack now, hurried away to meet her rival.

'It's a very near thing,' said John again, 'but she's still a wee bit ahead.'

'And the wind's dropping,' said Roger, as if he were talking of someone dangerously ill.

The two little ships swept nearer and nearer to each other.

'We've got to keep out of their way,' murmured John to himself.

'Why?' said Titty. 'Why should we?'

'We're on port tack,' said John. 'Not that it makes any difference,' he added. 'She'll clear us easily.'

'You've caught up a lot too much,' shouted Captain Nancy, cheerfully, as the *Amazon* passed across the *Swallow*'s bows with twenty yards to spare.

'Not quite enough,' shouted Captain John.

Over his shoulder he was watching the promontory on the southern side of the entrance to the Amazon River. 'We mustn't stand on one second longer than we need,' he almost whispered.

'*Amazon*'s going about,' called Roger.

'She'll have to look out for us if we go about now,' said John, 'for then she'll be on port tack and we'll be on starboard.'

He glanced again over his shoulder at the promontory.

'There's shallow water off the end of it,' he murmured.

Titty was patting the main thwart, just to encourage *Swallow*. 'Go it! Go it!' she was saying.

'I think we can just do it,' said John. 'Ready about!'

'Too soon,' said Susan. 'Too soon. We can't head above the shallows.'

John said nothing, but took the mainsheet from Susan.

Amazon, on the port tack, was coming towards them, Nancy glancing now at *Swallow*, now at her own sail, now over her shoulder at the point. *Swallow* had made up a little and Nancy was not sure whether she could cross her bows. She could, perhaps, have just done it, but, instead, went about and, like John, headed for the mouth of the river.

The two little ships were now at last on the same course, and *Amazon* was only ten yards ahead.

'Oh, do go it!' said Titty.

'Don't forget the shallows,' said Susan.

'I haven't,' said John, and whispered to Susan. Susan stared at him.

'It's the only chance,' he said.

Susan whispered to the others. 'Hang on to something. Hang on tight, and keep just where you are whatever we do.'

'What for?' said Roger. But there was no time to explain.

Beyond the point they could already see the reed-beds on the northern side of the river, the reed-beds where Nancy and Peggy had lurked in *Amazon* the night of last year's war.

The wind fell away almost to nothing.

Titty whistled, bits of two different tunes.

'Shut up,' said John. 'We want a lull now more than anything.'

Close ahead of them was *Amazon*, now almost at the point, and Nancy was wishing she had held on a little longer before trying to head for the river. She, too, remembered the shallows, and was thinking of the centreboard deep below the keel of her ship. There was no doubt about it. She would have to make one more short board out into the lake to be able to clear the shallows and get into the river.

'They're going about again,' shouted Roger.

Just and only just *Amazon* cleared *Swallow* as she headed out once more.

'You'll be running aground,' shouted Peggy, as *Swallow* held on her way.

'I can see the bottom,' shouted Roger.

'Now then, Susan,' said John.

'Hold tight, Roger,' said Susan.

Just as *Swallow* came over the shallows at the point, Susan and John threw all their weight over on her lee side and brought her gunwale so low that a few drops lapped across it. This, of course, lifted her keel.

The wind had dropped to next to nothing, and so, on her beam ends, *Swallow* slid across the shallows and into the river.

'Deep water,' said Susan, and in a moment John had flung his weight back to windward and *Swallow* rose again to an even keel, just in time to meet a little puff that carried her up the river to the Beckfoot boathouse. The same puff caught the *Amazon*, but that last short board out into the lake had lost her twenty yards and more, and *Swallow* slipped past the boathouse a full two lengths ahead of her.

'Well done, little ship,' cried Titty. 'Well done! Well done!'

'Would we have lost if we'd touched?' asked Susan.

'I don't know,' said John. 'But anyhow, we didn't touch.'

'You could see the minnows running away,' said Roger.

'Well done, Skipper,' shouted Captain Nancy. 'I thought you'd made a mistake and headed in too soon. I never guessed you'd done it on purpose. Shiver my timbers. If only I'd thought of pulling up the centreboard over the shoals we might have done you. But I don't know. I saw as soon as we went about for the river that we should have to make another tack, so I let her go a bit free. Perhaps I couldn't have cleared the point itself. Jolly good race, anyhow.'

'I was a proper donkey running down outside Wild Cat Island and having to crawl back inside with no wind.'

'What about me never thinking that with this wind you might do better through the narrow channel than by coming into Rio Bay?'

'Good, good, good little ship,' said Titty.

'Lower away,' said Susan. 'Take the yard as it comes, Titty. Gather in the sail, Roger. No. Don't try to get up.'

*

'So here you are,' said Mrs Blackett. 'And who won?'

'Who won?' asked the ship's baby.

'Who won?' asked Mrs Walker.

All three of them had come down to the boathouse to find the crews of the *Swallow* and the *Amazon* already stowing their sails.

'Hullo, Mother.'

'Hullo, Bridgie.'

'How do you do?'

'Well, you scaramouches.'

'Who won?' said Bridget again.

'You did,' said Peggy. 'At least your ship did.'

'John did what you told us Father did in that race when he slipped over the shoals on his beam ends,' said Susan.

'It was jolly good work,' said Nancy, 'and a fine race. We'll have lots more.'

'And *Swallow*'s better than ever she was,' said Titty.

'She certainly looks very smart,' said Mrs Blackett.

'I do believe she's a wee bit better than *Amazon* in going to windward when there's a squall,' said Nancy. 'But when it comes to running, and we pick up our centreboard, *Amazon* simply slips away from her.'

'Hurry up now and come along to take part in the feast,' said Mrs Blackett. 'You must all be hungry by now.'

'We are,' said Nancy. 'Bring out the roasted ox and broach a puncheon of Jamaica. It was great sailing.'

36

Wild Cat Island Once Again

THE feast came slowly to an end. Even Roger said
that he thought he had had enough ice-cream.
There had been plenty of everything for everybody.
It had been a very happy feast. Almost, it might have
been somebody's birthday. It was the sort of feast that
there is when everybody knows that the school term
has come to an end and that holidays begin tomorrow.
Of course, *Swallow* was afloat again, new rigged, new
painted, and sailing just as well as ever. That would
have been enough for the happiness of John, Susan,
Titty, and Roger. They were shipwrecked mariners no
longer, but able to sail once more. Bridget, the ship's

baby, with her mouth red with crushed raspberries, would have been happy anyhow just to be at a feast with the rest of the crew, as if she were old enough to go to sea like Roger himself. The Amazons were happy to be enjoying once more the freedom of ruthless and black-hearted pirates. But there was something in the happiness of this feast that was shared by Swallows and Amazons and their elders all alike. It was like the end of one of those heavy days full of thunder, when the clouds have cleared away and the air feels light and clean. It was as if shutters had been suddenly opened, letting the sunshine into a room that has been dark for a long time.

Yet there had been very little talk, really, about the going away of the great-aunt.

'Where did she sit?' Titty had asked Peggy privately.

'Just where Roger is sitting now.'

Titty had looked at Roger, but he was showing no signs of being a boy who was sitting in what had been the special chair of the great-aunt. Perhaps that was because he did not know. For a moment she had thought of getting him to move, but then she had decided that perhaps it was just as well not to tell him. The chair had been chosen for him because of its arms, on one of which he could lean his crutch, from which he refused to be parted.

Mrs Blackett, chattering happily to Mrs Walker ('Mother's fairly letting herself go again,' said Nancy), did say something about the way in which children used to be brought up and how much better it was now that children could be the friends of their elders instead of their terrified subjects.

This was too much for Nancy. 'What she really means,' she broke in, 'is that it's lucky that we are bringing ourselves up instead of being brought up by the G.A.'

'Nancy, Nancy,' said Mrs Blackett, and then laughed at herself. 'Well,' she said, 'it is a relief to be able to call you Nancy now and again without being reminded that you were christened Ruth.'

'The trouble now would be if Mother were to call me Ruth and I had to do something fierce to show that I was really Nancy.'

But little else was said about the great-aunt, though, when the feast was over and they were all in the garden, Roger, who liked Mrs Blackett and remembered what he had heard about the great-aunt always pointing out the weeds, stumped up to her and said, 'It's a very nice lawn, and the daisies are nice too. A lawn without any daisies would be awfully dull.'

Mrs Blackett stared at him for a moment, not in

the least knowing what he meant, and then suddenly laughed.

'Well, it's very kind of you to say so,' she said.

It was soon after that that Susan heard one of the mothers say, 'It all depends what sort of children they are,' and the other reply, 'It certainly works with yours.'

It was the mother of the Swallows who first spoke of going home.

'You'll have a lot to do when you get back to camp,' she said, 'and I want to beg a passage for myself and Bridget, as far as Holly Howe.'

'Come the whole way to Swallowdale,' said Titty.

'Do, please,' said Susan.

'Wait till you're back on the island and Mrs Blackett and I will come and spend a night with you, just to see how you manage.'

'And I'm coming,' said the ship's baby.

'Of course.'

'Well done, Mother,' said Nancy. 'We'll take care of you, and you shan't get in a row from anybody.'

'Will Captain Flint come too?' asked Roger.

'I expect he will if he's asked,' said Mrs Blackett.

'He must be bursting to come,' said Nancy.

'Well,' said Peggy, 'I do think he might have turned up for the feast.'

Mrs Blackett and Mrs Walker looked at each other.

'He's in a hurry to get back aboard his house-boat, after having to be proper all this time,' said Nancy.

Again Mrs Blackett looked at Mrs Walker. 'And I suppose all of you are in a hurry to get back to your island.'

'We don't want to waste a minute,' said Nancy.

'Swallowdale's a fine camp,' said John, 'but it's not the same thing.'

'It isn't an island,' said Titty.

'No harbour,' said Roger.

'It was quite all right while we hadn't got *Swallow*,' said John.

'Come on,' said Nancy, 'and we'll begin getting things ready for portage. It'll take us all day tomorrow if we don't begin on it tonight.'

'Come on,' said Peggy. 'Suppose someone else grabbed the island.'

'No one has,' said Titty. 'I looked.'

'Anybody might,' said Nancy, 'with none of us there to defend it. Look how you came last year and we had to have a war with you.'

'Come on,' said John. 'We'll be back there tomorrow and then we'll have another.'

Some of the *Swallow*'s crew sailed in the *Amazon* for the passage to Holly Howe. This was to make more room for Mrs Walker and the ship's baby.

'We'll lend you our A.B. and the ship's boy,' said Captain John.

'Skip aboard,' said Captain Nancy.

'Aye, aye, sir,' sang out Roger and Titty together, and were presently stowing themselves one on each side of the centreboard case.

'Of course there's really room in *Swallow* for all six of us,' said Captain John.

'No point in overcrowding,' called Nancy. 'Besides, you and your mate sailed with us the other day and your fo'c'sle hands never have.'

'No fog today,' said Roger.

'Good thing, too,' said Nancy. 'It's horrid, groping about.'

'Goodbye, and thank you very much for the feast,' called the Swallows.

'Goodbye, Mother,' called the Amazons. 'You're invited to a corroboree on Wild Cat Island any time you like.'

'Long pig and plenty of it,' called Peggy, as they drifted out towards the mouth of the river.

'We'll pretend it's great-aunt steak,' called Nancy, but Mrs Blackett pretended not to hear.

*

'Was she really as bad as all that?' said Mrs Walker quietly, as the *Swallow* slipped away.

'We never really saw her,' said John, 'but she must have been.'

'She probably didn't mean to be,' said Susan, 'but she just was.'

'Well, I wonder,' said Mother, 'in thirty years' time, when I come to stay with you. . . .'

'We'll never let you go away,' said Susan.

'There won't be any coming about it,' said John, 'because there won't be any going. You're fixed.'

*

The wind was dropping as the afternoon turned into evening. It had freshened up after the race was over, but now there was only enough to keep the sheet stretched and the boom well out. There was not enough even for that when, half-way between the river and the Rio Islands they met a steamer, and the wash from it set both little ships rolling and tossing their booms about as if in an ocean swell.

In *Swallow* the ship's baby was being allowed to help the mate to steer.

Amazon had passed *Swallow* outside the river, and, with the following wind, was adding foot after foot to her lead. She was being steered by Roger and Titty in turn. They were trying who could leave the straightest wake, now that the real captain and mate had changed places with their borrowed crew and were lying down on each side of the centreboard case, pretending that it was their watch below and that they were asleep in their cabins.

'Wake us up when we come to Rio Bay,' said Nancy.

'What for?' asked Roger.

'You should never say "What for?" to the captain,' said Titty.

'All right. I mean, aye, aye, sir. But if you hadn't gone and said that I wouldn't have made that waggle in our wake.'

'Count it my waggle,' said Titty. 'That's two with the one I made myself. And you've made three, two in your last turn and one in this.'

'No quarrelling on deck,' said Captain Nancy in a growling voice from down on the bottom boards, 'or there'll be keel-hauling and hanging from the yard-arm.'

'Aye, aye, sir,' said Titty.

'Why didn't you say "No, no, sir"?' asked Roger. 'You meant "No".'

'You think of your steering,' said Titty, 'or you'll make another waggle. You have. That's two waggles in this turn. Let me have a try for a bit.'

'All right,' said Roger, 'and I'll talk.'

'You're both wrong, really,' said Mate Peggy, lying on her back and looking up at the sky from the bottom of the boat. 'You ought never to talk to the man at the wheel, and you've both been doing it.'

'But there isn't a wheel,' said Roger.

*

The two little ships took the Rio passage, and John pointed out to Mother the island with the landing stage, where they had tied up and slept after beating to and fro in the dark a year ago.

'The night you were very nearly duffers?'

'Yes,' said John.

Then they were slipping across Rio Bay, outside the yacht moorings and close by the reeds where the natives anchor and fish.

'That's the yard where they mended *Swallow*,' said John, and called out to Nancy in the other boat. Nancy was sitting up now and being the pilot, taking *Amazon* through the bay. Titty was steering. Both ships turned across towards the boatyards and sailed along close to that shore with its wooden jetties, and slipways and sheds full of boats being built.

John sniffed the air.

'Yes, you can smell it. Tarred rope. Just sniff for a minute, Mother.'

And Mother sniffed and remembered that same smell drifting from the open doors of the little shops along the water front, and from the sailing ships in Australian harbours long ago.

A man who was looking at the new paintwork on a motor boat saw them passing, and called out to John, 'Is she all right?'

'That's the boatbuilder,' said John, and shouted back, 'Better than ever. Thank you very much.'

'You made a good job of the mast between you,' the boatbuilder shouted back. 'I had a good look at it, when we brought her down yesterday.'

They sailed on round the promontory and into Holly Howe Bay. Both vessels tied up to the jetty for a minute or two while Mother and Bridget went ashore to go home to the farm for the night, and the able-seaman and the boy left the *Amazon* and rejoined their own ship.

'Goodbye, Mother. Goodbye, Mrs Walker. Goodbye, Bridgie.'

Bridget, waving goodbye, nearly made a pierhead jump at the last moment without meaning it, if Mother had not caught her in time.

'Come and see us on the island tomorrow night,' called Susan.

'Glook, glook,' said the best of all natives.

The little ships pushed off from the jetty and sailed out of the bay, close together, under the Peak of Darien.

*

Titty looked up at the Peak, remembering how last year they had watched the island day after day from the top of it, waiting for the telegram from Daddy to say they might put to sea. She remembered how, day after day, they had watched the boats of natives fishing or rowing about, and how, when any boat went too near the island, they had been afraid that someone else was going to land there before they could. And then she remembered the finding of the fireplace when they landed there, and the coming of the Amazons who had made it. She remembered how first they had seen Peggy and Nancy, once their enemies and now their closest allies, and she looked happily across the water to the *Amazon* slipping quietly along beside the *Swallow*. And then, as they sailed on and left the Peak astern and could see into Houseboat Bay, she remembered their first sight of the retired pirate and the parrot.

'We'll sail in to tell Uncle Jim how you won the

race,' called Nancy, and the two ships changed course and headed directly for the houseboat.

'He isn't there,' said Peggy a moment later. 'There's no flag up.'

'And there's no rowing boat,' said Nancy.

The *Swallow* and the *Amazon* sailed close under the stern of the houseboat and Nancy and Peggy shouted 'Houseboat ahoy!' but there was no answer.

'He had the launch with him this morning,' said John.

'Of course he had,' said Nancy. 'That's it. I was forgetting he'd have to go back to Beckfoot in her. He must have missed us going through the islands. Oh, well, never mind. We'll tell him tomorrow.'

They sailed out of Houseboat Bay and now set a course a little west of south to take them straight to Horseshoe Cove.

'We don't want to waste any time,' said Susan. 'Let's all get to bed early. It'll take us all day tomorrow to get everything shifted across.'

They were well out in the middle of the lake, and more than half-way from Houseboat Bay to Cormorant Island, when Roger, who was being a look-out man, though, with his crutch, Mate Susan wouldn't let him go before the mast, suddenly shouted, 'Smoke, smoke! There's smoke on Wild Cat Island.'

Peggy, in the *Amazon*, had seen it at the same moment, a thin cloud of blue smoke, drifting away from the trees. They would have seen it before if it had not been that the wind was northerly and was blowing the smoke away from them to the south of the island.

'Too late, too late!' wailed Titty. 'Someone's got it after all.'

'We ought to have taken it today instead of racing,' said John.

'We couldn't,' said Susan. 'We'd promised to go to Beckfoot.'

'There's very little smoke,' said John. 'Someone may just have boiled a kettle there and left his fire smouldering. Natives often do.'

Nancy Blackett took command.

'Don't alter course more than a little at a time,' she said quietly across the water. 'Don't let them think we've seen it. We'll sail on just as we are, working over a bit that way when we can. Keep a sharp look-out, everybody. There may be nobody there. We'll make sure. It's no good taking risks. There may be a whole crowd of them.'

'We can't let them have it,' said Titty.

'We won't,' said Nancy. 'We'll keep together, working over that way, as if we were sailing for pleasure. Don't let them see that we're taking any notice.'

'How would it be for one of us to go across towards Shark Bay and down the inner channel? You can see right into the camp from there.'

'It would give us away at once,' said Nancy. 'They'd see that we'd come to look at them. No. We'll keep together and work over that way, pretending we aren't really altering course. Look here. There's a steamer coming. We'll change course the moment the steamer's between us and the island.'

So it was done. The long passenger steamer churned up the lake, and while it was passing completely hid the *Swallow* and the *Amazon* from anyone who might be watching on the island. They changed course and headed east of south, and when the steamer had passed, there they were, sailing together as before. No one who had not been looking at them very carefully could have been sure that they had not been heading in that direction before the steamer had shut them out of sight.

'Shan't we be able to go back to Wild Cat Island at all?' said Roger.

'Of course not, if there are a lot of strange natives on it,' said Titty. 'There's only room for one camp anyhow, and they'll be using our fireplace.'

'It may be just a fire someone's left,' said Susan. 'If it's a fire that's being used it's funny there's not more smoke.'

'Hullo,' said John, 'Nancy's putting her centreboard down. She must be meaning to reach across below the island.'

A hoarse whisper came over the water.

'It's so as to keep station and not run away from you. Any donkey'd know I was waiting for you if I go on monkeying about with my sail.'

Now that the centreboard was down, *Amazon* no longer moved faster than *Swallow*, in spite of the following wind. It was much easier now for the two ships to keep together.

'Can you see anyone there?' asked John.

'No. But there's no doubt about the smoke.'

'Watch for a branch to move low down. Someone's bound to stir the leaves if they're looking out. Watch the clumps of heather along the edge of the rock.'

'There *is* someone there. There *is* someone there,' cried Titty, pushing the telescope into Susan's hands. 'There's a lantern on our lighthouse tree.'

There it was, to be seen even without the telescope, hanging below the lofty branch at the top of the long straight stem of the tall pine at the north end of the island. Whoever was on the island meant to stay, or they would never have taken the trouble to climb those thirty feet of smooth trunk to hang a rope over the bough for hoisting the lantern to its place.

'That settles it,' said Captain Nancy. 'They weren't there this morning, or we'd have seen something. We mustn't let them settle down. We must drive them out tonight. We must give them no sleep. We must scuttle their ships. We must drive them into the sea.'

'But how?' said John.

'I don't believe they're any good at being explorers or pirates or they'd be keeping a look-out. And I don't think they are. Then, what galoots to leave the lantern up there not lit, instead of hoisting it up when they want it. They're no good at camping, or they'd have a better fire. They probably haven't discovered the harbour at all. They're probably the sort of pigs who just eat sandwiches and leave paper about. They little know what's coming to them.'

'I wish we had a cannon,' said Roger.

'Too much noise,' said Nancy. 'We'll creep on them like snakes and it'll all be over before they've had time to open their mouths. Then we'll spare their lives and let them get into their boats and row away. They'll row away as fast as ever they can and never bother us again.'

It sounded very good, but there were misgivings in both ships. Supposing it wasn't all over when the rightful discoverers of Wild Cat Island leapt out upon their enemies, what then? Still, there was nothing for it but to try, and no doubts were spoken aloud.

The two boats sailed on side by side, all the time edging over towards the eastern side of the lake. Cormorant Island was already astern. They were nearing the southern end of Wild Cat Island and still had seen no sign of anyone moving on it. But they had seen that lantern hanging from the tall pine, and wisps of smoke still kept blowing away out of the trees.

'Perhaps they've left a guard and sailed away, meaning to come back at night,' said Peggy.

'That would explain the lantern,' said John.

'It'll be all the easier for us if they have,' said Nancy. She laughed. The others looked at her. They did not feel like laughing. Nancy explained. 'I was remembering last year, and thinking we mustn't make the mistake we made when we let your able-seaman capture our ship.'

They passed the southern end of the island.

'Haul your wind, Captain John,' said Nancy. 'We'll stand across till we can see into the harbour.'

Both steersmen put their helms down and hauled in on their mainsheets, and the *Swallow* and the *Amazon*, changing course once more, stood in as if for the harbour.

'Keep a look-out for anyone hiding among the rocks.'

Everybody was watching. Not a wagtail could have moved among those rocks without being seen. But nothing stirred.

'The harbour's empty,' said Nancy, the moment she could see in. 'They haven't found it. Their boats must be at the old landing-place.'

She brought *Amazon* suddenly up into the wind.

'Not a yard farther,' she said, 'or they might see us from the landing-place. I don't believe they've spotted us at all. We'll go into the harbour. Lower away, Peggy. Up with the centreboard. Out oars. Quietly now. Quietly! . . .'

John was doing exactly what he saw Nancy do, and now Titty and Susan were stowing the sail. Then, very quietly, John lifted the rudder inboard, put out an oar, and sculling over the stern brought *Swallow* through the channel between the rocks while Susan, watching the marks, warned him when they were out of line. *Amazon* had hardly touched before *Swallow* was slipping into the harbour beside her.

'Quietly,' said John. 'Don't let her bump.'

'Roger,' said Susan, 'that's a clean handkerchief. Don't wipe the dirt off your crutch with it.'

'I'm not. I'm muffling the foot of my crutch, so it won't make a noise on the stones. It's ready now.'

He fended off with his crutch that now had a stout pad of handkerchief over its foot. He then hopped ashore, and stood there, propped on the crutch, holding *Swallow* from slipping back or grinding on the beach.

Nancy and Peggy were looking quickly here and there among the rocks round the harbour to make sure that no able-seaman of the enemy was lurking there to seize the ships. Titty, Susan, and John, one by one, joined Roger on the beach, when they lifted *Swallow*'s nose and hauled her up as silently as if they were pulling her out over cotton-wool instead of over hard stones.

'Let's cut them off from the landing-place,' said John.

'No, no,' said Nancy. 'We *want* them to take to their boats and go away. We'll creep through the under-growth above the western shore until we're close to the camp. Have you got a whistle?'

'The mate has.'

'So has Peggy. Whistle when you hear her whistle, and then dash out for all you're worth.'

'I can smell their fire,' said Titty.

'Listen.'

There was no noise at all.

'They may be asleep.'

'Or hogging. Come on, anyway.'

The Swallows and Amazons left the harbour and slipped into the undergrowth. Even the path was not the path it had been last year when Titty had trimmed it. Once more the honeysuckles and brambles had made it into a jungle track rather than a path. 'It's no wonder they didn't find the harbour,' said Susan. 'Lucky we hadn't cleared the path before we were shipwrecked,' said John.

There was a whisper from close ahead. ''Sh, 'sh!' and Nancy turned and waited. 'Tents!' she said below her breath.

The others crept up to her. Through the trees and between the tops of the bushes they could see the pale flash of tents, more than one of them.

'They've put up their tents in our very camp,' said Titty bitterly.

'There's nothing else for it,' hissed Nancy. 'We've *got* to drive them out. If we don't it'll never be our island any more. Are you ready? Swallows and Amazons for ever! Mates, blow your whistles and COME ON!'

Two whistles sounded shrilly, and the whole party burst out through the bushes and charged with a yell into their ancient camping ground. Five tents had been set up there, four small ones, where the Swallows' tents had been before the shipwreck, and one large one, where the Amazons' tent had been the year before. A sixth tent was behind the others, among the trees.

'They've got tents just like ours,' said Roger, as he swung desperately from foot to crutch and from crutch to foot, determined not to be last.

Nancy and Peggy charged at the big tent. The others rushed past the fireplace, across the open ground.

'But they *are* ours,' said Susan.

'Pretty Polly!' said a harsh voice.

The camp had no defenders. The fire in Susan's old fireplace had burned very low, and at the farther side of the camp with his back propped against a tree, was Captain Flint, just opening his eyes, while the ship's parrot, perched beside him on one of the roots of the tree, was trying to pull his pipe to pieces.

'Hullo,' said Captain Flint, 'what time is it? I sat down for a minute to play with old Polly. Hot work, you know, shifting all these things down to the launch, and that tree takes some climbing, too. Why, what on earth's the matter with you all?'

The Swallows and Amazons looked at each other.

'Oh, nothing,' said Captain Nancy. 'We mistook you for somebody else.'

*

Captain Flint stretched himself, and felt for his pipe.

THE CHARGE

'Back at your old tricks again, eh, Polly? I must have been asleep.'

'Fast asleep,' said Roger.

'And did you bring the whole caboodle across by yourself?' asked Nancy.

'Mary Swainson helped, and a young man, a friend of hers who seemed to have a day off.'

'I expect Peter Duck lent a hand,' said Titty, 'with the things in his cave.'

'He must have done,' said Captain Flint, 'but I may have put the wrong bags in the wrong tents or something like that at this end. Mary Swainson's going to have another look round up there, and if anything's left she'll bring it down to the farm.'

'Let's go across tomorrow and make her come to tea,' said Titty.

'There's another hole coming in my knickerbockers,' said Roger.

'But whatever made you think of doing it?' asked Nancy.

'Well,' said Captain Flint, 'it was just as well to make sure of your island, and besides that there'll be grouse-shooting all over those moors tomorrow, and both your mothers seemed to think you'd be best out of the way.'

'So that was why they hadn't put a place for you at

the feast,' said Nancy. 'But you haven't asked who won the race. We lost, if you want to know.'

'I thought *Swallow* had a good chance when I saw you go into Rio Bay while John went up the other side of the islands.'

'But you don't know what John did with her at the end.'

There was the whole story of the race to tell him, and after that they changed their minds and told him how they had seen the lantern and the smoke on the island and had thought the island had been taken by enemies.

'And now we've got it for ever and ever,' said Roger.

'Until you have to go away,' said Captain Flint. 'And if I don't go away at once I shall be getting into trouble.'

'But she's gone,' said Titty.

Captain Flint laughed.

'Cook's nearly as bad,' he said.

A few minutes later he was aboard the launch, chug, chugging away past Look-Out Point, while everybody shouted their thanks after him and asked him to come again tomorrow.

'You can give me supper,' he shouted back. 'I'll be sleeping in the houseboat tomorrow night. Oh, yes, and I was to tell you that Mrs Dixon will have milk for you in the morning.'

The Swallows and Amazons went down again into their camp.

'Well,' said Nancy, 'the holidays have really begun now.'

'We've got a good lot to put on our map already,' said Titty.

'Pouf!' said Susan, raking the sticks together in the fireplace. 'Isn't it a blessing to get home?'

SWALLOWS·AND·AMAZONS·FOR·EVER!

Postscript

We have often been asked which year we climbed Kanchenjunga. It was, of course, 1930, the second year of the Alliance, the year after Uncle Jim's book was published, and thirty years after mother climbed the Matterhorn. But, by mistake, Mr Ransome wrote 1931, which was the year he wrote it all down, and that got everything else wrong. So now you know.

N.B.

DISCOVERY

SWALLOWDALE

The Backstory

Discover how much of *Swallowdale* was based
on real places and events and learn some
seafaring vocabulary!

VINTAGE CLASSICS

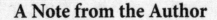

A Note from the Author

I have often been asked how I came to write *Swallows and Amazons*. The answer is that it had its beginning long, long ago when, as children, my brother, my sisters, and I spent most of our holidays on a farm at the south end of Coniston. We played in or on the lake or on the hills above it, finding friends in the farmers and shepherds and charcoal-burners whose smoke rose from the coppice woods along the shore. We adored the place. Coming to it, we used to run down to the lake, dip our hands in and wish, as if we had just seen the new moon. Going away from it, we were half drowned in tears. While away from it, as children and as grown-ups, we dreamt about it. No matter where I was, wandering about the world, I used at night to look for the North Star and, in my mind's eye, could see the beloved skyline of great hills beneath it. *Swallows and Amazons* grew out of those old memories. I could not help writing it. It almost wrote itself.

A.R.

Haverthwaite

May 19th, 1958

A Duffers' Guide to the Main Characters

John Walker: eldest of the Walkers and captain of the *Swallow*

Susan Walker: second eldest of the Walkers and mate of the *Swallow*

Titty Walker: Able-seaman of the *Swallow*

Roger Walker: youngest of the sailing Walkers and ship's boy of the *Swallow*

Bridget Walker: youngest of the Walkers and ship's baby of the *Swallow*

Nancy Blackett (Ruth): Captain of the *Amazon*

Peggy Blackett (Margaret): Nancy's younger sister and mate of the *Amazon*

James Turner: Nancy and Peggy's Uncle Jim. Known to the children as 'Captain Flint'

Mother: best of natives and mother to John, Susan, Titty, Roger and Bridget.

Maria Turner: Nancy and Peggy's fearsome great-aunt. She's a stickler for rules and likes girls to behave like young ladies

Mary Swainson: the granddaughter of the elderly Mr and Mrs Swainson. She runs the farm where the children get their milk whilst camping in Swallowdale

The Billies: Old Billy and Young Billy are father and son charcoal-burners who help Titty and Roger on the moor

VINTAGE CLASSICS

Swallows and Amazons forever!
Could you pass as a shipmate? Take this quiz to find out.
(Turn to the back for answers. No cheating!)

1) What kind of sailing has mother banned after last year's escapades?

2) Why do Titty and Roger set off on the exploration that ends in their discovery of Swallowdale?

3) What is the name of the rock that shipwrecks *Swallow*?

4) What are the favourite pastimes of the elderly Mr and Mrs Swainson?

5) What two names are carved into the wall of the cave by Captain Flint and Titty?

6) What item of clothing gives away the Amazons' position when they attempt to attack Swallowdale?

7) What sound mystifies Great-Aunt Maria when she hears it on the lawn of the Blacketts' house?

8) What does Roger spot which causes him to slip on the rock face?

Who was Arthur Ransome?

Arthur Ransome was born in Leeds in 1884. He had an adventurous life – as a baby he was carried by his father to the top of the Old Man of Coniston, a peak that is 2,276ft high!

He went to Russia in 1913 to study folklore and in 1914, at the start of World War I he became a foreign correspondent for the *Daily News*. In 1917 when the Russian Revolution began he became a journalist and was a special correspondent of the *Guardian* newspaper. He knew many of the leading Bolshevik figures, including Lenin, Trotsky and the latter's secretary, Evgenia Shvelpina. These contacts led to persistent but unproven accusations that he 'spied' for both the Bolsheviks and Britain.

Ransome married Evgenia and returned to England in 1924. He bought a cottage near Windermere in the Lake District in the late 1920s and worked as a foreign correspondent and highly-respected angling columnist for the *Manchester Guardian*.

He wrote *Swallows and Amazons* in 1930. And that was just the beginning of a series of twelve books which feature the same beloved characters and adventures with boats. The sequel *Swallowdale* followed in 1931 and starts with an unfortunate shipwreck and the dreadful great-aunt's attempts to ruin their holiday. Next up is *Peter Duck* (1932) which takes the adventure to the Caribbean. *Winter Holiday* (1933) introduces us to Dick and Dorothea Callum. *Coot Club* (1934) moves the adventures to Norfolk. *Pigeon Post* (1935)

CLASSICS

includes tales of gold-prospecting in the Lake District and *We Didn't Mean to Go to Sea* (1937) sees the children on a hairy adventure across the North Sea. *Secret Water* (1939) moves the action to the Essex coast and *The Big Six* (1940) is a detective story set in Norfolk. In *Missee Lee* (1941) the children are on a round the world trip with Captain Flint and they have a run-in with some frightening Chinese pirates. *The Picts and the Martyrs* (1943) brings back the fearsome great-aunt. The final book in the series, *Great Northern?* (1947), sees the Swallows and Amazons, the Ds and Captain Flint sailing in the Hebrides and trying to outwit the nasty Mr Jemmerling.

Arthur Ransome died in 1967 and is buried at Rusland in the Lake District.

How much of *Swallowdale* was based on real life?

Real children?

In 1928 Arthur Ransome's childhood friend Dora Altounyan came to stay in the Lake District with her husband and five children. That summer Ransome got to know the children whilst helping to teach them to sail. On the day of their departure they came to Ransome's house to give him a birthday present, a beautiful pair of slippers. He later wrote: 'was just then that I thought what fun it would be if I could write them a book about the "Swallow" and the lake and the island that was their playground, as it had been ours and that of our parents before us'. So Ransome began to write *Swallows and Amazons*, a novel about a group of children and their adventures on a lake. He based the characters on the Altounyan children and borrowed some of their names. The sequel, *Swallowdale*, which features the same main characters, followed in 1931.

Real boats?

With their father, Ransome taught the Altounyan children to sail in two small boats called *Swallow* and *Mavis*. After the family had gone home Ransome continued to sail *Swallow* himself. In his books *Mavis* was renamed *Amazon*.

Real place?

The lake and the surrounding countryside in Swallowdale is a mixture of two real-life lakes in the Lake District – Windermere and Coniston Water. Ransome spent a good deal of his childhood and adult life in this part of the world and it was there that he first met the Altounyan children. As for Wild Cat Island, some say it bears more than a passing resemblance to Peel Island which is on Coniston Water.

Real mountain?

Ransome enjoyed climbing a mountain in the Lake District called the Old Man of Coniston and he drew on his experiences of hiking to the summit when he came to write *Swallowdale*. In the story the children call the mountain Kanchenjunga. The reason for this is that there is in fact a real mountain called Kanchenjunga — it's in the Himalayas and the third highest mountain in the world. At the time that Ransome was writing *Swallowdale* expeditions to Kanchenjunga were frequently in the news.

Cannon-firing Captain Flint, fearsome pirate Nancy Blackett, butter-making Mary Swainson… *Swallowdale* features a motley crew of characters. Can you work out who said…?

1) 'Pieces of eight!'
2) 'What about adders?'
3) 'You come down to the farm and I'll darn that. It won't be the first by a long count.'
4) 'Then you can all go to look at the rock after dinner while I'm sweeping out the larder.'
5) 'Lurk! Lurk for your lives!'
6) 'There's a rare good song about that…'
7) 'It was probably Peter Duck who knocked the lantern over.'
8) 'Lost a mast? Holed her too? Well, these things will happen.'

Answers:

1) Polly the parrot
2) Roger
3) Mary Swainson
4) Susan
5) John
6) Mr Swainson
7) Titty
8) Captain Flint

VINTAGE CLASSICS

A few more interesting facts about *Swallowdale*

How Titty got her name: The character of Titty was based on Mavis Altounyan, one of the children that Arthur Ransome took sailing in the summer of 1928. She loved the story of 'Titty Mouse and Tatty Mouse' and identified with Titty Mouse, which is how she came to be known as Titty, both in the books and in real life.

How *Swallowdale* got its pictures: *Swallowdale* wouldn't be the same without its illustrations, all of which were done by Arthur Ransome himself. The book was originally illustrated by someone else but it was important to Ransome that the pictures were realistic and accurate and so in 1938 he redrew the illustrations. They became very popular and have remained in the story to this day, although he wasn't keen on drawing faces. Taqui Altounyan, the oldest of the Altounyan children once said 'He shirked drawing faces and got over that difficulty with back views of shaggy heads of hair or hats.'

Turn to, my hearties and learn some seafaring *Swallowdale* vocabulary

aft – the back of a ship.

amidships – the middle part of a ship.

ballast – heavy weights in the bottom of the boat to stop it capsizing .

boom – the pole along the bottom of a sail.

bows – the very front outside part of a ship.

fo'c'sle – the front inside part of a ship, before the mast.

gunwhale – top edge of the side of a boat.

halyard – rope used to raise or lower the sail.

hull – the watertight body of a ship.

jibe – to turn a ship with the wind behind you.

keel – the lowest part of a ship – the backbone.

mast – the upright pole that supports the sail.

painter – rope attached to bow of the boat for tying up or towing.

pennant – flag.

pigs – ballast weights (not really shaped like pigs).

port – left side of a ship.

reef – to make the sail smaller so it catches less wind.

starboard – right side of a ship.

stern – the back outside part of a ship.

skipper – captain.

thwart – a plank crosswise on a ship for strength.

Answers to the Swallowdale quiz – how did you do?

1) Night sailing

2) Because Peggy, Nancy, John and Susan spend ages talking.

3) Pike Rock

4) Mrs Swainson makes patchwork quilts and Mr Swainson loves to sing

5) Benn Gunn (carved by Captain Flint as a young man) and Peter Duck (written by Titty)

6) Their red caps

7) The sound of John hooting like an owl in the middle of the day

8) Wild goats

Visit **www.worldofstories.co.uk**